The Annotated H. P. Lovecraft

annotations by S. T. Joshi

A Dell Trade Paperback

A DELL TRADE PAPERBACK

Published by
Dell Publishing
a division of
Bantam Doubleday Dell Publishing Group, Inc.
1540 Broadway
New York, NY 10036

Edited by Leigh Grossman; copyedited by Nancy C. Hanger; proofread by Steven J. Albrecht.

Library of Congress Cataloging-in-Publication Data

Lovecraft, H. P. (Howard Phillips), 1890–1937.
        The annotated H. P. Lovecraft / annotated and with an
    introduction by S. T. Joshi.
            p.   cm.
        ISBN 0-440-50660-3
        1. Horror tales, American.   I. Joshi, S. T., 1958–   .   II. Title.
    PS3523.0833A6   1997b
    813'.52—DC21   96-53689
                                                                            CIP

Printed in the United States of America

Published simultaneously in Canada

August 1997

10 9 8 7 6 5 4 3 2
FFG

Typeset by Windhaven Press: Editorial Services, Auburn, NH

Acknowledgments

The texts of these stories are derived from the recent Arkham House corrected edition of Lovecraft's collected fiction (1984–86) produced under my editorship. This edition was founded upon consultation of autograph manuscripts, typescripts, and early publications, and eliminated many errors from previous editions. The texts as presented here correct a few further errors. The editor and publisher are grateful to Arkham House Publishers, Inc., for permission to reprint the stories.

For assistance in the annotations, I am grateful to Donald R. Burleson, Stefan Dziemianowicz, Jason C. Eckhardt, Margaretha M. Eckhardt, Nancy C. Hanger, Ben P. Indick, Steven J. Mariconda, Will Murray, Robert M. Price, and David E. Schultz.

For permission to use photographs and other illustrative materials in this book, I am grateful to Donald R. and Mollie L. Burleson, Daniel W. Lorraine, Steven J. Mariconda, Marc A. Michaud, and Will Murray.

—STJ

List of Illustrations

Introduction

H. P. Lovecraft has now become the victim of his own posthumous celebrity. In his lifetime he was almost entirely ignored by the literary mainstream, and achieved fleeting popularity only in the tiny realms of amateur journalism and pulp fiction. Now, almost sixty years after his death, his work has been translated into more than a dozen languages (including Japanese and Russian), his tales have been adapted for film, television, comic books, role-playing games, and even interactive computer games, and he has been the subject of more scholarly study than any other writer of horror fiction except (and perhaps even including) his great mentor Edgar Allan Poe. Lovecraft is by no means well ensconced as a legitimate American author, but this is chiefly the result of the vagaries of academic criticism—which has always held all horror literature in low esteem, and which today seems to be putting more emphasis on the race, gender, or sexual orientation of authors than on their pure literary merits—and Lovecraft has in any event already been acknowledged as this century's greatest contributor to the literature of the weird.

But inevitably accompanying this renown is myth, legendry, and in some cases outright falsehood regarding his life, work, and philosophy. Lovecraft the "eccentric recluse," the occultist, the racist, the mystic, the closet homosexual, the founder of the "Cthulhu Mythos"—all these labels and many others are common currency among horror fans. Some of them are true, but others—and these are the most dangerous—are only half-true, and few casual readers have the patience to sift truth from falsity, perhaps because they fear that in doing so Lovecraft will somehow become less interesting. But they need not worry: Lovecraft may by no means be as peculiar as many have believed him to be, but as a man and writer he becomes ever more compelling the more we know about him. He is a writer

whose life, work, and thought are so inextricably united that it is impossible to study the one without studying the others.

Howard Phillips Lovecraft was born on August 20, 1890, in Providence, Rhode Island. His father's ancestry was British (his great-grandfather had left Devonshire in the 1820s to settle in Rochester, New York), and his mother's ancestry was of old-time Yankee stock that could trace its roots back to the seventeenth century. The family was quite well-to-do: Lovecraft's grandfather Whipple V. Phillips was a prominent industrialist who pioneered land development in Idaho, and as a boy Lovecraft was indulged in every new hobby or interest that came to him. And these interests were many: he was reading by age four, writing at six, learning Latin at seven, and had become interested in the sciences well before entering high school—first chemistry at the age of eight, then astronomy at twelve. The enormous amount of literary work Lovecraft was producing in his early years—scientific "journals" and treatises, works on history and mythology, poetry and translations, horror tales (some inspired by Poe, others by dime-novels), detective stories, even some proto-science-fiction tales—bespeaks a formidable intellect and, more significantly, a burning curiosity in almost every academic subject. He would pass through a succession of interests—first the *Arabian Nights*, then classical antiquity, then eighteenth-century poetry, then Poe, then chemistry and astronomy—but, although one or two interests would perhaps be paramount at any given time, it was rare that he would wholly abandon any of them.

There were, of course, disruptions in his idyllic boyhood. His father, Winfield Scott Lovecraft, a traveling salesman, broke down in 1893 and spent the remaining five years of his life in Butler Hospital; it is now clear that he died of syphilis. At the time the nature and proper treatment of this disease were not known, so he was merely deemed insane and locked up in a madhouse. There is little doubt

that his wife, Sarah
Susan Phillips Love-
craft, was trauma-
tized by the event
and herself began
that mental decline
that would land
her in the same
hospital twenty
years later.

But the true
blow—the great-
est, Lovecraft con-
fessed, he ever suffered—came as a result of his
grandfather's death in 1904. Subsequent mismanagement
of his estate forced the family to sell the great Victorian
home at 454 Angell Street in which Lovecraft had been
born and to move to a smaller house at 598 Angell Street.
The loss of his birthplace was shattering to Lovecraft, and
he even contemplated suicide for a time, taking long
bicycle rides and looking wistfully at the watery depths
of the Barrington River. What prevented him, characteristically, was intellectual curiosity. Although he had attended elementary school for only two years (1898–99 and
1902–03), high school was in the offing, and Lovecraft re-
alized that there were too many things—about history,
philosophy, science, and literature—that he did not know.
Could a "gentleman" really leave this world with such
gaps in his knowledge? Perhaps it was worth living at
least for a year or two so that these gaps could be filled.

Lovecraft ended up having a great time at Hope Street
High School, and this period was perhaps the most "normal" of his entire life: he had many friends, played many
games (this was the heyday of the Providence Detective
Agency and of the Blackstone Military Band, in which
Lovecraft played some curious harmonicalike instrument
called the zobo), and hectographed his scientific journals,

The Rhode Island Journal of Astronomy and *The Scientific Gazette,* for friends and family. Of course, his intellect would always segregate him from his fellows: this was also the period when Lovecraft first achieved print, as he wrote astronomy columns for two different newspapers in the area, the *Pawtuxet Valley Gleaner* (1906–07?) and the *Providence Tribune* (1906–08). He was still writing fiction voluminously, but made no efforts to secure its publication.

But more trauma was in the offing. Lovecraft—always susceptible to various nervous (or perhaps psychosomatic) illnesses whose nature is now difficult to ascertain—suffered some sort of nervous breakdown in the summer of 1908, causing him to withdraw from high school after finishing only three years (he had sat out the whole of the 1905–06 school year with another breakdown). Naturally, having failed to gain a high school diploma, he could not even think of attending nearby Brown University; and for the next five years Lovecraft descended into a state of hermitry from which little could arouse him. Here, for perhaps the only time in his life, he really was the "eccentric recluse" many have thought him to be. He ceased writing fiction, and in fact destroyed all his earlier tales except two, "The Beast in the Cave" (1905) and "The Alchemist" (1908).

The unfortunate fact is that Lovecraft's family, never being in financial difficulties until 1904, did not train him to earn an income; and the result was an ever-increasing poverty, as he eked out a living from writing and from a dwindling inheritance. Around 1912 he attempted a correspondence course in chemistry, but it led nowhere. He had been living alone with his mother since 1904, and their relationship seems to have deteriorated increasingly with the years: Susie, beset by financial worries and perhaps horrified by her husband's illness and death, developed a love-hate relationship with her son, telling friends that he did not like to go out during the daytime because of his "hideous" face. One can only conjecture the effects on Lovecraft's psyche of this sort of emotional abuse.

Lovecraft finally did emerge from this dark period, and did so in a somewhat peculiar way. Although thoroughly familiar with the great literature of Greece, Rome, and England, he had developed—from so early a date as 1905— a habit of literary slumming by reading the cheap magazines of the Munsey chain, notably the *Argosy* and the *All-Story*. In 1913 Lovecraft was so disgusted with the sentimental love stories of one popular *Argosy* writer, Fred Jackson, that he wrote a sizzling letter attacking him; the subsequent battle of wits played out in the letter column— with many of the participants, including Lovecraft, writing satiric squibs in verse—came to the attention of Edward F. Daas, then Official Editor of the United Amateur Press Association (UAPA); he invited Lovecraft to join, and Lovecraft did so with alacrity in the spring of 1914.

The amateur journalism movement of the late nineteenth and early twentieth centuries is now such a little-known phenomenon—and one that was so typical of its time—that it is now difficult to recapture its essence; but we should make the effort to do so, for it was perhaps the most important force in Lovecraft's adult life, more so than his subsequent involvement in pulp fiction. There were two main groups, the UAPA, founded in 1895, and the older National Amateur Press Association (NAPA), founded in 1876. Neither group, even in their heyday, contained more than about 250 members, but these amateur journalists were all devoted to the cause. They spanned every age group, every part of the country, and every socio-economic class, from professor to farm laborer. Some wished to write, others wished to practice their expertise as printers; and they produced hundreds of little magazines, some very crude but some quite distinguished in appearance and contents. It may be the case that most of these writers were "amateurs" because they were unable to publish their work professionally; but a small number were in fact fairly well-established writers who wrote merely for the sake of self-expression without thought of remuneration. Certainly Lovecraft—who nurtured himself on the eighteenth-century ideal of the gentleman and who was also brought up with Victorian standards of courtesy, honor, and dignity—always scorned the idea of writing for pay, and found in the amateur world an ideal setting for expressing his views and receiving feedback on them in a relatively nonthreatening and nonacademic environment.

In other words, amateur journalism was exactly the right thing for Lovecraft at this time. Lost in his own world, scarcely aware that the twentieth century existed, and having developed very peculiar and old-fashioned views about life and literature, Lovecraft was in 1914 simply not prepared to face the real world; and the world of amateur journalism, where he quickly became prominent because of his intellectual superiority, slowly helped to acclimate him to present-day realities. He published his own journal, *The Conservative*, for thirteen issues (1915–23); he came into contact with individuals who would become lifelong friends (Rheinhart Kleiner, James F. Morton, Alfred Galpin, Maurice W. Moe); and he flexed his literary muscles by writing oceans of frankly mediocre essays, poetry, and reviews. Gradually his views underwent modification as he encountered opinions very different from his own; and he also emerged from physical reclusiveness by receiving amateurs who visited him in Providence and by taking short excursions himself.

In 1917 he had allowed his two surviving early tales to be printed in the amateur press; W. Paul Cook, a longtime amateur, was so impressed by them that he urged Lovecraft to recommence the writing of fiction. Lovecraft was quite rusty after a nine-year hiatus, but he took the plunge by writing "The Tomb" and "Dagon" in the summer of 1917. Even so, fiction was slow to emerge; only one story was written in 1918, and only five in 1919. But in 1920 he wrote more than a dozen, and gradually poetry and essays faded from his aesthetic horizons and fiction took over.

Lovecraft, however, still had no thought of professionally publishing his fiction; he was continuing, evidently, to read the Munsey magazines, but did not submit to them. Then an amateur colleague named George Julian Houtain decided to found a humor magazine entitled *Home Brew,* and asked Lovecraft to write a six-part series of tales under the generic title "Grewsome Tales." "You can't make them too morbid!" said Houtain, and Lovecraft obliged by writing "Herbert West—Reanimator" in 1921–22. This story—now having achieved a dubious fame from the Stuart Gordon film *Re-Animator* and its amusing but very un-Lovecraftian spinoffs—in fact is a successful self-parody, and in 1922 Lovecraft wrote a scarcely less parodic story, "The Lurking Fear," for *Home Brew.*

Just prior to his commencement of "Herbert West" Lovecraft's personal life lay in shambles. On May 24, 1921, his mother died after two years spent in Butler Hospital, and for weeks he was emotionally shaken. Gradually he came out of it, and at an amateur journalism convention in July he met the vivacious Sonia H. Greene, a widowed Russian Jewish woman seven years his elder. Sonia clearly pursued Lovecraft by frequently visiting him in Providence, by persuading him to come to New York on two occasions in 1922, and by writing reams of letters. Finally the two decided to marry, but when they did so on March 3, 1924, they told neither their friends nor Lovecraft's two aunts, Lillian D. Clark and Annie E. Phillips Gamwell, until the ceremony was over. Did Lovecraft and Sonia fear that the aunts would not approve of a dynamic businesswoman who was also not a member of the New England Yankee establishment? No one can say, but their silence on the matter is provocative.

In 1923 *Weird Tales* was founded, and Lovecraft was urged by many friends to submit to it; he sent in five stories at once, and all were accepted by editor Edwin Baird. Lovecraft's career as reluctant pulp writer had begun. It is maintained that "The Rats in the Walls" (1923) was one of the first stories written explicitly for a pulp market. Care must be taken in making such an assertion: firstly, Lovecraft rarely wrote a story for any single reason; secondly, he frequently stated expressly that he scorned the idea of writing for the pulps, and he never became a "pulp writer" in the sense of mechanically grinding out reams of hackwork for money. If a story submitted to a professional magazine was accepted, well and good; if it was not, Lovecraft would never revise it merely to make it more saleable. The "art for art's sake" attitude that Lovecraft had adopted from Poe and Oscar Wilde became the foundation of his aesthetics; he rejected the business of writing for cash and condemned the formula-ridden nature of pulp fiction, with its frenzied "action" plots, its wooden characterization, its slipshod style, and its fundamental lack of any vital connection with real life and real emotions. Artistic sincerity was everything to Lovecraft: he would rather fail at writing genuine literature than succeed at writing hackwork.

As for "The Rats in the Walls," Lovecraft himself confessed that it was "suggested by a very commonplace incident—the cracking of wall-paper late at night, and the chain of imaginings resulting from it" (*Selected Letters*, V, 181)—a statement that indicates how occasionally remote are the images or conceptions that inspired Lovecraft's fiction, since this particular image does not even appear as such in the story. Manifestly, also, "The

Rats in the Walls" is a homage to Poe: it could be regarded as a sort of updating of "The Fall of the House of Usher," but with a very modern overlay—the spectacularly rapid descent of the narrator upon the evolutionary scale, a scenario that could only have occurred to a writer who had accepted the truth of the Darwinian theory. "The Rats in the Walls" is a nearly flawless example of the short story in its condensation, its narrative pacing, its thunderous climax, and its mingling of horror and poignancy. Lovecraft may subsequently have written tales of greater scope and depth, but he rarely excelled this one in perfection of technique.

Lovecraft's marriage meant another uprooting—this time to his wife Sonia's lavish flat at 259 Parkside Avenue in Brooklyn. But almost immediately things began to go badly for the couple: the hat shop which Sonia had started went bankrupt, and shortly thereafter her own health gave way and she was forced to spend time in various rest homes; Lovecraft, having had no salaried position and earning only a meager income from freelance revision and ghost-writing, could not find a job, and also began to find the crowds and giganticism of New York wearying to his small-town New England temperament.

Sonia finally secured a job in Cleveland at the beginning of 1925, and for the next year or so returned to New York only infrequently; Lovecraft moved into a single-room apartment in the decaying Brooklyn Heights area at 169 Clinton Street, where he was bothered by mice, unsavory neighbors, and a burglary that deprived him of nearly all his suits and coats. In spite of the many friends he had in the city—this was the heyday of the "Kalem Club," so named because most of the members' names began with K, L, or M—Lovecraft became increasingly depressed. Finally, in early 1926, his aunts invited him to return home to Providence. He naturally accepted the offer, but no one seemed to know where Sonia fit into these plans. The aunts firmly declared that they could not countenance her

opening a shop in Providence: it would be too severe a blow to their genteel status to have a tradeswoman wife for their nephew. For his part, Lovecraft seems to have stood shiftlessly by and let his aunts make all his decisions for him. The inevitable occurred: a separation was had, and a divorce was filed in 1929.

Lovecraft's ecstatic return to Providence in April 1926 triggered a tremendous outburst of fiction writing such as he never experienced before or after: in less than a year he had written "The Call of Cthulhu" (1926), *The Dream-Quest of Unknown Kadath* (1926–27), *The Case of Charles Dexter Ward* (1927), "The Colour Out of Space" (1927), and several other stories. "The Call of Cthulhu," of course, definitively introduced what has come to be called the "Cthulhu Mythos." This is perhaps not the place to treat the vexed questions surrounding this most controversial creation of Lovecraft's—indeed, one of the most vexed questions is whether there even is such a thing as the "Cthulhu Mythos" (the term was created not by Lovecraft but by August Derleth), and whether anything is to be gained by grouping some of Lovecraft's stories as part of the mythos or not. Perhaps the most straightforward way of exploring this issue is to examine, in very condensed fashion, Lovecraft's basic philosophy of life. His early scientific interests, as well as his readings in ancient philosophy, led him to adopt the philosophy of mechanistic materialism. What this means is that the universe is a mechanism that runs without any external aid (in other words, there is no

God), and that all entity is material—there is no such thing as the immaterial "soul," no life after death, no "spiritual" substances. Not only do the radical discoveries of modern astrophysics—specifically, Einstein's theory of relativity—not overturn these beliefs, but they in fact confirm them:

> The truth is, that the discovery of matter's identity with energy—and of its consequent lack of vital intrinsic difference from empty space—is an absolute coup de grace to the primitive and irresponsible myth of "spirit". For matter, it appears, really is exactly what "spirit" was always supposed to be. Thus it is proved that wandering energy always has a detectable form—that if it doesn't take the form of waves or electron-streams, it becomes matter itself; and that the absence of matter or any other detectable energy-form indicates not the presence of spirit, but the absence of anything whatever. (Selected Letters, II, 266–67)

Lovecraft found that the most powerful way to express his philosophy in literary terms was through what he termed *cosmicism*. This is the idea that, given the vastness of the universe both in space and in time, the human race (now no longer regarded as the special creation of a divine being) is of complete inconsequence *in the universe-at-large*, although it may well be of some importance on the earthly scale. With this basic aesthetic framework, it is scarcely surprising that human beings occupy no very important place in his work. When asked why he did not write more about "ordinary people," Lovecraft responded:

> I could not write about "ordinary people" because I am not in the least interested in them. Without interest there can be no art. Man's relations to man do not captivate my fancy. It is man's relation to the

> *cosmos—to the unknown—which alone arouses in*
> *me the spark of creative imagination. The*
> *humanocentric pose is impossible to me, for I can-*
> *not acquire the primitive myopia which magnifies*
> *the earth and ignores the background.*[1]

Specifically, this meant—in such tales as "The Call of Cthulhu" (1926) and its successors—the depiction of vast gulfs of time and space by the creation of huge monsters who rule the universe and who, far from being hostile to human beings, are utterly indifferent to them and occasionally destroy them as we might heedlessly destroy ants underfoot. These entities are not to be taken *literally* (as occultists who now believe in the "truth" of the Cthulhu Mythos do), but as *symbols* for the eternal mysteries of a boundless cosmos. They are worshipped as "gods" by their human followers, but in reality most of them are mere extraterrestrials who are guided by their own motives and purposes. Lovecraft's scorn for religious dupes comes forth with especial clarity in his many degraded cults and covens. In effect, if the "Cthulhu Mythos" can be said to be anything, it is a series of plot devices—an imagined pantheon of gods; mythical books of occult lore (chiefly the *Necronomicon*); a fictitious New England topography (Arkham, Kingsport, Dunwich, Innsmouth)—designed to facilitate Lovecraft's cosmicism. These plot devices are indeed of some interest in themselves, but they are subordinate to the philosophy behind them.

What Lovecraft hoped to convey was the utter mystery of a cosmos of which we can grasp only the smallest fraction in our tiny solar system. This is not a mystical position, for as a materialist Lovecraft was well aware that our sensory limitations prevent us from ever probing fully

---

[1] "The Defence Remains Open!" (1921), in *In Defence of Dagon* (West Warwick, RI: Necronomicon Press, 1985), p. 21.

the depths of the universe. As an enthusiast of science, he believed that fiction—even (indeed, especially) weird fiction—must obey the most recent findings of biology, chemistry, and physics. Gone were the days when a writer could get much mileage out of the conventional vampire, ghost, or werewolf: these stock figures too clearly defied scientific fact as we know it, and they could no longer pass the test of verisimilitude. For Lovecraft, weird fiction must present "*supplements* rather than *contradictions* of the visible & mensurable universe" (*Selected Letters* III, 295–96), and must also rely on "subtle suggestion"[2] rather than plain statement to convince the skeptical reader that the impossible is actually occurring.

Lovecraft perhaps never succeeded better in fulfilling these criteria than in "The Colour Out of Space," which remained to the end of his life his favorite story. This tale—an exquisite union of horror and the nascent field of science fiction (it was first published in *Amazing Stories*)—is also a magical evocation of that New England landscape which Lovecraft had been exploring his whole life, and which he enthusiastically rediscovered upon his return from New York. The evocation of that wild terrain "west of Arkham" is at the heart of the story, as we witness the fate of the hapless Nahum Gardner and his family, who through no fault of their own suffer a loathsome fate as a meteorite containing an entity (or entities) from the deepest gulfs of space—where the laws of Nature must be very different from what they are in our world—lands on their property and slowly withers everything to a powdery gray dust.

It is in "The Colour Out of Space" that Lovecraft has, perhaps better than anywhere else in his work, exemplified another important principle structuring his fiction. He

---

[2] "Notes on Writing Weird Fiction" (c. 1933), *Uncollected Prose and Poetry 3* (West Warwick, RI: Necronomicon Press, 1982), p. 44.

expounds this principle in a letter to Farnsworth Wright of *Weird Tales,* accompanying the submittal of "The Call of Cthulhu" in the summer of 1927:

> *Now all my tales are based on the fundamental premise that common human laws and interests and emotions have no validity or significance in the vast cosmos-at-large. To me there is nothing but puerility in a tale in which the human form—and the local human passions and conditions and standards—are depicted as native to other worlds or other universes. To achieve the essence of real externality, whether of time or space or dimension, one must forget that such things as organic life, good and evil, love and hate, and all such local attributes of a negligible and temporary race called mankind, have any existence at all.* (Selected Letters II, 150)

This utterance has perhaps been somewhat over-interpreted, or even misconstrued: it does not mean that Lovecraft's fiction as a whole is somehow "beyond good and evil," or lacking in moral focus; rather, it merely maintains that extraterrestrial entities should not be endowed with physical, moral, or emotional qualities specifically pertaining to human beings. What Lovecraft was combating was the already well-established pulp convention of depicting extraterrestrials as quasi-human both in appearance and in mental and psychological makeup; Lovecraft cast this convention to the winds, to the degree that we are entirely ignorant not only of the physical properties of the entities in "The Colour Out of Space" but of their goals, purposes, and motivations. They cannot simplistically be branded as "evil" for causing the destruction they do; for who can say whether that destruction is merely the unanticipated but inevitable by-product of the juxtaposition of their physical composition with our own?

It is the utterly baffling nature of the meteorite and its inhabitants—who may not be conscious, organic, or even alive in any sense we recognize—that produces the deeply metaphysical horror in "The Colour Out of Space."

Lovecraft was much less successful in his next story, "The Dunwich Horror," written in the summer of 1928. It might be said that there are two basic influences on this tale, one topographical and one literary. The vivid evocation of both the allure and the lurking menace of the New England landscape is largely derived from an excursion Lovecraft made to the home of an amateur colleague, Edith Miniter, in Wilbraham, Massachusetts, earlier that summer, while the core notion of the tale—the union of a monster or "god" and a human being—seems to have been taken quite directly from Arthur Machen's "The Great God Pan." There are nods to other literary predecessors as well, notably Machen's "The White People" and Algernon Blackwood's "The Wendigo." But, in spite of its popularity, there are a number of logical and aesthetic problems with this story. "The Dunwich Horror" seems to defy Lovecraft's own strictures against a stock good-versus-evil scenario with humans as the self-evident "heroes" and extraterrestrials as self-evident "villains." Dr. Henry Armitage, the learned librarian who puts down the threat of Yog-Sothoth and his minions, the Whateley family, to "clear off the earth" of human beings and usher in the reign of the Old Ones, would make a very good parody of the pompous and valiant "hero" of hackneyed adventure fiction were it not so obvious that Lovecraft intends us to take him seriously; and his concluding actions—involving the muttering of spells to banish the invisible monster raised up by Wilbur Whateley—unwittingly laid the groundwork for many later such absurdities in the "Cthulhu Mythos" fiction of Lovecraft's talentless imitators. An interesting case has been made that the tale is in fact a parody,[3] but my feeling is that "The

---

[3] See Donald R. Burleson, "The Mythic Hero Archetype in 'The Dunwich Horror,'" *Lovecraft Studies* No. 4 (Spring 1981): 3–9.

Dunwich Horror" is simply an aesthetic mistake on Lovecraft's part.

Nevertheless, there are memorable passages in the story. The lengthy quotation from the mythical *Necronomicon* of the mad Arab Abdul Alhazred—that all-purpose book of demonology, occult lore, and magic from which Lovecraft would cite in tale after tale, and of whose reality many gullible and not-so-gullible people would become convinced—is full of ponderous resonance, recalling at once the stately prose of Lord Dunsany and the obscure philosophical aphorisms of Friedrich Nietzsche. The death of Wilbur Whateley, although by no means the true climax of the tale, is a triumph of loathsomeness, and the still more bizarre death of his invisible twin contains an exquisite parody of the crucifixion of Jesus that only a cynical atheist could have conceived.

Lovecraft's next tale, "The Whisperer in Darkness" (1930), is a still richer evocation of the New England landscape, this time the spectral remoteness of Vermont; but in his next fictional work, the short novel *At the Mountains of Madness* (1931), Lovecraft makes a radical departure, capturing the frigid wastes of Antarctica in what may represent the pinnacle of his craft as weird fictionist. Lovecraft had been fascinated by the Great White South for decades: as a boy he had, around the turn of the century, written little treatises (no longer extant) on the expeditions of Charles Wilkes and James Clark Ross, two pioneering explorers of the 1840s; he had avidly followed newspaper reports of the voyages of Borchgrevink, Scott, and others; and, of course, he had long been fascinated with Poe's *Narrative of Arthur Gordon Pym* (1838), especially its concluding section set in Antarctica, although Lovecraft's own novel cannot be regarded as any sort of true "sequel" to that work.[4] It would be facile to say that

---

[4] See, however, the interesting article by Marc A. Cerasini, "Thematic Links in *Arthur Gordon Pym, At the Mountains of Madness* and *Moby Dick*," *Crypt of Cthulhu* No. 49 (Lammas 1987): 3–20. William Fulwiler has made a suggestive but not entirely

Lovecraft's own anomalous sensitivity to cold—a malady or condition still not properly understood, but one which prevented him from venturing outside when the temperature was below 20°—was even a contributory factor in his interest; rather, it was merely that the Antarctic was, even by the 1920s, one of the last *unexplored* regions of the earth, where large stretches of territory had never seen the tread of human feet. Contemporary maps of the continent show a number of provocative blanks, and Lovecraft could exercise his imagination in filling them in with titanic mountains and cities built by extraterrestrial races, with little fear of immediate contradiction.

But *At the Mountains of Madness* is more than merely a fictionalized treatise on Antarctic exploration; it is pivotal to his evolving conception of weird fiction and of his pseudomythology. It is exactly at this time that Lovecraft was speaking of the need to introduce "supplements rather than contradictions" of known phenomena in the weird tale, with the result being a new type of work—nothing less than *"non-supernatural cosmic art"* (*Selected Letters* III, 296). The force of this statement cannot be overemphasized. There is nothing in *At the Mountains of Madness* that cannot be accounted for by an appeal to science—or, at least, a plausible extension of science. It is here, better than anywhere else, that Lovecraft has produced that fusion of weird fiction and science fiction which was to be the hallmark of his later work; and this accounts for the very painstaking scientific groundwork that Lovecraft feels compelled to lay at the outset of the tale, where his prodigious knowledge of geography, geology, and biology establish the most convincing atmosphere of verisimilitude and allow for the subtle, almost imperceptible incursion of the bizarre.

---

convincing case for the influence of Edgar Rice Burroughs's *At the Earth's Core* (serialized in the *Argosy* for 1914, where Lovecraft undoubtedly read it) on the novel. See "E. R. B. and H. P. L.," *ERB-dom* No. 80 (February 1975): 41, 44.

At the Mountains of Madness is also the culmination of what has been termed his "demythologizing"[5] of the "gods" of his mythos. While it may be true that some members of this invented pantheon—notably Azathoth—remain "godlike," this novel emphatically confirms what had been evident all along: that most of the "gods" are mere extraterrestrials whom human beings began to worship through sheer ignorance of their origins and purpose. When the narrator of *At the Mountains of Madness,* seeing the star-headed "Old Ones," declares, "They were . . . above all doubt the originals of the fiendish elder myths which things like the Pnakotic Manuscripts and the *Necronomicon* affrightedly hint about," he is resoundingly declaring that Alhazred simply failed to understand the true nature of these creatures, and that all the ponderous pseudoreligious invocations he had uttered in the *Necronomicon* (such as that celebrated passage in "The Dunwich Horror") are merely a product of error.

But *At the Mountains of Madness* goes still further than this. The casual mention that the Old Ones created all earth life "as jest or mistake" is not meant exactly literally—Lovecraft is not being the Erich van Däniken of his time—but rather as another example of Lovecraft's independence from conventional morality. The writer who, a decade before, had whimsically wondered, "Who ever wrote a story from the point of view that man is a blemish on the cosmos, who ought to be eradicated?",[6] has perfectly embodied his misanthropy in providing a degrading origin of our species. "The Shadow out of Time" (1934–35) takes this notion one step further, by positing that all the great accomplishments of the human intellect were the

---

[5] Robert M. Price, "Demythologizing Cthulhu," *Lovecraft Studies* No. 8 (Spring 1984: 3–9, 14. In several later articles Price has maintained that this "demythologizing" had been occurring from the earliest of Lovecraft's "mythic" tales.

[6] Letter to Edwin Baird, c. October 1923; *Uncollected Letters* (West Warwick, RI: Necronomicon Press, 1986), p. 8.

result of mind-exchange with the Great Race, an alien species of spectacular mental capacity.

Lovecraft's last ten years were relatively uneventful: he wrote only a handful of stories, although they are

largely the ones on which his reputation rests; he traveled widely to antiquarian oases up and down the eastern seaboard, from Quebec to Charleston to St. Augustine; he was the hub of a complex network of epistolary ties with other writers in the horror and science fiction fields (August Derleth, Donald Wandrei, Robert E. Howard, Robert Bloch, and Fritz Leiber, to mention only a few); he lived in comparative security, although on a perilously small income,

in two houses in the old part of Providence, and ended his years in a delightful post-colonial home (c. 1825) at the very crown of College Hill. But his poor diet—he ate only two meals a day, and most of these consisted of ice cream, sugar, beans, canned foods, and other ill-nourishing products—no doubt contributed to the cancer of the intestine that he had contracted perhaps as early as 1934, and which inexorably enfeebled him in the last year of his life. Either too poor or too heedless to consult a doctor over what he continued to pass off as "indigestion" or "grippe," Lovecraft entered the hospital on March 10, 1937, by which time it was too late to do anything except give him painkillers; he died five days later.

The posthumous resurrection of his work—inspired initially by Derleth and Wandrei, who founded Arkham House for the sole purpose of preserving his fiction within hardcovers, and carried on later by many able hands—needs no rehearsal here. Nor need we rehash the sorry story of the "Cthulhu Mythos," which (thanks largely to Derleth's rabid enthusiasm) took on a life of its own and inspired a legion of hacks to produce unwitting parodies of the writer they were misguidedly attempting to honor. Lovecraft's work does not require these half-baked imitations to claim a place in weird fiction; it stands on its own, and both its virtues and its flaws are clearly displayed for all to see. As for Lovecraft the man, he too will slough off facile charges that he was an "eccentric," a recluse, an occultist, or whatever other misconstruals a casual, superficial, or incomplete study of his life may engender. To be sure, he was not "normal"; but no person of intellect or creative imagination ever is. That he has left as a legacy one of the most distinctive bodies of literature ever written is all the defense he now requires.

—S. T. JOSHI

I discovered Lovecraft at age thirteen, and was never the same thereafter. As a rule, dense prose and long-winded paragraphs full of peculiar words like "eldritch" and "foeter" and "nacreous" tended to put me off, but I waded through because this Lovecraft guy was telling about another reality that impinged on ours, knowledge of which could drive you start raving mad; a dimension of perverse logic and bizarre geometry, full of godlike creatures with unpronouncable names, aloof and yet decidedly inimical.

. . .
This was Cosmic Horror . . . and it was cool.
It's still cool.

—F. Paul Wilson

"The Rats in the Walls" was probably written in late August or early September 1923, as Lovecraft announces its completion in a letter of September 4 (Selected Letters, I, 250). It was first published in Weird Tales for March 1924 and reprinted in the issue for June 1930. It had been initially submitted to Argosy-Allstory Weekly, but editor Robert H. Davis rejected it as being (in Lovecraft's words) *"too horrible for the tender sensibilities of a delicately nurtured publick"* (Selected Letters, I, 259). Its only other appearance in Lovecraft's lifetime was in the anthology Switch on the Light, edited by Christine Campbell Thomson (London: Selwyn & Blount, 1931).

Late in life Lovecraft declared that the story was *"suggested by a very commonplace incident—the cracking of wall-paper late at night, and the chain of imaginings resulting from it"* (Selected Letters, V, 181). He recorded the kernel of the idea in his commonplace book: *"Wall paper cracks off in sinister shape—man dies of fright"* (entry 107). As mentioned in the introduction, this image does not actually appear in the story. An earlier entry (79) in the commonplace book is also suggestive: *"Horrible secret in crypt of ancient castle—discovered by dweller."* *"The Rats in the Walls"* may then be a fusion of images and conceptions that had been percolating in his mind for years. It is perhaps the pinnacle of his work in the Gothic/Poe-esque vein.

Weird Tales

THE UNIQUE MAGAZINE

The SPIRIT FAKERS
of HERMANNSTADT
by

HOUDINI

The Most Miraculous
True Story Ever Written

MARCH 1924   25¢

The Rats in the Walls

On July 16, 1923, I moved into Exham Priory[1] after the last workman had finished his labours. The restoration had been a stupendous task, for little had remained of the deserted pile but a shell-like ruin; yet because it had been the seat of my ancestors I let no expense deter me. The place had not been inhabited since the reign of James the First,[2] when a tragedy of intensely hideous, though largely unexplained, nature had struck down the master, five of his children, and several servants; and driven forth under a cloud of suspicion and terror the third son, my lineal progenitor and the

---

[1] *Exham Priory*: The name Exham Priory may be derived from the British town of Hexham in Northumberland, which is mentioned in Lovecraft's *The Case of Charles Dexter Ward* (1927).

[2] *James the First*: King of England (1603–25) and Scotland (1567–1625). Among his many writings is a treatise on witchcraft, *Daemonologie* (1597).

only survivor of the abhorred line. With this sole heir denounced as a murderer, the estate had reverted to the crown, nor had the accused man made any attempt to exculpate himself or regain his property. Shaken by some horror greater that that of conscience or the law, and expressing only a frantic wish to exclude the ancient edifice from his sight and memory, Walter de la Poer,[3] eleventh Baron Exham, fled to Virginia and there founded the family which by the next century had become known as Delapore.

Exham Priory had remained untenanted, though later allotted to the estates of the Norrys family and much studied because of its peculiarly composite architecture; an architecture involving Gothic towers resting on a Saxon or Romanesque[4] substructure, whose foundation in turn was of a still earlier order or blend of orders—Roman, and even Druidic or native Cymric,[5] if legends speak truly. This foundation was a very singular thing, being merged on one side with the solid limestone of the precipice from whose brink the priory overlooked a desolate valley three miles west of the village of Anchester.[6] Architects and antiquarians loved

---

[3] *de la Poer*: The name *de la Poer* seems clearly derived from Edgar Allan Poe. Lovecraft referred to Poe as his "God of Fiction" (*Selected Letters*, I, 20); he had first read him at the age of eight. As Barton L. St. Armand (*The Roots of Horror in the Fiction of H. P. Lovecraft* [Elizabethtown, NY: Dragon Press, 1977], 11) points out, Poe's one-time fiancée Sarah Helen Whitman once traced a common genealogy between herself (whose maiden name was Power) and Poe to an ancient Celtic-Norman line named Poer or de le Poer. See Caroline Ticknor, *Poe's Helen* (New York: Charles Scribner's Sons, 1916), 159. Lovecraft had this book in his library.

[4] *Romanesque:* the architecture of the eleventh and twelfth centuries in Europe. For the Saxons, see below (note 20).

[5] *Cymric:* Cymru is the native name for Wales. The term Cymric was formerly used as a general designation for one of the two Celtic inhabitants of Britain, who lived in the south, as contrasted with the other Celtic group, the Gaels, who lived in the north. It was once believed that the Gaelic people came to England first from the mainland and were subsequently driven north by the Cymric people, but there is now reason to doubt this reconstruction. Cymric is also an archaic designation for a group of languages (comprising Welsh and Cornish) now denoted by the term Brythonic, as distinguished from another group (comprising Irish, Gaelic, and Manx) now denoted by the term Goidelic. See also note 53 below. For Druids, see note 14 below.

[6] *Anchester:* Either a fictitious name or an error for the town of Ancaster in Lincolnshire

to examine this strange relic of forgotten centuries, but the country folk hated it. They had hated it hundreds of years before, when my ancestors lived there, and they hated it now, with the moss and mould of abandonment on it. I had not been a day in Anchester before I knew I came of an accursed house.[7] And this week workmen have blown up Exham Priory, and are busy obliterating the traces of its foundations.

The bare statistics of my ancestry I had always known, together with the fact that my first American forbear had come to the colonies under a strange cloud. Of details, however, I had been kept wholly ignorant through the policy of reticence always maintained by the Delapores. Unlike our planter neighbors, we seldom boasted of crusading ancestors or other mediaeval and Renaissance heroes; nor was any kind of tradition handed down except what may have been recorded in the sealed envelope left before the Civil War by every squire to his eldest son for posthumous opening. The glories we cherished were those achieved since the migration; the glories of a proud and honourable, if somewhat reserved and unsocial Virginia line.

During the war our fortunes were extinguished and our whole existence changed by the burning of Carfax,[8] our home on the banks of the James. My grandfather, advanced in years, had perished in that incendiary outrage, and with him the envelope that bound us all to the past. I can recall that fire today as I saw it then at the age of seven, with the Federal soldiers shouting, the women screaming, and the negroes howling and praying. My father was in the army, defending

---

(where a Roman fort was located) or Alchester in Oxfordshire. Since Lovecraft in a letter declares the setting of the tale to be in the south of England (see note 53 below), Alchester seems the more likely setting if the site is indeed not meant to be imaginary.

[7] *house*: The usage is parallel to Poe's in "The Fall of the House of Usher," referring simultaneously to the family line and the structure itself.

[8] *Carfax*: St. Armand in *Roots of Horror* (note 3 above) points out the parallel to Carfax Abbey in Bram Stoker's *Dracula* (1897).

Richmond, and after many formalities my mother and I were
passed through the line to join him. When the war ended
we all moved north, whence my mother had come; and I
grew to manhood, middle age, and ultimate wealth as a stolid
Yankee.[9] Neither my father nor I ever knew what our hereditary envelope had contained, and as I merged into the grey-
ness of Massachusetts business life I lost all interest in the
mysteries which evidently lurked far back in my family tree.
Had I suspected their nature, how gladly I would have left
Exham Priory to its moss, bats, and cobwebs!

My father died in 1904,[10] but without any message to leave
me, or to my only child, Alfred,[11] a motherless boy of ten. It
was this boy who reversed the order of family information;
for although I could give him only jesting conjectures about
the past, he wrote me of some very interesting ancestral
legends when the late war took him to England in 1917 as
an aviation officer.[12] Apparently the Delapores had a
colourful and perhaps sinister history, for a friend of my
son's, Capt. Edward Norrys of the Royal Flying Corps, dwelt
near the family seat at Anchester and related some peasant
superstitions which few novelists could equal for wildness
and incredibility. Norrys himself, of course, did not take
them seriously; but they amused my son and made good
material for his letters to me. It was this legendry which

---

[9] *Yankee*: Lovecraft himself, although a lifelong Yankee, had Confederate leanings: he reports
that he and his childhood friend Harold Munroe were "Confederates in sympathy, & used to
act out all the battles of the War in Blackstone Park" in Providence (Lovecraft to Lillian D.
Clark, [May 2, 1929]; ms., John Hay Library, Brown University).

[10] In fact, it was not Lovecraft's father but his grandfather, Whipple Van Buren Phillips
(1833–1904), who died on March 28, 1904. Lovecraft's father had been hospitalized in
1893 and died in 1898, and Whipple Phillips had in effect become his father.

[11] *Alfred*: the name is possibly derived from Lovecraft's young friend Alfred Galpin
(1901–1983). They had come into contact in 1918 and remained voluminous and close
correspondents to the end of Lovecraft's life. When Lovecraft first met Galpin in Cleveland in August 1922, he addressed him as "my Son Alfredus" (*Selected Letters*, I, 191).

[12] The United States declared war on Germany on April 6, 1917, and a draft bill was
signed on May 18. Lovecraft had attempted to enlist first in the Rhode Island National
Guard and then in the U.S. Army, but he was rejected for health reasons.

definitely turned my attention to my transatlantic heritage, and made me resolve to purchase and restore the family seat which Norrys shewed to Alfred in its picturesque desertion, and offered to get for him at a surprisingly reasonable figure, since his own uncle was the present owner.

I bought Exham Priory in 1918, but was almost immediately distracted from my plans of restoration by the return of my son as a maimed invalid. During the two years that he lived I thought of nothing but his care, having even placed my business under the direction of partners. In 1921, as I found myself bereaved and aimless, a retired manufacturer no longer young, I resolved to divert my remaining years with my new possession. Visiting Anchester in December, I was entertained by Capt. Norrys, a plump, amiable young man who had though much of my son, and secured his assistance in gathering plans and anecdotes to guide in the coming restoration. Exham Priory itself I saw without emotion, a jumble of tottering mediaeval ruins covered with lichens and honeycombed with rooks' nests, perched perilously upon a precipice, and denuded of floors or other interior features save the stone walls of the separate towers.[13]

As I gradually recovered the image of the edifice as it had been when my ancestor left it over three centuries before, I began to hire workmen for the reconstruction. In every case I was forced to go outside the immediate locality, for the Anchester villagers had an almost unbelievable fear and hatred of the place. This sentiment was so great that it was sometimes communicated to the outside labourers, causing numerous desertions; whilst its scope appeared to include both the priory and its ancient family.

My son had told me that he was somewhat avoided during his visits because he was a de la Poer, and I now found

---

[13] The description of Exham Priory corresponds remarkably with a structure called St. Patrick's Purgatory as cited in Sabine Baring-Gould's *Curious Myths of the Middle Ages* (1866–68; rev. ed. London: Rivington's, 1869), a volume Lovecraft is known to have read: "In that charming medieval romance, 'Fortunatus and his Sons,' is an account of a visit paid by the favored youth to that cave of mystery in Lough Derg, the Purgatory of S. Patrick.

myself subtly ostracised for a like reason until I convinced
the peasants how little I knew of my heritage. Even then
they sullenly disliked me, so that I had to collect most of
the village traditions through the mediation of Norrys. What
the people could not forgive, perhaps, was that I had come
to restore a symbol so abhorrent to them; for, rationally or
not, they viewed Exham Priory as nothing less than a haunt
of fiends and werewolves.

Piecing together the tales which Norrys collected for me,
and supplementing them with the accounts of several
savants who had studied the ruins, I deduced that Exham
Priory stood on the site of a prehistoric temple; a Druidical
or ante-Druidical thing which must have been contemporary with Stonehenge.[14] That indescribable rites had been
celebrated there, few doubted; and there were unpleasant
tales of the transference of these rites into the Cybele-
worship which the Romans had introduced.[15] Inscriptions
still visible in the sub-cellar bore such unmistakable letters
as "DIV . . . OPS . . . MAGNA. MAT . . . "[16] sign of
the Magna Mater whose dark worship was once vainly forbidden to Roman citizens. Anchester had been the camp of
the third Augustan legion,[17] as many remains attest, and it
was said that the temple of Cybele was splendid and thronged
with worshippers who performed nameless ceremonies at

Fortunatus, we are told, has heard in his travels of how two days' journey from the town,
Valdric, in Ireland, was a town, Vernic, where was the entrance to the Purgatory; so
thither he went with many servants. He found a great abbey, and behind the altar of the
church a door, which led into the dark cave which is called the Purgatory of S. Patrick"
(Baring-Gould, 1869, 230). See, in general, Steven J. Mariconda, "Baring-Gould and the
Ghouls: The Influence of *Curious Myths of the Middle Ages* on 'The Rats in the Walls,'"
Crypt of Cthulhu No. 14 (St. John's Eve 1983):3–7, 27.

[14] The Druids were a religious order amongst the Celts of Gaul, Britain, and Ireland.
Their influence in England theoretically waned after the Roman general C. Suetonius
Paulinus attacked their stronghold on the island of Mona (Anglesea) in A.D. 61. Stonehenge
is a circular rock enclosure in the Salisbury Plain, now believed to have been built by
Celts, possibly for druidical rites, around 1900–1400 B.C.

[15] The cult of Cybele was introduced to Roman Britain probably in the third century A.D.
It had been introduced to Rome in 204 B.C., during the war with Hannibal. Up to the time
of the Emperor Claudius (A.D. 41–54) the priesthood was prohibited to Roman citizens.

the bidding of a Phrygian priest. Tales added that the fall of the old religion did not end the orgies at the temple, but that the priests lived on in the new faith without real change. Likewise was it said that the rites did not vanish with the Roman power,[18] and that certain among the Saxons added to what remained of the temple, and gave it the essential outline it subsequently preserved, making it the centre of a cult feared through half the heptarchy.[19] About 1000 A.D. the place is mentioned in a chronicle as being a substantial stone priory housing a strange and powerful monastic order and surrounded by extensive gardens which needed no walls to exclude a frightened populace. It was never destroyed by the Danes, though after the Norman Conquest it must have declined tremendously; since there was no impediment when Henry the Third granted the site to my ancestor, Gilbert de la Poer, First Baron Exham, in 1261.[20]

Cybele was a goddess of fertility emerging in Anatolia and Phrygia (Turkey). Her cult was brought to the Greek mainland no later than the fifth century B.C.

[16] It is possible to conjecture what Lovecraft had in mind in presenting these fragmentary Latin words: "div" may suggest *divinum* ("divine") or *dives* ("wealthy"); "ops" may refer to Ops, the goddess of plenty or riches; for Magna Mater means "Great Mother," attribute of Cybele.

[17] Lovecraft is in error: it is the Second Augustan Legion that was stationed in Britain, its base the enormous legionary fortress at Isca Silurum (Caerleon-on-Usk) in what is now Wales. He repeated the error in the fragment called "The Descendant" (1927?; *Dagon and Other Macabre Tales* [Sauk City, WI: Arkham House, 1986], 361). He later learned of his error from reading Arthur Machen, many of whose works use Roman Britain as a backdrop, and Arthur Weigall's *Wanderings in Roman Britain* (1926), which he read in 1933. It is possible that this is a deliberate change on Lovecraft's part, but if so it is too much at variance with the known facts to be plausible.

[18] In 410, the Emperor Honorius ordered the Roman citizens of Britain to fend for themselves; most of the soldiers in the two or three legions customarily stationed in Britain had been withdrawn long before.

[19] *heptarchy*: Greek for "rule of seven," i.e., the seven kingdoms of Anglo-Saxon England: Northumbria, Mercia, East Anglia, Wessex, Kent, Essex, and Sussex.

[20] Lovecraft has here supplied an encapsulation of the early history of England. The Angles and Saxons had driven out or conquered the Romans by around 550; the "Danes" (really the Vikings) invaded England in 838 and had established footholds throughout the country by the end of the ninth century; the Norman Conquest (i.e., the invasion of England from the French region of Normandy) canonically dates to 1066, when William of Normandy became

Of my family before this date there is no evil report, but something strange must have happened then. In one chronicle there is a reference to a de la Poer as "cursed of God" in 1307, whilst village legendry had nothing but evil and frantic fear to tell of the castle that went up on the foundations of the old temple and priory. The fireside tales were of the most grisly description, all the ghastlier because of their frightened reticence and cloudly evasiveness. They represented my ancestors as a race of hereditary daemons beside whom Gilles de Retz and the Marquis de Sade[21] would seem the veriest tyros, and hinted whisperingly at their responsibility for the occasional disappearance of villagers through several generations.

The worst characters, apparently, were the barons and their direct heirs; at least, most was whispered about these. If of healthier inclinations, it was said, an heir would early and mysteriously die to make way for another more typical scion. There seemed to be an inner cult in the family, presided over by the head of the house, and sometimes closed except to a few members. Temperament rather than ancestry was evidently the basis of this cult, for it was entered by several who married into the family. Lady Margaret Trevor from Cornwall, wife of Godfrey, the second son of the fifth baron, became a favourite bane of children all over the countryside, and the daemon heroine of a particularly horrible old

---

William I ("the Conquerer"); Henry III was king of England from 1216 to 1272. One wonders whether the dating of the first Baron Exham to 1261 is a nod to the great Irish *fantaisiste* Lord Dunsany (1878–1957), whose work Lovecraft admired: the first Lord Dunsany dates to the twelfth century.

[21] *Gilles de Retz*: Sometimes referred to as Gilles de Rais (c. 1396–1440), a compatriot of Joan of Arc who was accused (probably falsely) of necromancy, child-kidnapping, and murder. His purported crimes gave rise to the legend of Bluebeard.

Marquis de Sade: Donatien Alphonse François (1740–1814), notorious writer of sexually explicit works including *The 120 Days of Sodom* (written c. 1785; published 1931–35) and *Justine* (1791). He is known to have played various sex-torture games with prostitutes and servants, for which he was incarcerated in the Bastille and other prisons during much of his adult life. The word *sadism* is derived from his name.

ballad not yet extinct near the Welsh border. Preserved in balladry, too, though not illustrating the same point, is the hideous tale of Lady Mary de la Poer, who shortly after her marriage to the Earl of Shrewsfield[22] was killed by him and his mother, both of the slayers being absolved and blessed by the priest to whom they confessed what they dared not repeat to the world.

These myths and ballads, typical as they were of crude superstition, repelled me greatly. Their persistence, and their application to so long a line of my ancestors, were especially annoying; whilst the imputations of monstrous habits proved unpleasantly reminiscent of the one known scandal of my immediate forbears—the case of my cousin, young Randolph Delapore of Carfax, who went among the negroes and became a voodoo priest after he returned from the Mexican War.[23]

I was much less disturbed by the vaguer tales of wails and howlings in the barren, windswept valley beneath the limestone cliff; of the graveyard stenches after the spring rains; of the floundering, squealing white thing on which Sir John Clave's horse had trod one night in a lonely field; and of the servant who had gone mad at what he saw in the priory in the full light of day. These things were hackneyed spectral lore, and I was at that time a pronounced sceptic. The accounts of vanished peasants were less to be dismissed, though not especially significant in view of mediaeval custom. Prying curiosity meant death, and more than one severed head had been publicly shewn on the bastions—now effaced—around Exham Priory.

A few of the tales were exceedingly picturesque, and made

---

[22] *Earl of Shrewsfield*: A mythical peerage, although there were earls of Shrewsbury from the eleventh to the seventeenth centuries.

[23] *Mexican War*: A war fought between the United States and Mexico (1845–48) as a result of a dispute over the western border of the new state of Texas. After the U.S. victory, Mexico ceded a large portion of territory now covering all or part of the states of California, Nevada, Utah, Arizona, New Mexico, and Colorado.

me wish I had learnt more of comparative mythology in my
youth. There was, for instance, the belief that a legion of
bat-winged devils kept Witches' Sabbath each night at the
priory—a legion whose sustenance might explain the dis-
proportionate abundance of coarse vegetables harvested in
the vast gardens. And, most vivid of all, there was the dramatic epic of the rats—the scampering army of obscene vermin which had burst forth from the castle three months
after the tragedy that doomed it to desertion—the lean, filthy,
ravenous army which had swept all before it and devoured
fowl, cats, dogs, hogs, sheep, and even two hapless human
beings before its fury was spent. Around that unforgettable
rodent army a whole separate cycle of myths revolves, for it
scattered among the village homes and brought curses and
horrors in its train.[24]

---

[24] This tale of the rats seems similarly derived from the legend of Bishop Hatto as narrated in
Baring-Gould's *Curious Myths of the Middle Ages* (see note 13). Bishop Hatto was an abbot of
Fulda in Germany in the tenth century. A famine occurred in the year 970, but Hatto refused
to feed the people. Instead, he locked them into a barn and set fire to it. As revenge, rats
overrun his estate:

> Then there came a man to him from his farm, with a countenance pale with
> fear, to tell him that the rats had devoured all the corn in his granaries. And
> presently there came another servant, to inform him that a legion of rats was on
> its way to his palace. The Bishop looked from his window, and saw the road and
> fields dark with the moving multitude; neither hedge nor wall impeded their
> progress, as they made straight for his mansion. Then, full of terror, the prelate
> fled by his postern, and, taking a boat, was rowed out to his tower in the river …

> He listen'd and look'd—it was only the cat;
> But the Bishop he grew more fearful for that,
> For she sat screaming, mad with fear,
> At the army of rats that were drawing near.

> For they have swum over the river so deep,
> And they have climb'd the shores so steep,
> And now by thousands up they crawl
> To the holes and windows in the wall.

> Down on his knees the Bishop fell,
> And faster and faster his beads did tell,
> As louder and louder, drawing near,
> The saw of their teeth without he could hear.

> And in at the windows, and in at the door,
> And through the walls by the thousands they pour,

Such was the lore that assailed me as I pushed to completion, with an elderly obstinacy, the work of restoring my
ancestral home. It must not be imagined for a moment that
these tales formed my principal psychological environment.
On the other hand, I was constantly praised and encouraged
by Capt. Norrys and the antiquarians who surrounded and
aided me. When the task was done, over two years after its
commencement, I viewed the great rooms, wainscotted
walls, vaulted ceilings, mullioned windows, and broad stair-
cases with a pride which fully compensated for the prodigious expense of the restoration. Every attribute of the
Middle Ages was cunningly reproduced, and the new parts
blended perfectly with the original walls and foundations.
The seat of my fathers was complete, and I looked forward
to redeeming at last the local fame of the line which ended
in me. I would reside here permanently, and prove that a de
la Poer (for I had adopted again the original spelling of the
name) need not be a fiend. My comfort was perhaps augmented by the fact that, although Exham Priory was
mediaevally fitted, its interior was in truth wholly new and
free from old vermin and old ghosts alike.

As I have said, I moved in on July 16, 1923. My household
consisted of seven servants and nine cats, of which latter
species I am particularly fond. My eldest cat, "Nigger-
Man",[25] was seven years old and had come with me from my

And down from the ceiling, and up through the floor,
And from the right and the left, from behind and before,
From within and without, from above and below,
And all at once to the Bishop they go.

They have whetted their teeth against the stones,
And now they pick the Bishop's bones;
They gnaw'd the flesh from every limb,
For they were sent to do judgment on him.

(Baring-Gould, 1869, 448–50)

[25] Lovecraft himself had a cat by this name, which disappeared in 1904. At the turn of the
century the use of the term "nigger" was not regarded as offensive.

home in Bolton, Massachusetts;[26] the others I had accumulated whilst living with Capt. Norrys' family during the restoration of the priory. For five days our routine proceeded with the utmost placidity, my time being spent mostly in the codification of old family data. I had now obtained some very circumstatial accounts of the final tragedy and flight of Walter de la Poer, which I conceived to be the probable contents of the hereditary paper lost in the fire at Carfax. It appeared that my ancestor was accused with much reason of having killed all the other members of his household, except four servant confederates, in their sleep, about two weeks after a shocking discovery which changed his whole demeanour, but which, except by implication, he disclosed to no one save perhaps the servants who assisted him and afterward fled beyond reach.

This deliberate slaughter, which included a father, three brothers, and two sisters, was largely condoned by the villagers, and so slackly treated by the law that its perpetrator escaped honoured, unharmed, and undisguised to Virginia; the general whispered sentiment being that he had purged the land of an immemorial curse. What discovery had prompted an act so terrible, I could scarcely even conjecture. Walter de la Poer must have known for years the sinister tales about his family, so that this material could have given him no fresh impulse. Had he, then, witnessed some appalling ancient rite, or stumbled upon some frightful and revealing symbol in the priory or its vicinity? He was reputed to have been a shy, gentle youth in England. In Viriginia he seemed not so much hard or bitter as harassed and apprehensive. He was spoken of in the diary of another gentleman-adventurer, Francis Harley of Bellview,[27] as a man of unexampled justice, honour, and delicacy.

---

[26] *Bolton, Massachusetts*: A small town in east central Massachusetts. Lovecraft cites it in several other stories.

[27] *Francis Harley of Bellview*: It is not certain how Lovecraft came up with this name. Clearly he wished to create a name typical of an old Virginia family. Compare the name Harley Warren (a Southerner) in an early story, "The Statement of Randolph Carter" (1919).

On July 22 occurred the first incident which, though lightly dismissed at the time, takes on a preternatural significance in relation to later events. It was so simple as to be almost negligible, and could not possibly have been noticed under the circumstances; for it must be recalled that since I was in a building practically fresh and new except for the walls, and surrounded by a well-balanced staff of servitors, apprehension would have been absurd despite the locality. What I afterward remembered is merely this—that my old black cat, whose moods I know so well, was undoubtedly alert and anxious to an extent wholly out of keeping with his natural character. He roved from room to room, restless and disturbed, and sniffed constantly about the walls which formed part of the old Gothic structure. I realise how trite this sounds—like the inevitable dog in the ghost story, which always growls before his master sees the sheeted figure—yet I cannot consistently suppress it.

The following day a servant complained of restlessness among all the cats in the house. He came to me in my study, a lofty west room on the second story, with groined arches, black oak panelling, and a triple Gothic window overlooking the limestone cliff and desolate valley; and even as he spoke I saw the jetty form of Nigger-Man creeping along the west wall and scratching at the new panels which overlaid the ancient stone. I told the man that there must be some singular odour or emanation from the old stonework, imperceptible to human senses, but affecting the delicate organs of cats even through the new woodwork. This I truly believed, and when the fellow suggested the presence of mice or rats, I mentioned that there had been no rats there for three hundred years, and that even the field mice of the surrounding country could hardly be found in these high walls, where they had never been known to stray. That afternoon I called on Capt. Norrys, and he assured me that it would be quite incredible for field mice to infest the priory in such a sudden and unprecedented fashion.

That night, dispensing as usual with a valet, I retired in

the west tower chamber which I had chosen as my own,
reached from the study by a stone staircase and short gallery—the former partly ancient, the latter entirely restored.
This room was circular, very high, and without wainscot-
ting, being hung with arras[28] which I had myself chosen in
London. Seeing that Nigger-Man was with me, I shut the
heavy Gothic door and retired by the light of the electric
bulbs which so cleverly counterfeited candles, finally switching off the light and sinking on the carved and canopied
four-poster, with the venerable cat in his accustomed place
across my feet.[29] I did not draw the curtains, but gazed out
at the narrow north window which I faced. There was a
suspicion of aurora in the sky, and the delicate traceries of
the window were pleasantly silhouetted.

At some time I must have fallen quietly asleep, for I recall
a distinct sense of leaving strange dreams, when the cat
started violently from his placid position. I saw him in the
faint auroral glow, head strained forward, fore feet on my
ankles, and hind feet stretched behind. He was looking
intensely at a point on the wall somewhat west of the window, a point which to my eye had nothing to mark it, but
toward which all my attention was now directed. And as I
watched, I knew that Nigger-Man was not vainly excited.
Whether the arras actually moved I cannot say. I think it
did, very slightly. But what I can swear to is that behind it I
heard a low, distinct scurrying as of rats or mice. In a moment

---

[28] *arras*: "A rich tapestry fabric, in which figures and scenes are woven in colours"
(*Oxford English Dictionary*). This is a clear nod to Poe, especially "Metzengerstein":
"The rich although faded tapestry hangings which swung gloomily upon the walls,
represented the shadowy and majestic forms of a thousand illustrious ancestors." Later
the figure of a horse and rider appearing on this tapestry vanishes from it, only to emerge
supernaturally at the end of the story. Extensive use is also made of tapestries in "Ligeia"
and "The Fall of the House of Usher." See *Collected Works of Edgar Allan Poe*, ed. Thomas
Ollive Mabbott (Cambridge, MA: Harvard University Press, 1978), 2:21–24, 322.

[29] Cf. Lovecraft's account of a visit to Boston in August 1923: "… a coal-black cat came
in & slept across my feet …" (*Selected Letters*, I, 248). This letter was written on September
4, 1923; later on in the letter he writes: "I have writ two hideous tales—'The Unnamable'
and 'The Rats in the Walls'" (*Selected Letters*, I, 250).

the cat had jumped bodily on the screening tapestry, bringing the affected section to the floor with his weight, and exposing a damp, ancient wall of stone; patched here and there by the restorers, and devoid of any trace of rodent prowlers. Nigger-Man raced up and down the floor by this part of the wall, clawing the fallen arras and seemingly trying at times to insert a paw between the wall and the oaken floor. He found nothing, and after a time returned wearily to his place across my feet. I had not moved, but I did not sleep again that night.

In the morning I questioned all the servants, and found that none of them had noticed anything unusual, save that the cook remembered that actions of a cat which had rested on her windowsill. This cat had howled at some unknown hour of the night, awaking the cook in time for her to see him dart purposefully out of the open door down the stairs. I drowsed away the noontime, and in the afternoon called again on Capt. Norrys, who became exceedingly interested in what I told him. The odd incidents—so slight yet so curious—appealed to his sense of the picturesque, and elicited from him a number of reminiscences of local ghostly lore. We were genuinely perplexed at the presence of rats, and Norrys lent me some traps and Paris green,[30] which I had the servants place in strategic localities when I returned.

I retired early, being very sleepy, but was harassed by dreams of the most horrible sort. I seemed to be looking down from an immense height upon a twilit grotto, knee-deep with filth, where a white-bearded daemon swineherd drove about with his staff a flock of fungous, flabby beasts whose appearance filled me with unutterable loathing. Then, as the swineherd paused and nodded over his task, a mighty

---

[30] *Paris green:* An insecticide in powder form prepared from arsenic trioxide and acetate of copper. Cf. Lovecraft's comment in 1934 on a colleague's cat, "who ate some Paris green in the cellar, was seized with a sort of frenzy, and dashed out of the house, never to be seen again" (*Selected Letters*, V, 72).

swarm of rats rained down on the stinking abyss and fell
to devouring beasts and man alike.[31]

From this terrific vision I was abruptly awaked by the
motions of Nigger-Man, who had been sleeping as usual
across my feet. This time I did not have to question the
source of his snarls and hisses, and of the fear which made
him sink his claws into my ankle, unconscious of their effect; for on every side of the chamber the walls were alive
with nauseous sound—the verminous slithering of ravenous, gigantic rats. There was now no aurora to shew the
state of the arras—the fallen section of which had been
replaced—but I was not too frightened to switch on the light.

As the bulbs leapt into radiance I saw a hideous shaking
all over the tapestry, causing the somewhat peculiar designs
to execute a singular dance of death. This motion disappeared almost at once, and the sound with it. Springing out
of bed, I poked at the arras with the long handle of a warm-
ing-pan that rested near, and lifted one section to see what
lay beneath. There was nothing but the patched stone wall,
and even the cat had lost his tense realisation of abnormal
presences. When I examined the circular trap that had been
placed in the room, I found all of the openings sprung, though
no trace remained of what had been caught and had escaped.

Further sleep was out of the question, so, lighting a candle,
I opened the door and went out in the gallery toward the
stairs to my study, Nigger-Man following at my heels. Before
we had reached the stone steps, however, the cat darted ahead
of me and vanished down the ancient flight. As I descended
the stairs myself, I became suddenly aware of sounds in
the great room below; sounds of a nature which could not

---

[31] St. Armand (note 3 above) cites Lovecraft's account of a dream he had in early 1920:
"I was alone in black space, when suddenly, ahead of me, there arose out of some hidden
pit a huge, white-robed man with a bald head and snowy beard. Across his shoulders was
slung the corpse of a younger man—cleanshaven, and grizzled of hair, and clad in a
similar robe. A sound as of rushing wind or a roaring furnace accompanied this spectacular ascent—an ascent which seemed accomplished by some occult species of levita-
tion. When I awaked, I had an idea for a story—but queerly enough, the idea had
nothing to do with the dream!" (*Selected Letters*, I, 102).

be mistaken. The oak-panelled walls were alive with rats, scampering and milling, whilst Nigger-Man was racing about with the fury of a baffled hunter. Reaching the bottom, I switched on the light, which did not this time cause the noise to subside. The rats continued their riot, stampeding with such force and distinctness that I could finally assign to their motions a definite direction. These creatures, in numbers apparently inexhaustible, were engaged in one stupendous migration from inconceivable heights to some depth conceivably, or inconceivably, below.

I now heard steps in the corridor, and in another moment two servants pushed open the massive door. They were searching the house for some unknown source of distrubance which had thrown all the cats into a snarling panic and caused them to plunge precipitately down several flights of stairs and squat, yowling, before the closed door to the sub-cellar. I asked them if they had heard the rats, but they replied in the negative. And when I turned to call their attention to the sounds in the panels, I realised that the noise had ceased. With the two men, I went down to the door of the sub-cellar, but found the cats already dispersed. Later I resolved to explore the crypt below, but for the present I merely made a round of the traps. All were sprung, yet all were tenantless. Satisfying myself that no one had heard the rats save the felines and me, I sat in my study till morning; thinking profoundly, and recalling every scrap of legend I had unearthed concerning the building I inhabited.

I slept some in the forenoon, leaning back in the one comfortable library chair which my mediaeval plan of furnishing could not banish. Later I telephoned to Capt. Norrys, who came over and helped me explore the sub-cellar. Absolutely nothing untoward was found, although we could not repress a thrill at the knowledge that this vault was built by Roman hands. Every low arch and massive pillar was Roman—not the debased Romanesque of the bungling Saxons, but the severe and harmonious classicism of the age of the Caesars; indeed, the walls abounded with inscriptions familiar to the antiquarians who had repeatedly explored the place—things like "P. GETAE. PROP ...TEMP ... DONA ..." and "L. PRAEC ... VS ... PONTIFI ... ATYS...."[32]

The reference to Atys made me shiver, for I had read Catullus[33] and knew something of the hideous rites of the Eastern god, whose worship was so mixed with that of Cybele.[34] Norrys and I, by the light of lanterns, tried to interpret the odd and nearly effaced designs on certain irregularly rectangular blocks of stone generally held to be altars, but could make nothing of them. We remembered that one pattern, a sort of rayed sun, was held by students to imply a non-Roman origin, suggesting that these altars had merely been adopted by the Roman priests from some older and perhaps aboriginal temple on the same site. On one of these blocks were some brown stains which made me wonder. The largest, in the centre of the room, had certain features on the upper surface which indicated its connexion with fire—probably burnt offerings.

Such were the sights in that crypt before whose door the cats had howled, and where Norrys and I now determined

---

[32] Again it is possible to guess at some of the words Lovecraft has here given fragmentarily: "P. Getae" and "L. Praec ... vs" are parts of proper names; "temp" is probably meant to signify *templum* ("temple"); "dona" signifies *dona* ("gifts"); "pontifi" is a form of *pontifex* ("priest"). For "Atys" see note 34 below.

[33] The reference is to poem 63 of Catullus, frequently referred to as the "Attis" poem. It narrates, in the first person, the story of Attis' maddened self-mutilation in the course of rites to his mother-lover Cybele, the Great Mother. Lovecraft may have derived the spelling "Atys" from the entry "Attis" in the 9th edition of the *Encyclopaedia Britannica*, which gives "Atys" as a variant form.

[34] Aside from Catullus, Lovecraft probably derived his knowledge of Attis/Atys and Cybele from Sir James George Frazer's landmark work of anthropology, *The Golden Bough* (1890f.). Consider this suggestive passage: "At Rome the new birth and the remission of sins by the shedding of bull's blood appear to have been carried out above all at the sanctuary of the Phrygian goddess [Cybele] on the Vatican Hill, at or near the spot where the great basilica of St. Peter's now stands; for many inscriptions relating to the rites were found when the church was being enlarged in 1608 or 1609" (*The Golden Bough: A Study in Magic and Religion* [New York: Macmillan, 1922], 352). See Hubert Van Calenbergh, "The Roots of Horror in *The Golden Bough*," *Lovecraft Studies* No. 26 (Spring 1992): 21–23.

to pass the night. Couches were brought down by the servants, who were told not to mind any nocturnal actions of the cats, and Nigger-Man was admitted as much for help as for companionship. We decided to keep the great oak door— a modern replica with slits for ventilation—tightly closed; and, with this attended to, we retired with lanterns still burning to await whatever might occur.

The vault was very deep in the foundations of the priory, and undoubtedly far down on the face of the beetling limestone cliff overlooking the waste valley. That it had been the goal of the scuffling and unexplainable rats I could not doubt, though why, I could not tell. As we lay there expectantly, I found my vigil occasionally mixed with half-formed dreams from which the uneasy motions of the cat across my feet would rouse me. These dreams were not wholesome, but horribly like the one I had had the night before. I saw again the twilit grotto, and the swineherd with his unmentionable fungous beasts wallowing in filth, and as I looked at these things they seemed nearer and more distinct—so distinct that I could almost observe their features.[35] Then I did observe the flabby features of one of them—and awaked with such a scream that Nigger-Man started up, whilst Capt. Norrys, who had not slept, laughed considerably. Norrys might have laughed more—or perhaps less— had he known what it was that made me scream. But I did not remember myself till later. Ultimate horror often paralyses memory in a merciful way.

---

[35] This entire passage seems partially derived from the legend of St. Patrick's Purgatory as related by Baring-Gould (see note 13 above). Baring-Gould quotes Froissart's conversation with Sir William Lisle, who made a pilgrimage to the Purgatory: "'[Lisle] said that when he and his companion passed through the gate of the Purgatory of S. Patrick, that they had descended as though into a cellar, and that a hot vapour rose towards them, and so affected their heads, that they were obliged to sit down on the stone steps. And after sitting there awhile they felt heavy with sleep, and so fell asleep, and slept all night.... [Lisle said] that they had been oppressed with many fancies and wonderful dreams, different from those they were accustomed to in their own chambers; and in the morning when they went out, in a short while they had clean forgotten their dreams and visions; wherefore he concluded that the whole matter was fancy'" (Baring-Gould, 1869, 240–41).

Norrys waked me when the phenomena began. Out of the same frightful dream I was called by his gentle shaking and his urging to listen to the cats. Indeed, there was much to listen to, for beyond the closed door at the head of the stone steps was a veritable nightmare of feline yelling and clawing, whilst Nigger-Man, unmindful of his kindred outside, was running excitedly around the bare stone walls, in which I heard the same babel of scurrying rats that had troubled me the night before.

An acute terror now rose within me, for here were anomalies which nothing normal could well explain. These rats, if not the creatures of a madness which I shared with the cats alone, must be burrowing and sliding in Roman walls I had thought to be of solid limestone blocks ... unless perhaps the action of water through more than seventeen centuries had eaten winding tunnels which rodent bodies had worn clear and ample.... But even so, the spectral horror was no less; for if these were living vermin why did not Norrys hear their disgusting commotion? Why did he urge me to watch Nigger-Man and listen to the cats outside, and why did he guess wildly and vaguely at what could have aroused them?

By the time I had managed to tell him, as rationally as I could, what I though I was hearing, my ears gave me the last fading impression of the scurrying; which had retreated *still downward,* far underneath this deepest of sub-cellars till it seemed as if the whole cliff below were riddled with questing rats. Norrys was not as sceptical as I had anticipated, but instead seemed profoundly moved. He motioned to me to notice that the cats at the door had ceased their clamour, as if giving up the rats for lost; whilst Nigger-Man had a burst of renewed restlessness, and was clawing frantically around the bottom of the large stone altar in the centre of the room, which was nearer Norrys' couch than mine.

My fear of the unknown was at this point very great. Something astounding had occurred, and I saw that Capt. Norrys, a younger, stouter, and presumably more naturally materialistic man, was affected fully as much as myself—

perhaps because of his lifelong and intimate familiarity
with local legend. We could for the moment do nothing
but watch the old black cat as he pawed with decreasing
fevour at the base of the altar, occasionally looking up and
mewing to me in that persuasive manner which he used
when he wished me to perform some favour for him.

Norrys now took a lantern close to the altar and examined the place where Nigger-Man was pawing; silently kneel-
ing and scraping away the lichens of centuries which joined
the massive pre-Roman block to the tessellated floor. He
did not find anything, and was about to abandon his effort
when I noticed a trivial circumstance which made me shudder, even though it implied nothing more than I had already
imagined. I told him of it, and we both looked at its almost
imperceptible manifestation with the fixedness of fascinated
discovery and acknowledgment. It was only this—that the
flame of the lantern set down near the altar was slightly but
certainly flickering from a draught of air which it had not
before received, and which came indubitably from the crev-
ice between floor and altar where Norrys was scraping away
the lichens.

We spent the rest of the night in the brilliantly lighted
study, nervously discussing what we should do next. The
discovery that some vault deeper than the deepest known
masonry of the Romans underlay this accursed pile—some
vault unsuspected by the curious antiquarians of three centuries—would have been sufficient to excite us without any
background of the sinister. As it was, the fascination became twofold; and we paused in doubt whether to abandon
our search and quit the priory forever in superstitious caution, or to gratify our sense of adventure and brave whatever horrors might await us in the unknown depths. By
morning we had compromised, and decided to go to London
to gather a group of archaeologists and scientific men fit to
cope with the mystery. It should be mentioned that before
leaving the sub-cellar we had vainly tried to move the central
altar which we now recognised as the gate to a new pit of

nameless fear. What secret would open the gate, wiser men than we would have to find.

During many days in London Capt. Norrys and I presented our facts, conjectures, and legendary anecdotes to five eminent authorities, all men who could be trusted to respect any family disclosures which future explorations might develop. We found most of them little disposed to scoff, but instead intensely interested and sincerely sympathetic. It is hardly necessary to name them all, but I may say that they included Sir William Brinton, whose excavations in the Troad[36] excited most of the world in their day. As we all took the train for Anchester I felt myself poised on the brink of frightful revelations, a sensation symbolised by the air of mourning among the many Americans at the unexpected death of the President on the other side of the world.[37]

On the evening of August 7th we reached Exham Priory, where the servants assured me that nothing unusual had occurred. The cats, even old Nigger-Man, had been perfectly placid; and not a trap in the house had been sprung. We were to begin exploring on the following day, awaiting which I assigned well-appointed rooms to all my guests. I myself retired in my own tower chamber, with Nigger-Man across my feet. Sleep came quickly, but hideous dreams assailed me. There was a vision of a Roman feast like that of Trimalchio,[38] with a horror in a covered platter. Then came that damnable, recurrent thing about the swineherd and his filthy drove in the twilit grotto. Yet when I awoke

---

[36] *Troad*: The region around Troy, in Asia Minor (now Turkey). Troy had been excavated by Heinrich Schliemann between 1870 and 1890. After Wilhelm Dörpfeld's excavations of 1893–94 there was little work done on the site until the 1930s.

[37] Warren Gamaliel Harding, 29th President of the United States (1921–23), died on August 2, 1923, of coronary thrombosis. In reference to a stamp of Harding, Lovecraft remarks: "Harding was a handsome bimbo—I'm sure sorry he had the good luck to get clear of this beastly planet" (*Selected Letters*, I, 253).

[38] *Trimalchio*: A character in Petronius' eccentric novel, *Satyricon* (c. A.D. 60), of which only a relatively small portion survives. The central tableau of this surviving section is an enormous and lavish banquet given by Trimalchio, a former slave from Asia Minor who becomes a fabulously wealthy businessman.

it was full daylight, with normal sounds in the house below. The rats, living or spectral, had not troubled me; and Nigger-Man was quietly asleep. On going down, I found that the same tranquillity had prevailed elsewhere; a condition which one of the assembled savants—a fellow named Thornton, devoted to the psychic—rather absurdly laid to the fact that I had now been shewn the thing which certain forces had wished to shew me.

All was now ready, and at 11 a.m. our entire group of seven men, bearing powerful electric searchlights and implements of excavation, went down to the sub-cellar and bolted the door behind us. Nigger-Man was with us, for the investigators found no occasion to despise his excitability, and were indeed anxious that he be present in case of obscure rodent manifestations. We noted the Roman inscriptions and unknown altar designs only briefly, for three of the savants had already seen them, and all knew their characteristics. Prime attention was paid to the momentous central altar, and within an hour Sir William Brinton had caused it to tilt backward, balanced by some unknown species of counterweight.

There now lay revealed such a horror as would have overwhelmed us had we not been prepared. Through a nearly square opening in the tiled floor, sprawling on a flight of stone steps so prodigiously worn that it was little more than an inclined plane at the centre, was a ghastly array of human or semi-human bones. Those which retained their collocation as skeletons shewed attitudes of panic fear, and over all were the marks of rodent gnawing. The skulls denoted nothing short of utter idiocy, cretinism,[39] or primitive semi-apedom. Above the hellishly littered

---

[39] These terms are not synonymous, but are quite specific psychological classifications. In 1910 the American Association for the Study of the Feeble-minded defined an idiot as "a mentally-defective person usually having a mental age of less than 3 years or, if a child, an intelligence quotient of less than 20." Idiocy is not a disease, but a condition in which the intellectual faculties are never developed. Cretinism is a medical classification denoting severe mental retardation produced when hypothyroidism in infants goes untreated.

steps arched a descending passage seemingly chiselled from the solid rock, and conducting a current of air. This current was not a sudden and noxious rush as from a closed vault, but a cool breeze with something of freshness in it. We did not pause long, but shiveringly began to clear a passage down the steps. It was then that Sir William, examining the hewn walls, made the odd observation that the passage, according to the direction of the strokes, must have been chiselled *from beneath*.[40]

I must be very deliberate now, and choose my words.

After ploughing down a few steps amidst the gnawed bones we saw that there was light ahead; not any mystic phosphorescence, but a filtered daylight which could not come except from unknown fissures in the cliff that overlooked the waste valley. That such fissures had escaped notice from outside was hardly remarkable, for not only is the valley wholly uninhabited, but the cliff is so high and beetling that only an aeronaut could study its face in detail. A few steps more, and our breaths were literally snatched from us by what we saw; so literally that Thornton, the psychic investigator, actually fainted in the arms of the dazed man who stood behind him. Norrys, his plump face utterly white and flabby, simply cried out inarticulately; whilst I think that what I

---

[40] St. Armand (note 3 above) has pointed out that this entire scene is remarkably similar to a dream experienced by Carl Gustav Jung as related in *Man and His Symbols* (Garden City, NY: Doubleday, 1964): "I had a dream when I was working with Freud…. I dreamed that I was in 'my home,' apparently on the first floor, in a cosy, pleasant sitting room furnished in the manner of the 18th century. I was astonished that I had never seen this room before, and began to wonder what the ground floor was like. I went downstairs and found the place was rather dark, with paneled walls and heavy furniture dating from the 16th century or even earlier. My surprise and curiosity increased. I wanted to see more of the whole structure of this house. So I went down to the cellar, where I found a door opening onto a flight of stone steps that led to a large vaulted room. The floor consisted of large slabs of stone and the walls seemed very ancient. I examined the mortar and found it was mixed with splinters of brick. Obviously the walls were of Roman origin. I became increasingly excited. In one corner, I saw an iron ring on a stone slab. I pulled up the slab and saw yet another narrow flight of stone steps leading to a kind of cave, which seemed to be a prehistoric tomb, containing two skulls, some bones, and broken shards of pottery" (Jung, 1964, 56). It is impossible that either Lovecraft or Jung could have known of each other's work at this time; this parallelism is a case of what Jung himself would have called synchronicity.

did was to gasp or hiss, and cover my eyes. The man behind me—the only one of the party older than I—croaked
the hackneyed "My God!" in the most cracked voice I ever
heard. Of seven cultivated men, only Sir William Brinton
retained his composure; a thing more to his credit because
he led the party and must have seen the sight first.

It was a twilit grotto of enormous height, stretching
away farther than any eye could see; a subterraneous world
of limitless mystery and horrible suggestion. There were
buildings and other architectural remains—in one terrified glance I saw a weird pattern of tumuli, a savage circle
of monoliths, a low-domed Roman ruin, a sprawling Saxon
pile, and an early English edifice of wood—but all these
were dwarfed by the ghoulish spectacle presented by the
general surface of the ground. For yards about the steps
extended an insane tangle of human bones, or bones at
least as human as those on the steps. Like a foamy sea
they stretched, some fallen apart, but others wholly or
partly articulated as skeletons; these latter invariably in
postures of daemoniac frenzy, either fighting off some
menace or clutching other forms with cannibal intent.

When Dr. Trask, the anthropologist, stooped to classify
the skulls, he found a degraded mixture which utterly baffled
him. They were mostly lower than the Piltdown man[41] in
the scale of evolution, but in every case definitely human.
Many were of higher grade, and a very few were the skulls
of supremely and sensitively developed types. All the bones
were gnawed, mostly by rats, but somewhat by others of
the half-human drove. Mixed with them were many tiny
bones of rats—fallen members of the lethal army which
closed the ancient epic.

[41] Lovecraft also refers to the Piltdown man in "Dagon" (1917). In 1912, a human brain
case remarkably like that of modern man but with a jawbone resembling an ape's was
found in a field near the small English town of Piltdown, south of London, by Charles
Dawson; the discovery was publicized by Sir Arthur Woodward Smith, and was the
source of much debate as to its authenticity and its place in the anthropological record.
For many years most anthropologists who accepted the find placed it in the Pleistocene

I wonder that any man among us lived and kept his sanity through that hideous day of discovery. Not Hoffmann[42] or Huysmans[43] could conceive a scene more wildly incredible, more frenetically repellent, or more Gothically grotesque than the twilit grotto through which we seven staggered; each stumbling on revelation after revelation, and trying to keep for the nonce from thinking of the events which must have taken place there three hundred years, or a thousand, or two thousand, or ten thousand years ago. It was the antechamber of hell, and poor Thornton fainted again when Trask told him that some of the skeleton things must have descended as quadrupeds through the last twenty or more generations.

Horror piled on horror as we began to interpret the architectural remains. The quadruped things—with their occasional recruits from the biped class—had been kept in stone pens, out of which they must have broken in their last delirium of hunger or rat-fear. There had been great herds of them, evidently fattened on the coarse vegetables whose remains could be found as a sort of poisonous ensilage[44] at the bottom of huge stone bins older than Rome. I knew now why

---

age. It was not revealed to be a hoax (the brain case and jawbone were from different species) until 1953. There is still debate as to who the perpetrator of the hoax was. One recent authority (Frank Spencer, *Piltdown: A Scientific Forgery* [New York: Oxford University Press, 1990]) accuses the distinguished anthropologist Sir Arthur Keith (who is glancingly mentioned in Lovecraft's "The Whisperer in Darkness" [1930]), but another scholar (Lord Zuckerman, "A Phony Ancestor," *New York Review of Books*, November 8, 1990, 12–16) suggests an eccentric scientist named Martin Hinton.

[42] *Hoffman*: Ernst Theodor Amadeus Hoffmann (1776–1822), German writer of the grotesque and a significant influence on Poe. Lovecraft says of him in "Supernatural Horror in Literature" (1927) that his works "are a byword for mellowness of background and maturity of form, though they incline to levity and extravagance, and lack the exalted moments of stark, breathless terror which a less sophisticated writer might have achieved" (*Dagon and Other Macabre Tales*, 389–90).

[43] *Huysmans*: Joris-Karl Huysmans (1848–1907), French novelist. Lovecraft read and was much influenced by his two weird novels, *Là-Bas* (1891; translated as *Down There*) and *A Rebours* (1884; usually translated as *Against the Grain*), the latter serving as a partial model for "The Hound" (1922).

my ancestors had had such excessive gardens—would to heaven I could forget! The purpose of the herds I did not have to ask.

Sir William, standing with his searchlight in the Roman ruin, translated aloud the most shocking ritual I have ever known; and told of the diet of the antediluvian cult which the priests of Cybele found and mingled with their own. Norrys, used as he was to the trenches, could not walk straight when he came out of the English building. It was a butcher shop and kitchen—he had expected that—but it was too much to see familiar English implements in such a place, and to read familiar English *graffiti* there, some as recent as 1610. I could not go in that building—that building whose daemon activities were stopped only by the dagger of my ancestor Walter de la Poer.

What I did venture to enter was the low Saxon building, whose oaken door had fallen, and there I found a terrible row of ten stone cells with rusty bars. Three had tenants, all skeletons of high grade, and on the bony forefinger of one I found a seal ring with my own coat-of-arms. Sir William found a vault with far older cells below the Roman chapel, but these cells were empty. Below them was a low crypt with cases of formally arranged bones, some of them bearing terrible parallel inscriptions carved in Latin, Greek, and the tongue of Phrygia.[45] Meanwhile, Dr. Trask had opened one of the prehistoric tumuli,[46] and brought to light skulls which were slighty more human than a gorilla's, and which bore indescribable ideographic carvings. Through all this horror my cat stalked unperturbed. Once I saw him

---

[44] *ensilage*: The primary meaning is "The process of preserving green fodder in a silo or pit, without having previously dried it"; here used in its secondary meaning: "The material resulting from the process" (*Oxford English Dictionary*).

[45] *the tongue of Phrygia*: Little is known about the Phrygian language save that it is Indo-European; its alphabet resembles Greek and the earliest surviving documents date from the eighth century B.C.

[46] *tumulus*: A sepulchral mound or barrow.

monstrously perched atop a mountain of bones, and wondered at the secrets that might lie behind his yellow eyes.

Having grasped to some slight degree the frightful revelations of this twilit area—an area so hideously foreshadowed by my recurrent dream—we turned to that apparently boundless depth of midnight cavern where no ray of light from the cliff could penetrate. We shall never know what sightless Stygian[47] worlds yawn beyond the little distance we went, for it was decided that such secrets are not good for mankind. But there was plenty to engross us close at hand, for we had not gone far before the searchlights shewed that accursed infinity of pits in which the rats had feasted, and whose sudden lack of replenishment had driven the ravenous rodent army first to turn on the living herds of starving things, and then to burst forth from the priory in that historic orgy of devastation which the peasants will never forget.

God! those carrion black pits of sawed, picked bones and opened skulls! Those nightmare chasms choked with the pithecanthropoid,[48] Celtic, Roman, and English bones of countless unhallowed centuries! Some of them were full, and none can say how deep they had once been. Others were still bottomless to our searchlights, and peopled by unnamable fancies. What, I thought, of the hapless rats that stumbled into such traps amidst the blackness of their quests in this grisly Tartarus?[49]

Once my foot slipped near a horribly yawning brink, and I had a moment of ecstatic fear. I must have been musing a long time, for I could not see any of the party but the plump Capt. Norrys. Then there came a sound from that inky, boundless, farther distance that I thought I knew; and I saw

---

[47] *Stygian*: Adjectival form of Styx, one of the five rivers in the Greek underworld.

[48] *pithecanthropoid*: Pithecanthrope was a neo-Greek coinage (*pithekos*, ape, and *anthropos*, man) invented by the German scientist Ernst Haeckel (1834–1919) for the putative link between man and ape. The suffix *-oid* means "like or resembling."

[49] *Tartarus*: A region in the Greek underworld.

my old black cat dart past me like a winged Egyptian god,[50] straight into the illimitable gulf of the unknown. But I was not far behind, for there was no doubt after another second. It was the eldritch scurrying of those fiend-born rats, always questing for new horrors, and determined to lead me on even unto those grinning caverns of earth's centre where Nyarlathotep,[51] the mad faceless god, howls blindly to the piping of two amorphous idiot flute-players.[52]

My searchlight expired, but still I ran. I heard voices, and yowls, and echoes, but above all there gently rose that impious, insidious scurrying; gently rising, rising, as a stiff bloated corpse gently rises above an oily river that flows under endless onyx bridges to a black, putrid sea. Something bumped into me—something soft and plump. It must have

---

[50] Perhaps Lovecraft was thinking of Bast, an Egyptian cat-headed goddess, although Bast did not have wings. Only a few of Egypt's principal gods were winged; among them are Re (or Ra) (hawk), the sun-god; Horus (hawk), the sky-god; Mentu (hawk), the war-god; and Nekhbet (vulture), sovereign over Upper Egypt.

[51] *Nyarlathotep*: The name had occurred to Lovecraft in a dream, and he had written the prose-poem "Nyarlathotep" (1920) around this enigmatic figure. There he portrays him as "swarthy, slender, and sinister," and as one who "looked like a Pharaoh" (Lovecraft, *Miscellaneous Writings* [Sauk City, WI: Arkham House, 1995], 32). He recurs in many later tales as a sort of all-purpose figure of cosmic chaos, notably in *The Dream-Quest of Unknown Kadath* (1926–27), "The Whisperer in Darkness" (1930), and "The Haunter of the Dark" (1935). In a recent article ("Behind the Mask of Nyarlathotep," *Lovecraft Studies* No. 25 [Fall 1991]:25–29) Will Murray suggests that the figure of Nyarlathotep in the prose-poem was partially inspired by Nikola Tesla (1856–1943), the eccentric scientist and inventor who created a sensation at the turn of the century with his electrical demonstrations. The name may have been derived (perhaps unconsciously) from two names in the work of Lord Dunsany: Alhireth-Hotep, a prophet in *The Gods of Pegana* (1905; rpt. Boston: John W. Luce, 1916), 53; and Mynarthitep, a god in "The Sorrow of Search," in *Time and the Gods* (1906; rpt. in *The Book of Wonder* [New York: Boni & Liveright/ Modern Library, 1918]), 132.

[52] These flute-players are among the most nebulous of Lovecraft's creations. They are first alluded to in the prose-poem "Nyarlathotep" (1920), which contains a reference to the "thin, monotonous whine of blasphemous flutes from inconceivable, unlighted chambers beyond Time" (*Miscellaneous Writings*, 34); but later the flute-players become associated with the god that stands at the pinnacle of Lovecraft's invented pantheon, Azathoth, "that last amorphous blight of nethermost confusion which blasphemes and bubbles at the centre of all infinity ... who gnaws hungrily in inconceivable, unlighted chambers beyond time amidst the muffled, maddening beat of vile drums and the thin, monotonous whine of accursed flutes" (*The Dream-Quest of Unknown Kadath* [1926–27]; *At the Mountains of Madness and Other Novels* [Sauk City, WI: Arkham House, 1985], 308).

been the rats; the viscous, gelatinous, ravenous army that feast on the dead and the living.... Why shouldn't rats eat a de la Poer as a de la Poer eats forbidden things? ... The war ate my boy, damn them all ... and the Yanks ate Carfax with flames and burnt Grandsire Delapore and the secret ... No, no, I tell you, I am *not* that daemon swineherd in the twilit grotto! It was *not* Edward Norrys' fat face on that flabby, fungous thing! Who says I am a de la Poer? He lived, but my boy died! ... Shall a Norrys hold the lands of a de la Poer? ... It's voodoo, I tell you ... that spotted snake ... Curse you, Thornton, I'll teach you to faint at what my family do! ... 'Sblood, thou stinkard, I'll learn ye how to gust ... wolde ye swynke me thilke wys? ... *Magna Mater! Magna Mater!* ... Atys ... *Dia ad aghaidh 's ad aodann ... agus bas dunach ort! Dhonas 's dholas ort, agus leat-sa! ... Ungl ... ungl ... rrrlh ... chchch ...* [53]

That is what they say I said when they found me in the blackness after three hours; found me crouching in the blackness over the plump, half-eaten body of Capt. Norrys, with my own cat leaping and tearing at my throat. Now they have blown up Exham Priory, taken my Nigger-Man away from me, and shut me into this barred room at Hanwell[54] with fearful whispers about my heredity and experiences. Thornton is in the next room, but they pre-

---

[53] The progression of languages is archaic English (" 'Sblood, thou stinkard ..."), Middle English ("wolde ye swynke ..."), Latin ("*Magna Mater!* ..."), Gaelic ("*Dia ad aghaidh* ..."), and primitive grunts; the purported effect is the narrator's sudden reversal on the evolutionary scale. The Gaelic in this passage is taken from "The Sin-Eater" by Fiona Macleod (pseudonym of William Sharp, 1856–1905), which Lovecraft read in Joseph Lewis French's *The Best Psychic Stories* (New York: Boni & Liveright/Modern Library, 1920): "'But, Andrew Blair, I will say this: when you fare abroad, *Droch caoidh ort!* and when you go upon the water, *Gaoth gun direadh ort!* Ay, ay, Anndra-mhic-Adam, *Dia ad aghaid 's ad aodann ... agus bas dunach ort! Dhonas 's dholas ort, agus leat-sa!*'" (French, 1920, 146). In a footnote Macleod translates this as follows: "Droch caoidh ort! 'May a fatal accident happen to you' (*lit.* 'bad moan on you'). Gaoth gun direadh ort! 'May you drift to your drowning' (*lit.* 'wind without direction on you'). Dia ad aghaidh, etc., 'God against thee and in thy face ... and may a death of woe be yours ... Evil and sorrow to thee and thine!'"

vent me from talking to him. They are trying, too, to suppress most of the facts concerning the priory. When I speak of poor Norrys they accuse me of a hideous thing, but they must know that I did not do it. They must know it was the rats; the slithering, scurrying rats whose scampering will never let me sleep; the daemon rats that race behind the padding in this room and beckon me down to greater horrors than I have ever known; the rats they can never hear; the rats, the rats in the walls.

Lovecraft, in a letter to Frank Belknap Long acknowledging the borrowing, remarked: "... the only objection to the phrase is that it's *Gaelic* instead of *Cymric* as the south-of-England locale demands. But as with anthropology—details don't count. Nobody will ever stop to note the difference" (*Selected Letters*, I, 258). In this he was wrong: when the tale was reprinted in *Weird Tales* for June 1930, Robert E. Howard wrote to editor Farnsworth Wright: "And I note from the fact that Mr. Lovecraft has his character speaking Gaelic instead of Cymric, in denoting the Age of the Druids, that he holds to Lluyd's theory as to the settling of Britain by the Celts" (*Selected Letters 1923-1930*, ed. Glenn Lord, et al. [West Warwick, RI: Necronomicon Press, 1989], 48). Wright passed the letter on to Lovecraft, and the two authors began a voluminous six-year correspondence.

[54] A real insane asylum in England at the time, although Lovecraft probably learned of it from its mention in Lord Dunsany's "The Coronation of Mr. Thomas Shap" (in *The Book of Wonder* [London: William Heinemann, 1912]).

H. P. Lovecraft is one of the absolute masters of the tale of supernatural dread and visionary horror, and among the writers whose work has been most crucial to the development of the field. His achievement is frequently underrated or misunderstood. He did indeed invent a mythos—the Cthulhu Mythos, as later writers called it—which united science fiction and the occult, but enviable and considerable though this was, it was by no means all he did. His work unites the British and American traditions of the weird tale, founding itself in the best of Blackwood and Machen and Dunsany as well as Poe and Bierce, as part of his search for a perfect form for stories in the genre. In the course of his career he explored various prose styles and handled so many of the themes of the weird tale that his fiction, along with his study Supernatural Horror in Literature, goes a long way to demonstrating the breadth of the field. Some of his tricks of style—his fondness for certain words, his runs of adjectives, his use of extended fantastic metaphors—may seem easy to imitate or parody, but not so the careful structures of which these elements are a part, nor the way he orchestrates his prose. Few other writers in the field have his power to communicate the awe and terror and alienness of the rest of the universe, nor the sense he conveys of something larger than his stories can contain. On a personal note, if I had not had his work on which to model my first serious efforts while learning my craft, I might well never have been heard of as a writer.

—Ramsey Campbell

"The Colour Out of Space" was written in March 1927 and first published in Amazing Stories for September 1927. Lovecraft referred to it "as an atmospheric study rather than as a tale" (Selected Letters, II, 127), and later came to regard it as perhaps his best story. He received, however, a payment of only $25 (about 1/5¢ per word) from editor Hugo Gernsback, leading Lovecraft in later years to refer to him as "Hugo the Rat." The tale was given a three-star rating in the 1928 edition of Edward J. O'Brien's prestigious series, The Best Short Stories ... and the Yearbook of the American Short Story; although the story itself was not reprinted, a "Biographical Notice" written by Lovecraft was printed in the back of the volume.

Lovecraft always remained proud of this story, frequently ranking it as his favorite among his works. He was particularly pleased with the depiction of the nebulous extraterrestrial entity (or entities) in the tale: "Most of my monsters fail altogether to satisfy my sense of the cosmic—the abnormally chromatic entity in 'The Colour Out of Space' being the only one of the lot which I take any pride in" (Selected Letters, II, 316). Because of its "cosmic" perspective and its publication in Amazing Stories, "The Colour Out of Space" has become a cornerstone in the development of science fiction. Fritz Leiber has testified that the story "gave me the gloomy creeps for weeks as a kid, when it turned up as a dark intruder in Amazing" ("Through Hyperspace with Brown Jenkin," in Lovecraft's The Dark Brotherhood and Other Pieces [Sauk City, WI: Arkham House, 1966], 170). Its inclusion in Groff Conklin's Omnibus of Science Fiction (1952) has ensured its place as a landmark in the field.

The Colour
Out of Space

West of Arkham[1] the hills rise wild, and there are valleys with deep woods that no axe has ever cut. There are dark narrow glens where the trees slope fantastically, and where thin brooklets trickle without ever having caught the glint of sunlight. On the gentler slopes there are farms, ancient and rocky, with squat, moss-coated cottages brooding eternally over old New England secrets in the lee of great ledges;

[1] *Arkham*: It is difficult to know how far "west" of Arkham the setting for this story is, especially as it is not clear where exactly Arkham itself is situated; but as characters are seen walking back from the Nahum Gardner farmhouse to Arkham, one assumes that the setting of the tale is not very far west of the imaginary city. In earlier stories Arkham seems clearly to be an inland town in central Massachusetts; in later stories it is identified loosely with the coastal town of Salem. Here an inland setting seems more likely. See note 44 below.

but these are all vacant now, the wide chimneys crumbling and the shingled sides bulging perilously beneath low gambrel roofs.[2]

The old folk have gone away, and foreigners do not like to live there. French-Canadians have tried it, Italians have tried it, and the Poles have come and departed.[3] It is not because of anything that can be seen or heard or handled, but because of something that is imagined. The place is not good for the imagination, and does not bring restful dreams at night. It must be this which keeps the foreigners away, for old Ammi Pierce has never told them of anything he recalls from the strange days. Ammi,[4] whose head has been a little queer for years, is the only one who still remains, or who ever talks of the strange days; and he dares to do this because his house is so near the open fields and the travelled roads around Arkham.

There was once a road over the hills and through the

---

[2] This opening passage, as Donald R. Burleson (*H. P. Lovecraft: A Critical Study* [Westport, CT: Greenwood Press, 1983], 136) has pointed out, bears some affinities to a passage in John Milton's "Il Penseroso" (c. 1631):

> And, when the sun begins to fling
> His flaring beams, me, Goddess, bring
> To arched walks of twilight groves,
> And shadows brown, that Sylvan loves,
> Of pine, or monumental oak,
> Where the rude axe with heaved stroke
> Was never heard the nymphs to daunt,
> Or fright them from their hallowed haunt.
> There, in close covert, by some brook,
> Where no profaner eye may look,
> Hide me from day's garish eye ... (ll. 131–41)

[3] These are three of the major ethnic minorities in New England. French Canadians are a significant force in the Rhode Island town of Woonsocket, while Providence has heavy Italian and Polish districts. Lovecraft's "The Haunter of the Dark" (1935) is largely set in the Italian district of Providence known as Federal Hill.

[4] The name Ammi is probably derived from Ben-Ammi, one of the children begot from the incestuous union of Lot and his daughters (Genesis 19:38). Robert M. Price, in "A Biblical Antecedent for 'The Colour Out of Space,'" *Lovecraft Studies* No. 25 (Fall 1991):23–25, makes an interesting case for the influence of the entire story of Lot in Sodom (Genesis 18 and 19) on this tale.

valleys, that ran straight where the blasted heath[5] is now; but people ceased to use it and a new road was laid curving far toward the south. Traces of the old one can still be found amidst the weeds of a returning wilderness, and some of them will doubtless linger even when half the hollows are flooded for the new reservoir.[6] Then the dark woods will be cut down and the blasted heath will slumber far below blue waters whose surface will mirror the sky and ripple in the sun. And the secrets of the strange days will be one with the deep's secrets; one with the hidden lore of old ocean, and all the mystery of primal earth.

When I went into the hills and vales to survey for the new reservoir they told me the place was evil. They told me

---

[5] *blasted heath*: See note 10 below.

[6] This "new reservoir" is based in part on the Quabbin Reservoir in the Swift River Valley of central Massachusetts, plans for which had begun in 1926, although it was not completed until 1939. Lovecraft surely knew of this project, designed to supply drinking water for Boston; but note this remark in a letter of 1935: "The trip through the doomed Swift River Valley must have held more than a slight touch of melancholy. I went through it 8 years ago, not long after its doom was first pronounced, & well-nigh groaned at the future destruction of exquisite old villages like Dana & its neighbours.... We have had a similar experience in Rhode Island, where a vast amount of rural territory was flooded in 1926 for a reservoir. It was that flooding which caused me to use the reservoir element in 'The Colour Out of Space'" (Lovecraft to Richard Ely Morse, October 13, 1935; ms., John Hay Library). (Lovecraft is here referring to the Scituate Reservoir in central Rhode Island.) The building of the Quabbin Reservoir caused the razing and immersion of entire towns in central Massachusetts, including Greenwich, Enfield, Dana, and Prescott.

this in Arkham, and because that is a very old town full of witch legends I thought the evil must be something which grandams had whispered to children through centuries. The name "blasted heath" seemed to me very odd and theatrical, and I wondered how it had come into the folklore of a Puritan people. Then I saw that dark westward tangle of glens and slopes for myself, and ceased to wonder at anything besides its own elder mystery. It was morning when I saw it, but shadow lurked always there. The trees grew too thickly, and their trunks were too big for any healthy New England wood. There was too much silence in the dim alleys between them, and the floor was too soft with the dank moss and mattings of infinite years of decay.

In the open spaces, mostly along the line of the old road, there were little hillside farms; sometimes with all the buildings standing, sometimes with only one or two, and sometimes with only a lone chimney or fast-filling cellar. Weeds and briers reigned, and furtive wild things rustled in the undergrowth. Upon everything was a haze of restlessness and oppression; a touch of the unreal and the grotesque, as if some vital element of perspective or chiaroscuro[7] were awry. I did not wonder that the foreigners would not stay, for this was no region to sleep in. It was too much like a landscape of Salvator Rosa;[8] too much like some forbidden woodcut in a tale of terror.[9]

But even all this was not so bad as the blasted heath. I knew it the moment I came upon it at the bottom of a spacious valley; for no other name could fit such a thing, or any other thing fit such a name. It was as if the poet had coined

---

[7] *chiaroscuro*: A technical term in painting, derived from two Italian words, *chiaro* ("clear") and *oscuro* ("dark"); in other words, the treatment of light and shade in a picture.

[8] *Salvator Rosa*: Italian painter (1615–1673). Many of Rosa's paintings feature wild and desolate landscapes full of rocky cliffs, trees clawing in the air, thunder and lightning, and witches. Several of his paintings are in the Metropolitan Museum in New York, where Lovecraft probably saw them.

[9] The phrase "tale of terror," referring to the eighteenth-century Gothic novel, may have been suggested by Edith Birkhead's *The Tale of Terror* (1921), which Lovecraft used as a major source for "Supernatural Horror in Literature" (1927).

the phrase from having seen this one particular region.[10] It must, I thought as I viewed it, be the outcome of a fire; but why had nothing new ever grown over those five acres of grey desolation that sprawled open to the sky like a great spot eaten by acid in the woods and fields? It lay largely to the north of the ancient road line, but encroached a little on the other side. I felt an odd reluctance about approaching, and did so at last only because my business took me through and past it. There was no vegetation of any kind on that broad expanse, but only a fine grey dust or ash which no wind seemed ever to blow about. The trees near it were sickly and stunted, and many dead trunks stood or lay rotting at the rim. As I walked hurriedly by I saw the tumbled bricks and stones of an old chimney and cellar on my right, and the yawning black maw of an abandoned well whose stagnant vapours played strange tricks with the hues of the sunlight. Even the long, dark woodland climb beyond seemed welcome in contrast, and I marvelled no more at the frightened whispers of Arkham people. There had been no house or ruin near; even in the old days the place must have been lonely and remote. And at twilight, dreading to repass that ominous spot, I walked circuitously back to the town by the curving road on the south. I vaguely wished some clouds would gather, for an odd timidity about the deep skyey voids above had crept into my soul.

In the evening I asked old people in Arkham about the blasted heath, and what was meant by that phrase "strange days" which so many evasively muttered. I could not, however, get any good answers, except that all the mystery was much more recent than I had dreamed. It was not a matter of old legendry at all, but something within the lifetime of

---

[10] Perhaps Lovecraft was unaware that at least two major poets had used this phrase. In Shakespeare's *Macbeth* Macbeth says to the witches: "Say from whence / You owe this strange intelligence, or why / Upon this blasted heath you stop our way / With such prophetic greeting" (I, iii, 75–78). But probably Lovecraft was thinking of the passage in Milton's *Paradise Lost* that reads: "... as, when Heaven's fire / Hath scathed the forest oaks or mountain pines, / With singed top their stately growth, though bare, / Stands on the blasted heath" (I, 612–15).

those who spoke. It had happened in the 'eighties, and a family had disappeared or was killed. Speakers would not be exact; and because they all told me to pay no attention to old Ammi Pierce's crazy tales, I sought him out the next morning, having heard that he lived alone in the ancient tottering cottage where the trees first begin to get thick. It was a fearsomely archaic place, and had begun to exude the faint miasmal odour which clings about houses that have stood too long. Only with persistent knocking could I rouse the aged man, and when he shuffled timidly to the door I could tell he was not glad to see me. He was not so feeble as I had expected; but his eyes drooped in a curious way, and his unkempt clothing and white beard made him seem very worn and dismal.[11] Not knowing just how he could best be launched on his tales, I feigned a matter of business; told him of my surveying, and asked vague questions about the district. He was far brighter and more educated than I had been led to think, and before I knew it had grasped quite as much of the subject as any man I had talked with in Arkham. He was not like other rustics I had known in the sections where reservoirs were to be. From him there were no protests at the miles of old wood and farmland to be blotted out, though perhaps there would have been had not his home lain outside the bounds of the future lake. Relief was all that he shewed; relief at the doom of the dark ancient valleys through which he had roamed all his life. They were better under water now—better under water since the strange days. And with this opening his husky voice sank low, while his body leaned forward and his right forefinger began to point shakily and impressively.

---

[11] Cf. Lovecraft's description of the unnaturally aged cannibal in "The Picture in the House" (1920): "His face, almost hidden by a long beard which grew high on the cheeks, seemed abnormally ruddy and less wrinkled than one might expect; while over a high forehead fell a shock of white hair little thinned by the years. His blue eyes, though a trifle bloodshot, seemed inexplicably keen and burning. But for his horrible unkemptness the man would have been as distinguished-looking as he was impressive" (*The Dunwich Horror and Others* [Sauk City, WI: Arkham House, 1984], 120).

It was then that I heard the story, and as the rambling voice scraped and whispered on I shivered again and again despite the summer day. Often I had to recall the speaker from ramblings, piece out scientific points which he knew only by a fading parrot memory of professors' talk, or bridge over gaps where his sense of logic and continuity broke down. When he was done I did not wonder that his mind had snapped a trifle, or that the folk of Arkham would not speak much of the blasted heath. I hurried back before sunset to my hotel, unwilling to have the stars come out above me in the open; and the next day returned to Boston to give up my position. I could not go into that dim chaos of old forest and slope again, or face another time that grey blasted heath where the black well yawned deep beside the tumbled bricks and stones. The reservoir will soon be built now, and all those elder secrets will be safe forever under watery fathoms. But even then I do not believe I would like to visit that country by night—at least, not when the sinister stars are out; and nothing could bribe me to drink the new city water of Arkham.

It all began, old Ammi said, with the meteorite. Before that time there had been no wild legends at all since the witch trials,[12] and even then these western woods were not feared half so much as the small island in the Miskatonic where the devil held court beside a curious stone altar older than the Indians.[13] These were not haunted woods, and their fantastic dusk was never terrible till the strange days. Then

---

[12] The Salem witch trials occurred in Salem Village (now Danvers), Massachusetts, in 1692. The incident began when young girls accused a West Indian slave, Tituba, of bewitching them. In the subsequent hysteria the accusations spread and many townspeople were accused of witchcraft. Hundreds were arrested, nineteen were hanged, and one man was "pressed" to death (no witches were burned in the United States, as they were in Europe). See also note 18 to "The Dunwich Horror."

[13] This "small island" is mentioned again in "The Dreams in the Witch House" (1932): " … there was a clearly visible living figure on that desolate island, and a second glance told him it was certainly the strange old woman whose sinister aspect had worked itself so disastrously into his dreams" (*At the Mountains of Madness and Other Novels*, 274).

there had come that white noontide cloud, that string of explosions in the air, and that pillar of smoke from the valley far in the wood. And by night all Arkham had heard of the great rock that fell out of the sky and bedded itself in the ground beside the well at the Nahum Gardner[14] place. That was the house which had stood where the blasted heath was to come—the trim white Nahum Gardner house amidst its fertile gardens and orchards.

Nahum had come to town to tell people about the stone, and had dropped in at Ammi Pierce's on the way. Ammi was forty then, and all the queer things were fixed very strongly in his mind. He and his wife had gone with the three professors from Miskatonic University who hastened out the next morning to see the weird visitor from unknown stellar space, and had wondered why Nahum had called it so large the day before. It had shrunk, Nahum said as he pointed out the big brownish mound above the ripped earth and charred grass near the archaic well-sweep[15] in his front yard; but the wise men answered that stones do not shrink. Its heat lingered persistently, and Nahum declared it had glowed faintly in the night. The professors tried it with a geologist's hammer and found it was oddly soft. It was, in truth, so soft as to be almost plastic; and they gouged rather than chipped a specimen to take back to the college for testing. They took it in an old pail borrowed from Nahum's kitchen, for even the small piece refused to grow cool. On the trip back they stopped at Ammi's to rest, and seemed thoughtful when Mrs. Pierce remarked that the fragment

---

[14] *Nahum Gardner*: Nahum is the title of a book in the Old Testament; Nahum the Elkoshite is the seventh of the minor prophets. The name also clearly suggests backwoods rusticity. Gardner is a city in north-central Massachusetts, near Athol (see note 29 to "The Dunwich Horror").

[15] *well-sweep*: A pump-handle. Cf. Lovecraft's visit in 1936 to the Thomas Clemence house (1654) near Manton, Rhode Island: "In the yard the old well-sweep still remains—one of the relatively few left in this colony" (Lovecraft to Edward H. Cole, August 15, 1936; ms., John Hay Library).

was growing smaller and burning the bottom of the pail.
Truly, it was not large, but perhaps they had taken less than
they thought.

The day after that—all this was in June of '82—the professors had trooped out again in a great excitement. As they
passed Ammi's they told him what queer things the specimen had done, and how it had faded wholly away when
they put it in a glass beaker. The beaker had gone, too, and
the wise men talked of the strange stone's affinity for silicon.[16] It had acted quite unbelievably in that well-ordered
laboratory; doing nothing at all and shewing no occluded
gases[17] when heated on charcoal, being wholly negative in
the borax bead,[18] and soon proving itself absolutely
non-volatile at any producible temperature, including that
of the oxy-hydrogen blowpipe.[19] On an anvil it appeared
highly malleable, and in the dark its luminosity was very
marked. Stubbornly refusing to grow cool, it soon had the
college in a state of real excitement; and when upon heating before the spectroscope[20] it displayed shining bands

---

[16] *silicon*: Silicon (Si) is one of the principal constituents of glass.

[17] *occluded gases*: Gases retained within certain substances (chiefly metals); usually
released when the metal is heated to a sufficient temperature.

[18] *borax bead*: "Beads made of borax [$Na_2B_4O_7$], used in blowpipe analysis to distinguish
the metallic oxides, and test minerals by the characteristic colours which they give in the
oxidizing and the reducing flame" (*Oxford English Dictionary*).

[19] *oxy-hydrogen blowpipe*: An instrument, invented by Robert Hare in 1813 and used for
welding, glass-blowing, and chemical analysis, with a flame utilizing a mixture of oxygen and
hydrogen. Such a flame produces an exceptionally high temperature, up to 2000° C. At the
time of this story's events, this was the highest temperature that could be achieved by a flame;
but by the early twentieth century the oxyacetylene blowpipe, which could reach temperatures of 3300° C (5972° F), had largely replaced the earlier instrument.

[20] *spectroscope*: An instrument designed to separate light into its constituent wavelengths so
as to form a spectrum. This spectrum displays all the wavelengths visible to the human eye;
those of a higher frequency are ultraviolet, those of a lower frequency are infrared. Spectro-
scopes can also be used to resolve waves of electromagnetic radiation into a spectrum. A
band spectrum is produced by molecules, as distinguished from a line spectrum (produced
by atoms) and a continuous spectrum (produced by dense matter).

The reference here to "shining bands unlike any known colours of the normal spectrum" (as
well as the mention below [p. 88] of an "unknown spectrum") is a deliberate paradox; for

unlike any known colours of the normal spectrum there was much breathless talk of new elements,[21] bizarre optical properties, and other things which puzzled men of science[22] are wont to say when faced by the unknown.

Hot as it was, they tested it in a crucible with all the proper reagents.[23] Water did nothing. Hydrochloric acid[24] was the same. Nitric acid and even aqua regia[25] merely hissed and spattered against its torrid invulnerability. Ammi had difficulty in recalling all these things, but recognised some

---

the "colour" in this story *can* be seen by the human eye, even if it is unusual, and yet it does not appear in any conventional form on the spectrum.

Lovecraft did much spectroscopic analysis as a youth as part of his enthusiasm for chemistry: "One phase of chemistry in which I dabbled was spectrum-analysis, & I still have my spectroscope—a rather low-priced diffraction instrument costing $15.00. I have also a still cheaper *pocket* spectroscope, which was the delight of my fellow students at H[ope] S[treet] H[igh] S[chool]. It is unbelievably tiny—will go into a vest pocket without making much of a bulge— yet gives a neat, bright little spectrum, with clear Frauenhofer lines when directed at sunlight" (Lovecraft to Alfred Galpin, August 29, 1918; ms., John Hay Library).

[21] *new elements*: At the time of the writing of this story, ninety of the ninety-two elements occurring in nature had been discovered, although atomic weights of six of these had not yet been determined. At least thirteen more elements not now occurring in nature have been found, and some scientists believe that there may be a total of 168 possible elements.

[22] *men of science*: i.e., scientists. Lovecraft preferred this usage, since the word "scientist" (although first attested in 1840, according to the *Oxford English Dictionary*) was still regarded as a neologism or colloquialism at this time. Lovecraft uses the word in "Dagon" (1917), but when John Ravenor Bullen read the story in 1921, he suggested a change to "man of science"; Lovecraft, in "The Defence Remains Open!" (1921), acknowledges: "The suggestions anent the dubious word *scientist* ... are good, and will be acted on if the yarn is ever republished" (*In Defence of Dagon* [West Warwick, RI: Necronomicon Press, 1985], 14). In fact, Lovecraft never revised the word in "Dagon."

[23] *reagent*: A substance used in chemical analysis to determine the presence of some other substance by means of a reaction.

[24] *hydrochloric acid*: HCl, a compound of hydrogen and chlorine. Hydrochloric acid, nitric acid, and their combined forms (see notes 25–26 below) have highly corrosive properties. They are very active against metals, but relatively safe against stone and glass. In testing the meteorite, the scientists would not have expected silicaceous matter to be as affected as metallic iron, a common ingredient of meteorites.

[25] *nitric acid*: HNO_3, a compound of hydrogen, nitrogen, and oxygen; formerly called *aqua fortis*. Cf. Marinus Willett's translation of a Latin message in Saxon minuscules in *The Case of Charles Dexter Ward* (1927): "Curwen must be killed. The body must be dissolved in aqua fortis, nor must anything be retained" (*At the Mountains of Madness and Other Novels*, 220).

aqua regia: A mixture of nitric and hydrochloric acid.

solvents as I mentioned them in the usual order of use. There were ammonia and caustic soda, alcohol and ether, nauseous carbon disulphide[26] and a dozen others; but although the weight grew steadily less as time passed, and the fragment seemed to be slightly cooling, there was no change in the solvents to shew that they had attacked the substance at all. It was a metal, though, beyond a doubt. It was magnetic, for one thing; and after its immersion in the acid solvents[27] there seemed to be faint traces of the Widmannstätten figures[28] found on meteoric iron. When the cooling had grown very considerable, the testing was carried on in glass; and it was in a glass beaker that they left all the chips made of the original fragment during the work. The next morning both chips and beaker were gone without trace, and only a charred spot marked the place on the wooden shelf where they had been.

All this the professors told Ammi as they paused at his door, and once more he went with them to see the stony messenger from the stars, though this time his wife did not accompany them. It had now most certainly shrunk, and even the sober professors could not doubt the truth of what they saw. All around the dwindling brown earth had caved in; and whereas it had been a good seven feet across the day before, it was now scarcely five. It was still hot, and the

---

[26] *ammonia*: NH_3, a compound of nitrogen and hydrogen.

caustic soda: Sodium hydroxide (NaOH).

alcohol: Presumably ethyl alcohol (C_2H_5OH).

ether: $C_4H_{10}O$. Both alcohol and ether are solvents of organic materials.

carbon disulphide: CS_2, a compound of carbon and sulphur. Lovecraft refers to it as "nauseous" because it has a foetid odor, like that of rotten eggs. It is a toxic gas.

[27] *acid solvents*: Those solvents that are compounds of hydrogen; these include (of those mentioned above) ammonia, caustic soda, alcohol, and ether.

[28] *Widmannstätten figures*: Patterns of intersecting bands revealed when polished surfaces of most iron meteorites are etched in nitric acid. Named after Aloys von Widmannstätten (1754–1849), who discovered them.

sages studied its surface curiously as they detached another and larger piece with hammer and chisel. They gouged deeply this time, and as they pried away the smaller mass they saw that the core of the thing was not quite homogeneous.

They had uncovered what seemed to be the side of a large coloured globule imbedded in the substance. The colour, which resembled some of the bands in the meteor's strange spectrum, was almost impossible to describe; and it was only by analogy that they called it colour at all.[29] Its texture was glossy, and upon tapping it appeared to promise both brittleness and hollowness. One of the professors gave it a smart blow with a hammer, and it burst with a nervous little pop. Nothing was emitted, and all trace of the thing vanished with the puncturing. It left behind a hollow spherical space about three inches across, and all thought it probable that others would be discovered as the enclosing substance wasted away.

Conjecture was vain; so after a futile attempt to find additional globules by drilling, the seekers left again with their new specimen—which proved, however, as baffling in the laboratory as its predecessor had been. Aside from being almost plastic, having heat, magnetism, and slight luminosity, cooling slightly in powerful acids, possessing an unknown spectrum, wasting away in air, and attacking silicon compounds with mutual destruction as a result, it presented no identifying features whatsoever; and at the end of the tests the college scientists were forced to own that they could not place it. It was nothing of this earth, but a piece

---

[29] Cf. Ambrose Bierce's "The Damned Thing":

At each end of the solar spectrum the chemist can detect the presence of what are known as "actinic" rays. They represent colors—integral colors in the composition of light—which we are unable to discern. The human eye is an imperfect instrument; its range is but a few octaves of the real "chromatic scale." I am not mad; there are colors that we cannot see.

And, God help me! the Damned Thing is of such a color! (*Can Such Things Be?* [1893; rpt. Secaucus, NJ: Citadel Press, 1974], 139)

of the great outside; and as such dowered[30] with outside properties and obedient to outside laws.

That night there was a thunderstorm, and when the professors went out to Nahum's the next day they met with a bitter disappointment. The stone, magnetic as it had been, must have had some peculiar electrical property; for it had "drawn the lightning",[31] as Nahum said, with a singular persistence. Six times within an hour the farmer saw the lightning strike the furrow in the front yard, and when the storm was over nothing remained but a ragged pit by the ancient well-sweep, half-choked with caved-in earth. Digging had borne no fruit, and the scientists verified the fact of the utter vanishment. The failure was total; so that nothing was left to do but go back to the laboratory and test again the disappearing fragment left carefully encased in lead. That fragment lasted a week, at the end of which nothing of value had been learned of it. When it had gone, no residue was left behind, and in time the professors felt scarcely sure they had indeed seen with waking eyes that cryptic vestige of the fathomless gulfs outside; that lone, weird message from other universes and other realms of matter, force, and entity.

As was natural, the Arkham paper made much of the incident with its collegiate sponsoring, and sent reporters to talk with Nahum Gardner and his family. At least one

---

[30] *dowered*: Endowed or furnished with a given quality; from the noun *dower*, which can refer either to the portion of a deceased husband's estate given to his widow upon his death or the money or property a wife brings to her husband; in this latter meaning the word *dowry* is more commonly used.

[31] As Will Murray ("Sources for 'The Colour Out of Space,'" *Crypt of Cthulhu* No. 28 [Yuletide 1984]:3–5) has pointed out, this is perhaps an echo of Charles Fort's account of "thunderstones," small stones that may or may not have fallen from the sky and which cause lightning to strike them repeatedly. See *The Book of the Damned* (1919), in *The Books of Charles Fort* (New York: Fortean Society/Henry Holt, 1941), 101f. Charles Fort (1874–1932) was an American author of several books in which he collected newspaper and other accounts of strange occurrences (e.g., blood raining from the sky) in an effort to jolt scientists out of what he believed to be their dogmatic skepticism in regard to anomalous or unexplained phenomena.

Boston daily also sent a scribe, and Nahum quickly became a kind of local celebrity. He was a lean, genial person of about fifty, living with his wife and three sons on the pleasant farmstead in the valley. He and Ammi exchanged visits frequently, as did their wives; and Ammi had nothing but praise for him after all these years. He seemed slightly proud of the notice his place had attracted, and talked often of the meteorite in the succeeding weeks. That July and August were hot, and Nahum worked hard at his haying in the ten-acre pasture[32] across Chapman's Brook;[33] his rattling wain[34] wearing deep ruts in the shadowy lanes between. The labour tired him more than it had in other years, and he felt that age was beginning to tell on him.

Then fell the time of fruit and harvest. The pears and apples slowly ripened, and Nahum vowed that his orchards were prospering as never before. The fruit was growing to phenomenal size and unwonted gloss, and in such abundance that extra barrels were ordered to handle the future crop. But with the ripening came sore disappointment; for of all that gorgeous array of specious lusciousness not one single jot was fit to eat. Into the fine flavour of the pears and apples had crept a stealthy bitterness and sickishness, so that even the smallest of bites induced a lasting disgust. It was the same with the melons and tomatoes, and Nahum sadly saw that his entire crop was lost. Quick to connect events, he declared that the meteorite had poisoned the soil, and thanked heaven that most of the other crops were in the upland lot along the road.

Winter came early, and was very cold. Ammi saw Nahum less often than usual, and observed that he had begun to look worried. The rest of his family, too, seemed to have

---

[32] *ten-acre pasture*: Cf. Ten-Acre Meadow in "The Dunwich Horror" (p. 143).

[33] *Chapman's Brook*: A "Chapman farmhouse" is mentioned in "Herbert West— Reanimator." (1921–22)

[34] *wain*: wagon.

grown taciturn; and were far from steady in their chuchgoing or their attendance at the various social events of the countryside. For this reserve or melancholy no cause could be found, though all the household confessed now and then to poorer health and a feeling of vague disquiet. Nahum himself gave the most definite statement of anyone when he said he was disturbed about certain footprints in the snow. They were the usual winter prints of red squirrels, white rabbits, and foxes, but the brooding farmer professed to see something not quite right about their nature and arrangement. He was never specific, but appeared to think that they were not as characteristic of the anatomy and habit of squirrels and rabbits and foxes as they ought to be. Ammi listened without interest to this talk until one night when he drove past Nahum's house in his sleigh on the way back from Clark's Corners. There had been a moon, and a rabbit had run across the road, and the leaps of the rabbit were longer than either Ammi or his horse liked. The latter, indeed, had almost run away when brought up by a firm rein. Thereafter Ammi gave Nahum's tales more respect, and wondered why the Gardner dogs seemed so cowed and quivering every morning. They had, it developed, nearly lost the spirit to bark.

In February the McGregor boys from Meadow Hill were out shooting woodchucks, and not far from the Gardner place bagged a very peculiar specimen. The proportions of its body seemed slightly altered in a queer way impossible to describe, while its face had taken on an expression which no one ever saw in a woodchuck before. The boys were genuinely frightened, and threw the thing away at once, so that only their grotesque tales of it ever reached the people of the countryside. But the shying away of the horses near Nahum's house had now become an acknowledged thing, and all the basis for a cycle of whispered legend was fast taking form.

People vowed that the snow melted faster around Nahum's than it did anywhere else, and early in March there was an awed discussion in Potter's general store in Clark's

Corners. Stephen Rice[35] had driven past Gardner's in the morning, and had noticed the skunk-cabbages[36] coming up through the mud by the woods across the road. Never were things of such size seen before, and they had held strange colours that could not be put into any words. Their shapes were monstrous, and the horse had snorted at an odour which struck Stephen as wholly unprecedented. That afternoon several persons drove past to see the abnormal growth, and all agreed that plants of that kind ought never to sprout in a healthy world. The bad fruit of the fall before was freely mentioned, and it went from mouth to mouth that there was poison in Nahum's ground. Of course it was the meteorite; and remembering how strange the men from the college had found that stone to be, several farmers spoke about the matter to them.

One day they paid Nahum a visit; but having no love of wild tales and folklore were very conservative in what they inferred. The plants were certainly odd, but all skunk-cabbages are more or less odd in shape and odour and hue. Perhaps some mineral element from the stone had entered the soil, but it would soon be washed away. And as for the footprints and frightened horses—of course this was mere country talk which such a phenomenon as the aërolite[37] would be certain to start. There was really nothing for serious men to do in cases of wild gossip, for superstitious rustics will say and believe anything. And so all through the strange days the professors stayed away in contempt. Only one of them, when given two phials of dust for analysis in a police job over a year and a half later, recalled that the queer colour of that skunk-cabbage had been very like one of the anomalous

---

[35] Cf. Professor Warren Rice, a character in "The Dunwich Horror." See note 72 to that story.

[36] *skunk-cabbages*: *Symplocarpus foetidus*, a stemless plant of the arum family that gives off an offensive odor, especially when bruised. The plant is common in the Northeast.

[37] *aërolite*: meteorite. The *Oxford English Dictionary* states, "In recent usage, the name *aerolite* has been confined to those meteorites which consist of stone or other substance other than meteoric iron," and considers *aerolith* ("stone from the air") a more correct form.

bands of light shewn by the meteor fragment in the college spectroscope, and like the brittle globule found imbedded in the stone from the abyss. The samples in this analysis case gave the same odd bands at first, though later they lost the property.

The trees budded prematurely around Nahum's, and at night they swayed ominously in the wind. Nahum's second son Thaddeus, a lad of fifteen, swore that they swayed also when there was no wind; but even the gossips would not credit this. Certainly, however, restlessness was in the air. The entire Gardner family developed the habit of stealthy listening, though not for any sound which they could consciously name. The listening was, indeed, rather a product of moments when consciousness seemed half to slip away. Unfortunately such moments increased week by week, till it became common speech that "something was wrong with all Nahum's folks". When the early saxifrage[38] came out it had another strange colour; not quite like that of the skunk-cabbage, but plainly related and equally unknown to anyone who saw it. Nahum took some blossoms to Arkham and shewed them to the editor of the *Gazette*,[39] but that dignitary did no more than write a humorous article about them, in which the dark fears of rustics were held up to polite ridicule. It was a mistake of Nahum's to tell a stolid city man about the way the great, overgrown mourning-cloak butterflies[40] behaved in connexion with these saxifrages.

April brought a kind of madness to the country folk, and

---

[38] *saxifrage*: A name for several plants of the genus *Saxifraga*, a type of dwarf herb, commonly blooming in late spring and early summer.

[39] *Gazette*: This is the only mention in Lovecraft's work of this newspaper, evidently a predecessor to the *Arkham Advertiser* (see note 49 to "The Dunwich Horror"). The first newspaper in Providence was the *Providence Gazette and Country-Journal* (1762–1820?), the entire run of which Lovecraft read at the Providence Public Library. In 1915 Lovecraft wrote a series of astronomy articles for the *Asheville* (NC) *Gazette-News*.

[40] *mourning-cloak butterflies*: *Nymphalis antiopa*, a butterfly with brown wings flecked with blue and with a yellow band on the outer edges; sometimes colloquially called the Yellow Edge butterfly. It is common throughout the Americas and Europe.

began that disuse of the road past Nahum's which led to its ultimate abandonment. It was the vegetation. All the orchard trees blossomed forth in strange colours, and through the stony soil of the yard and adjacent pasturage there sprang up a bizarre growth which only a botanist could connect with the proper flora of the region. No sane wholesome colours were anywhere to be seen except in the green grass and leafage; but everywhere those hectic and prismatic variants of some diseased, underlying primary tone without a place among the known tints of earth. The Dutchman's breeches[41] became a thing of sinister menace, and the blood-roots[42] grew insolent in their chromatic perversion. Ammi and the Gardners thought that most of the colours had a sort of haunting familiarity, and decided that they reminded one of the brittle globule in the meteor. Nahum ploughed and sowed the ten-acre pasture and the upland lot, but did nothing with the land around the house. He knew it would be of no use, and hoped that the summer's strange growths would draw all the poison from the soil. He was prepared for almost anything now, and had grown used to the sense of something near him waiting to be heard. The shunning of his house[43] by neighbours told on him, of course; but it told on his wife more. The boys were better off, being at school each day; but they could not help being frightened by the gossip. Thaddeus, an especially sensitive youth, suffered the most.

In May the insects came, and Nahum's place became a nightmare of buzzing and crawling. Most of the creatures seemed not quite usual in their aspects and motions, and their nocturnal habits contradicted all former experience. The Gardners took to watching at night—watching in all

---

[41] *Dutchman's breeches: Dicentra cucullaria*, a type of herb, usually with white flowers tipped with yellow and roughly shaped like a pair of trousers. Native to the Northeast.

[42] *bloodroots: Sanguinaria canadensis*, an herb with white flowers sometimes tinged with pink. The plant contains a red juice that was formerly used as a paint by the Indians.

[43] Cf. Lovecraft's "The Shunned House" (1924).

directions at random for something . . . they could not tell what. It was then that they all owned that Thaddeus had been right about the trees. Mrs. Gardner was the next to see it from the window as she watched the swollen boughs of a maple against a moonlit sky. The boughs surely moved, and there was no wind. It must be the sap. Strangeness had come into everything growing now. Yet it was none of Nahum's family at all who made the next discovery. Familiarity had dulled them, and what they could not see was glimpsed by a timid woodmill salesman from Bolton[44] who drove by one night in ignorance of the country legends. What he told in Arkham was given a short paragraph in the *Gazette*; and it was there that all the farmers, Nahum included, saw it first. The night had been dark and the buggy-lamps faint, but around a farm in the valley which everyone knew from the account must be Nahum's the darkness had been less thick. A dim though distinct luminosity seemed to inhere in all the vegetation, grass, leaves, and blossoms alike, while at one moment a detached piece of the phosphorescence appeared to stir furtively in the yard near the barn.

The grass had so far seemed untouched, and the cows were freely pastured in the lot near the house, but toward the end of May the milk began to be bad. Then Nahum had the cows driven to the uplands, after which the trouble ceased. Not long after this the change in grass and leaves became apparent to the eye. All the verdure was going grey, and was developing a highly singular quality of brittleness. Ammi was now the only person who ever visited the place, and his visits were becoming fewer and fewer. When school closed the Gardners were virtually cut off from the world, and sometimes let Ammi do their errands in town. They were failing curiously both physically and mentally, and no one was surprised when the news of Mrs. Gardner's madness stole around.

---

[44] *Bolton*: A small town in east central Massachusetts. The mention of this town supports the belief that Arkham is situated in central Massachusetts, not on the coast.

It happened in June, about the anniversary of the meteor's fall, and the poor woman screamed about things in the air which she could not describe. In her raving there was not a single specific noun, but only verbs and pronouns.[45] Things moved and changed and fluttered, and ears tingled to impulses which were not wholly sounds. Something was taken away—she was being drained of something—something was fastening itself on her that ought not to be—someone must make it keep off—nothing was ever still in the night—the walls and windows shifted. Nahum did not send her to the county asylum, but let her wander about the house as long as she was harmless to herself and others. Even when her expression changed he did nothing. But when the boys grew afraid of her, and Thaddeus nearly fainted at the way she made faces at him, he decided to keep her locked up in the attic.[46] By July she had ceased to speak and crawled on all fours, and before that month was over Nahum got the mad notion that she was slightly luminous in the dark, as he now clearly saw was the case with the nearby vegetation.

It was a little before this that the horses had stampeded. Something had aroused them in the night, and their neighing and kicking in the stall had been terrible. There seemed virtually nothing to do to calm them, and when Nahum

---

[45] This is perhaps reminiscent of the madman Klenze's ravings in "The Temple" (1920): "*He* is calling! *He* is calling! I hear him! We must go!" (*Dagon and Other Macabre Tales*, 65).

[46] Shortly after writing this tale, Lovecraft notes in a letter: "Living things—usually insane or idiotic members of the family—concealed in the garrets or secret rooms of old houses are or at least have been literal realities in rural New England—I was told by someone of how he stopped at a lone farmhouse on some errand years ago, and was nearly frightened out of his wits by the opening of a sliding panel in the kitchen wall, and the appearance at the aperture of the most horrible, dirt-caked, and matted-bearded face he had ever conceived possible to exist!" (Lovecraft to Bernard Austin Dwyer, [June 1927]; *Selected Letters*, II, 139). Lovecraft may also have been thinking of Charlotte Perkins Gilman's celebrated tale, "The Yellow Wall Paper" (1892), which, as he notes in "Supernatural Horror in Literature," "rises to a classic level in subtly delineating the madness which crawls over a woman dwelling in the hideously papered room where a madwoman was once confined" (*Dagon and Other Macabre Tales*, 410). Gilman (1860–1935) was a Connecticut-born author and reformer who was much involved in the women's rights movement in the early decades of this century. She also wrote a utopian feminist novel, *Herland* (posthumously published in 1979).

opened the stable door they all bolted out like frightened woodland deer. It took a week to track all four, and when found they were seen to be quite useless and unmanageable. Something had snapped in their brains, and each one had to be shot for its own good. Nahum borrowed a horse from Ammi for his haying, but found it would not approach the barn. It shied, balked, and whinnied, and in the end he could do nothing but drive it into the yard while the men used their own strength to get the heavy wagon near enough the hayloft for convenient pitching. And all the while the vegetation was turning grey and brittle. Even the flowers whose hue had been so strange were greying now, and the fruit was coming out grey and dwarfed and tasteless. The asters and goldenrod bloomed grey and distorted, and the roses and zinneas and hollyhocks in the front yard were such blasphemous-looking things that Nahum's oldest boy Zenas[47] cut them down. The strangely puffed insects died about that time, even the bees that had left their hives and taken to the woods.

By September all the vegetation was fast crumbling to a greyish powder, and Nahum feared that the trees would die before the poison was out of the soil. His wife now had spells of terrific screaming, and he and the boys were in a constant state of nervous tension. They shunned people now, and when school opened the boys did not go. But it was Ammi, on one of his rare visits, who first realised that the well water was no longer good. It had an evil taste that was not exactly foetid nor exactly salty, and Ammi advised his friend to dig another well on higher ground to use till the soil was good again. Nahum, however, ignored the warning, for he had by that time become calloused to strange and unpleasant things. He and the boys continued to use the tainted supply, drinking it as listlessly and mechanically as they ate their meagre and ill-cooked meals and did

---

[47] *Zenas*: The name of a lawyer briefly cited in Titus 3:13.

their thankless and monotonous chores through the aimless days. There was something of stolid resignation about them all, as if they walked half in another world between lines of nameless guards to a certain and familiar doom.

Thaddeus went mad in September after a visit to the well. He had gone with a pail and had come back empty-handed, shrieking and waving his arms, and sometimes lapsing into an inane titter or a whisper about "the moving colours down there". Two in one family was pretty bad, but Nahum was very brave about it. He let the boy run about for a week until he began stumbling and hurting himself, and then he shut him in an attic room across the hall from his mother's. The way they screamed at each other from behind their locked doors was very terrible, especially to little Merwin,[48] who fancied they talked in some terrible language that was not of earth. Merwin was getting frightfully imaginative, and his restlessness was worse after the shutting away of the brother who had been his greatest playmate.

Almost at the same time the mortality among the livestock commenced. Poultry turned greyish and died very quickly, their meat being found dry and noisome[49] upon cutting. Hogs grew inordinately fat, then suddenly began to undergo loathsome changes which no one could explain. Their meat was of course useless, and Nahum was at his wit's end. No rural veterinary would approach his place, and the city veterinary from Arkham was openly baffled. The swine began growing grey and brittle and falling to pieces before they died, and their eyes and muzzles developed singular alterations. It was very inexplicable, for they had never been fed from the tainted vegetation. Then something struck the cows. Certain areas or sometimes the whole body would be uncannily shrivelled or compressed, and atrocious collapses or disintegrations were common. In the last stages—

---

[48] *Merwin*: The source or origin of this name is uncertain.

[49] *noisome*: Ill-smelling.

and death was always the result—there would be a greying
and turning brittle like that which beset the hogs. There
could be no question of poison, for all the cases occurred in
a locked and undisturbed barn. No bites of prowling things
could have brought the virus, for what live beast of earth
can pass through solid obstacles? It must only be natural
disease—yet what disease could wreak such results was
beyond any mind's guessing. When the harvest came there
was not an animal surviving on the place, for the stock and
poultry were dead and the dogs had run away. These dogs,
three in number, had all vanished one night and were never
heard of again. The five cats had left some time before, but
their going was scarcely noticed since there now seemed to
be no mice, and only Mrs. Gardner had made pets of the
graceful felines.

On the nineteenth of October Nahum staggered into
Ammi's house with hideous news. The death had come to
poor Thaddeus in his attic room, and it had come in a way
which could not be told. Nahum had dug a grave in the railed
family plot behind the farm, and had put therein what he
found. There could have been nothing from outside, for the
small barred window and locked door were intact; but it was
much as it had been in the barn. Ammi and his wife consoled
the stricken man as best they could, but shuddered as they
did so. Stark terror seemed to cling around the Gardners and
all they touched, and the very presence of one in the house
was a breath from regions unnamed and unnamable.[50] Ammi
accompanied Nahum home with the greatest reluctance, and
did what he might to calm the hysterical sobbing of little
Merwin. Zenas needed no calming. He had come of late to
do nothing but stare into space and obey what his father told
him; and Ammi thought that his fate was very merciful.
Now and then Merwin's screams were answered faintly from

---

[50] Cf. the final sentence of Lovecraft's "The Hound" (1922): " … I shall seek with my revolver
the oblivion which is my only refuge from the unnamed and unnamable" (*Dagon and Other
Macabre Tales*, 178). Cf. also Lovecraft's story "The Unnamable" (1923).

the attic, and in response to an inquiring look Nahum said that his wife was getting very feeble. When night approached, Ammi managed to get away; for not even friendship could make him stay in that spot when the faint glow of the vegetation began and the trees may or may not have swayed without wind. It was really lucky for Ammi that he was not more imaginative. Even as things were, his mind was bent ever so slightly; but had he been able to connect and reflect upon all the portents around him he must inevitably have turned a total maniac. In the twilight he hastened home, the screams of the mad woman and the nervous child ringing horribly in his ears.

Three days later Nahum lurched into Ammi's kitchen in the early morning, and in the absence of his host stammered out a desperate tale once more, while Mrs. Pierce listened in a clutching fright. It was little Merwin this time. He was gone. He had gone out late at night with a lantern and pail for water, and had never come back. He'd been going to pieces for days, and hardly knew what he was about. Screamed at everything. There had been a frantic shriek from the yard then, but before the father could get to the door, the boy was gone. There was no glow from the lantern he had taken, and of the child himself no trace. At the time Nahum thought the lantern and pail were gone too; but when dawn came, and the man had plodded back from his all-night search of the woods and fields, he had found some very curious things near the well. There was a crushed and apparently somewhat melted mass of iron which had certainly been the lantern; while a bail and twisted iron hoops beside it, both half-fused, seemed to hint at the remnants of the pail. That was all. Nahum was past imagining, Mrs. Pierce was blank, and Ammi, when he had reached home and heard the tale, could give no guess. Merwin was gone, and there would be no use in telling the people around, who shunned all Gardners now. No use, either, in telling the city people at Arkham who laughed at everything. Thad had gone, and now Mernie was gone. Something was creeping and creeping and waiting to be seen and felt and heard. Nahum would go soon, and he wanted Ammi to look after his wife and Zenas if they survived him. It must all be a judgment of some sort; though he could not fancy what for, since he had always walked uprightly in the Lord's ways so far as he knew.[51]

For over two weeks Ammi saw nothing of Nahum; and then, worried about what might have happened, he overcame his fears and paid the Gardner place a visit. There was no smoke from the great chimney, and for a moment the visitor was apprehensive of the worst. The aspect of the whole farm was shocking—greyish withered grass and leaves on the ground, vines falling in brittle wreckage from archaic walls and gables, and great bare trees clawing up at the grey November sky with a studied malevolence which Ammi could not but feel had come from some subtle change in the tilt of the branches. But Nahum was alive, after all. He was weak, and lying on a couch in the low-ceiled kitchen, but perfectly conscious and able to give simple orders to Zenas. The room was deadly cold; and as Ammi visibly shivered, the host shouted huskily to Zenas for more wood. Wood, indeed, was sorely needed; since the cavernous fireplace was unlit and empty, with a cloud of soot blowing about in the chill wind that came down the chimney. Presently Nahum asked him if the extra wood had made him any more comfortable, and then Ammi saw what had happened. The stoutest cord had broken at last, and the hapless farmer's mind was proof against more sorrow.

Questioning tactfully, Ammi could get no clear data at all about the missing Zenas. "In the well—he lives in the well—" was all that the clouded father would say. Then there flashed across the visitor's mind a sudden thought of the mad wife, and he changed his line of inquiry. "Nabby?

---

[51] Cf. Psalm 15:11: "For the Lord God is a sun and shield: the Lord will give grace and glory: no good thing will be withheld from them that walk uprightly."

Why, here she is!" was the surprised response of poor Nahum, and Ammi soon saw that he must search for himself. Leaving the harmless babbler on the couch, he took the keys from their nail beside the door and climbed the creaking stairs to the attic. It was very close and noisome up there, and no sound could be heard from any direction. Of the four doors in sight, only one was locked, and on this he tried various keys on the ring he had taken. The third key proved the right one, and after some fumbling Ammi threw open the low white door.

It was quite dark inside, for the window was small and half-obscured by the crude wooden bars; and Ammi could see nothing at all on the wide-planked floor. The stench was beyond enduring, and before proceeding further he had to retreat to another room and return with his lungs filled with breathable air. When he did enter he saw something dark in the corner, and upon seeing it more clearly he screamed outright. While he screamed he thought a momentary cloud eclipsed the window, and a second later he felt himself brushed as if by some hateful current of vapour. Strange colours danced before his eyes; and had not a present horror numbed him he would have thought of the globule in the meteor that the geologists hammer had shattered, and of the morbid vegetation that had sprouted in the spring. As it was he thought only of the blasphemous monstrosity which confronted him, and which all too clearly had shared the nameless fate of young Thaddeus and the livestock. But the terrible thing about this horror was that it very slowly and perceptibly moved as it continued to crumble.[52]

Ammi would give me no added particulars to this scene, but the shape in the corner does not reappear in his tale as a

---

[52] This passage is very similar to that of Arthur Machen's "The Novel of the White Powder" (a segment of the episodic novel *The Three Impostors* [1895]) in which a young man named Francis Leicester unwittingly takes a drug that reduces him to a formless mass. His physician, Dr. Haberden, breaks into his locked room: "There upon the floor was a dark and putrid mass, seething with corruption and hideous rottenness, neither liquid nor solid, but melting and changing before our eyes, and bubbling with unctuous oily bubbles like boiling pitch.

moving object. There are things which cannot be mentioned, and what is done in common humanity is sometimes cruelly judged by the law. I gathered that no moving thing was left in that attic room, and that to leave anything capable of motion there would have been a deed so monstrous as to damn any accountable being to eternal torment. Anyone but a stolid farmer would have fainted or gone mad, but Ammi walked conscious through that low doorway and locked the accursed secret behind him. There would be Nahum to deal with now; he must be fed and tended, and removed to some place where he could be cared for.

Commencing his descent of the dark stairs, Ammi heard a thud below him. He even thought a scream had been suddenly choked off, and recalled nervously the clammy vapour which had brushed by him in that frightful room above. What presence had his cry and entry started up? Halted by some vague fear, he heard still further sounds below. Indubitably there was a sort of heavy dragging, and a most detestably sticky noise as of some fiendish and unclean species of suction. With an associative sense goaded to feverish heights, he thought unaccountably of what he had seen upstairs. Good God! What eldritch[53] dream-world was this into which he had blundered? He dared move neither backward nor forward, but stood there trembling at the black curve of the boxed-in staircase. Every trifle of the scene burned itself into his brain. The sounds, the sense of dread expectancy, the darkness, the steepness of the narrow steps— and merciful heaven! . . . the faint but unmistakable luminosity of all the woodwork in sight; steps, sides, exposed lathes, and beams alike!

And out of the midst of it shone two burning points like eyes, and I saw a writhing and stirring as of limbs, and something moved and lifted up what might have been an arm. The doctor took a step forward, raised the iron bar and struck at the burning points; he drove in the weapon, and struck again and again in the fury of loathing" (*Tales of Horror and the Supernatural* [New York: Alfred A. Knopf, 1948], 55).

[53] *eldritch*: One of Lovecraft's favorite descriptives. The *Oxford English Dictionary* defines it as "Weird, unnatural, frightful, hideous," and states that its etymology is doubtful, but that it may be related to *elf*.

Then there burst forth a frantic whinny from Ammi's horse outside, followed at once by a clatter which told of a frenzied runaway. In another moment horse and buggy had gone beyond earshot, leaving the frightened man on the dark stairs to guess what had sent them. But that was not all. There had been another sound out there. A sort of liquid splash—water—it must have been the well. He had left Hero untied near it, and a buggy-wheel must have brushed the coping and knocked in a stone. And still the pale phosphorescence glowed in that detestably ancient woodwork. God! how old the house was! Most of it built before 1670, and the gambrel roof[54] not later than 1730.

A feeble scratching on the floor downstairs now sounded distinctly, and Ammi's grip tightened on a heavy stick he had picked up in the attic for some purpose.[55] Slowly nerving himself, he finished his descent and walked boldly toward the kitchen. But he did not complete the walk, because what he sought was no longer there. It had come to meet him, and it was still alive after a fashion. Whether it had crawled or whether it had been dragged by any external force, Ammi could not say; but the death had been at it. Everything had happened in the last half-hour, but collapse, greying, and disintegration were already far advanced. There was a horrible brittleness, and dry fragments were scaling off. Ammi could not touch it, but looked horrifiedly into the distorted parody that had been a face.[56] "What was it, Nahum—what was it?" He whispered, and the cleft, bulging lips were just able to crackle out a final answer.

---

[54] *gambrel roof*: An architectural design specific to New England in the late seventeenth and early eighteenth centuries, in the shape of a reversed V with an additional obtuse angle in each of the slanting sides. Cf. *The Case of Charles Dexter Ward* (1927): "He would hesitate gingerly down vertical Jenckes Street [in Providence] with its bank walls and colonial gables to the shady Benefit Street corner, where before him was a wooden antique with an Ionic-pilastered pair of doorways, and beside him a prehistoric gambrel-roofer with a bit of primal farmyard remaining ..." (*At the Mountains of Madness and Other Novels*, 113–14).

[55] The suggestion is that Ammi had used this stick to beat Nabby to death, just as Dr. Haberden had beaten Francis Leicester with an iron bar in Machen's "The Novel of the White Powder."

"Nothin' ... nothin' ... the colour ... it burns ... cold an' wet ... but it burns ... it lived in the well ... I seen it ... a kind o' smoke ... jest like the flowers last spring ... the well shone at night ... Thad an' Mernie an' Zenas ... everything alive ... suckin' the life out of everthing ... in that stone ... it must a' come in that stone ... pizened[57] the whole place ... dun't know what it wants ... that round thing them men from the college dug outen the stone ... they smashed it ... it was that same colour ... jest the same, like the flowers an' plants ... must a' ben more of 'em ... seeds ... seeds ... they growed ... I seen it the fust time this week ... must a' got strong on Zenas ... he was a big boy, full o' life ... it beats down your mind an' then gits ye ... burns ye up ... in the well water ... you was right about that ... evil water ... Zenas never come back from the well ... can't git away ... draws ye ... ye know summ'at's comin', but 'tain't no use ... I seen it time an' agin senct Zenas was took ... whar's Nabby, Ammi? ... my head's no good ... dun't know how long senct I fed her ... it'll git her ef we ain't keerful ... jest a colour ... her face is gettin' to hev that colour sometimes towards night ... an' it burns an' sucks ... it come from some place whar things ain't as they is here ... one o' them professors said so ... he was right ... look out, Ammi, it'll do suthin' more ... sucks the life out...."

But that was all. That which spoke could speak no more because it had completely caved in. Ammi laid a red checked tablecloth over what was left and reeled out the back door into the fields. He climbed the slope to the ten-acre pasture and stumbled home by the north road and the woods. He could not pass that well from which his horse had run

---

[56] Cf. Lovecraft's "The Outsider" (1921): " ... I saw in its eaten-away and bone-revealing outlines a leering, abhorrent travesty on the human shape" (*The Dunwich Horror and Others*, 51); also "The Thing on the Doorstep" (1933), in reference to the reanimated corpse of Asenath Waite: " ... who was this foul, stunted parody?" (*The Dunwich Horror and Others*, 301).

[57] *pizened*: Lovecraft's attempt to render phonetically Nahum's dialectic pronunciation of "poisoned."

away. He had looked at it through the window, and had seen that no stone was missing from the rim. Then the lurching buggy had not dislodged anything after all—the splash had been something else—something which went into the well after it had done with poor Nahum....

When Ammi reached his house the horse and buggy had arrived before him and thrown his wife into fits of anxiety. Reassuring her without explanations, he set out at once for Arkham and notified the authorities that the Gardner family was no more. He indulged in no details, but merely told of the deaths of Nahum and Nabby, that of Thaddeus already being known, and mentioned that the cause seemed to be the same strange ailment which had killed the livestock. He also stated that Merwin and Zenas had disappeared. There was considerable questioning at the police station, and in the end Ammi was compelled to take three officers to the Gardner farm, together with the coroner, the medical examiner, and the veterinary who had treated the diseased animals. He went much against his will, for the afternoon was advancing and he feared the fall of night over that accursed place, but it was some comfort to have so many people with him.

The six men drove out in a democrat-wagon,[58] following Ammi's buggy, and arrived at the pest-ridden farmhouse about four o'clock. Used as the officers were to gruesome experiences, not one remained unmoved at what was found in the attic and under the red checked tablecloth on the floor below. The whole aspect of the farm with its grey desolation was terrible enough, but those two crumbling objects were beyond all bounds. No one could look long at them, and even the medical examiner admitted that there was very little to examine. Specimens could be analysed, of course, so he busied himself in obtaining them—and here it develops

---

[58] *democrat-wagon*: "A light four-wheeled cart with several seats one behind the other, and usually drawn by two horses" (*Oxford English Dictionary*).

that a very puzzling aftermath occurred at the college laboratory where the two phials of dust were finally taken. Under the spectroscope both samples gave off an unknown spectrum, in which many of the baffling bands were precisely like those which the strange meteor had yielded in the previous year. The property of emitting this spectrum vanished in a month, the dust thereafter consisting mainly of alkaline phosphates and carbonates.[59]

Ammi would not have told the men about the well if he had thought they meant to do anything then and there. It was getting toward sunset, and he was anxious to be away. But he could not help glancing nervously at the stony curb by the great sweep, and when a detective questioned him he admitted that Nahum had feared something down there— so much so that he had never even thought of searching it for Merwin or Zenas. After that nothing would do but that they empty and explore the well immediately, so Ammi had to wait trembling while pail after pail of rank water was hauled up and splashed on the soaking ground outside. The men sniffed in disgust at the fluid, and toward the last held their noses against the foetor they were uncovering. It was not so long a job as they had feared it would be, since the water was phenomenally low. There is no need to speak too exactly of what they found. Merwin and Zenas were both there, in part, though the vestiges were mainly skeletal. There were also a small deer and a large dog in about the same state, and a number of bones of smaller animals. The ooze and slime at the bottom seemed inexplicably porous and bubbling, and a man who descended on hand-holds with a long pole found that he could sink the wooden shaft to

---

[59] This is a very complex chemical conception. The meteorite, although nonreactive, was alkaline, so that it must have had alkali metals in pure form (the most common of which are sodium and potassium) in its composition. These metals, in their elemental form, are highly reactive; it is interesting that they did not react when tested with acids, so perhaps they were present in some chemically impervious combination. In time their residue, combined with elements of either the remains of the meteorite or of the earth or other organic matter, appears to have produced inert phosphate and carbonate compounds.

any depth in the mud of the floor without meeting any solid obstruction.

Twilight had now fallen, and lanterns were brought from the house. Then, when it was seen that nothing further could be gained from the well, everyone went indoors and conferred in the ancient sitting-room while the intermittent light of a spectral[60] half-moon played wanly on the grey desolation outside. The men were frankly nonplussed by the entire case, and could find no convincing common element to link the strange vegetable conditions, the unknown disease of livestock and humans, and the unaccountable deaths of Merwin and Zenas in the tainted well. They had heard the common country talk, it is true; but could not believe that anything contrary to natural law had occurred.[61] No doubt the meteor had poisoned the soil, but the illness of persons and animals who had eaten nothing grown in that soil was another matter. Was it the well water? Very possibly. It might be a good idea to analyse it. But what peculiar madness could have made both boys jump into the well? Their deeds were so similar—and the fragments shewed that they had both suffered from the grey brittle death. Why was everything so grey and brittle?

It was the coroner, seated near a window overlooking the yard, who first noticed the glow about the well. Night had fully set in, and all the abhorrent grounds seemed faintly luminous with more than the fitful moonbeams; but this new glow was something definite and distinct, and appeared to shoot up from the black pit like a softened ray from a searchlight, giving dull reflections in the little ground pools where the water had been emptied. It had a very queer colour, and as all the men clustered round the window Ammi gave a violent start. For this strange beam of ghastly miasma was

---

[60] *spectral*: The primary meaning of this adjective is "ghostly" (derived from the noun *spectre*), but there is clearly also a pun on *spectrum*, referring to the unknown colors that show up in the spectrum as mentioned earlier in the tale.

[61] See note 56 to *At the Mountains of Madness*.

to him of no unfamiliar hue. He had seen that colour before, and feared to think what it might mean. He had seen it in the nasty brittle globule in the aërolite two summers ago, had seen it in the crazy vegetation of the springtime, and had thought he had seen it for an instant that very morning against the small barred window of that terrible attic room where nameless things had happened. It had flashed there a second, and a clammy and hateful current of vapour had brushed past him—and then poor Nahum had been taken by something of that colour. He had said so at the last—said it was the globule and the plants. After that had come the runaway in the yard and the splash in the well—and now that well was belching forth to the night a pale insidious beam of the same daemoniac tint.

It does credit to the alertness of Ammi's mind that he puzzled even at that tense moment over a point which was essentially scientific. He could not but wonder at his gleaning of the same impression from a vapour glimpsed in the daytime, against a window opening on the morning sky, and from a nocturnal exhalation seen as a phosphorescent mist against the black and blasted landscape. It wasn't right—it was against Nature—and he thought of those terrible last words of his stricken friend, "It come from some place whar things ain't as they is here . . . one o' them professors said so. ..."

All three horses outside, tied to a pair of shrivelled saplings by the road, were now neighing and pawing frantically. The wagon driver started for the door to do something, but Ammi laid a shaky hand on his shoulder. "Dun't go out thar," he whispered. "They's more to this nor what we know. Nahum said somethin' lived in the well that sucks your life out. He said it must be some'at growed from a round ball like one we all seen in the meteor stone that fell a year ago June. Sucks an' burns, he said, an' is jest a cloud of colour like that light out thar now, that ye can hardly see an' can't tell what it is. Nahum thought it feeds on everything livin' an' gits stronger all the time. He said he seen it this last week. It must be somethin' from away off in the sky like

the men from the college last year says the meteor stone
was. The way it's made an' the way it works ain' like no
way o' God's world. It's some'at from beyond."

So the men paused indecisively as the light from the well
grew stronger and the hitched horses pawed and whinnied in
increasing frenzy. It was truly an awful moment; with terror in that ancient and accursed house itself, four monstrous
sets of fragments—two from the house and two from the well—
in the woodshed behind, and that shaft of unknown and unholy
iridescence from the slimy depths in front. Ammi had
restrained the driver on impulse, forgetting how uninjured
he himself was after the clammy brushing of that coloured
vapour in the attic room, but perhaps it is just as well that
he acted as he did. No one will ever know what was abroad
that night; and though the blasphemy from beyond had not
so far hurt any human of unweakened mind, there is no telling what it might not have done at that last moment, and with
its seemingly increased strength and the special signs of purpose
it was soon to display beneath the half-clouded moonlit sky.

All at once one of the detectives at the window gave a
short, sharp gasp. The others looked at him, and then
quickly followed his own gaze upward to the point at which
its idle straying had been suddenly arrested. There was no
need for words. What had been disputed in country gossip
was disputable no longer, and it is because of the thing
which every man of that party agreed in whispering later
on that the strange days are never talked about in Arkham.
It is necessary to premise that there was no wind at that
hour of the evening. One did arise not long afterward, but
there was absolutely none then. Even the dry tips of the
lingering hedge-mustard,[62] grey and blighted, and the fringe
on the roof of the standing democrat-wagon were unstirred.
And yet amidst that tense, godless calm the high bare
boughs of all the trees in the yard were moving. They
were twitching morbidly and spasmodically, clawing in

---

[62] *hedge-mustard: Sisymbrium officinale*, a weed with small yellow flowers.

convulsive and epileptic madness at the moonlit clouds; scratching impotently in the noxious air as if jerked by some alien and bodiless line of linkage with subterrene horrors writhing and struggling below the black roots.

Not a man breathed for several seconds. Then a cloud of darker depth passed over the moon, and the silhouette of clutching branches faded out momentarily. At this there was a general cry; muffled with awe, but husky and almost identical from every throat. For the terror had not faded with the silhouette, and in a fearsome instant of deeper darkness the watchers saw wriggling at that treetop height a thousand tiny points of faint and unhallowed radiance, tipping each bough like the fire of St. Elmo or the flames that came down on the apostles' heads at Pentecost.[63] It was a monstrous constellation of unnatural light, like a glutted swarm of corpse-fed fireflies dancing hellish sarabands[64] over an accursed marsh; and its colour was that same nameless intrusion which Ammi had come to recognise and dread. All the while the shaft of phosphorescence from the well was getting brighter and brighter, bringing to the minds of the huddled men a sense of doom and abnormality which far outraced any image their conscious minds could form. It was no longer *shining* out, it was *pouring* out; and as the shapeless stream of unplaceable colour left the well it seemed to flow directly into the sky.

---

[63] *the fire of St. Elmo*: A bluish light that sometimes is seen on the tips of trees, ship masts, or other tall objects during a thunderstorm; caused by an accumulation of positive charge as a result of the negative charge in storm clouds. The name derives from a fourth-century saint, Erasmus, who became a patron of sailors.

Pentecost: From the Greek *pentekoste* ("fiftieth"), originally a Hebrew agricultural festival (the fiftieth day after Passover). On the first Pentecost after the death and resurrection of Jesus, the apostles congregated in Jerusalem; there was a sudden sound from heaven as of rushing wind and "there appeared unto them cloven tongues like as of fire, and it sat upon each of them" (Acts 2:3).

[64] *sarabands*: The primary meaning of this term is "A slow and stately Spanish dance in triple time" (*Oxford English Dictionary*). Cf. "The Shadow over Innsmouth" (1931): "And yet I saw them in a limitless stream ... surging inhumanly through the spectral moonlight in a grotesque, malignant saraband of fantastic nightmare" (*The Dunwich Horror and Others*, 360).

The veterinary shivered, and walked to the front door to drop the heavy extra bar across it. Ammi shook no less, and had to tug and point for lack of a controllable voice when he wished to draw notice to the growing luminosity of the trees. The neighing and stamping of the horses had become utterly frightful, but not a soul of that group in the old house would have ventured forth for any earthly reward. With the moments the shining of the trees increased, while their restless branches seemed to strain more and more toward verticality. The wood of the well-sweep was shining now, and presently a policeman dumbly pointed to some wooden sheds and bee-hives near the stone wall on the west. They were commencing to shine, too, though the tethered vehicles of the visitors seemed so far unaffected. Then there was a wild commotion and clopping in the road, and as Ammi quenched the lamp for better seeing they realised that the span of frantic greys had broke their sapling and run off with the democrat-wagon.

The shock served to loosen several tongues, and embarrassed whispers were exchanged. "It spreads on everything organic that's been around here," muttered the medical examiner. No one replied, but the man who had been in the well gave a hint that his long pole must have stirred up something intangible. "It was awful," he added. "There was no bottom at all. Just ooze and bubbles and the feeling of something lurking under there." Ammi's horse still pawed and screamed deafeningly in the road outside, and nearly drowned its owner's faint quaver as he mumbled his formless reflections. "It come from that stone ... it growed down thar ... it got everything livin' ... it fed itself on 'em, mind and body ... Thad an' Mernie, Zenas an' Nabby ... Nahum was the last ... they all drunk the water ... it got strong on 'em ... it come from beyond, whar things ain't like they be here ... now it's goin' home...."

At this point, as the column of unknown colour flared suddenly stronger and began to weave itself into fantastic suggestions of shape which each spectator later described

differently, there came from poor Hero such a sound as no
man before or since ever heard from a horse. Every person
in that low-pitched sitting room stopped his ears, and Ammi
turned away from the window in horror and nausea. Words
could not convey it—when Ammi looked out again the hapless beast lay huddled inert on the moonlit ground between
the splintered shafts of the buggy. That was the last of Hero
till they buried him next day. But the present was no time
to mourn, for almost at this instant a detective silently called
attention to something terrible in the very room with them.
In the absence of the lamplight it was clear that a faint phosphorescence had begun to pervade the entire apartment. It
glowed on the broad-planked floor and the fragment of rag
carpet, and shimmered over the sashes of the small-paned
windows. It ran up and down the exposed corner-posts, cor-
uscated about the shelf and mantel, and infected the very
doors and furniture. Each minute saw it strengthen, and at
last it was very plain that healthy living things must leave
that house.

Ammi shewed them the back door and the path up through
the fields to the ten-acre pasture. They walked and stumbled
as in a dream, and did not dare look back till they were far
away on the high ground. They were glad of the path, for
they could not have gone the front way, by that well. It was
bad enough passing the glowing barn and sheds, and those
shining orchard trees with the gnarled, fiendish contours;
but thank heaven the branches did their worst twisting high
up. The moon went under some very black clouds as they
crossed the rustic bridge over Chapman's Brook, and it was
blind groping from there to the open meadows.

When they looked back toward the valley and the distant
Gardner place at the bottom they saw a fearsome sight. All
the farm was shining with the hideous unknown blend of
colour; trees, buildings, and even such grass and herbage as
had not been wholly changed to lethal grey brittleness. The
boughs were all straining skyward, tipped with tongues of
foul flame, and lambent[65] tricklings of the same monstrous

fire were creeping about the ridgepoles of the house, barn, and sheds. It was a scene from a vision of Fuseli,[66] and over all the rest reigned that riot of luminous amorphousness, that alien and undimensioned rainbow of cryptic poison from the well—seething, feeling, lapping, reaching, scintillating, straining, and malignly bubbling in its cosmic and unrecognisable chromaticism.

Then without warning the hideous thing shot vertically up toward the sky like a rocket or meteor, leaving behind no trail and disappearing through a round and curiously regular hole in the clouds before any man could gasp or cry out. No watcher can ever forget that sight, and Ammi stared blankly at the stars of Cygnus, Deneb twinkling above the others, where the unknown colour had melted into the Milky Way.[67] But his gaze was the next moment called swiftly to earth by the crackling in the valley. It was just that. Only a wooden ripping and crackling, not an explosion, as so many others of the party vowed. Yet the outcome was the same, for in one feverish, kaleidoscopic instant there burst up from that doomed and accursed farm a gleamingly eruptive cataclysm of unnatural sparks and substance; blurring the glance of the few who saw it, and sending forth to the zenith a bombarding cloudburst of such coloured and fantastic fragments as our

---

[65] *lambent*: "Shining with a soft clear light and without fierce heat" (*Oxford English Dictionary*).

[66] *Fuseli*: Henry Fuseli (Heinrich Füssli, 1741–1825), Swiss-born painter who spent most of his life in England. His painting "The Nightmare" (1782) is one of the icons of weird art. Cf. "Pickman's Model" (1926): "I don't have to tell you why a Fuseli really brings a shiver while a cheap ghost-story frontispiece really brings a laugh" (*The Dunwich Horror and Others*, 13). Interestingly, Fuseli engaged in a several-year affair with Mary Wollstonecraft, mother of Mary Shelley.

[67] Lovecraft, an ardent amateur astronomer in youth, knew that Cygnus (the swan), although best seen in summer, would still be visible in the western sky in November. In an astronomy article Lovecraft explains the meaning of Deneb: "The word 'deneb' is the Arabic word for 'tail,' and is applied to stars in the tails of more than one imaginary constellation figure. That in the tail of Cygnus, however, is most frequently called Deneb, and unless some qualifying adjective be present, the term may be considered to apply exclusively to it" ("November Skies," *Providence Evening News* [October 31, 1916], 2).

universe must needs disown. Through quickly re-closing vapours they followed the great morbidity that had vanished, and in another second they had vanished too. Behind and below was only a darkness to which the men dared not return, and all about was a mounting wind which seemed to sweep down in black, frore[68] gusts from interstellar space. It shrieked and howled, and lashed the fields and distorted woods in a mad cosmic frenzy, till soon the trembling party realised it would be no use waiting for the moon to shew what was left down there at Nahum's.

Too awed even to hint theories, the seven shaking men trudged back toward Arkham by the north road. Ammi was worse than his fellows, and begged them to see him inside his own kitchen, instead of keeping straight on to town. He did not wish to cross the nighted, wind-whipped woods alone to his home on the main road. For he had had an added shock that the others were spared, and was crushed forever with a brooding fear he dared not even mention for many years to come. As the rest of the watchers on that tempestuous hill had stolidly set their faces toward the road, Ammi had looked back an instant at the shadowed valley of desolation so lately sheltering his ill-starred friend.[69] And from that stricken, far-away spot he had seen something feebly rise, only to sink down again upon the place from which the great shapeless horror had shot into the sky. It was just a colour—but not any colour of our earth or heavens. And because Ammi recognised that colour, and knew that this last faint remnant must still lurk down there in the well, he has never been quite right since.

---

[68] *frore*: "Intensely cold" (*Oxford English Dictionary*). Cf. Milton, *Paradise Lost*: "The parching air / Burns frore, and cold performs th' effect of Fire" (II, 594–95).

[69] This seems a clear echo of the story of Lot in Genesis 19:1–38. Lot, son of Haran and nephew of Abraham, had settled in Sodom. Two angels appeared to him and announced Sodom's imminent destruction, urging him to flee. Lot, his wife, and his two daughters left the town, but Lot's wife looked back at their lost property; as punishment she was turned into a pillar of salt. Later the towns of Sodom and Gomorrah were destroyed. Robert M. Price (note 4 above) points to Genesis 19:27–28: "And Abraham gat up early in the morning to the

Ammi would never go near the place again. It is over half a century now since the horror happened,[70] but he has never been there, and will be glad when the new reservoir blots it out. I shall be glad, too, for I do not like the way the sunlight changed colour around the mouth of that abandoned well I passed. I hope the water will always be very deep—but even so, I shall never drink it. I do not think I shall visit the Arkham country hereafter. Three of the men who had been with Ammi returned the next morning to see the ruins by daylight, but there were not any real ruins. Only the bricks of the chimney, the stones of the cellar, some mineral and metallic litter here and there, and the rim of that nefandous[71] well. Save for Ammi's dead horse, which they towed away and buried, and the buggy which they shortly returned to him, everything that had ever been living had gone. Five eldritch acres of dusty grey desert remained, nor has anything ever grown there since. To this day it sprawls open to the sky like a great spot eaten by acid in the woods and fields, and the few who have ever dared glimpse it in spite of the rural tales have named it "the blasted heath".

The rural tales are queer. They might be even queerer if city men and college chemists could be interested enough to analyse the water from that disused well, or the grey dust that no wind seems ever to disperse. Botanists, too, ought to study the stunted flora on the borders of that spot, for they might shed light on the country notion that the blight

---

place where he stood before the Lord: And he looked toward Sodom and Gomorrah, and toward all the land of the plain, and beheld, and, lo, the smoke of the country went up as the smoke of a furnace." Cf. Dyer's and Danforth's glance backward at the shoggoth in *At the Mountains of Madness* (p. 321), where, significantly, Lot's wife is mentioned.

[70] The original reading of the passage is: "It is forty-four years now since the horror happened ..." Lovecraft made the alteration c. 1934 for a proposed reprinting of the story as a pamphlet by F. Lee Baldwin.

[71] *nefandous*: From the Latin *nefandus*; derived from *ne-fari*, "not to be mentioned, unmentionable" (Lewis and Short, *A Latin Dictionary* [1879]), hence unspeakable or abominable.

is spreading—little by little, perhaps an inch a year. People say the colour of the neighbouring herbage is not quite right in the spring, and that wild things leave queer prints in the light winter snow. Snow never seems quite so heavy on the blasted heath as it is elsewhere. Horses—the few that are left in this motor age—grow skittish in the silent valley; and hunters cannot depend on their dogs too near the splotch of greyish dust.

They say the mental influences are very bad, too. Numbers went queer in the years after Nahum's taking, and always they lacked the power to get away. Then the stronger-minded folk all left the region, and only the foreigners tried to live in the crumbling old homesteads. They could not stay, though; and one sometimes wonders what insight beyond ours their wild, weird stores of whispered magic have given them. Their dreams at night, they protest, are very horrible in that grotesque country; and surely the very look of the dark realm is enough to stir a morbid fancy. No traveller has ever escaped a sense of strangeness in those deep ravines, and artists shiver as they paint thick woods whose mystery is as much of the spirit as of the eye. I myself am curious about the sensation I derived from my one lone walk before Ammi told me his tale. When twilight came I had vaguely wished some clouds would gather, for an odd timidity about the deep skyey voids above had crept into my soul.

Do not ask me for my opinion. I do not know—that is all. There was no one but Ammi to question; for Arkham people will not talk about the strange days, and all three professors who saw the aërolite and its coloured globule are dead. There were other globules—depend upon that. One must have fed itself and escaped, and probably there was another which was too late. No doubt it is still down the well—I know there was something wrong with the sunlight I saw above that miasmal brink. The rustics say the blight creeps an inch a year, so perhaps there is a kind of growth or nourishment even now. But whatever daemon hatchling is there, it must be tethered to something or else it would quickly spread. Is it fastened to the roots of those trees that claw the air? One of the current Arkham tales is about fat oaks that shine and move as they ought not to do at night.

What it is, only God knows. In terms of matter I suppose the thing Ammi described would be called a gas, but this gas obeyed laws that are not of our cosmos.[72] This was no fruit of such worlds and suns as shine on the telescopes and photographic plates of our observatories. This was no breath from the skies whose motions and dimensions our astronomers measure or deem too vast to measure. It was just a colour out of space—a frightful messenger from unformed realms of infinity beyond all Nature as we know it; from realms whose mere existence stuns the brain and numbs us with the black extra-cosmic gulfs it throws open before our frenzied eyes.

I doubt very much if Ammi consciously lied to me, and I do not think his tale was all a freak of madness as the townfolk had forewarned. Something terrible came to the hills and valleys on that meteor, and something terrible—though I know not in what proportion—still remains. I shall be glad to see the water come.[73] Meanwhile I hope nothing will happen to Ammi. He saw so much of the thing—and its influence was so insidious. Why has he never been able to move away? How clearly he recalled those dying words of Nahum's—"can't git away . . . draws ye . . . ye know summ'at's comin', but 'tain't no use. . . ." Ammi is such a

---

[72] Cf. a letter of 1916: "How do we know that that form of atomic and molecular motion called 'life' is the highest of all forms? Perhaps the dominant creature—the most rational and God-like of all beings—is an invisible gas!" (*Selected Letters*, I, 24). In "Celephaïs" (1920) Kuranes visits in dream "a part of space where form does not exist, but where glowing gases study the secrets of existence. And a violet-coloured gas told him that this part of space was outside what he had called infinity" (*Dagon and Other Macabre Tales*, 87). In *The Dream-Quest of Unknown Kadath* (1926–27) Kuranes notes that "The violet gas S'ngac had told him terrible things of the crawling chaos Nyarlathotep ..." (*At the Mountains of Madness and Other Novels*, 355). See Murray, "Sources for 'The Colour Out of Space'" (note 31 above).

[73] A reference to the imminent construction of the reservoir.

good old man—when the reservoir gang gets to work I must write the chief engineer to keep a sharp watch on him. I would hate to think of him as the grey, twisted, brittle monstrosity which persists more and more in troubling my sleep.

In his stories and letters Lovecraft often expressed outrage at what he called, I believe, the "galling limitations" of spacetime. This is something that we, his readers, take for granted about Lovecraft—that he aspired to attain or simulate an impossible omniscience, a long-distance view of all the real and unreal universes from their inception to their extinction and at every point in between. This is an astonishing attitude for a writer, especially an American writer of that time, to convey in his works and to experience with a peculiar intensity in his life. It is the sort of ambition that propels a new religion or at least occasions a revolutionary turn in the history of human consciousness. However hard I try I cannot overstate my amazement at this quality in Lovecraft—the desire to project oneself out of a particular time and place, to contemplate all the pyrotechnic mutations of phenomena from a point outside of everything. And this is only one of those incredible qualities which have come to be called Lovecraftian, and which we so infrequently credit with their true value of precious strangeness. It is really stupifying how even we, Lovecraft's devoted readers, can take so many things for granted in his universe, which ultimately seems superior to that other one.

—Tom Ligotti

"The Dunwich Horror" was written from July to August 1928. It was first published in Weird Tales, April 1929. Although Lovecraft declares that the story "is so fiendish that [Farnsworth] Wright [editor of Weird Tales] may not dare to print it" (Selected Letters, II, 240), it was accepted readily by Wright and Lovecraft received a payment of $240, the largest single amount he had received for original fiction up to this time.

There are a great many influences, both literary and personal, on the story. The dominant literary influence appears to be Arthur Machen's novelette "The Great God Pan" (in Machen's The Great God Pan and The Inmost Light [1894]), which Lovecraft read in 1923. This tale, like Lovecraft's, involves the offspring of a human woman and a "god." Certain other touches in the tale seem to derive from Algernon Blackwood's "The Wendigo" (in The Lost Valley and Other Stories [1910]) and from Anthony M. Rud's "Ooze," published in the first issue of Weird Tales (March 1923). Lovecraft takes notice of this story in a letter of comment published in Weird Tales, March 1924.

But the immediate inspiration for the story appears to have been a trip Lovecraft took to Wilbraham, Massachusetts, in the south-central part of the state, to visit a friend from the amateur journalism movement, Edith Miniter. As he was writing the story he told August Derleth: "The action takes place amongst the wild domed hills of the upper Miskatonic Valley, far northwest of Arkham, & is based on several old New England legends—one of which I heard only last month during my sojourn in Wilbraham" (Lovecraft to August Derleth, August 4, 1928; ms., State Historical Society of Wisconsin). Elsewhere he remarks provocatively that the story "belongs to the Arkham cycle" (Selected Letters, II, 246). The thrust of this comment is not entirely clear, but it at least suggests that Lovecraft considered some of his tales linked in some fashion, perhaps by setting. Whether the "Arkham cycle" corresponds to what August Derleth and others later termed the "Cthulhu Mythos" is by no means clear.

Weird Tales

The Unique Magazine

The DEVIL'S ROSARY

by SEABURY QUINN

APRIL 1929

25¢
25¢ IN CANADA

HUGH RANKIN

The Dunwich Horror

"Gorgons, and Hydras, and Chimaeras[1]—dire stories of Celaeno and the Harpies—may reproduce themselves in the brain of superstition—but they were there before. They are transcripts, types—the

---

[1] The reference is to various monsters from Greek myth. Gorgons (from *gorgos*, "grim, fierce") were female monsters, usually with snakes for hair; the most famous one was Medusa, whose glance turned people into stone. She was slain by Perseus. Cf. the incantation in Lovecraft's "The Horror at Red Hook" (1925): " … Gorgo, Mormo, thousand-faced moon, look favourably on our sacrifices!" (*Dagon and Other Macabre Tales*, 255).

The Hydra (from *hydor*, "water") was a poisonous water-snake with many heads; when one head was cut off, two more would grow in its place. It was slain by Herakles (Hercules).

The Chimaera (from *chimaira*, "she-goat") was a fire-breathing monster with the head of a lion, the body of a she-goat, and the tail of a snake. It was killed by Bellerophon mounted on the winged horse Pegasus.

archtypes[2] *are in us, and eternal. How else should the recital of that which we know in a waking sense to be false come to affect us at all? Is it that we naturally conceive terror from such objects, considered in their capacity of being able to inflict upon us bodily injury? O, least of all!* These terrors are of older standing. They date beyond body—*or without the body, they would have been the same ... That the kind of fear here treated is purely spiritual—that it is strong in proportion as it is objectless on earth, that it predominates in the period of our sinless infancy—are difficulties the solution of which might afford some probable insight into our ante-mundane condition, and a peep at least into the shadowland of pre-existence.*"

— Charles Lamb: *"Witches and Other Night-Fears"*[3]

The Harpies (*harpuiai*, "snatchers") were birdlike creatures with the faces of women, one of whom was Celaeno (*Kelaino*, "dark"). For the influence of Greek mythology on Lovecraft, see Will Murray, "The Dunwich Chimera and Others: Correlating the Cthulhu Mythos," *Lovecraft Studies* No. 8 (Spring 1984):10–24.

[2] Barton L. St. Armand, in *The Roots of Horror in the Fiction of H. P. Lovecraft* (see note 3 to "The Rats in the Walls"), quotes Carl Gustav Jung's *Memories, Dreams, Reflections* (New York: Vintage, 1965): "The concept of the archetype ... is derived from the repeated observation that, for instance, the myths and fairytales of world literature contain definite motifs which crop up everywhere.... These typical images and associations are what I call archetypal ideas.... They have their origin in the archetype, which in itself is an irrepresentable unconscious, pre-existent form that seems to be part of the inherited structure of the psyche and can therefore manifest itself spontaneously anywhere, at any time" (p. 392). This conception is central to Jung's theory of the collective unconscious.

[3] "Witches, and Other Night-Fears" appears in *Elia* (1823; later titled *The Essays of Elia* by Charles Lamb (1775–1834). Lovecraft had an 1874 edition of Lamb's *Complete Works in Prose and Verse* in his library. The italics were introduced by Lovecraft. The ellipses omit a passage about the devils in Dante and a quotation from Coleridge's *Rime of the Ancient Mariner*. Lovecraft should have placed ellipses after "affect us at all?", for he has omitted a brief quotation: "—Names, whose sense we see not, / Fray us with things that be not?"

I.

When a traveller in north central Massachusetts[4] takes the wrong fork at the junction of the Aylesbury pike[5] just beyond Dean's Corners[6] he comes upon a lonely and curious country. The ground gets higher, and the brier-bordered stone walls press closer and closer against the ruts of the dusty, curving road. The trees of the frequent forest belts seem too large, and the wild weeds, brambles, and grasses attain a luxuriance not often found in settled regions. At the same time the planted fields appear singularly few and barren; while the sparsely scattered houses wear a surprisingly uniform aspect of age, squalor, and dilapidation. Without knowing why, one hesitates to ask directions from the gnarled, solitary figures spied now and then on crumbling doorsteps or on the sloping, rock-strown meadows. Those figures are so silent and furtive that one feels somehow confronted by forbidden things, with which it would be better

---

[4] Actually, Lovecraft states that the real topographical source for Dunwich is a cluster of cities in south-central Massachusetts (see note 14 below), but other topographical details are indeed taken from sites in the north-central part of the state. See, in general, Donald R. Burleson, "Humour beneath Horror: Some Sources for 'The Dunwich Horror' and 'The Whisperer in Darkness,'" *Lovecraft Studies* No. 2 (Spring 1980):5–15.

[5] It is not entirely clear what real sites, if any, the fictitious name Aylesbury is based on. There is an Aylesbury in Buckinghamshire in England, but none in New England. There is an Amesbury on the North Shore of Massachusetts, near Newburyport. Lovecraft visited the town in 1923 (see Lovecraft to Samuel Loveman, April 29, 1923; *Letters to Samuel Loveman and Vincent Starrett*, 20). Aside from this story, Aylesbury is mentioned only in two sonnets in the *Fungi from Yuggoth* sequence (1929–30); in one of these, "The Familiars" (XXVI), it is mentioned in conjunction with a John Whateley, and might have some connection with "The Dunwich Horror."

[6] *Dean's Corners*: Fictitious; never mentioned in any other work by Lovecraft. There are a number of towns in western Massachusetts with "Corners" in their names (e.g., Worthington Corners, Moores Corner). Cf. Clark's Corners in "The Colour Out of Space" (p. 72–73). Dean's Corners may not be a town as such, but merely a region; the term Corners is a holdover from the crossroads laid out during the colonial settlement of the region.

to have nothing to do. When a rise in the road brings the mountains in view above the deep woods, the feeling of strange uneasiness is increased. The summits are too rounded and symmetrical to give a sense of comfort and naturalness, and sometimes the sky silhouettes with especial clearness the queer circles of tall stone pillars with which most of them are crowned.[7]

Gorges and ravines of problematical depth intersect the way, and the crude wooden bridges always seem of dubious safety. When the road dips again there are stretches of marshland that one instinctively dislikes, and indeed almost fears at evening when unseen whippoorwills chatter and the

---

[7] This is the first of many references in this story to these megalithic sites, which can be found throughout New England. One of them is located at Dogtown, an area between Gloucester and Rockport. Lovecraft visited this region in 1927 (see Lovecraft to Zealia Bishop, September 8, 1927; *Selected Letters*, II, 166), although he does not mention Dogtown or any megaliths seen there. In spite of several articles (e.g., Andrew E. Rothovius, "Lovecraft and the New England Megaliths," in Lovecraft's *The Dark Brotherhood and Other Pieces* [1966]) asserting that Lovecraft was intimately familiar with such sites, there is little evidence that he visited very many of them prior to writing the story. It is worth noting that Mystery Hill, in Salem, New Hampshire, is a bogus megalithic site, being instead an Indian settlement of the seventeenth century with a nineteenth-century farmer's "folly" built on top of it to create the impression of a prehistoric ruin. Lovecraft did not visit this site until the 1930s.

fireflies[8] come out in abnormal profusion to dance to the raucous, creepily insistent rhythms of stridently piping bull-frogs. The thin, shining line of the Miskatonic's upper reaches[9] has an oddly serpent-like suggestion as it winds close to the feet of the domed hills among which it rises.

   As the hills draw nearer, one heeds their wooded sides more than their stone-crowned tops. Those sides loom up so darkly and precipitously that one wishes they would keep their distance, but there is no road by which to escape them. Across a covered bridge[10] one sees a small village huddled between the stream and the vertical slope of Round Mountain,[11] and wonders at the cluster of rotting gambrel roofs[12] bespeaking an earlier architectural period than that of the neighbouring region. It is not reassuring to see, on a closer glance, that most of the houses are deserted and falling to ruin, and that the broken-steepled church now harbours the one slovenly mercantile establishment of the hamlet.[13]

---

[8] While in Wilbraham, Massachusetts, in June and July of 1928 (see note 14 below), Lovecraft saw an "absolutely marvellous *firefly* display ... All agree that it was unprecedented, even for Wilbraham. Level fields & woodland aisles were alive with dancing lights, till all the night seemed one restless constellation of nervous witch-fire. They leaped in the meadows, & under the spectral old oaks at the bend of the road. They danced tumultuously in the swampy hollow, & held witches' sabbaths beneath the gnarled, ancient trees of the orchard" (Lovecraft to Lillian D. Clark, July 1, 1928; ms., John Hay Library). Cf. "The Colour out of Space": "It was a monstrous constellation of unnatural light, like a glutted swarm of corpse-fed fireflies dancing hellish sarabands over an accursed marsh ..." (see p. 92).

[9] *Miskatonic*: The word *Miskatonic* was first cited in "The Picture in the House" (1920) and is probably an adaptation of several Indian place-names in New England, most notably Housatonic, a river in western Massachusetts and Connecticutt.

[10] A reference to bridges that are covered with a wooden enclosure to form a tunnel. A fair number of them remain in western Massachusetts, although they are now very rare elsewhere in New England. Lovecraft encountered one on his visit to Vermont in 1927: "By an ancient covered bridge we ride back through decades and enter the enchanted city of our fathers' world" ("Vermont—A First Impression" [1927], in *Miscellaneous Writings*, 294).

[11] *Round Mountain*: Fictitious; but Lovecraft mentions a (fictitious) Round Hill in Vermont frequently in "The Whisperer in Darkness" (1930).

[12] *gambrel roofs*: See note 54 to "The Colour Out of Space." See also note 43 below.

[13] Cf. the Brooklyn church that has been turned into a dance-hall in "The Horror at Red Hook" (1925).

One dreads to trust the tenebrous tunnel of the bridge, yet there is no way to avoid it. Once across, it is hard to prevent the impression of a faint, malign odour about the village street, as of the massed mould and decay of centuries. It is always a relief to get clear of the place, and to follow the narrow road around the base of the hills and across the level country beyond till it rejoins the Aylesbury pike. Afterward one sometimes learns that one has been through Dunwich.[14]

---

[14] *Dunwich*: There has been much speculation as to the origin of this name. It is thought that Lovecraft was aware of the now-vanished English town of Dunwich in East Anglia (now Suffolk) on the shore of the North Sea; it is the subject of Algernon Charles Swinburne's poem "By the North Sea," which is included in the edition of his *Poems* (Modern Library, 1919) owned by Lovecraft, although the name Dunwich never appears in the poem. This Dunwich is also mentioned in Arthur Machen's short novel, *The Terror* (1917), which Lovecraft is known to have read. (For the history of this town see Rowland Parker's *Men of Dunwich* [1979].) But the English Dunwich—a coastal city that slowly sank into the sea because of the erosion of the shoreline—seems more reminiscent of Lovecraft's decaying seaport Innsmouth (featured in "The Shadow over Innsmouth" [1931]). If the English Dunwich is not the source of the name, then there are any number of New England towns with the *-wich* ending, notably Ipswich, near Salem on the North Shore of Massachusetts, and East and West Greenwich, Rhode Island. A Greenwich in Massachusetts was one of the towns obliterated in the building of the Quabbin Reservoir (see note 6 to "The Colour Out of Space").

As to the location of Dunwich, Lovecraft declares that "the place [is] a vague echo of the decadent Massachusetts countryside around Springfield—say Wilbraham, Monson, and Hampden" (*Selected Letters*, III, 432–33). This area—which Lovecraft visited in the summer of 1928, staying with his colleague Edith Miniter in Wilbraham—is in south-central Massachusetts. Lovecraft describes his first impressions of Wilbraham in a letter: "The scenery is lovely in the extreme, with just the right balance of hill & plain. It is not so vivid as Vermont, but much richer & statelier; with larger trees and more luxuriant vegetation generally. The houses are old, but not notable. The population is quite sharply divided—the good families are maintaining their old standards whilst the common folk are going downhill" (Lovecraft to Lillian D. Clark, July 1, 1928; ms., John Hay Library). There is, however, reason to think that certain topographical and historical details are derived from other parts of the state (see notes 18, 19, 29, 52, 72, and 95 below).

One final query is the pronunciation of the name Dunwich. In accordance with English (and Rhode Island) practice, it would be pronounced "DUN-nich" rather than "DUN-wich" (although the Massachusetts Greenwich was actually pronounced "GREEN-wich"). Lovecraft gives no clue in letters as to its pronunciation, and the only other appearance of the name in Lovecraft's work—the poem "The Ancient Track" (1929)—does not help to settle the question.

[15] Cf. "The Ancient Track": "There was the milestone that I knew— / 'Two miles to Dunwich'—now the view / Of distant spire and roofs would dawn / With ten more

Outsiders visit Dunwich as seldom as possible, and since a certain season of horror all the signboards pointing toward it have been taken down.[15] The scenery, judged by any ordinary aesthetic canon, is more than commonly beautiful; yet there is no influx of artists or summer tourists. Two centuries ago, when talk of witch-blood, Satan-worship, and strange forest presences was not laughed at, it was the custom to give reasons for avoiding the locality. In our sensible age—since the Dunwich horror of 1928 was hushed up by those who had the town's and the world's welfare at heart—people shun it without knowing exactly why. Perhaps one reason—though it cannot apply to uninformed strangers—is that the natives are now repellently decadent, having gone far along that path of retrogression so common in many New England backwaters. They have come to form a race by themselves, with the well-defined mental and physical stigmata of degeneracy and inbreeding. The average of their intelligence is woefully low, whilst their annals reek of overt viciousness and of half-hidden murders, incests, and deeds of almost unnamable violence and perversity.[16] The old gentry, representing the two or

---

upward paces gone . . ." (*The Fantastic Poetry* [West Warwick, RI: Necronomicon Press, 1993], 58).

[16] Cf. the description of Joe Slater and his fellow denizens of the Catskill Mountains in "Beyond the Wall of Sleep" (1919): " ... Slater ... was ... one of those strange, repellent scions of a primitive colonial peasant stock whose isolation for nearly three centuries in the hilly fastnesses of a little travelled countryside has caused them to sink to a kind of barbaric degeneracy, rather than advance with their more fortunately placed brethren of the thickly settled districts. Among these odd folks, who correspond exactly to the decadent element of 'white trash' in the South, law and morals are non-existent; and their general mental status is probably below that of any other section of the native American people" (*Dagon and Other Macabre Tales*, 26). "The Lurking Fear" (1922) is set in the same locale, and there we find this description: "Simple animals they were, gently descending the evolutionary scale because of their unfortunate ancestry and stultifying isolation" (*Dagon and Other Macabre Tales*, 186). For the later contrast between the "decayed" and "undecayed" families or branches of families in Dunwich, cf. Lovecraft's initial reaction to the people of Wilbraham (note 14 above).

three armigerous[17] families which came from Salem in 1692,[18] have kept somewhat above the general level of decay; though many branches are sunk into the sordid populace so deeply that only their names remain as a key to the origin they disgrace. Some of the Whateleys and Bishops[19] still send their eldest sons to Harvard and Miskatonic, though those sons seldom return to the mouldering gambrel roofs under which they and their ancestors were born.

No one, even those who have the facts concerning the recent horror, can say just what is the matter with Dunwich; though old legends speak of unhallowed rites and conclaves of the Indians, amidst which they called forbidden shapes of shadow out of the great rounded hills, and made wild orgiastic prayers that were answered by loud crackings and rumblings from the ground below. In 1747 the Reverend Abijah Hoadley,[20] newly come to the Congregational

---

[17] *armigerous*: "Entitled to bear (heraldic) arms" (*Oxford English Dictionary*). Lovecraft, who liked to trace his lineage to Devonshire yeomen in the fifteenth century, occasionally signed himself "H. Lovecraft, Armiger."

[18] Lovecraft has picked the date by design to indicate that Dunwich was founded by those individuals who fled from the witchcraft trials in Salem; the suggestion being that Dunwich was founded by actual witches. Lovecraft, influenced by Margaret A. Murray's *The Witch-Cult in Western Europe* (1921), believed that there may actually have been a witch-cult of sorts existing in Salem:

> Another and highly important factor in accounting for Massachusetts witch-belief and daemonology is the fact, now widely emphasised by anthropologists, that the traditional features of witch-practice and Sabbat-orgies *were by no means mythical.* ... *Something actual was going on under the surface*, so that people really stumbled on *concrete experiences* from time to time which confirmed all they had ever heard of the witch species. ... Miss Murray, the anthropologist, believes that the witch-cult actually established a "coven" (its only one in the New World) in the Salem region about 1690.... For my part—I doubt if a compact coven existed, but certainly think that people had come to Salem who had a direct personal knowledge of the cult, and who were perhaps initiated members of it. I think that some of the rites and formulae of the cult must have been talked about secretly among certain elements, and perhaps furtively practiced by the few degenerates involved. ... Most of the people hanged were probably innocent, yet I do think there was a concrete, sordid background not present in any other New England witchcraft case. (*Selected Letters*, III, 178, 182–83)

Will Murray ("In Search of Arkham Country Revisited," *Lovecraft Studies* Nos. 19/20 [Fall 1989]:65–69) has pointed out that the town of New Salem (in north-central Massachusetts, near Athol and the Quabbin Reservoir) *was* founded by settlers who left Salem in 1737, forty-five years after the witch trials.

Church[21] at Dunwich Village, preached a memorable sermon on the close presence of Satan and his imps; in which
he said:

> *"It must be allow'd, that these Blasphemies of an
> infernall Train of Daemons are Matters of too com-
> mon Knowledge to be deny'd; the cursed Voices of
> Azazel and Buzrael, of Beelzebub and Belial,[22] being
> heard now from under Ground by above a Score of
> credible Witnesses now living. I my self did not more
> than a Fortnight ago catch a very plain Discourse of
> evill Powers in the Hill behind my House; wherein
> there were a Rattling and Rolling, Groaning, Screech-
> ing, and Hissing, such as no Things of this Earth cou'd
> raise up, and which must needs have come from those
> Caves that only black Magick can discover, and only
> the Divell[23] unlock."*

---

[19] Bishop is (as Burleson [note 4 above] has pointed out) a prominent name in the
history of Athol, as are Wheeler, Farr, Frye, and Sawyer. Bishops and Fryes also figure in
the early history of Salem.

[20] Both Hoadly and his sermon are imaginary, although there was an eighteenth-century
playwright and critic named Benjamin Hoadly (1706–1757) with whom Lovecraft may have
been familiar. A John Hoadly (1678–1746) was archbishop of Armagh and Chaplain in Ordinary to King George I; he published several sermons.

[21] The Congregational sect is an important religious group in New England, especially in
Massachusetts and Connecticut. In Massachusetts the Congregationalists had become the
dominant religious sect by the later seventeenth century, but their influence waned after 1833
when the state officially decreed the separation of church and state. Nevertheless, by Lovecraft's
time the Congregational church was still often the social center for New England towns, as
they are to this day. Congregational tall steeples dominate most town centers—standing in
white contrast to the traditional "town greens."

[22] Azazel is a demon variously mentioned in the Old Testament (Leviticus 16:1–28;
Enoch 6, 8, 10). Buzrael is a name invented here by Lovecraft. Beelzebub is a name used
interchangeably with Satan in the New Testament (e.g., Matthew 12:24–27). The term
probably means "lord of the flies" in Hebrew. Belial is mentioned only once in the New
Testament (II Corinthians 6:15) as a synonym for Satan. It appears to refer to various
types of threats to the social and cosmic order. Azazel, Beelzebub, and Belial are all cited
in the first book of Milton's *Paradise Lost*, although the three of them do not appear
together in any single passage.

[23] *Divell*: Archaic spelling of "Devil."

Mr. Hoadley disappeared soon after delivering this sermon; but the text, printed in Springfield,[24] is still extent. Noises in the hills[25] continued to be reported from year to year, and still form a puzzle to geologists and physiographers.[26]

Other traditions tell of foul odours near the hill-crowning circles of stone pillars, and of rushing airy presences to be heard faintly at certain hours from stated points at the bottom of the great ravines; while still others try to explain the Devil's Hop Yard[27]—a bleak, blasted hillside where no tree, shrub, or grass-blade will grow. Then too, the natives are mortally afraid of the numerous whippoorwills which grow vocal on warm nights. It is vowed that the birds are psychopomps lying in wait for the souls of the dying, and that they time their eerie cries in unison with the sufferer's

---

[24] *Springfield*: See note 14 above.

[25] The reference is to the so-called "Moodus noises," named after the town of Moodus, Connecticut, where they have been particularly common, although other localities have reported similar phenomena. Lovecraft probably derived his information on this matter from a chapter entitled "Moodus Noises" in Charles M. Skinner's *Myths and Legends of Our Own Land* (Philadelphia: J. B. Lippincott Co., 1896), 2:43–46. Skinner writes: "As early as 1700, and for thirty years after, there were crackings and rumblings that were variously compared to fusillades, to thunder, to roaring in the air, to the breaking of rocks, to reports of cannon. ... Houses shook and people feared." Cf. Lovecraft to F. Lee Baldwin, December 23, 1934 (ms., John Hay Library): "Did you ever hear of the 'Moodus Noises' in Connecticut about 200 years ago? These noises consisted of alarming rumblings in the earth near some lonely hills, & the colonists swore they were either devices of the Devil or indications of the wrath of God. Later geologists decided that they were caused by certain harmless but unusual settlings in connexion with 'faults' in the rock strata. They have had a tendency to return at long intervals—decades apart—& only a few weeks ago a fresh example of them was reported. This time, however, there were no fears, & no speculations as to the 'work o' the Devil' or the 'wrath o' Jehovy.' "

There is also a brief mention of the Moodus noises in Charles Fort's *New Lands* (1923), which Lovecraft read around September 1927 (*Selected Letters*, II, 174).

[26] *physiographers*: A scientist specializing in physiography—the description and analysis of the physical features of the earth.

[27] *Devil's Hop Yard*: This term was derived by Lovecraft from the very next chapter of Skinner's *Myths and Legends of Our Own Land* (see n. 25 above) following that on "Moodus Noises." In "Haddam Enchantments," Skinner tells of supposed gatherings of witches in the town of Haddam, Connecticut: " ... there were dances of old crones at Devils' Hop Yard, Witch Woods, Witch Meadows, Giant's Chair, Devil's Footprint, and Dragon's Rock.... In Devils' Hop Yard was a massive oak that never bears leaves or acorns, for it has been enchanted since the time that one of the witches, in the form of

struggling breath. If they can catch the fleeing soul when it leaves the body, they instantly flutter away chittering in daemonic laughter; but if they fail, they subside gradually into a disappointed silence.[28]

These tales, of course, are obsolete and ridiculous; because they come down from very old times. Dunwich is indeed ridiculously old—older by far than any of the communities within thirty miles of it. South of the village one may still spy the cellar walls and chimney of the ancient Bishop house, which was built before 1700; whilst the ruins of the mill at the falls, built in 1806, form the most modern piece of architecture to be seen. Industry did not flourish here, and the nineteenth-century factory movement proved short-lived. Oldest of all are the great rings of rough-hewn stone columns on the hill-tops, but these are more generally attributed to the Indians than to the settlers. Deposits of skulls and bones, found within these circles and around the sizeable table-like rock on Sentinel Hill,[29]

---

a crow, perched on the topmost branch, looked to the four points of the compass, and flew away. That night the leaves fell off, the twigs shrivelled, sap ceased to run, and moss began to beard its skeleton limbs" (Skinner, 1896, 47–48). The term "hop yard" is a variant of "hop-garden," a plot of land devoted to the cultivation of hops. The description is clearly reminiscent of the "blasted heath" in "The Colour Out of Space" (see p. 60).

[28] This is an actual legend in the Wilbraham area and was told to Lovecraft either by Edith Miniter or her friend Evanore Beebe. Cf. his essay, "Mrs. Miniter: Estimates and Recollections" (1934): "I saw the ruinous, deserted old Randolph Beebe house where the whippoorwills cluster abnormally, and learned that these birds are feared by the rustics as evil psychopomps. It is whispered that they linger and flutter around houses where death is approaching, hoping to catch the soul of the departed as it leaves. If the soul eludes them, they disperse in quiet disappointment; but sometimes they set up a chorused clamour which makes the watchers turn pale and mutter—with that air of hushed, awestruck portentousness which only a backwoods Yankee can assume—'They got 'im!'" (*Miscellaneous Writings*, 477). In this story, the whippoorwills prove to be a central unifying motif, manifesting themselves at the deaths of each member of the Whateley family.

The word *psychopomp* is adapted from the Greek *psychopompos* ("conductor of souls" [i.e., to the underworld]), applied variously to Charon or Hermes in Greek myth. Cf. Lovecraft's discussion, in "Supernatural Horror in Literature," of the "strange cat" in Hawthorne's *The House of the Seven Gables*: "It is clearly the psychopomp of primeval myth, fitted and adapted with infinite deftness to its latter-day setting" (*Dagon and Other Macabre Tales*, 405). In 1918 Lovecraft wrote a long poem entitled "Psychopompos," but it is an adaptation of the conventional werewolf legend.

sustain the popular belief that such spots were once the burial-places of the Pocumtucks;[30] even though many ethnologists, disregarding the absurd improbability of such a theory, persist in believing the remains Caucasian.

II.

It was in the township of Dunwich, in a large and partly inhabited farmhouse set against a hillside four miles from the village and a mile and a half from any other dwelling,

---

[29] *Sentinel Hill*: Cf. W. Paul Cook: "During most of the years of my acquaintance with Lovecraft I was living in a north central Massachusetts town [Athol] which was the most absolutely devoid of historical, architectural, scenic, archeological or sentimental interest of any town I ever saw anywhere. Receptive to impressions as he was, and on the outlook for local color as he was, Lovecraft would spend days tramping around that town and its environs without being able to express himself as enthused, much as he would have liked to flatter his host. The only thing he carried away from the town itself for literary use was the name 'Sentinel Hill,' but he had to move that hill several miles down into the doomed valley in order to get it into a romantic environment" (*In Memoriam: Howard Phillips Lovecraft* [1941; rpt. West Warwick, RI: Necronomicon Press, 1991], 18–19). There does not seem to be an actual landmark named Sentinel Hill in Athol; but near West Hill there is a farm called Sentinel Elm Farm, and this is probably the source of the name. The topographical source for Sentinel Hill is probably Wilbraham Mountain near Wilbraham, Massachusetts. Lovecraft, visiting the region in 1928, states in a letter: "Far to the west, across marshy meadows where at evening the fireflies dance in incredibly fantastic profusion, the benign bulk of Wilbraham Mountain rises purple and mystical" (*Selected Letters*, II, 246).

[30] *Pocumtucks*: or Pocumtucs, one of the seven aboriginal Indian tribes of Massachusetts. They settled the entire Connecticut River Valley, and their chief settlement was near the present-day town of Deerfield in north-central Massachusetts.

that Wilbur Whateley[31] was born at 5 a.m. on Sunday, the
second of February, 1913. This date was recalled because
it was Candlemas,[32] which people in Dunwich curiously
observe under another name;[33] and because the noises in
the hills had sounded, and all the dogs of the countryside
had barked persistently, throughout the night before. Less
worthy of notice was the fact that the mother was one of
the decadent Whateleys, a somewhat deformed, unattrac-
tive albino woman of thirty-five,[34] living with an aged and
half-insane father about whom the most frightful tales of
wizardry had been whispered in his youth. Lavinia
Whateley had no known husband, but according to the

---

[31] *Wilbur Whateley*: It is not certain where Lovecraft got the name Whateley. There is a
small town in northwestern Massachusetts named Whately, and it is not far from the
Mohawk Trail, which Lovecraft traversed on a number of occasions, including the
summer of 1928. Burleson (see note 4 above) conjectures that Lovecraft may have had
the English theologian Richard Whately (1787–1863) in mind, but there is no evidence
that Lovecraft knew of this figure.

[32] *Candlemas*: February 2. In Christian theology, Candlemas commemorates the presen-
tation of Christ in the Temple. This is the first of many mentions of Christian feast days
in this story, but some of these also correspond to the four important celebrations of the
Witches' Sabbath: Candlemas, May Eve, Lammas, and Halloween. The most significant
of these were May Eve and Halloween. These latter two festivals have their origin in
primitive times, specifically in certain rituals of the Celtic tribes. Sir James George
Frazer, noting that May Eve and Halloween do not correspond either to the solstices or
equinoxes of the year nor to the time of planting of grain nor of the harvest, writes: "Yet
the first of May and the first of November mark turning-points of the year in Europe; the
one ushers in the genial heat and the rich vegetation of summer, the other heralds, if it
does not share, the cold and barrenness of winter. Now these particular points of the year
… while they are of comparatively little moment to the European husbandman, do
deeply concern the European huntsman; for it is on the approach of summer that he
drives his cattle out into the open to crop the fresh grass, and it is on the approach of
winter that he leads them back to the safety and shelter of the stall. Accordingly it seems
not improbable that the Celtic bisection of the year into two halves at the beginning of
May and the beginning of November dates from a time when the Celts were mainly a
pastoral people, dependent for their subsistence on their herds, and when accordingly
the great epochs of the year for them were the days on which the cattle went forth from
the homestead in early summer and returned to it again in early winter" (Frazer, *The
Golden Bough*, 633). See notes 40, 47, and 54 below.

[33] The import of this remark is not entirely clear; perhaps the suggestion is that the
Dunwich denizens are using an older name for this festival, whose origins can be traced
to rituals before the dawn of civilization.

[34] Lovecraft's mother, Sarah Susan Lovecraft, was almost thirty-three when Lovecraft was born.

custom of the region made no attempt to disavow the child; concerning the other side of whose ancestry the country folk might—and did—speculate as widely as they chose. On the contrary, she seemed strangely proud of the dark, goatish-looking[35] infant who formed such a contrast to her own sickly and pink-eyed albinism, and was heard to mutter many curious prophecies about its unusual powers and tremendous future.

Lavinia was one who would be apt to mutter such things, for she was a lone creature given to wandering amidst thunderstorms in the hills and trying to read the great odorous books which her father had inherited through two centuries of Whateleys, and which were fast falling to pieces with age and worm-holes. She had never been to school, but was filled with disjointed scraps of ancient lore that Old Whateley had taught her. The remote farmhouse had always been feared because of Old Whateley's reputation for black magic, and the unexplained death by violence of Mrs. Whateley when Lavinia was twelve years old had not helped to make the place popular. Isolated among strange influences, Lavinia was fond of wild and grandiose day-dreams and singular occupations; nor was her leisure much taken up by household cares in a home from which all standards of order and cleanliness had long since disappeared.

There was a hideous screaming which echoed above even the hill noises and the dogs' barking on the night Wilbur was born, but no known doctor or midwife presided at his coming. Neighbours knew nothing of him till a week afterward, when Old Whateley drove his sleigh through the snow into Dunwich Village[36] and discoursed incoherently to the group of loungers at Osborn's general store. There seemed

---

[35] *goatish-looking*: A clear suggestion of the demonic attributes of Wilbur Whateley. The Devil in the form of a goat was said to preside over the Witches' Sabbath.

[36] *Dunwich Village*: In many New England towns, the word "Village" is added to the name to denote the downtown section. Recall that it was in Salem Village, the original settlement (now a separate community called Danvers), where the Salem witch trials actually took place.

to be a change in the old man—an added element of furtiveness in the clouded brain which subtly transformed him from an object to a subject of fear[37]—though he was not one to be perturbed by any common family event. Amidst it all he shewed some trace of the pride later noticed in his daughter, and what he said of the child's paternity was remembered by many of his hearers years afterward.

"I dun't keer what folks think—ef Lavinny's boy looked like his pa, he wouldn't look like nothin' ye expeck. Ye needn't think the only folks is the folks hereabaouts. Lavinny's read some, an' has seed some things the most o' ye only tell abaout. I calc'late her man is as good a husban' as ye kin find this side of Aylesbury; an' ef ye knowed as much abaout the hills as I dew, ye wouldn't ast no better church weddin' nor her'n. Let me tell ye suthin'—*some day yew folks'll hear a child o' Lavinny's a-callin' its father's name on the top o' Sentinel Hill!*"

The only persons who saw Wilbur during the first month of his life were old Zechariah Whateley, of the undecayed Whateleys, and Earl Sawyer's common-law wife, Mamie Bishop. Mamie's visit was frankly one of curiosity, and her subsequent tales did justice to her observations; but Zechariah came to lead a pair of Alderney cows[38] which Old Whateley had bought of his son Curtis. This marked the beginning of a course of cattle-buying on the part of small Wilbur's family which ended only in 1928, when the Dunwich horror came and went; yet at no time did the ramshackle Whateley barn seem overcrowded with livestock. There came a period when people were curious enough to steal up and count the herd that grazed precariously on

---

[37] Cf. the reverse idea in Lovecraft's "The Statement of Randolph Carter" (1919): "But I do not fear him now, for I suspect that he has known horrors beyond my ken. Now I fear *for* him" (*At the Mountains of Madness and Other Novels*, 300).

[38] *Alderney cows*: A name formerly used for two distinct breeds of dairy cattle, Jersey and Guernsey, originally raised on the Channel Islands off the southeast coast of England. Guernseys were first imported to the U.S. in 1830, Jerseys in 1850.

the steep hillside above the old farmhouse, and they could never find more than ten or twelve anaemic, bloodless-looking specimens.[39] Evidently some blight or distemper, perhaps sprung from the unwholesome pasturage or the diseased fungi and timbers of the filthy barn, caused a heavy mortality amongst the Whateley animals. Odd wounds or sores, having something of the aspect of incisions, seemed to inflict the visible cattle; and once or twice during the earlier months certain callers fancied they could discern similar sores about the throats of the grey, unshaven old man and his slatternly, crinkly-haired albino daughter.

In the spring after Wilbur's birth Lavinia resumed her customary rambles in the hills, bearing in her misproportioned arms the swarthy child. Public interest in the Whateleys subsided after most of the country folk had seen the baby, and no one bothered to comment on the swift development which that newcomer seemed every day to exhibit. Wilbur's growth was indeed phenomenal, for within three months of his birth he had attained a size and muscular power not usually found in infants under a full year of age. His motions and even his vocal sounds shewed a restraint and deliberateness highly peculiar in an infant, and no one was really unprepared when, at seven months, he began to walk unassisted, with falterings which another month was sufficient to remove.

It was somewhat after this time—on Hallowe'en[40]—that

---

[39] The idea is that the monster is being fed on the flesh and blood of the cattle. Cf. *The Case of Charles Dexter Ward* (1927), alluding to large numbers of prisoners secretly kept by Joseph Curwen: "[The townsfolk] did not like the large number of livestock which thronged the pastures, for no such number of livestock was needed to keep a lone old man and a very few servants in meat, milk, and wool" (*At the Mountains of Madness and Other Novels*, 119). The idea may have been derived from Anthony M. Rud's "Ooze" (*Weird Tales*, March 1923; rpt. January 1952, p. 255), where similarly a monstrous entity is being secretly kept and fed: " … Rori had furnished certain indispensables in way of food to the Cranmer household. At first, these salable articles had been exclusively vegetable—white and yellow turnip, sweet potatoes, corn and beans—but later, *meat!* Yes, meat especially—whole lambs, slaughtered and quartered, the coarsest variety of piney-woods pork and beef, all in immense quantity!"

[40] *Hallowe'en*: October 31; sometimes referred to as All Hallow's Eve, the evening preceding the Feast of All Saints (Hallowmass). As noted earlier (note 32 above), Halloween

a great blaze[41] was seen at midnight on the top of Sentinel Hill where the old table-like stone stands amidst its tumulus of ancient bones. Considerable talk was started when Silas Bishop—of the undecayed Bishops—mentioned having seen the boy running sturdily up that hill ahead of his mother about an hour before the blaze was remarked. Silas was rounding up a stray heifer, but he nearly forgot his mission when he fleetingly spied the two figures in the dim light of his lantern. They darted almost noiselessly through the underbrush, and the astonished watcher seemed to think they were entirely unclothed. Afterward he could not be sure about the boy, who may have had some kind of a fringed belt and a pair of dark trunks or trousers on. Wilbur was never subsequently seen alive and conscious without complete and tightly buttoned attire, the disarrangement or threatened disarrangement of which always seemed to fill him with anger and alarm. His contrast with his squalid mother and grandfather in this respect was thought very notable until the horror of 1928 suggested the most valid of reasons.

The next January gossips were mildly interested in the fact that "Lavinny's black brat" had commenced to talk, and at the age of only eleven months. His speech was somewhat remarkable both because of its difference from the

---

and May Eve are the two great festivals of the Celtic tribes. Sir James George Frazer in *The Golden Bough* elaborates: "Not only among the Celts but throughout Europe, Hallowe'en, the night which marks the transition from autumn to winter, seems to have been of old the time of year when the souls of the departed were supposed to revisit their old homes in order to warm themselves by the fire and to comfort themselves with the good cheer provided for them in the kitchen or the parlour by their affectionate kinsfolk. It was, perhaps, a natural thought that the approach of winter should drive the poor shivering hungry ghosts from the bare fields and the leafless woodlands to the shelter of the cottage with its familiar fireside.... But it is not only the souls of the departed who are supposed to be hovering unseen on the day 'when autumn to winter resigns the pale year.' Witches then speed on their errands of mischief, some sweeping through the air on besoms, others galloping along the roads on tabby-cats, which for that evening are turned into coal-black steeds. The fairies, too, are all let loose, and hobgoblins of every sort roam freely about" (Frazer, 1922, 634).

[41] Lighting fires, especially on hilltops, was a significant feature of ancient celebrations of Halloween.

ordinary accents of the region, and because it displayed a freedom from infantile lisping of which many children or three or four might well be proud. The boy was not talkative, yet when he spoke he seemed to reflect some elusive element wholly unpossessed by Dunwich and its denizens. The strangeness did not reside in what he said, or even in the simple idioms he used; but seemed vaguely linked with his intonation or with the internal organs that produced the spoken sounds. His facial aspect, too, was remarkable for its maturity; for though he shared his mother's and grandfather's chinlessness, his firm and precociously shaped nose united with the expression of his large, dark, almost Latin eyes to give him an air of quasi-adulthood and well-nigh preternatural intelligence. He was, however, exceedingly ugly despite his appearance of brilliancy; there being something almost goatish or animalistic about his thick lips, large-pored, yellowish skin, coarse crinkly hair, and oddly elongated ears. He was soon disliked even more decidedly than his mother and grandsire, and all conjectures about him were spiced with references to the bygone magic of Old Whateley, and how the hills once shook when he shrieked the dreadful name of *Yog-Sothoth*[42] in the midst of a circle of stones with a great book open in his arms before him. Dogs abhorred the boy, and he was always obliged to take various defensive measures against their barking menace.

III.

Meanwhile Old Whateley continued to buy cattle without measurably increasing the size of his herd. He also

---

[42] *Yog-Sothoth*: The name had first been cited by Lovecraft in *The Case of Charles Dexter Ward* (1927), but the entity is very ill-defined there. It first appears in a letter by Joseph Curwen ("I laste Night strucke on ye Wordes that bringe up YOGGE-SOTHOTHE" [*At the Mountains of Madness and Other Novels*, 151]), then in various incantations. Although mentioned in a number of later tales, Yog-Sothoth is a central figure only in "The Dunwich Horror."

cut timber and began to repair the unused parts of his house—a spacious, peaked-roofed[43] affair whose rear end was buried entirely in the rocky hillside, and whose three least-ruined ground-floor rooms had always been sufficient for himself and his daughter. There must have been prodigious reserves of strength in the old man to enable him to accomplish so much hard labour; and though he still babbled dementedly at times, his carpentry seemed to shew the effects of sound calculation. It had already begun as soon as Wilbur was born, when one of the many tool-sheds had been put suddenly in order, clapboarded,[44] and fitted with a stout fresh lock. Now, in restoring the abandoned upper story of the house, he was a no less thorough craftsman. His mania shewed itself only in his tight boarding-up of all the windows in the reclaimed section— though many declared that it was a crazy thing to bother with the reclamation at all. Less inexplicable was his fitting up of another downstairs room for his new grandson— a room which several callers saw, though no one was ever admitted to the closely boarded upper story. This chamber he lined with tall, firm shelving; along which he began gradually to arrange, in apparently careful order, all the rotting ancient books and parts of books which during his own day had been heaped promiscuously in odd corners of the various rooms.

"I made some use of 'em," he would say as he tried to

---

[43] *peaked-roofed*: An architectural form prevalent in New England in the middle seventeenth century, preceding that of the gambrel roof (see note 11 above) and presenting a very sharp inverted V-shape at the roofline. The so-called Witch House (1642) at 310½ Essex Street is of this type, as is the house (c. 1660) upon which Hawthorne based *The House of the Seven Gables*, also in Salem. Cf. Lovecraft's "An Account of a Trip to the Antient Fairbanks House, in Dedham ..." (1929): "This oldest of all New-England houses ... is built of massive timbers from Old England ... [I]n the early 1700's the peaked roofs of the wings (but not that of the original part) were made gambrel according to the universal fashion of that time" (ms., John Hay Library).

[44] *clapboarded*: To clapboard means to cover with clapboards, a series of wooden boards each overlapping the one below.

mend a torn black-letter[45] page with paste prepared on the rusty kitchen stove, "but the boy's fitten to make better use of 'em. He'd orter hev 'em as well sot as he kin, for they're goin' to be all of his larnin'."

When Wilbur was a year and seven months old—in September of 1914—his size and accomplishments were almost alarming. He had grown as large as a child of four, and was a fluent and incredibly intelligent talker. He ran freely about the fields and hills, and accompanied his mother on all her wanderings. At home he would pore diligently over the queer pictures and charts in his grandfather's books, while Old Whateley would instruct and catechise him through long, hushed afternoons.[46] By this time the restoration of the house was finished, and those who watched it wondered why one of the upper windows had been made into a solid plank door. It was a window in the rear of the east gable end, close against the hill; and no one could imagine why a cleated wooden runway was built up to it from the ground. About the period of this work's completion people noticed that the old toolhouse, tightly locked and windowlessly clapboarded since Wilbur's birth, had been abandoned again. The door swung listlessly open, and when Earl Sawyer once stepped within after a cattle-selling call on Old Whateley he was quite discomposed by the singular odour he encountered—such a stench, he averred, as he had never before smelt in all his life except near the Indian circles on the hills, and which could not come from anything sane or of this earth.

---

[45] *black-letter*. A very ornate type of font that came into use around 1600, principally in Germany and Scandinavia, chiefly for liturgical texts, based on earlier, mediaeval, calligraphic hands.

[46] The scene is curiously reminiscent of Lovecraft's own youthful reading of old books in the attic of his grandfather Whipple Phillips's house at 454 Angell Street in Providence. "The books which I used were not modern reprints, but musty old volumes written with 'long s's'.... Latin came quite naturally to me, and in other studies my mother, aunts, and grandfather helped me greatly. To my grandfather I owe much" (*Selected Letters*, I, 7–8).

But then, the homes and sheds of Dunwich folk have never been remarkable for olfactory immaculateness.

The following months were void of visible events, save that everyone swore to a slow but steady increase in the mysterious hill noises. On May-Eve[47] of 1915 there were tremors which even the Aylesbury people felt, whilst the following Hallowe'en produced an underground rumbling queerly synchronised with bursts of flame—"them witch Whateleys' doin's"—from the summit of Sentinel Hill. Wilbur was growing up uncannily, so that he looked like a boy of ten as he entered his fourth year. He read avidly by himself now; but talked much less than formerly. A settled taciturnity was absorbing him, and for the first time people began to speak specifically of the dawning look of evil in his goatish face. He would sometimes mutter an unfamiliar jargon, and chant in bizarre rhythms which chilled the listener with a sense of unexplainable terror. The aversion displayed toward him by dogs had now become a matter of wide remark, and he was obliged to carry a pistol in order to traverse the countryside in safety. His occasional use of the weapon did not enhance his popularity amongst the owners of canine guardians.

The few callers at the house would often find Lavinia alone on the ground floor, while odd cries and footsteps resounded in the boarded-up second story. She would never tell what her father and the boy were doing up there, though once she turned pale and displayed an abnormal degree of fear when a jocose fish-peddler tried the locked door leading to the stairway. That peddler told the store loungers at Dunwich Village that he thought he heard a horse stamping on that floor above. The loungers reflected, thinking of the door and runway, and of the cattle that so swiftly disappeared.

---

[47] *May-Eve*: April 30, the evening before May Day. The day was also known in Germany as *Walpurgisnacht* ("the night of St. Walpurga"), and is so mentioned by Lovecraft in "The Horror at Red Hook" (1925), "The Dreams in the Witch House" (1932), and other stories. See also note 32 above.

Then they shuddered as they recalled tales of Old Whateley's youth, and of the strange things that are called out of the earth when a bullock is sacrificed at the proper time to certain heathen gods. It had for some time been noticed that dogs had begun to hate and fear the whole Whateley place as violently as they hated and feared young Wilbur personally.

In 1917 the war came, and Squire Sawyer Whateley, as chairman of the local draft board, had hard work finding a quota of young Dunwich men fit even to be sent to a development camp.[48] The government, alarmed at such signs of wholesale regional decadence, sent several officers and medical experts to investigate; conducting a survey which New England newspaper readers may still recall. It was the publicity attending this investigation which set reporters on the track of the Whateleys, and caused the *Boston Globe* and *Arkham Advertiser*[49] to print flamboyant Sunday stories of young Wilbur's precociousness, Old Whateley's black magic, the shelves of strange books, the sealed second story of the ancient farmhouse, and the weirdness of the whole region and its hill noises. Wilbur was four and a half then, and looked like a lad of fifteen. His lips and cheeks were fuzzy with a coarse dark down, and his voice had begun to break.

Earl Sawyer went out to the Whateley place with both sets of reporters and camera men, and called their attention to the queer stench which now seemed to trickle down from the sealed upper spaces. It was, he said, exactly like a smell he had found in the toolshed abandoned when the house was finally repaired; and like the faint odours which he

---

[48] *development camp*: In the summer of 1917, when the United States declared war on Germany, development camps were established across the country to train soldiers for war duty. Recall Lovecraft's own rejection for army service during World War I (see note 12 to "The Rats in the Walls").

[49] *Arkham Advertiser*: A mythical newspaper; first cited here, then in "The Whisperer in Darkness" (1930) and *At the Mountains of Madness* (p. 184). In "The Colour Out of Space," an *Arkham Gazette* is cited, evidently a newspaper of earlier date (see note 39 to that story).

sometimes thought he caught near the stone circles on the mountains. Dunwich folk read the stories when they appeared, and grinned over the obvious mistakes. They wondered, too, why the writers made so much of the fact that Old Whateley always paid for his cattle in gold pieces of extremely ancient date.[50] The Whateleys had received their visitors with ill-concealed distaste, though they did not dare court further publicity by violent resistance or refusal to talk.

IV.

For a decade the annals of the Whateleys sink indistinguishably into the general life of a morbid community used to their queer ways and hardened to their May-Eve and All-Hallows orgies. Twice a year they would light fires on the top of Sentinel Hill, at which times the mountain rumblings would recur with greater and greater violence; while at all seasons there were strange and portentous doings at the lonely farmhouse. In the course of time callers professed to hear sounds in the sealed upper story even when all the family were downstairs, and they wondered how swiftly or how lingeringly a cow or bullock was usually sacrificed. There was talk of a complaint to the Society for the Prevention of Cruelty to Animals;[51] but nothing ever came of it, since Dunwich folk are never anxious to call the outside world's attention to themselves.

About 1923, when Wilbur was a boy of ten whose mind, voice, stature, and bearded face gave all the impressions

---

[50] Cf. Lovecraft's "The Terrible Old Man" (1920): " ... [the Terrible Old Man] pays for his few necessities at the village store with Spanish gold and silver minted two centuries ago" (*The Dunwich Horror and Others*, 273).

[51] Properly, the American Society for the Prevention of Cruelty to Animals, founded in 1866. The first such society was founded in England in 1824.

of maturity, a second great siege of carpentry went on at
the old house. It was all inside the sealed upper part, and
from bits of discarded lumber people concluded that the
youth and his grandfather had knocked out all the partitions and even removed the attic floor, leaving only one
vast open void between the ground story and the peaked
roof. They had torn down the great central chimney, too,
and fitted the rusty range with a flimsy outside tin stove-
pipe.

In the spring after this event Old Whateley noticed the
growing number of whippoorwills that would come out of
Cold Spring Glen[52] to chirp under his window at night. He
seemed to regard the circumstance as one of great significance, and told the loungers at Osborn's that he thought his
time had almost come.

"They whistle jest in tune with my breathin' naow," he
said, "an' I guess they're gittin' ready to ketch my soul. They
know it's a-goin' aout, and dun't calc'late to miss it. Yew'll
know, boys, arter I'm gone, whether they git me er not. Ef
they dew, they'll keep up a-singin' an' laffin' till break o'
day. Ef they dun't they'll kinder quiet daown like. I expeck
them an' the souls they hunts fer hev some pretty tough
tussles[53] sometimes."

On Lammas[54] Night, 1924, Dr. Houghton[55] of Aylesbury
was hastily summoned by Wilbur Whateley, who had lashed
his one remaining horse through the darkness and tele-

---

[52] *Cold Spring Glen*: The name seems derived from Coldbrook Springs, a small town in
central Massachusetts, or perhaps from Cold Spring Harbor, Long Island, the site of a
celebrated laboratory devoted to genetics and eugenics.

[53] *tough tussles*: Cf. the title of Ambrose Bierce's story, "A Tough Tussle" (in *Tales of
Soldiers and Civilians* [1891]).

[54] *Lammas:* August 1. Its origin and significance in Christian theology are debated: it
refers either to the tribute of first-ripe grain at Mass or of first-year lambs at Mass. The
ceremony is still performed in the Anglican church. See also note 32 above.

[55] *Houghton*: A common New England name, as in the Houghton Library at Harvard (see
note 58 below) and the Boston publishing firm Houghton Mifflin. Burleson (note 4
above) points out that there was a Houghton's Block in Athol.

phoned from Osborn's in the village. He found Old Whateley in a very grave state, with a cardiac action and stertorous[56] breathing that told of an end not far off. The shapeless albino daughter and oddly bearded grandson stood by the bedside, whilst from the vacant abyss overhead there came a disquieting suggestion of rhythmical surging or lapping, as of the waves on some level beach. The doctor, though, was chiefly disturbed by the chattering night birds outside; a seemingly limitless legion of whippoorwills that cried their endless message in repetitions timed diabolically to the wheezing gasps of the dying man. It was uncanny and unnatural—too much, thought Dr. Houghton, like the whole of the region he had entered so reluctantly in response to the urgent call.

Toward one o'clock Old Whateley gained consciousness, and interrupted his wheezing to choke out a few words to his grandson.

"More space, Willy, more space soon. Yew grows—an' *that* grows faster. It'll be ready to sarve ye soon, boy. Open up the gates to Yog-Sothoth with the long chant that ye'll find on page 751 *of the complete edition,* an' *then* put a match to the prison. Fire from airth can't burn it nohaow."

He was obviously quite mad. After a pause, during which the flock of whippoorwills outside adjusted their cries to the altered tempo while some indications of the strange hill noises came from afar off, he added another sentence or two.

"Feed it reg'lar, Willy, an' mind the quantity; but dun't let it grow too fast fer the place, fer ef it busts quarters or gits aout afore ye opens to Yog-Sothoth, it's all over an' no use. Only them from beyont kin make it multiply an' work.... Only them, the old uns as wants to come back...."

But speech gave place to gasps again, and Lavinia

---

[56] *stertorous*: Characterized by a stertor, or a heavy snoring sound.

screamed at the way the whippoorwills followed the change. It was the same for more than an hour, when the final throaty rattle came. Dr. Houghton drew shrunken lids over the glazing grey eyes as the tumult of birds faded imperceptibly to silence. Lavinia sobbed, but Wilbur only chuckled whilst the hill noises rumbled faintly.

"They didn't git him," he muttered in his heavy bass voice.

Wilbur was by this time a scholar of really tremendous erudition in his one-sided way, and was quietly known by correspondence to many librarians in distant places where rare and forbidden books of old days are kept. He was more and more hated and dreaded around Dunwich because of certain youthful disappearances which suspicion laid vaguely at his door; but was always able to silence inquiry through fear or through use of that fund of old-time gold which still, as in his grandfather's time, went forth regularly and increasingly for cattle-buying. He was now tremendously mature of aspect, and his height, having reached the normal adult limit, seemed inclined to wax beyond that figure. In 1925, when a scholarly correspondent from Miskatonic University called upon him one day and departed pale and puzzled, he was fully six and three-quarters feet tall.

Through all the years Wilbur had treated his half-deformed albino mother with a growing contempt, finally forbidding her to go to the hills with him on May-Eve and Hallowmass; and in 1926 the poor creature complained to Mamie Bishop of being afraid of him.

"They's more abaout him as I knows than I kin tell ye, Mamie," she said, "an' naowadays they's more nor what I know myself. I vaow afur Gawd, I dun't know what he wants nor what he's a-tryin' to dew."

That Hallowe'en the hill noises sounded louder than ever, and fire burned on Sentinel Hill as usual; but people paid more attention to the rhythmical screaming of vast flocks of unnaturally belated whippoorwills which seemed to be assembled near the unlighted Whateley farmhouse. After midnight their shrill notes burst into a kind of pandaemoniac cachinnation[57] which filled all the countryside, and not until dawn did they finally quiet down. Then they vanished, hurrying southward where they were fully a month overdue. What this meant, no one could quite be certain till later. None of the country folk seemed to have died—but poor Lavinia Whateley, the twisted albino, was never seen again.

In the summer of 1927 Wilbur repaired two sheds in the farmyard and began moving his books and effects out to them. Soon afterward Earl Sawyer told the loungers at Osborn's that more carpentry was going on in the Whateley farmhouse. Wilbur was closing all the doors and windows on the ground floor, and seemed to be taking out partitions as he and his grandfather had done upstairs four years before. He was living in one of the sheds, and Sawyer thought he seemed unusually worried and tremulous. People generally suspected him of knowing something about his mother's disappearance, and very few ever approached his neighbourhood now. His height had increased to more than seven feet, and shewed no signs of ceasing its development.

V.

The following winter brought an event no less strange than Wilbur's first trip outside the Dunwich region. Correspondence with the Widener Library at Harvard, the Bibliothèque Nationale in Paris, the British Museum, the

---

[57] *cachinnation*: From the Latin *cachinno*, "to laugh aloud" (Lewis and Short, *A Latin Dictionary*); hence, "loud or immoderate laughter" (*Oxford English Dictionary*). Here the meaning seems more broadly to be merely a loud chattering.

University of Buenos Ayres, and the Library of Miskatonic
University of Arkham[58] had failed to get him the loan of a
book he desperately wanted; so at length he set out in person, shabby, dirty, bearded, and uncouth of dialect, to consult the copy at Miskatonic, which was the nearest to him
geographically.[59] Almost eight feet tall, and carrying a cheap
new valise from Osborn's general store, this dark and goatish
gargoyle appeared one day in Arkham in quest of the
dreaded volume kept under lock and key at the college
library—the hideous *Necronomicon*[60] of the mad Arab

---

[58] Lovecraft has certainly cited several of the most important libraries in the world in this list. The Widener Library (built 1913–15) was in 1928 both the main and the rare book library of Harvard University (the Houghton Library now houses rare books and manuscripts); the Bibliothèque Nationale is the national library of France, as the British Museum in London (the library part of which is now called the British Library) is, along with the Bodleian Library at Oxford, one of the national libraries of England, where all books published in France and England, respectively, must be sent for registration of copyright. It is not clear why Lovecraft selected the University of Buenos Ayres (archaic spelling of *Aires*), whose exact name is the Universidad Nacional de Buenos Aires. Its library was not notable at the time, even among South American countries; however, the Biblioteca Nacional de Argentina, the country's national library, was a distinguished institution.

[59] The fact that Miskatonic University is, of the institutions owning the *Necronomicon*, mentioned as being "nearest" to Dunwich once again suggests that Arkham must be located in the central part of Massachusetts and not at or near Salem; if it were at Salem, then the Widener Library would be closer to Dunwich.

[60] The *Necronomicon* is the most celebrated mythical book invented by Lovecraft. It was first cited by name in "The Hound" (1922), while Abdul Alhazred had been mentioned in "The Nameless City" (1921). In "History of the *Necronomicon*" (1927) Lovecraft provides a tongue-in-cheek history of the volume. He says there that the book as written in the eighth century A.D. by Alhazred was entitled *Al Azif* (a term Lovecraft had derived from Samuel Henley's notes to William Beckford's *Vathek* [1786], referring to the nocturnal buzzing of insects) and was translated into Greek under the title *Necronomicon* by Theodorus Philetas in A.D. 950.

In a late letter Lovecraft gives a purported derivation of the Greek term *Necronomicon*: "*nekros*, corpse; *nomos*, law; *eikon*, image = An Image [or Picture] of the Law of the Dead" (*Selected Letters*, V, 418). Unfortunately for Lovecraft, whose knowledge of Greek was limited, this derivation is almost entirely wrong. According to the rules of Greek etymology, the derivation is: *nekros*, corpse; *nemo*, to divide [hence, to classify or study]; *-ikon*, neuter adjectival suffix = A Study (or Classification) of the Dead. It should also be pointed out that Lovecraft's limited knowledge of Arabic has produced a linguistic monstrosity in the name Abdul Alhazred, since the *-ul* of "Abdul" is cognate with the *-al* of "Alhazred"; a more correct (but perhaps less charismatic) rendering would have been Abd-el-Hazred (analogous to Haroun al-Raschid).

Olaus Wormius was first mentioned as the Latin translator of the *Necronomicon* in "The Festival" (1923). In "History of the *Necronomicon*" Lovecraft makes the curious mistake of

Abdul Alhazred in Olaus Wormius' Latin version, as printed in Spain in the seventeenth century. He had never seen a city before, but had no thought save to find his way to the university grounds; where, indeed, he passed heedlessly by the great white-fanged watchdog that barked with unnatural fury and enmity, and tugged frantically at its stout chain.

Wilbur had with him the priceless but imperfect copy of Dr. Dee's English version[61] which his grandfather had bequeathed him, and upon receiving access to the Latin copy he at once began to collate the two texts with the aim of discovering a certain passage which would have come on the 751st page of his own defective volume. This much he could not civilly refrain from telling the librarian—the same erudite Henry Armitage[62] (A.M. Miskatonic, Ph. D. Princeton, Litt. D. Johns Hopkins) who had once called at the farm, and who now politely plied him with

---

dating this translation to 1228, when in fact Wormius (Ole Worm, 1588–1654) was a Danish doctor and scientist who lived in the seventeenth century and wrote treatises on Danish antiquities, medicine, and the philosopher's stone. This mistake seems to have occurred from Lovecraft's erroneous reading of a passage in Hugh Blair's *A Critical Dissertation on the Poems of Ossian* (1763), where Wormius is mentioned. See S. T. Joshi, "Lovecraft, Regner Lodbrog, and Olaus Wormius," *Crypt of Cthulhu* No. 89 (Eastertide 1995):3–7. In a late letter Lovecraft seems to date this translation to 1623 (see Lovecraft to James Blish and William Miller, Jr., May 13, 1936; *Uncollected Letters* [West Warwick, RI: Necronomicon Press, 1986], 37).

[61] Dee's English translation of the *Necronomicon* had been invented by Frank Belknap Long in "The Space-Eaters" (*Weird Tales*, July 1928), where it was cited as an epigraph (omitted in many reprints of the story). Long was working on the tale around September 1927 (cf. *Selected Letters*, II, 171–72), and Lovecraft had read the story in ms. no later than January 1928 (*Selected Letters*, II, 217).

John Dee (1527–1608) was an English mathematician and astrologer who for a time was physician to Queen Elizabeth I. In later life he engaged extensively in necromancy, claiming to have discovered the philosopher's stone and to have raised spirits from the dead. Among his many works are *Monas Hieroglyphica* (1564), a treatise on astrology, and *A True and Faithful Relation of What Passed for Many Yeers between Dr. John Dee ... and Some Spirits* (1659). *The Necronomicon*, ed. George Hay (1978), purports to print Dee's translation from a manuscript in the British Library. It is one of the most exquisite hoaxes of modern times.

[62] It is not certain where Lovecraft derived the name Armitage, although it is a common New England name. Burleson (note 4 above) suggests a Wisconsin bishop, William Edmond Armitage (1830–1873), but again there is no evidence that Lovecraft knew of this individual.

questions. He was looking, he had to admit, for a kind of formula or incantation containing the frightful name *Yog-Sothoth,* and it puzzled him to find discrepancies, duplications, and ambiguities which made the matter of determination far from easy. As he copied the formula he finally chose, Dr. Armitage looked involuntarily over his shoulder at the open pages; the left-hand one of which, in the Latin version, contained such monstrous threats to the peace and sanity of the world.[63]

"Nor is it to be thought," ran the text as Armitage mentally translated it, "that man is either the oldest or the last of earth's masters, or that the common bulk of life and substance walks alone. The Old Ones were, the Old Ones are, and the Old Ones shall be. Not in the spaces we know, but between them, They walk serene and primal, undimensioned and to us unseen. Yog-Sothoth *knows the gate.* Yog-Sothoth *is the gate.* Yog-Sothoth *is the key and guardian of*

---

[63] The following passage is the most exhaustive excerpt from the *Necronomicon* to be found in Lovecraft's work. Indeed, aside from the "unexplainable couplet" ("That is not dead which can eternal lie, / And with strange aeons even death may die") first cited in "The Nameless City" (1921), Lovecraft provides relatively few actual quotations from the *Necronomicon*. Other authors have not been so reticent. Many of the earlier passages invented by Clark Ashton Smith, August Derleth, and others are included in Lin Carter's "H. P. Lovecraft: The Books," in Lovecraft's *The Shuttered Room and Other Pieces* (Sauk City, WI: Arkham House, 1959), 229–39.

[64] Cf. *The Dream-Quest of Unknown Kadath* (1926–27): "It is known that in disguise the younger among the Great Ones often espouse the daughters of men, so that around the borders of the cold waste wherein stands Kadath the peasants must all bear their blood. This being so, the way to find that waste must be to see the stone face on Ngranek and mark the features; then, having noted them with care, to search for such features among living men" (*At the Mountains of Madness and Other Novels*, 313). Cf. also Lord Dunsany, "A Pretty Quarrel": "The demi-gods are they that were born of earthly women, but their sires are the elder gods who walked of old among men" (*Tales of Three Hemispheres* [Boston: John W. Luce, 1919], 31). Cf. also Lovecraft's comment in "Supernatural Horror in Literature" on Hawthorne's *The Marble Faun* and its "glimpses of fabulous blood in mortal veins" (*Dagon and Other Macabre Tales*, 402). The conception, of course, goes back to Greco-Roman and other early mythologies.

the gate. Past, present, future, all are one in Yog-
Sothoth. *He knows where the Old Ones broke
through of old, and where They shall break through
again. He knows where They have trod earth's
fields, and where They still tread them, and why
no one can behold Them as They tread. By Their
smell can men sometimes know Them near, but of
Their semblance can no man know,* saving only in
the features of those They have begotten on mankind;[64] *and of those are there many sorts, differing
in likeness from man's truest eidolon[65] to that shape
without sight or substance which is* Them. *They
walk unseen and foul in lonely places where the
Words have been spoken and the Rites howled
through at their Seasons. The wind gibbers with
Their voices, and the earth mutters with Their consciousness. They bend the forest and crush the city,
yet may not forest or city behold the hand that
smites. Kadath in the cold waste hath known
Them, and what man knows Kadath?[66] The ice*

---

[65]   *eidolon*: Lovecraft here seems to be using the term in its original Greek meaning ("image, likeness" [Liddell and Scott, *Greek-English Lexicon*]) rather than the English: "An unsubstantial image, spectre, phantom" (*Oxford English Dictionary*). Cf. Lovecraft's poem "The Eidolon" (1918); also "The Outsider" (1921): "the putrid, dripping eidolon of unwholesome revelation" (*The Dunwich Horror and Others*, 51).

[66]   *Kadath*: First cited in "The Other Gods" (1921), where, apparently, it is a mountain in some unspecified locale in the dim prehistory of the earth. It is said that the gods have gone there after having abandoned Mt. Ngranek (see note 64 above), and "suffer no man to tell that he hath looked upon them" (*Dagon and Other Macabre Tales*, 127). Cf. *The Dream-Quest of Unknown Kadath*: "It was lucky that no man knew where Kadath towers, for the fruits of ascending it would be very grave" (*At the Mountains of Madness and Other Novels*, 312). The generally oracular and rhetorical tone of the passage may derive from Lord Dunsany: "Some say that the Worlds and the Suns are but the echoes of the drumming of Skarl, and others say that they may be dreams that arise in the mind of MANA because of the drumming of Skarl, as one may dream whose rest is troubled by the sound of song, but none knoweth, for who hath heard the voice of MANA-YOOD-SUSHAI, or who hath seen his drummer?" (*The Gods of Pegana* [1905; rpt. Boston: John W. Luce, 1916], 3).

*desert of the South and the sunken isles of Ocean
hold stones whereon Their seal is engraven, but who
hath seen the deep frozen city or the sealed tower
long garlanded with seaweed and barnacles? Great
Cthulhu[67] is Their cousin, yet can he spy Them only
dimly. Iä! Shub-Niggurath![68] As a foulness shall ye
know Them. Their hand is at your throats, yet ye see
Them not; and Their habitation is even one with your
guarded threshold. Yog-Sothoth is the key to the gate,
whereby the spheres meet. Man rules now where They
ruled once; They shall soon rule where Man rules now.
After summer is winter, and after winter summer.
They wait patient and potent, for here shall They reign
again."*

Dr. Armitage, associating what he was reading with what he had heard of Dunwich and its brooding presences, and of Wilbur Whateley and his dim, hideous aura that stretched from a dubious birth to a cloud of probable matricide, felt a wave of fright as tangible as a draught of the tomb's cold clamminess. The bent, goatish giant before him seemed like the spawn of another planet or dimension; like something only partly of mankind, and linked to black gulfs of essence and entity that stretch like titan phantasms beyond all spheres of force and matter, space and time. Presently Wilbur raised his head and began speaking in that strange, resonant fashion which hinted at sound-producing organs unlike the run of mankind's.

"Mr. Armitage," he said, "I calc'late I've got to take that book home. They's things in it I've got to try under sarten conditions that I can't git here, an' it 'ud be a mortal sin to

---

[67] *Great Cthulhu*: The extraterrestrial entity introduced in "The Call of Cthulhu" (1926).

[68] This utterance first appears, of all places, in Lovecraft's revision of a story by Adolphe de Castro, "The Last Test" (1927). Later Shub-Niggurath becomes a sort of fertility goddess, and in a late letter Lovecraft declares that she is a "hellish cloud-like entity" and is the wife of Yog-Sothoth (see *Selected Letters*, V, 303). The name is very likely derived from Sheol Nugganoth, a god mentioned in Dunsany's "Idle Days on the Yann" (*A Dreamer's Tales* [1910; rpt. Boston: John W. Luce, 1916], 63).

let a red-tape rule hold me up. Let me take it along, Sir, an' I'll swar they wun't nobody know the difference. I dun't need to tell ye I'll take good keer of it. It wa'n't me that put this Dee copy in the shape it is...."

He stopped as he saw firm denial on the librarian's face, and his own goatish features grew crafty. Armitage, half-ready to tell him he might make a copy of what parts he needed, thought suddenly of the possible consequences and checked himself. There was too much responsibility in giving such a being the key to such blasphemous outer spheres. Whateley saw how things stood, and tried to answer lightly.

"Wal, all right, ef ye feel that way abaout it. Maybe Harvard wun't be so fussy as yew be." And without saying more he rose and strode out of the building, stooping at each doorway.

Armitage heard the savage yelping of the great watchdog, and studied Whateley's gorilla-like lope as he crossed the bit of campus visible from the window. He thought of the wild tales he had heard, and recalled the old Sunday stories in the *Advertiser;* these things, and the lore he had picked up from Dunwich rustics and villagers during his one visit there. Unseen things not of earth—or at least not of tri-dimensional earth—rushed foetid and horrible through New England's glens, and brooded obscenely on the mountain-tops. Of this he had long felt certain. Now he seemed to sense the close presence of some terrible part of the intruding horror, and to glimpse a hellish advance in the black dominion of the ancient and once passive nightmare. He locked away the *Necronomicon* with a shudder of disgust, but the room still reeked with an unholy and unidentifiable stench. "As a foulness shall ye know them," he quoted. Yes— the odour was the same as that which had sickened him at the Whateley farmhouse less than three years before. He thought of Wilbur, goatish and ominous, once again, and laughed mockingly at the village rumours of his parentage.

"Inbreeding?" Armitage muttered half-aloud to himself.

"Great God, what simpletons! Shew them Arthur Machen's Great God Pan[69] and they'll think it a common Dunwich scandal! But what thing—what cursed shapeless influence on or off this three-dimensioned earth—was Wilbur's father? Born on Candlemas—nine months after May-Eve of 1912, when the talk about the queer earth noises reached clear to Arkham— What walked on the mountains that May-Night? What Roodmas[70] horror fastened itself on the world in half-human flesh and blood?"

During the ensuing weeks Dr. Armitage set about to collect all possible data on Wilbur Whateley and the formless presences around Dunwich. He got in communication with Dr. Houghton of Aylesbury, who had attended Old Whateley in his last illness, and found much to ponder over in the grandfather's last words as quoted by the physician. A visit to Dunwich Village failed to bring out much that was new; but a close survey of the *Necronomicon,* in those parts which Wilbur had sought so avidly, seemed to supply new and terrible clues to the nature, methods, and desires of the strange evil so vaguely threatening this planet. Talks with several students of archaic lore in Boston, and letters to many others elsewhere, gave him a growing amazement which passed slowly through varied degrees of alarm to a state of really acute spiritual fear. As the summer drew on he felt dimly that something ought to be done about the lurking terrors of the upper Miskatonic valley, and about the monstrous being known to the human world as Wilbur Whateley.

---

[69] The reference is to "The Great God Pan," a novelette by Arthur Machen first published in *The Great God Pan and The Inmost Light* (1894). This story was manifestly an influence upon "The Dunwich Horror," as it tells of the sexual union between a young woman and the god Pan, whose offspring—the mysterious Helen Vaughan—wreaks physical and psychological havoc upon many individuals before perishing hideously. Lovecraft owned Machen's *The House of Souls* (1906; rpt. 1923), which contained the story.

[70] *Roodmas:* May 3; more commonly termed Holy Rood Day. In Roman Catholic and Orthodox theology, it commemorates the Invention (i.e., finding) of the Cross.

VI.

The Dunwich horror itself came between Lammas and the equinox[71] in 1928, and Dr. Armitage was among those who witnessed its monstrous prologue. He had heard, meanwhile, of Whateley's grotesque trip to Cambridge, and of his frantic efforts to borrow or copy from the *Necronomicon* at the Widener Library. Those efforts had been in vain, since Armitage had issued warnings of the keenest intensity to all librarians having charge of the dreaded volume. Wilbur had been shockingly nervous at Cambridge; anxious for the book, yet almost equally anxious to get home again, as if he feared the results of being away long.

Early in August the half-expected outcome developed, and in the small hours of the 3d Dr. Armitage was awakened suddenly by the wild, fierce cries of the savage watchdog on the college campus. Deep and terrible, the snarling, half-mad growls and barks continued; always in mounting volume, but with hideously significant pauses. Then there rang out a scream from a wholly different throat—such a scream as roused half the sleepers of Arkham and haunted their dreams ever afterward—such a scream as could come from no being born of earth, or wholly of earth.

Armitage, hastening into some clothing and rushing across the street and lawn to the college buildings, saw that others were ahead of him; and heard the echoes of a burglar-alarm still shrilling from the library. An open window shewed black and gaping in the moonlight. What had come had indeed completed its entrance; for the barking and the screaming, now fast fading into a mixed growling and moaning, proceeded unmistakably from within. Some instinct

---

[71] *the equinox*: the autumn equinox, which occurred on September 23 in 1928.

warned Armitage that what was taking place was not a thing for unfortified eyes to see, so he brushed back the crowd with authority as he unlocked the vestibule door. Among the others he saw Professor Warren Rice and Dr. Francis Morgan,[72] men to whom he had told some of his conjectures and misgivings; and these two he motioned to accompany him inside. The inward sounds, except for a watchful, droning whine from the dog, had by this time quite subsided; but Armitage now perceived with a sudden start that a loud chorus of whippoorwills among the shrubbery had commenced a damnably rhythmical piping, as if in unison with the last breaths of a dying man.

The building was full of a frightful stench which Dr. Armitage knew too well, and the three men rushed across the hall to the small genealogical reading-room[73] whence the low whining came. For a second nobody dared to turn on the light, then Armitage summoned up his courage and snapped the switch. One of the three—it is not certain which—shrieked aloud at what sprawled before them among disordered tables and overturned chairs. Professor Rice declares that he wholly lost consciousness for an instant, though he did not stumble or fall.[74]

The thing that lay half-bent on its side in a foetid pool of greenish-yellow ichor[75] and tarry stickiness was almost nine

[72] As Burleson (note 4 above) has pointed out, the names Rice and Morgan are significantly linked in the history of Athol. An H. H. Rice sold the mill power in the town to the Morgan Memorial in the nineteenth century. A Stephen Rice is mentioned in "The Colour Out of Space" (see note 35 to that story).

[73] Although genealogical reading rooms are common in New England libraries, one wonders whether Lovecraft is thinking specifically of the genealogical reading-room of the New York Public Library, where he spent much time reading up on Providence history during his stay in Brooklyn (1924–26).

[74] Cf. the reaction of the scientists at the sight of the twilit grotto in "The Rats in the Walls" (p. 48–49).

[75] *ichor.* "A watery acid discharge issuing from certain wounds and sores" (*Oxford English Dictionary*). Several commentators have noted that some ancient Greek writers mention ichor as the fluid that ran in the veins of the gods. Homer (*Iliad* 5, 340–42, 416) does not specify the color of ichor, but Apollonius Rhodius (*Argonautica* 3, 853) says it is "bloodlike," hence presumably red. A number of English writers (including Pope and Byron) adopt this usage.

feet tall, and the dog had torn off all the clothing and some of the skin. It was not quite dead, but twitched silently and spasmodically while its chest heaved in monstrous unison with the mad piping of the expectant whippoorwills outside. Bits of shoe-leather and fragments of apparel were scattered about the room, and just inside the window an empty canvas sack lay where it had evidently been thrown. Near the central desk a revolver had fallen, a dented but undischarged cartridge later explaining why it had not been fired. The thing itself, however, crowded out all other images at the time. It would be trite and not wholly accurate to say that no human pen could describe it, but one may properly say that it could not be vividly visualised by anyone whose ideas of aspect and contour are too closely bound up with the common life-forms of this planet and of the three known dimensions. It was partly human, beyond a doubt, with very man-like hands and head, and the goatish, chinless face had the stamp of the Whateleys upon it. But the torso and lower parts of the body were teratologically[76] fabulous, so that only generous clothing could ever have enabled it to walk on earth unchallenged or uneradicated.[77]

Above the waist it was semi-anthropomorphic;[78] though its chest, where the dog's rending paws still rested watchfully, had the leathery, reticulated[79] hide of a crocodile or alligator. The back was piebald with yellow and black, and dimly suggested the squamous[80] covering of certain snakes.

---

[76] *teratologically*: The noun form of the word (teratology) means simply the study of monsters (from the Greek *teratos*, "monster").

[77] Cf. Lovecraft's account of an individual named Jean Libbera (misspelled "Libera" by Lovecraft) whom he encountered at a freak show in New York in 1925: "The man in question … had a little anthropoid excrescence growing out of his abdomen which looked hellishly gruesome when uncovered. Clothed, he looked merely like a somewhat 'pot-bellied' individual" (*Selected Letters*, V, 33). Lovecraft mentioned this matter to Henry S. Whitehead, who based his story "Cassius" (1931; in *Jumbee and Other Uncanny Tales*, 1944) upon it.

[78] *semi-anthropomorphic*: Resembling a human being in shape or outline.

[79] *reticulated*: Skin marked so as to resemble a net or network.

[80] *squamous*: Scaly.

Below the waist, though, it was the worst; for here all human resemblance left off and sheer phantasy began. The skin was thickly covered with coarse black fur, and from the abdomen a score of long greenish-grey tentacles with red sucking mouths protruded limply. Their arrangement was odd, and seemed to follow the symmetries of some cosmic geometry unknown to earth or the solar system. On each of the hips, deep set in a kind of pinkish, ciliated[81] orbit, was what seemed to be a rudimentary eye; whilst in lieu of a tail there depended a kind of trunk or feeler with purple annular[82] markings, and with many evidences of being an undeveloped mouth or throat. The limbs, save for their black fur, roughly resembled the hind legs of prehistoric earth's giant saurians; and terminated in ridgy-veined pads that were neither hooves nor claws. When the thing breathed, its tail and tentacles rhythmically changed colour, as if from some circulatory cause normal to the non-human side of its ancestry. In the tentacles this was observable as a deepening of the greenish tinge, whilst in the tail it was manifest as a yellowish appearance which alternated with a sickly greyish-white in the spaces between the purple rings. Of genuine blood there was none; only the foetid greenish-yellow ichor which trickled along the painted floor beyond the radius of the stickiness, and left a curious discolouration behind it.[83]

---

[81] *ciliated*: Furnished with cilia ("Delicate hairs resembling eye-lashes, *esp.* such as form a fringe" [*Oxford English Dictionary*]).

[82] *annular*: Ringlike.

[83] This description is roughly similar to that of the boy Jervase Cradock as described in Arthur Machen's "The Novel of the Black Seal." Jervase is a fourteen-year-old boy (Wilbur is fifteen at the time of his death) born of a human mother and one of the "Little People" of Wales. At one point Professor Gregg describes him as follows: "I saw his body swell and become distended as a bladder, while the face blackened before my eyes ... Something pushed out from the body there on the floor, and stretched forth, a slimy, wavering tentacle, across the room, grasped the bust [of William Pitt] upon the cupboard, and laid it down on my desk" (*The Three Impostors* [London: John Lane; Boston: Roberts Brothers, 1895], 155–56). Murray (note 1 above) interestingly suggests that Wilbur is a sort of Chimaeralike figure, thereby relating him to the Charles Lamb epigraph.

As the presence of the three men seemed to rouse the dying thing, it began to mumble without turning or raising its head. Dr. Armitage made no written record of its mouthings, but asserts confidently that nothing in English was uttered. At first the syllables defied all correlation with any speech of earth, but toward the last there came some disjointed fragments evidently taken from the *Necronomicon,* that monstrous blasphemy in quest of which the thing had perished. These fragments, as Armitage recalls them, ran something like *"N'gai, n'gha'ghaa, bugg-shoggog, y'hah; Yog-Sothoth, Yog-Sothoth. . . ."*[84] They trailed off into nothingness as the whippoorwills shrieked in rhythmical crescendoes[85] of unholy anticipation.

Then came a halt in the gasping, and the dog raised its head in a long, lugubrious[86] howl. A change came over the yellow, goatish face of the prostrate thing, and the great black eyes fell in appallingly. Outside the window the shrilling of the whippoorwills had suddenly ceased, and above the murmurs of the gathering crowd there came the sound of a panic-struck whirring and fluttering. Against the moon vast clouds of feathery watchers rose and raced from sight, frantic at that which they had sought for prey.

All at once the dog started up abruptly, gave a frightened bark, and leaped nervously out of the window by which it had entered. A cry rose from the crowd, and Dr. Armitage shouted to the men outside that no one must be admitted till the police or medical examiner came. He was thankful that the windows were just too high to permit of peering in, and drew the dark curtains carefully down over each one. By this time two policemen had arrived; and Dr. Morgan, meeting them in the vestibule, was urging them for their

---

[84] Cf. the incantation in *The Case of Charles Dexter Ward* (1927) reading: "Y'ai 'ng'ngah, Yog-Sothoth" (*At the Mountains of Madness and Other Novels*, 216).

[85] *crescendoes*: A musical term: "A gradual increase of volume of tone in a passage or piece of music"; hence, "A gradual increase in loudness of tone" (*Oxford English Dictionary*).

[86] *lugubrious*: Mournful.

own sakes to postpone entrance to the stench-filled reading-room till the examiner came and the prostrate thing could be covered up.

Meanwhile frightful changes were taking place on the floor. One need not describe the *kind* and *rate* of shrinkage and disintegration that occurred before the eyes of Dr. Armitage and Professor Rice; but it is permissible to say that, aside from the external appearance of face and hands,[87] the really human element of Wilbur Whateley must have been very small. When the medical examiner came, there was only a sticky whitish mass on the painted boards, and the monstrous odour had nearly disappeared. Apparently Whateley had had no skull or bony skeleton; at least, in any true or stable sense. He had taken somewhat after his unknown father.

VII.

Yet all this was only the prologue of the actual Dunwich horror. Formalities were gone through by bewildered officials, abnormal details were duly kept from press and public, and men were sent to Dunwich and Aylesbury to look up property and notify any who might be heirs of the late Wilbur Whateley. They found the countryside in great agitation, both because of the growing rumblings beneath the domed hills, and because of the unwonted stench and the surging, lapping sounds which came increasingly from the great empty shell formed by Whateley's boarded-up farmhouse. Earl Sawyer, who tended the horse and cattle during Wilbur's absence, had developed a woefully acute case of

---

[87] Cf. "The Whisperer in Darkness" (1930): "For the things in the chair ... were the face and hands of Henry Wentworth Akeley" (*The Dunwich Horror and Others*, 271).

nerves. The officials devised excuses not to enter the noisome boarded place; and were glad to confine their survey of the deceased's living quarters, the newly mended sheds, to a single visit. They filed a ponderous report at the courthouse in Aylesbury, and litigations concerning heirship are said to be still in progress amongst the innumerable Whateleys, decayed and undecayed, of the upper Miskatonic valley.

An almost interminable manuscript in strange characters, written in a huge ledger and adjudged a sort of diary[88] because of the spacing and the variations in ink and penmanship, presented a baffling puzzle to those who found it on the old bureau which served as its owner's desk. After a week of debate it was sent to Miskatonic University, together with the deceased's collection of strange books, for study and possible translation; but even the best linguists soon saw that it was not likely to be unriddled with ease. No trace of the ancient gold with which Wilbur and Old Whateley always paid their debts has yet been discovered.

It was in the dark of September 9th that the horror broke loose. The hill noises had been very pronounced during the evening, and dogs barked frantically all night. Early risers on the 10th noticed a peculiar stench in the air. About seven o'clock Luther Brown, the hired boy at George Corey's,[89] between Cold Spring Glen and the village, rushed frenziedly back from his morning trip to Ten-Acre Meadow with the cows. He was almost convulsed with fright as he stumbled into the kitchen; and in the yard outside the no less

---

[88] Perhaps reminiscent of the little girl's diary in Arthur Machen's "The White People" (in *The House of Souls* [see note 69 above]) as she unwittingly narrates her nurse's inculcation of her into the witch-cult.

[89] The name is perhaps derived from Mary E. Wilkins Freeman's play, *Giles Corey, Yeoman* (1893), about the Salem witchcraft. Lovecraft read the play in 1924 (cf. *Selected Letters*, I, 360).

frightened herd were pawing and lowing pitifully, having followed the boy back in the panic they shared with him. Between gasps Luther tried to stammer out his tale to Mrs. Corey.[90]

"Up thar in the rud beyont the glen, Mis' Cory—they's suthin' ben thar! It smells like thunder, an' all the bushes an' little trees is pushed back from the rud like they'd a haouse ben moved along of it. An' that ain't the wust, nuther. They's *prints* in the rud, Mis' Corey—great raound prints as big as barrel-heads,[91] all sunk daown deep like a elephant had ben along, *only they's a sight more nor four feet could make!* I looked at one or two afore I run, an' I see every one was covered with lines spreadin' aout from

---

[90] The following New England backwoods dialect is first found in "The Picture in the House" (1920), and is used at great length in "The Shadow over Innsmouth" (1931). It is not clear where and how Lovecraft evolved this dialect. In 1929 he wrote in a letter: "As for Yankee farmers—oddly enough, I haven't noticed that the majority talk any differently from myself; so that I've never regarded them as a separate class to whom one must use a special dialect. If I were to say, 'Mornin', Zeke, haow ye be?' to anybody along the road during my numerous summer walks, I fancy I'd receive an icy stare in return—or perhaps a puzzled inquiry as to what theatrical troupe I had wandered out of!" (*Selected Letters*, II, 306). When in Vermont in the summer of 1928, however, Lovecraft wrote to his aunt: "Whether you believe it or not, the rustics hereabouts *actually* say 'caow', 'daown', 'araound', &c.—& employ in daily speech a thousand colourful country-idioms which we know only in literature" (Lovecraft to Lillian D. Clark, June 19, 1928; ms., John Hay Library). Jason C. Eckhardt believes that Lovecraft may have derived this dialect in part from a series of poems by James Russell Lowell, *The Biglow Papers* (1848–62). See Eckhardt's "The Cosmic Yankee," in *An Epicure in the Terrible*, ed. David E. Schultz and S. T. Joshi (Rutherford, NJ: Fairleigh Dickinson University Press, 1991), 89–90.

[91] *barrel-heads*: The flat end of a barrel. A barrel is a cask usually containing 105 dry quarts.

[92] Cf. Algernon Blackwood's "The Wendigo": " … before he had gone a quarter of a mile he came across the tracks of a large animal in the snow, and beside it the light and smaller tracks of what were beyond question human feet—the feet of Défago. The relief he at once experienced was natural, though brief; for at first sight he saw in these tracks a simple explanation of the whole matter: these big marks had surely been left by a bull moose that, wind against it, had blundered upon the camp, and uttered its singular cry of warning and alarm the moment its mistake was apparent.… [But] now that he examined them closer, these were not the tracks of a moose at all! … these were wholly different. They were big, round, ample, and with no pointed outline as of sharp hoofs.… And, stooping down to examine the marks more closely, he caught a faint whiff of that sweet yet pungent odour that made him instantly straighten up again, fighting a sensation almost of nausea" (*The Lost Valley and Other Stories* [London: Eveleigh Nash, 1910], 101–2).

one place, like as if big palm-leaf fans—twict or three times as big as any they is—hed of ben paounded daown into the rud.[92] An' the smell was awful, like what it is araound Wizard Whateley's ol' haouse...."

Here he faltered, and seemed to shiver afresh with the fright that had sent him flying home. Mrs. Corey, unable to extract more information, began telephoning the neighbours; thus starting on its round the overture of panic that heralded the major terrors. When she got Sally Sawyer, housekeeper at Seth Bishop's, the nearest place to Whateley's, it became her turn to listen instead of transmit; for Sally's boy Chauncey,[93] who slept poorly, had been up on the hill toward Whateley's, and had dashed back in terror after one look at the place, and at the pasturage where Mr. Bishop's cows had been left out all night.

"Yes, Mis' Corey," came Sally's tremulous voice over the party wire, "Cha'ncey he just come back a-postin', and couldn't haff talk fer bein' scairt! He says Ol' Whateley's haouse is all blowed up, with the timbers scattered raound like they'd ben dynamite inside; only the bottom floor ain't through, but is all covered with a kind o' tar-like stuff that smells awful an' drips daown offen the aidges onto the graoun' whar the side timbers is blown away. An' they's awful kinder marks in the yard, tew—great raound marks bigger raound than a hogshead,[94] an' all sticky with stuff like is on the blowed-up haouse. Cha'ncey he says they leads off into the medders, whar a great swath wider'n a barn is matted daown, an' all the stun walls tumbled every whichway wherever it goes.

"An' he says, says he, Mis' Corey, as haow he sot to look for Seth's caows, frightened ez he was; an' faound 'em in the

---

[93] Edith Miniter and Evanore Beebe had a hired boy named Chauncey (last name unknown); see note 14 above.

[94] *hogshead*: A cask of varying capacity. In medieval times a hogshead was established at 52½ imperial gallons (63 U.S. gallons). More recently its capacity varies from 100 to 140 gallons.

upper pasture nigh the Devil's Hop Yard in an awful shape. Haff on 'em's clean gone, an' nigh haff o' them that's left is sucked most dry o' blood, with sores on 'em like they's ben on Whateley's cattle ever senct Lavinny's black brat was born. Seth he's gone aout naow to look at 'em, though I'll vaow he wun't keer ter git very nigh Wizard Whateley's! Cha'ncey didn't look keerful ter see whar the big matted-daown swath led arter it leff the pasturage, but he says he thinks it p'inted towards the glen rud to the village.

"I tell ye, Mis' Corey, they's sunthin' abroad as hadn't orter be abroad, an' I for one think that black Wilbur Whateley, as come to the bad eend he desarved, is at the bottom of the breedin' of it. He wa'n't all human hisself, I allus says to everybody; an' I think he an' Ol' Whateley must a raised suthin' in that there nailed-up haouse as ain't even so human as he was. They's allus ben unseen things araound Dunwich—livin' things—as ain't human an' ain't good fer human folks.

"The graoun' was a-talkin' lass night, an' towards mornin' Cha'ncey he heered the whippoorwills so laoud in Col' Spring Glen he couldn't sleep nun. Then he thought he heered another faint-like saound over towards Wizard Whateley's—a kinder rippin' or tearin' o' wood, like some big box er crate was bein' opened fur off. What with this an' that, he didn't git to sleep at all till sunup, an' no sooner was he up this mornin', but he's got to go over to Whateley's an' see what's the matter. He see enough, I tell ye, Mis' Corey! This dun't mean no good, an' I think as all the men-folks ought to git up a party an' do suthin'. I know suthin' awful's abaout, an' feel my time is nigh, though only Gawd know jest what it is.

"Did your Luther take accaount o' whar them big tracks led tew? No? Wal, Mis' Corey, ef they was on the glen rud this side o' the glen, an' ain't got to your haouse yet, I calc'late they must go into the glen itself. They would do that. I allus says Col' Spring Glen ain't no healthy nor decent place. The whippoorwills an' fireflies there never did act like they was creaters o' Gawd, an' they's them as says ye kin hear strange things a-rushin' an' a-talkin' in the air daown thar ef ye stand in the right place, atween the rock falls an' Bear's Den."[95]

By that noon fully three-quarters of the men and boys of Dunwich were trooping over the roads and meadows between the new-made Whateley ruins and Cold Spring Glen, examining in horror the vast, monstrous prints, the maimed Bishop cattle, the strange noisome wreck of the farmhouse, and the bruised, matted vegetation of the fields and roadsides. Whatever had burst loose upon the world had assuredly gone down into the great sinister ravine; for all the trees on the bank were bent and broken, and a great avenue had been gouged in the precipice-hanging underbrush. It was

---

[95] *Bear's Den*: There actually is a site called the Bear's Den near North New Salem, Massachuetts, and Lovecraft's subsequent description of it is quite accurate. He saw it in the summer of 1928, and describes it as follows in a letter: "On Thursday evening [June 28] [H. Warner] Munn came down to dinner in his Essex Roadster & afterward took [W. Paul] Cook & me on a trip to one of the finest scenic spots I have ever seen—Bear's Den, in the woods southwest of Athol. There is a deep forest gorge there; approached dramatically from a rising path ending in a cleft boulder, & containing a magnificent terraced waterfall over the sheer bedrock. Above the tumbling stream rise high rock precipices crusted with strange lichens & honeycombed with alluring caves. Of the latter several extend far into the hillside, though too narrowly to admit a human being beyond a few yards. I entered the largest specimen—it being the first time I was ever in a real cave, notwithstanding the vast amount I have written concerning such things" (Lovecraft to Lillian D. Clark, July 1, 1928; ms., John Hay Library). Donald R. Burleson (see note 4 above) has rediscovered the site.

as though a house, launched by an avalanche, had slid down through the tangle growths of the almost vertical slope. From below no sound came, but only a distant, undefinable foetor;[96] and it is not to be wondered at that the men preferred to stay on the edge and argue, rather than descend and beard the unknown Cyclopean[97] horror in its lair. Three dogs that were with the party had barked furiously at first, but seemed cowed and reluctant when near the glen. Someone telephoned the news to the *Aylesbury Transcript*;[98] but the editor, accustomed to wild tales from Dunwich, did no more than concoct a humorous paragraph about it; an item soon afterward reproduced by the Associated Press.[99]

That night everyone went home, and every house and barn was barricaded as stoutly as possible. Needless to say, no cattle were allowed to remain in open pasturage. About two in the morning a frightful stench and the savage barking of the dogs awakened the household at Elmer Frye's, on the eastern edge of Cold Spring Glen, and all agreed that they could hear a sort of muffled swishing or lapping sound from somewhere outside. Mrs. Frye proposed telephoning the neighbours, and Elmer was about to agree when the noise of

---

[96] *foetor*: Archaic or British spelling of *fetor*, an offensive smell or stench.

[97] *Cyclopean*: An adjective used frequently by Lovecraft. Its principal meaning applies to architecture, and refers to structures made of very large stone blocks; the Greeks used the word in reference to ancient Mycenaean architecture, which they took to be built by the Cyclopes, the race of enormous men invented by Homer in the *Odyssey*. Polyphemus, the individual encountered by Odysseus and his men, is sometimes termed simply the Cyclops. Here the term is used to denote the sheer size of the monster, but its cognate meaning (of or pertaining to the Cyclops) is clearly evident. Cf. "Dagon" (1917): "Vast, Polyphemus-like, and loathsome, it darted like a stupendous monster of nightmares" (*Dagon and Other Macabre Tales*, 18). Also see the description of Cthulhu in "The Call of Cthulhu" (1926): " ... the titan Thing from the stars slavered and gibbered like Polypheme cursing the fleeing ship of Odysseus. Then, bolder than the storied Cyclops, great Cthulhu slid greasily into the water and began to pursue with vast wave-raising strokes of cosmic potency" (*The Dunwich Horror and Others*, 153).

[98] *Aylesbury Transcript*: Mythical; never again used by Lovecraft. In Lovecraft's day the *Boston Transcript* was one of the best-known papers in the country. Lovecraft's friend W. Paul Cook worked for many years for the *Athol Transcript*.

[99] *Associated Press*: The news agency was founded in 1848.

splintering wood burst in upon their deliberations. It came, apparently, from the barn; and was quickly followed by a hideous screaming and stamping amongst the cattle. The dogs slavered and crouched close to the feet of the fear-numbed family. Frye lit a lantern through force of habit, but knew it would be death to go out into that black farm-yard. The children and the womenfolk whimpered, kept from screaming by some obscure, vestigial instinct of defence which told them their lives depended on silence. At last the noise of the cattle subsided to a pitiful moaning, and a great snapping, crashing, and crackling ensued. The Fryes, huddled together in the sitting-room, did not dare to move until the last echoes died away far down in Cold Spring Glen. Then, amidst the dismal moans from the stable and the daemoniac piping of late whippoorwills in the glen, Selina Frye tottered to the telephone and spread what news she could of the second phase of the horror.

The next day all the countryside was in a panic; and cowed, uncommunicative groups came and went where the fiend-ish thing had occurred. Two titan paths of destruction stretched from the glen to the Frye farmyard, monstrous prints covered the bare patches of ground, and one side of the old red barn had completely caved in. Of the cattle, only a quarter could be found and identified. Some of these were in curious fragments, and all that survived had to be shot. Earl Sawyer suggested that help be asked from Aylesbury or Arkham, but others maintained it would be of no use. Old Zebulon Whateley, of a branch that hovered about half way between soundness and decadence, made darkly wild sug-gestions about rites that ought to be practiced on the hill-tops. He came of a line where tradition ran strong, and his memories of chantings in the great stone circles were not altogether connected with Wilbur and his grandfather.[100]

---

[100] A reference to the legends of the convocations of the witch-cult on hilltops or standing stones, both in New England and in Europe.

Darkness fell upon a stricken countryside too passive to organise for real defence. In a few cases closely related families would band together and watch in the gloom under one roof; but in general there was only a repetition of the barricading of the night before, and a futile, ineffective gesture of loading muskets and setting pitchforks handily about. Nothing, however, occurred except some hill noises; and when the day came there were many who hoped that the new horror had gone as swiftly as it had come. There were even bold souls who proposed an offensive expedition down in the glen, though they did not venture to set an actual example to the still reluctant majority.

When night came again the barricading was repeated, though there was less huddling together of families. In the morning both the Frye and the Seth Bishop households reported excitement among the dogs and vague sounds and stenches from afar, while early explorers noted with horror a fresh set of the monstrous tracks in the road skirting Sentinel Hill. As before, the sides of the road shewed a bruising indicative of the blasphemously stupendous bulk of the horror; whilst the conformation of the tracks seemed to argue a passage in two directions, as if the moving mountain[101] had come from Cold Spring Glen and returned to it along the same path. At the base of the hill a thirty-foot swath of crushed shrubbery saplings led steeply upward, and the seekers gasped when they saw that even the most perpendicular places did not deflect the inexorable trail. Whatever the horror was, it could scale a sheer stony cliff of almost complete verticality; and as the investigators climbed around to the hill's summit by safer routes they saw that the trail ended—or rather, reversed—there.

It was here that the Whateleys used to build their hellish fires and chant their hellish rituals by the table-like stone

---

[101] Cf. the description of Cthulhu in "The Call of Cthulhu": "A mountain walked or stumbled" (*The Dunwich Horror and Others*, 152).

on May-Eve and Hallowmass. Now that very stone formed the centre of a vast space thrashed around by the mountainous horror, whilst upon its slightly concave surface was a thick and foetid deposit of the same tarry stickiness observed on the floor of the ruined Whateley farmhouse when the horror escaped. Men looked at one another and muttered. Then they looked down the hill. Apparently the horror had descended by a route much the same as that of its ascent. To speculate was futile. Reason, logic, and normal ideas of motivation stood confounded. Only old Zebulon, who was not with the group, could have done justice to the situation or suggested a plausible explanation.

Thursday night began much like the others, but it ended less happily. The whippoorwills in the glen had screamed with such unusual persistence that many could not sleep, and about 3 a.m. all the party telephones[102] rang tremulously. Those who took down their receivers heard a fright-mad voice shriek out, "Help, oh, my Gawd! . . ." and some thought a crashing sound followed the breaking off of the exclamation. There was nothing more. No one dared do anything, and no one knew till morning whence the call came. Then those who had heard it called everyone on the line, and found that only the Fryes did not reply. The truth appeared an hour later, when a hastily assembled group of armed men trudged out to the Frye place at the head of the glen. It was horrible, yet hardly a surprise. There were more swaths and monstrous prints, but there was no longer any house. It had caved in like an egg-shell, and amongst the

---

[102] In 1928 there were only 16.32 telephones per 100 people in the United States, and even this was a much higher rate than in other parts of the world. Party lines were the earliest type of telephone system, in which two or more telephones were connected to a single telephone line. They were common in rural areas but by no means restricted to them at this time; many working-class families in large cities also used them because of the expense of installing private lines, which require one or more switching stations. As late as 1950, three out of four residence telephones in the United States were party lines. See John Brooks, *Telephone: The First Hundred Years* (New York: Harper & Row, 1976), 267.

ruins nothing living or dead could be discovered.[103] Only a stench and a tarry stickiness. The Elmer Fryes had been erased from Dunwich.

VIII.

In the meantime a quieter yet even more spiritually poignant phase of the horror had been blackly unwinding itself behind the closed door of a shelf-lined room in Arkham. The curious manuscript record or diary of Wilbur Whateley, delivered to Miskatonic University for translation, had caused much worry and bafflement among the experts in languages both ancient and modern; its very alphabet, notwithstanding a general resemblance to the heavily shaded Arabic used in Mesopotamia,[104] being absolutely unknown to any available authority. The final conclusion of the linguists was that the text represented an artificial alphabet, giving the effect of a cipher; though none of the usual methods of cryptographic solution seemed to furnish any clue, even when applied on the basis of every tongue the writer might conceivably have used. The ancient books taken from Whateley's quarters, while absorbingly interesting and in several cases promising to open up new and terrible lines of research among philosophers and men of

---

[103] Cf. Anthony M. Rud, "Ooze" (note 39 above): "Far more interesting were the traces of violence apparent on wall and what once had been a house. The latter seemed to have been ripped from its foundations by a giant hand, crushed out of semblance to a dwelling, and then cast in fragments about the base of wall—mainly on the south side, where heaps of twisted, broken timbers lay in profusion. On the opposite side there had been such heaps once, but now only charred sticks, coated with that gray-black, omnipresent coat of desiccation, remained ... no sign whatever of human remains was discovered" (Rud, 1952, 253).

[104] Probably a reference to the Kufic script, a formal and decorative script used throughout the Arab-speaking world (not only in Mesopotamia) from the eighth to the twelfth centuries A.D. Mesopotamia had been conquered by the Muslims by A.D. 641, who ruled there until being driven out by the Mongols in 1258.

science,[105] were of no assistance whatever in this matter. One of them, a heavy tome with an iron clasp, was in another unknown alphabet—this one of a very different cast, and resembling Sanscrit more than anything else. The old ledger was at length given wholly into the charge of Dr. Armitage, both because of his peculiar interest in the Whateley matter, and because of his wide linguistic learning and skill in the mystical formulae of antiquity and the Middle Ages.

Armitage had an idea that the alphabet might be something esoterically used by certain forbidden cults which have come down from old times, and which have inherited many forms and traditions from the wizards of the Saracenic world.[106] That question, however, he did not deem vital; since it would be unnecessary to know the origin of the symbols if, as he suspected, they were used as a cipher in a modern language. It was his belief that, considering the great amount of text involved, the writer would scarcely have wished the trouble of using another speech than his own, save perhaps in certain special formulae and incantations. Accordingly he attacked the manuscript with the preliminary assumption that the bulk of it was in English.

Dr. Armitage knew, from the repeated failures of his colleagues, that the riddle was a deep and complex one; and that no simple mode of solution could merit even a trial. All through late August he fortified himself with the massed lore of cryptography; drawing upon the fullest resources of his own library, and wading night after night amidst the arcana of Trithemius' *Poligraphia,* Giambattista Porta's *De Furtivis Literarum Notis,* De Vigénère's *Traité des Chiffres,* Falconer's *Cryptomenysis Patefacta,* Davys' and Thicknesse's eighteenth-century

---

[105] See note 22 to "The Colour Out of Space."

[106] *Saracenic world:* "Saracens" was a general term formerly used by Christians to denote Islamic peoples, chiefly Arabs and Turks.

treatises, and such fairly modern authorities as Blair, von Marten, and Klüber's *Kryptographik*.[107] He interspersed his study of the books with attacks on the manuscript itself, and in time became convinced that he had to deal with one of those subtlest and most ingenious of cryptograms, in which many separate lists of corresponding letters are arranged like the multiplication table, and the message built up with arbitrary key-words known only to the initiated. The older authorities seemed rather more helpful than the newer ones, and Armitage concluded that the code of the manuscript was one of great antiquity, no doubt handed down through a long line of mystical experimenters. Several times he seemed near daylight, only to be set back by some unforeseen obstacle. Then, as September approached, the clouds began to clear. Certain letters, as used in certain parts of the manuscript, emerged definitely and unmistakably; and it became obvious that the text was indeed in English.

On the evening of September 2nd the last major barrier

---

[107] These authors and titles are all cited, in this order, in the entry on "Cryptography" by John Eglinton Bailey in the 9th edition of the *Encyclopaedia Britannica*, which Lovecraft owned.

The *Polygraphia* of Johannes Trithemius (1462–1516) was first published in Latin in 1518 and translated into French in 1561. The treatise concerns cabbalistic writing.

De Furtivis Literarum Notis, a work on ciphers by Giovanni Battista della Porta (1535?–1615), was first published in 1563.

Traicté des Chiffres ou Secrètes d'Escrire by Blaise de Vigenère (1523–1596) was first published in 1586.

Cryptomenysis Patefacta; or, The Art of Secret Information Disclosed without a Key by John Falconer was first published in 1685.

An Essay on the Art of Decyphering by John Davys (1678–1724) was published in 1737.

Philip Thicknesse (1719–1792) published *A Treatise on the Art of Decyphering and of Writing in Cypher* in 1772.

William Blair wrote a lengthy article on "Cipher" for Abraham Rees's *Cyclopaedia* (1819).

G. von Marten published *Cours diplomatique* in 1801 (4th ed. 1851).

The *Kryptographik* of Johann Ludwig Klüber (1762–1837) dates to 1809.

See, in general, Lin Carter, "H. P. Lovecraft: The Books" (note 63 above). On the issue of cryptography, see Donald R. Burleson, "Lovecraft and the World as Cryptogram," *Lovecraft Studies* No. 16 (Spring 1988):14–18.

gave way, and Dr. Armitage read for the first time a continuous passage of Wilbur Whateley's annals. It was in
truth a diary, as all had thought; and it was couched in a
style clearly shewing the mixed occult erudition and general illiteracy of the strange being who wrote it. Almost
the first long passage that Armitage deciphered, an entry
dated November 26, 1916, proved highly startling and disquieting. It was written, he remembered, by a child of three
and a half who looked like a lad of twelve or thirteen.

> *"Today learned the Aklo[108] for the Sabaoth,"[109] it ran,
> "which did not like, it being answerable from the
> hill and not from the air. That upstairs more ahead
> of me than I had thought it would be, and is not like
> to have much earth brain. Shot Elam Hutchins' col-
> lie Jack when he went to bite me, and Elam says he
> would kill me if he dast.[110] I guess he won't. Grand-
> father kept me saying the Dho formula last night,
> and I think I saw the inner city at the 2 magnetic
> poles. I shall go to those poles when the earth is
> cleared off, if I can't break through with the Dho-
> Hna formula when I commit it. They from the air
> told me at Sabbat that it will be years before I can
> clear off the earth, and I guess grandfather will be
> dead then, so I shall have to learn all the angles of
> the planes and all the formulas between the Yr and
> Nhhngr.[111] They from outside will help, but they*

---

[108] *Aklo*: A term found in Arthur Machen's "The White People" (see notes 69, 88 above).
The little girl's diary states at one point: "I must not write down the real names of the days
and months which I found out a year ago, nor the way to make the Aklo letters, or the
Chian language, or the great beautiful Circles, nor the Mao Games, nor the chief songs"
(*The House of Souls* [New York: Alfred A. Knopf, 1923], 125).

[109] *Sabaoth*: A Hebrew word retained untranslated in the New Testament, meaning "The
Lord of Hosts"; later it erroneously became a variant spelling of "Sabbath," the Lord's
day. Here it means any day reserved for a religious ritual.

[110] *dast*: Dialectic past participle of "dare."

[111] Both terms are mythical and are never used again by Lovecraft.

*cannot take body without human blood. That
upstairs looks it will have the right cast. I can see it
a little when I make the Voorish sign[112] or blow the
powder of Ibn Ghazi[113] at it, and it is near like them
at May-Eve on the Hill. The other face may wear off
some. I wonder how I shall look when the earth is
cleared and there are no earth beings on it. He that
came with the Aklo Sabaoth said I may be transfig-
ured, there being much of outside to work on."*

Morning found Dr. Armitage in a cold sweat of terror and
a frenzy of wakeful concentration. He had not left the manuscript all night, but sat at his table under the electric light
turning page after page with shaking hands as fast as he could
decipher the cryptic text. He had nervously telephoned his
wife he would not be home, and when she brought him a
breakfast from the house he could scarcely dispose of a
mouthful. All that day he read on, now and then halted
maddeningly as a reapplication of the complex key became
necessary. Lunch and dinner were brought him, but he ate
only the smallest fraction of either. Toward the middle of
the next night he drowsed off in his chair, but soon woke
out of a tangle of nightmares almost as hideous as the truths
and menaces to man's existence that he had uncovered.

On the morning of September 4th Professor Rice and Dr.
Morgan insisted on seeing him for a while, and departed
trembling and ashen-grey. That evening he went to bed, but
slept only fitfully. Wednesday—the next day—he was back
at the manuscript, and began to take copious notes both

---

[112] *Voorish*: Another term derived from Machen's "The White People": "It was all so still
and silent, and the sky was heavy and grey and sad, like a wicked voorish dome in Deep
Dendo" (*The House of Souls* [1923], 128).

[113] *Ibn Ghazi*: A mythical Arabic name, perhaps intended to denote a sorcerer. In
"History of the *Necronomicon*" (note 60 above) Ebn Khallikan is said to be Abdul
Alhazred's twelfth-century biographer. In "The Festival" (1923) there is a reference to
one Ibn Schacabao (*Dagon and Other Macabre Tales*, 216).

from the current sections and from those he had already deciphered. In the small hours of that night he slept a little in an easy-chair in his office, but was at the manuscript again before dawn. Some time before noon his physician, Dr. Hartwell, called to see him and insisted that he cease work. He refused; intimating that it was of the most vital importance for him to complete the reading of the diary, and promising an explanation in due course of time.

That evening, just as twilight fell, he finished his terrible perusal and sank back exhausted. His wife, bringing his dinner, found him in a half-comatose state; but he was conscious enough to warn her off with a sharp cry when he saw her eyes wander toward the notes he had taken. Weakly rising, he gathered up the scribbled papers and sealed them all in a great envelope, which he immediately placed in his inside coat pocket. He had sufficient strength to get home, but was so clearly in need of medical aid that Dr. Hartwell was summoned at once. As the doctor put him to bed he could only mutter over and over again, *"But what, in God's name, can we do?"*

Dr. Armitage slept, but was partly delirious the next day. He made no explanations to Hartwell, but in his calmer moments spoke of the imperative need of a long conference with Rice and Morgan. His wilder wanderings were very startling indeed, including frantic appeals that something in a boarded-up farmhouse be destroyed, and fantastic references to some plan for the extirpation of the entire human race and all animal and vegetable life from the earth by some terrible elder of beings from another dimension.[114]

---

[114] Cf. "The Call of Cthulhu" and the prophecies of the Cthulhu cult when Cthulhu reemerges from the depths of R'lyeh: "The time would be easy to know, for then mankind would have become as the Great Old Ones; free and wild and beyond good and evil, with laws and morals thrown aside and all men shouting and killing and revelling in joy. Then the liberated Old Ones would teach them new ways to shout and kill and revel and enjoy themselves, and all the earth would flame with a holocaust of ecstasy and freedom" (*The Dunwich Horror and Others*, 141).

He would shout that the world was in danger, since the
Elder Things[115] wished to strip it and drag it away from the
solar system and cosmos of matter into some other plane
or phase of entity from which it had once fallen,
vigintillions[116] of aeons[117] ago. At other times he would
call for the dreaded *Necronomicon* and the *Daemonolatreia*
of Remigius,[118] in which he seemed hopeful of finding some
formula to check the peril he conjured up.

"Stop them, stop them!" he would shout. "Those
Whateleys meant to let them in, and the worst of all is
left! Tell Rice and Morgan we must do something—it's
a blind business, but I know how to make the powder....
It hasn't been fed since the second of August, when
Wilbur came here to his death, and at that rate...."

But Armitage had a sound physique despite his seventy-
three years, and slept off his disorder that night without
developing any real fever. He woke late Friday, clear of
head, though sober with a gnawing fear and tremendous
sense of responsibility. Saturday afternoon he felt able to
go over to the library and summon Rice and Morgan for a
conference, and the rest of that day and evening the three
men tortured their brains in the wildest speculation and
the most desperate debate. Strange and terrible books were
drawn voluminously from the stack shelves and from secure places of storage; and diagrams and formulae were

---

[115] *Elder Things*: See note 80 to *At the Mountains of Madness*.

[116] *vigintillions*: In American numeration, 10^{63}; in British numeration, 10^{120}. Cf. "The Call of Cthulhu": "After vigintillions of years great Cthulhu was loose again, and ravening for delight" (*The Dunwich Horror and Others*, 152).

[117] *aeon*: British spelling of *eon* (now archaic in the United States); from the Greek *aion*, "long space of time" (Liddell and Scott, *Greek-English Lexicon*).

[118] A real volume. Remigius is the Latinized form of the name Nicholas Remi (1530–1612). *Daemonolatreia* was published in Latin in 1595; there have been two translations, one in German in 1693 and one in English in 1930 (by Montague Summers; as *Daemonolatry*). The book is, like the *Malleus Maleficarum*, a sort of guidebook to witch-hunting for witchcraft judges. Lovecraft had first mentioned the work in "The Festival" (1923; *Dagon and Other Macabre Tales*, 211).

copied with feverish haste and in bewildering abundance. Of skepticism there was none. All three had seen the body of Wilbur Whateley as it lay on the floor in a room of that very building, and after that not one of them could feel even slightly inclined to treat the diary as a madman's raving.

Opinions were divided as to notifying the Massachusetts State Police, and the negative finally won. There were things involved which simply could not be believed by those who had not seen a sample, as indeed was made clear during certain subsequent investigations. Late at night the conference disbanded without having developed a definite plan, but all day Sunday Armitage was busy comparing formulae and mixing chemicals obtained from the college laboratory. The more he reflected on the hellish diary, the more he was inclined to doubt the efficacy of any material agent in stamping out the entity which Wilbur Whateley had left behind him—the earth-threatening entity which, unknown to him, was to burst forth in a few hours and become the memorable Dunwich horror.

Monday was a repetition of Sunday with Dr. Armitage, for the task in hand required an infinity of research and experiment. Further consultations of the monstrous diary brought about various changes of plan, and he knew that even in the end a large amount of uncertainty must remain. By Tuesday he had a definite line of action mapped out, and believed he would try a trip to Dunwich within a week. Then, on Wednesday, the great shock came. Tucked obscurely away in a corner of the *Arkham Advertiser* was a facetious little item from the Associated Press, telling what a record-breaking monster the bootleg whiskey[119] of

---

[119] *bootleg whiskey:* "The Dunwich Horror" was, of course, written in the midst of Prohibition (1919–33), when the passage of the Eighteenth Amendment made the production, sale, or consumption of alcoholic beverages illegal. Cf. "The Shadow over Innsmouth" (1931): "A quart bottle of whiskey was easily, though not cheaply, obtained in the rear of a dingy variety-store" (*The Dunwich Horror and Others*, 327). Lovecraft was a lifelong teetotaler and in his early years wrote several articles and poems on temperance and Prohibition, although he later came to doubt the efficacy of the measure in the face of widespread resistance to it. The Twenty-first Amendment repealed Prohibition in 1933.

Dunwich had raised up. Armitage, half stunned, could only telephone for Rice and Morgan. Far into the night they discussed, and the next day was a whirlwind of preparation on the part of them all. Armitage knew he would be meddling with terrible powers, yet saw that there was no other way to annul the deeper and more malign meddling which others had done before him.

IX.

Friday morning Armitage, Rice, and Morgan set out by motor for Dunwich, arriving at the village about one in the afternoon. The day was pleasant, but even in the brightest sunlight a kind of quiet dread and portent seemed to hover about the strangely domed hills and the deep, shadowy ravines of the stricken region. Now and then on some mountain-top a gaunt circle of stones could be glimpsed against the sky. From the air of hushed fright at Osborn's store they knew something hideous had happened, and soon learned of the annihilation of the Elmer Frye house and family. Throughout that afternoon they rode around Dunwich; questioning the natives concerning all that had occurred, and seeing for themselves with rising pangs of horror the drear Frye ruins with their lingering traces of the tarry stickiness, the blasphemous tracks in the Frye yard, the wounded Seth Bishop cattle, and the enormous swaths of disturbed vegetation in various places. The trail up and down Sentinel Hill seemed to Armitage of almost cataclysmic significance, and he looked long at the sinister altar-like stone on the summit.

At length the visitors, apprised of a party of State Police which had come from Aylesbury that morning in response to the first telephone reports of the Frye tragedy, decided to seek out the officers and compare notes as far as practicable. This, however, they found more easily planned than performed; since no sign of the party could be found in any direction. There had been five of them in a car, but now the car stood empty near the ruins in the Frye yard. The natives, all of whom had talked with policemen, seemed at first as perplexed as Armitage and his companions. Then old Sam Hutchins thought of something and turned pale, nudging Fred Farr and pointing to the dank, deep hollow that yawned close by.

"Gawd," he gasped, "I told 'em not ter go daown into the glen, an' I never thought nobody'd dew it with them tracks an' that smell an' the whippoorwills a-screechin' daown thar in the dark o' noonday ..."

A cold shudder ran through natives and visitors alike, and every ear seemed strained in a kind of instinctive, unconscious listening. Armitage, now that he had actually come upon the horror and its monstrous work, trembled with the responsibility he felt to be his. Night would soon fall, and it was then that the mountainous blasphemy lumbered upon its eldritch course. *Negotium perambulans in tenebris....*[120] The old librarian rehearsed the formulae he had memorised, and clutched the paper containing the alternative one he had not memorised. He saw that his electric flashlight was in working order. Rice, beside him, took from a valise a metal sprayer of the sort used in combating insects; whilst Morgan uncased the big-game rifle on which he relied despite his colleague's warnings that no material weapon would be of help.

Armitage, having read the hideous diary, knew painfully

---

[120] *Negotium perambulans in tenebris*: "The pestilence [lit., business] that walketh in darkness ...": from Psalm 91:6 (Vulgate 90:6). Cf. E. F. Benson's celebrated tale, "*Negotium Perambulans* ..." (in *Visible and Invisible* [London: Hutchinson, 1923]); Lovecraft notes in "Supernatural Horror in Literature" that the story's "unfolding reveals an abnormal monster from an ancient ecclesiastical panel which performs an act of miraculous vengeance in a lonely village on the Cornish coast" (*Dagon and Other Macabre Tales*, 416).

well what kind of a manifestation to expect; but he did not add to the fright of the Dunwich people by giving any hints or clues. He hoped that it might be conquered without any revelation to the world of the monstrous thing it had escaped. As the shadows gathered, the natives commenced to disperse homeward, anxious to bar themselves indoors despite the present evidence that all human locks and bolts were useless before a force that could bend trees and crush houses when it chose. They shook their heads at the visitors' plan to stand guard at the Frye ruins near the glen; and as they left, had little expectancy of ever seeing the watchers again.

There were rumblings under the hills that night, and the whippoorwills piped threateningly. Once in a while a wind, sweeping up out of Cold Spring Glen, would bring a touch of ineffable foetor to the heavy night air; such a foetor as all three of the watchers had smelled once before, when they stood above a dying thing that had passed for fifteen years and a half as a human being. But the looked-for terror did not appear. Whatever was down there in the glen was biding its time, and Armitage told his colleagues it would be suicidal to try to attack it in the dark.

Morning came wanly, and the night-sounds ceased. It was a grey, bleak day, with now and then a drizzle of rain; and heavier and heavier clouds seemed to be piling themselves up beyond the hills to the northwest. The men from Arkham were undecided what to do. Seeking shelter from the increasing rainfall beneath one of the few undestroyed Frye outbuildings, they debated the wisdom of waiting, or of taking the aggressive and going down into the glen in quest of their nameless, monstrous quarry. The downpour waxed in heaviness, and distant peals of thunder sounded from far horizons.[121] Sheet lighting shimmered, and then a forky bolt flashed near at hand, as if descending into

---

[121] Cf. "The Lurking Fear" (1922): "There was thunder in the air on the night I went to the deserted mansion atop Tempest Mountain to find the lurking fear" (*Dagon and Other Macabre Tales*, 179).

the accursed glen itself. The sky grew very dark, and the watchers hoped that the storm would prove a short, sharp one followed by clear weather.

It was still gruesomely dark when, not much over an hour later, a confused babel of voices sounded down the road. Another moment brought to view a frightened group of more than a dozen men, running, shouting, and even whimpering hysterically. Someone in the lead began sobbing out words, and the Arkham men started violently when those words developed a coherent form.

"Oh, my Gawd, my Gawd," the voice choked out. "It's a-goin' agin, *an' this time by day!* It's aout—it's aout an' a-movin' this very minute, an' only the Lord knows when it'll be on us all!"

The speaker panted into silence, but another took up his message.

"Nigh on a haour ago Zeb Whateley here heerd the 'phone a-ringin', an' it was Mis' Corey, George's wife, that lives daown by the junction. She says the hired boy Luther was aout drivin' in the caows from the storm arter the big bolt, when he see all the trees a-bendin' at the maouth o' the glen—opposite side ter this—an' smelt the same awful smell like he smelt when he faound the big tracks las' Monday mornin'. An' she says he says they was a swishin', lappin' saound, more nor what the bendin' trees an' bushes could make, an' all on a suddent the trees along the rud begun ter git pushed one side, an' they was a awful stompin' an' splashin' in the mud. But mind ye, Luther he didn't see nothin' at all, only just the bendin' trees an' underbrush.

"Then fur ahead where Bishop's Brook goes under the rud he heerd a awful creakin' an' strainin' on the bridge, an' says he could tell the saound o' wood a-startin' to crack an' split. An' all the whiles he never see a thing, only them trees an' bushes a-bendin'. An' when the swishin' saound got very fur off—on the rud towards Wizard Whateley's an' Sentinel Hill—Luther he had the guts ter step up whar he'd heerd it furst an' look at the graound. It was all mud an' water, an' the sky was dark, an' the rain was wipin' aout all tracks abaout as fast as could be; but beginnin' at the glen maouth, whar the trees had moved, they was still some o' them awful prints big as bar'ls like he seen Monday."

At this point the first excited speaker interrupted.

"But *that* ain't the trouble naow—that was only the start. Zeb here was callin' folks up an' everybody was a-listenin' in when a call from Seth Bishop's cut in. His haousekeeper Sally was carryin' on fit ter kill—she'd jest seen the trees a-bendin' beside the rud, an' says they was a kind o' mushy saound, like a elephant puffin' an' treadin', a-headin' fer the haouse. Then she up an' spoke suddent of a fearful smell, an' says her Cha'ncey was a-screamin' as haow it was jest like what he smelt up to the Whateley rewins Monday mornin'. An' the dogs was all barkin' an' whinin' awful.

"An' then she let aout a turrible yell, an' says the shed daown the rud had jest caved in like the storm hed blowed it over, only the wind wa'n't strong enough to dew that. Everybody was a-listenin', an' we could hear lots o' folks on the wire a-gaspin'. All to onct Sally she yelled agin, an' says the front yard picket fence hed just crumbled up, though they wa'n't no sign o' what done it. Then everybody on the line could hear Cha'ncey an' ol' Seth Bishop a-yellin' tew, an' Sally was shriekin' aout that suthin' heavy hed struck the haouse—not lightin' nor nothin', but suthin' heavy agin the front, that kep' a-launchin' itself agin an' agin, though ye couldn't see nothin' aout the front winders. An' then ... an' then ..."

Lines of fright deepened on every face; and Armitage, shaken as he was, had barely poise enough to prompt the speaker.

"An' then ... Sally she yelled aout, 'O help, the haouse is a-cavin' in' ... an' on the wire we could hear a turrible crashin', an' a hull flock o' screamin' ... jest like when Elmer Frye's place was took, only wuss...."

The man paused, and another of the crowd spoke.

"That's all—not a saound nor squeak over the 'phone arter that. Jest still-like. We that heerd it got aout Fords an' wagons an' raounded up as many able-bodied menfolks as we could git, at Corey's place, an' come up here ter see what yew thought best ter dew. Not but what I think it's the Lord's jedgment fer our iniquities, that no mortal kin ever set aside."

Armitage saw that the time for positive action had come, and spoke decisively to the faltering group of frightened rustics.

"We must follow it, boys." He made his voice as reassuring as possible. "I believe there's a chance of putting it out of business. You men know that those Whateleys were wizards—well, this thing is a thing of wizardry, and must be put down by the same means. I've seen Wilbur Whateley's diary and read some of the strange old books he used to read; and I think I know the right kind of spell to recite to make the thing fade away.[122] Of course, one can't be sure, but we can always take a chance. It's invisible—I knew it would be—but there's a powder in this long-distance sprayer that might make it shew up for a second. Later on we'll try it. It's a frightful thing to have alive, but it isn't as bad as what Wilbur would have let in if he'd lived longer. You'll never know what the world has escaped. Now we've only this one to fight, and it can't multiply. It can, though, do a lot of harm; so we mustn't hesitate to rid the community of it.

"We must follow it—and the way to begin is to go to the place that has just been wrecked. Let somebody lead the way—I don't know your roads very well, but I've got an idea there might be a shorter cut across lots. How about it?"

The men shuffled about a moment, and then Earl Sawyer spoke softly, pointing with a grimy finger through the steadily lessening rain.

"I guess ye kin git to Seth Bishop's quickest by cuttin' acrost the lower medder here, wadin' the brook at the low

---

[122] Cf., in *The Case of Charles Dexter Ward*, the two incantations (the "Dragon's Head," ascending node, and the "Dragon's Tail," descending node), the latter of which is used by Marinus Bicknell Willett to dispatch Joseph Curwen.

place, an' climbin' through Carrier's mowin' and the timber-lot beyont. That comes aout on the upper rud might nigh Seth's—a leetle t'other side."

Armitage, with Rice and Morgan, started to walk in the direction indicated; and most of the natives followed slowly. The sky was growing lighter, and there were signs that the storm had worn itself away. When Armitage inadvertently took a wrong direction, Joe Osborn warned him and walked ahead to shew the right one. Courage and confidence were mounting; though the twilight of the almost perpendicular wooded hill which lay toward the end of their short cut, and among whose fantastic ancient trees they had to scramble as if up a ladder, put these qualities to a severe test.

At length they emerged on a muddy road to find the sun coming out. They were a little beyond the Seth Bishop place, but bent trees and hideously unmistakable tracks shewed what had passed by. Only a few moments were consumed in surveying the ruins just around the bend. It was the Frye incident all over again, and nothing dead or living was found in either of the collapsed shells which had been the Bishop house and barn. No one cared to remain there amidst the stench and tarry stickiness, but all turned instinctively to the line of horrible prints leading on toward the wrecked Whateley farmhouse and the altar-crowned slopes of Sentinel Hill.

As the men passed the site of Wilbur Whateley's abode they shuddered visibly, and seemed again to mix hesitancy with their zeal. It was no joke tracking down something as big as a house that one could not see, but that had all the vicious malevolence of a daemon. Opposite the base of Sentinel Hill the tracks left the road, and there was a fresh bending and matting visible along the broad swath marking the monster's former route to and from the summit.

Armitage produced a pocket telescope[123] of considerable

---

[123] Lovecraft owned several telescopes, including a Bardon three-inch telescope that cost $50.00 in 1906. In a black enamel bag which he habitually carried with him on trips he would

power and scanned the steep green side of the hill. Then he handed the instrument to Morgan, whose sight was keener. After a moment of gazing Morgan cried out sharply, passing the glass to Earl Sawyer and indicating a certain spot on the slope with his finger. Sawyer, as clumsy as most non-users of optical devices are, fumbled a while; but eventually focussed the lenses with Armitage's aid. When he did so his cry was less restrained than Morgan's had been.

"Gawd almighty, the grass an' bushes is a-movin'! It's a-goin' up—slow-like—creepin' up ter the top this minute, heaven only knows what fur!"

Then the germ of panic seemed to spread among the seekers. It was one thing to chase the nameless entity, but quite another to find it. Spells might be all right—but suppose they weren't? Voices began questioning Armitage about what he knew of the thing, and no reply seemed quite to satisfy. Everyone seemed to feel himself in close proximity to phases of Nature and of being utterly forbidden, and wholly outside the sane experience of mankind.

X.

In the end the three men from Arkham—old, white-bearded Dr. Armitage, stocky, iron-grey Professor Rice, and lean, youngish Dr. Morgan—ascended the mountain alone. After much patient instruction regarding its focussing and use, they left the telescope with the frightened group that remained in the road; and as they climbed they were watched closely by those among whom the glass was passed around. It was hard going, and Armitage had to be

include a pocket telescope (see Lovecraft to Lillian D. Clark, May 13–14, 1929; ms., John Hay Library).

helped more than once. High above the toiling group the great swath trembled as its hellish maker re-passed with snail-like deliberateness. Then it was obvious that the pursuers were gaining.

Curtis Whateley—of the undecayed branch—was holding the telescope when the Arkham party detoured radically from the swath. He told the crowd that the men were evidently trying to get to a subordinate peak which overlooked the swath at a point considerably ahead of where the shrubbery was now bending. This, indeed, proved to be true; and the party were seen to gain the minor elevation only a short time after the invisible blasphemy had passed it.

Then Wesley Corey, who had taken the glass, cried out that Armitage was adjusting the sprayer which Rice held, and that something must be about to happen. The crowd stirred uneasily, recalling that this sprayer was expected to give the unseen horror a moment of visibility. Two or three men shut their eyes, but Curtis Whateley snatched back the telescope and strained his vision to the utmost. He saw that Rice, from the party's point of vantage above and behind the entity, had an excellent chance of spreading the potent powder with marvellous effect.

Those without the telescope saw only an instant's flash of grey cloud—a cloud about the size of a moderately large building—near the top of the mountain. Curtis, who held the instrument, dropped it with a piercing shriek into the ankle-deep mud of the road. He reeled, and would have crumpled to the ground had not two or three others seized and steadied him. All he could do was moan half-inaudibly,

"Oh, oh, great Gawd ... *that* ... *that* ... "

There was a pandemonium of questioning, and only Henry Wheeler thought to rescue the fallen telescope and wipe it clean of mud. Curtis was past all coherence, and even isolated replies were almost too much for him.

"Bigger'n a barn ... all made o' squirmin' ropes ... hull thing sort o' shaped like a hen's egg bigger'n anything, with dozens o' legs like hogsheads that haff shut up when they step ... nothin' solid abaout it—all like jelly, an' made o' sep'rit wrigglin' ropes pushed clost together[124] ... great bulgin' eyes all over it ... ten or twenty maouths or trunks a-stickin' aout all along the sides, big as stovepipes, an' all a-tossin' an' openin' an' shuttin' ... all grey, with kinder blue or purple rings ... *an' Gawd in heaven—that haff face on top! ...*"

This final memory, whatever it was, proved too much for poor Curtis; and he collapsed completely before he could say more. Fred Farr and Will Hutchins carried him to the roadside and laid him on the damp grass. Henry Wheeler, trembling, turned the rescued telescope on the mountain to see what he might. Through the lenses were discernible three tiny figures, apparently running toward the summit as fast as the steep incline allowed. Only these—nothing more. Then everyone noticed a strangely unseasonable noise in the deep valley behind, and even in the underbrush of Sentinel Hill itself. It was the piping of unnumbered whippoorwills, and in their shrill chorus there seemed to lurk a note of tense and evil expectancy.

Earl Sawyer now took the telescope and reported the three figures as standing on the topmost ridge, virtually level with the altar-stone but at a considerable distance from it. One figure, he said, seemed to be raising its hands above its head at rhythmic intervals; and as Sawyer mentioned the circumstance the crowd seemed to hear a faint, half-musical sound from the distance, as if a loud chant were accompanying the gestures. The weird silhouette on that remote peak must have been a spectacle of infinite grotesqueness and impressiveness, but no observer was in a mood for aesthetic appreciation. "I guess he's sayin' the spell," whispered Wheeler as he snatched back the telescope. The whippoorwills were

---

[124] Cf. Lovecraft's playful description of Yog-Sothoth in a late letter: "Yog doesn't *always* have long, ropy arms, since he assumes a variety of shapes—solid, liquid, gaseous—at will. Possibly, though, he's fondest of the form which does have 'em" (*Selected Letters*, V, 303).

piping wildly, and in a singularly curious irregular rhythm quite unlike that of the visible ritual.

Suddenly the sunshine seemed to lessen without the intervention of any discernible cloud. It was a very peculiar phenomenon, and was plainly marked by all. A rumbling sound brewing beneath the hills, mixed strangely with a concordant rumbling which clearly came from the sky. Lightning flashed aloft, and the wondering crowd looked in vain for the portents of storm. The chanting of the men from Arkham now became unmistakable, and Wheeler saw through the glass that they were all raising their arms in the rhythmic incantation. From some farmhouse far away came the frantic barking of dogs.

The change in the quality of the daylight increased, and the crowd gazed about the horizon in wonder. A purplish darkness, born of nothing more than a spectral deepening of the sky's blue, pressed down upon the rumbling hills. Then the lightning flashed again, somewhat brighter than before, and the crowd fancied that it had shewed a certain mistiness around the altar-stone on the distant height. No one, however, had been using the telescope at that instant. The whippoorwills continued their irregular pulsation, and the men of Dunwich braced themselves tensely against some imponderable menace with which the atmosphere seemed surcharged.

Without warning came those deep, cracked, raucous vocal sounds which will never leave the memory of the stricken group who heard them. Not from any human throat were they born, for the organs of man can yield no such acoustic perversions. Rather would one have said they came from the pit itself, had not their source been so unmistakably the altar-stone on the peak. It is almost erroneous to call them *sounds* at all, since so much of their ghastly, infra-bass timbre spoke to dim seats of consciousness and terror far subtler than the ear; yet one must do so, since their form was indisputably though vaguely that of half-articulate *words*. They were loud—loud as the rumblings and the thunder above which they echoed—yet did they come from no visible being. And because imagination might suggest a conjectural source in the world of non-visible beings, the huddled crowd at the mountain's base huddled still closer, and winced as if in expectation of a blow.

"Ygnaiih ... ygnaiih ... thflthkh'ngha ... Yog-Sothoth ..." rang the hideous croaking out of space. *"Y'bthnk ... h'ehye—n'grkdl'lh."*

The speaking impulse seemed to falter here, as if some frightful psychic struggle were going on. Henry Wheeler strained his eye at the telescope, but saw only the three grotesquely silhouetted human figures on the peak, all moving their arms furiously in strange gestures as their incantation drew near its culmination. From what black wells of Acherontic[125] fear or feeling, from what unplumbed gulfs of extra-cosmic consciousness or obscure, long-latent heredity, were those half-articulate thunder-croakings drawn? Presently they began to gather renewed force and coherence as they grew in stark, utter, ultimate frenzy.

"Eh-ya-ya-ya-yahaah—e'yayayayaaaa ... ngh'aaaaa ... ngh'aaaa ... h'yuh ... h'yuh ... HELP! HELP! ... ff—ff—ff—FATHER! FATHER! YOG-SOTHOTH! ..."[126]

But that was all. The pallid group in the road, still reeling at the *indisputably English* syllables that had poured thickly and thunderously down from the frantic vacancy beside that shocking altar-stone, were never to hear such syllables again. Instead, they jumped violently at the terrific report which seemed to rend the hills; the deafening, cataclysmic peal whose source, be it inner earth or sky, no hearer was ever able to place. A single lightning-bolt shot from the

---

[125] *Acherontic:* From Acheron, one of the five rivers in the Greek underworld.

[126] Perhaps an echo (or parody) of Jesus: "And when Jesus had cried with a loud voice, he said, Father, into thy hands I commend my spirit: and having said thus, he gave up the ghost" (Luke 23:46). Cf. also Mark 15:34 (= Matthew 27:46): "And at the ninth hour Jesus cried with a loud voice, saying, Eloi, Eloi, lama sabachthani? that is to say, My God, my God, why hast thou forsaken me?"

purple zenith to the altar-stone, and a great tidal wave of viewless force and indescribable stench swept down from the hill to all the countryside. Trees, grass, and underbrush were whipped into a fury; and the frightened crowd at the mountain's base, weakened by the lethal foetor that seemed about to asphyxiate them, were almost hurled off their feet. Dogs howled from the distance, green grass and foliage wilted to a curious, sickly yellow-grey, and over field and forest were scattered the bodies of dead whippoorwills.

The stench left quickly, but the vegetation never came right again. To this day there is something queer and unholy about the growths on and around that fearsome hill. Curtis Whateley was only just regaining consciousness when the Arkham men came slowly down the mountain in the beams of a sunlight once more brilliant and untainted. They were grave and quiet, and seemed shaken by memories and re-flections even more terrible than those which had reduced the group of natives to a state of cowed quivering. In reply to a jumble of questions they only shook their heads and reaffirmed one vital fact.

"The thing has gone forever," Armitage said. "It has been split up into what it was originally made of, and can never exist again. It was an impossibility in a normal world. Only the least fraction was really matter in any sense we know. It was like its father—and most of it has gone back to him in some vague realm or dimension outside our material universe; some vague abyss out of which only the most accursed rites of human blasphemy could ever have called him for a moment on the hills."

There was a brief silence, and in that pause the scattered senses of poor Curtis Whateley began to knit back into a sort of continuity; so that he put his hands to his head with a moan. Memory seemed to pick itself up where it had left off, and the horror of the sight that had prostrated him burst in upon him again.

"Oh, oh, my Gawd, that haff face—that haff face on top of it ... that face with the red eyes an' crinkly albino hair,

an' no chin, like the Whateleys ... It was a octopus, centi-pede, spider sort o' thing, but they was a haff-shaped man's face on top of it, an' it looked like Wizard Whateley's, only it was yards an' yards acrost...."

He paused exhausted, as the whole group of natives stared in a bewilderment not quite crystallised into fresh terror. Only old Zebulon Whateley, who wanderingly remembered ancient things but who had been silent heretofore, spoke aloud.

"Fifteen year' gone," he rambled, "I heerd Ol' Whateley say as haow some day we'd hear a child o' Lavinny's a-callin' its father's name on the top o' Sentinel Hill...."

But Joe Osborn interrupted him to question the Arkham men anew.

"*What was it anyhaow,* an' haowever did young Wizard Whateley call it aout o' the air it come from?"

Armitage chose his words very carefully.

"It was—well, it was mostly a kind of force that doesn't belong in our part of space; a kind of force that acts and grows and shapes itself by other laws than those of our sort of Nature.[127] We have no business calling in such things from outside, and only very wicked people and very wicked cults ever try to. There was some of it in Wilbur Whateley himself—enough to make a devil and a precocious monster of him, and to make his passing out a pretty terrible sight. I'm going to burn his accursed diary, and if you men are wise you'll dynamite that altar-stone up there, and pull down all the rings of standing stones on the other hills. Things like that brought down the beings those Whateleys were so fond of—the beings they were going to let in tangibly to wipe out the human race and drag the earth off to some nameless place for some nameless purpose.

---

[127] Cf. the "violet-coloured gas" encountered by Kuranes in "Celephaïs" (1920): "The gas had not heard of planets and organisms before, but identified Kuranes merely as one from the infinity where matter, energy, and gravitation exist" (*Dagon and Other Macabre Tales*, 87). See also note 72 to "The Colour Out of Space."

"But as to this thing we've just sent back—the Whateleys raised it for a terrible part in the doings that were to come. It grew fast and big from the same reason that Wilbur grew fast and big—but it beat him because it had a greater share of the *outsideness* in it. You needn't ask how Wilbur called it out of the air. He didn't call it out. *It was his twin brother, but it looked more like the father than he did.*"

It's been said that only six degrees of separation exist between any two people on earth at any given time; in my case, the degree of separation between myself and H. P. Lovecraft was one—Robert Bloch, with whom I corresponded sporadically during the late eighties to early nineties. While he and I never discussed Lovecraft, the latter writer has never been far from my thoughts in regard to my own work, for he was one of my (many) early influences: It was from him that I developed a fascination with unusual siblings (from his Dunwich Horror, *which in turn influenced my own novel* Dark Journey), *as well as an eagerness to delve into the darker, heretofore "forgotten" past (both my personal history, and that of the town I live in; the result was basically the entire body of my Ewerton-based stories and novels), thanks to his past-centered works like "Pickman's Model." I also remember that he was something of a fixture in 1970s film and TV; personally, the thing about him I treasure most was his love of cats, especially black ones. We cat people tend to stick together, regardless of the circumstances!*

—A. R. Morlan

At the Mountains of Madness, *the third of Lovecraft's short novels (the others are* The Dream-Quest of Unknown Kadath *[1926-27] and* The Case of Charles Dexter Ward *[1927]), was written between January and March 1931. It was rejected by* Weird Tales *for being (as Lovecraft quotes editor Farnsworth Wright) "'too long', 'not easily divisible into parts', 'not convincing'—& so on"* (Selected Letters, *III, 395). Lovecraft, discouraged, let the manuscript sit for years until the young Julius Schwartz, editor of* Fantasy Magazine *who was attempting to start a literary agency, persuaded Lovecraft to let him try to market the tale. It was readily accepted by F. Orlin Tremaine, editor of* Astounding Stories, *for $350 (with $35 going to Schwartz as his fee). It appeared in* Astounding *as a three-part serial in the issues for February, March, and April 1936.*

Lovecraft had been fascinated with the Antarctic continent since he was at least twelve years old, when he had written several small treatises on early Antarctic explorers. It is difficult to know what exactly inspired him to write At the Mountains of Madness *in early 1931. One possibility is a story that appeared in* Weird Tales *for November 1930, "A Million Years After" by Katharine Metcalf Roof. It was not that Lovecraft thought highly of this story (which involves the hatching of dinosaurs' eggs millions of years old); quite the reverse. For years he had advised Frank Belknap Long to write a story on this subject, but Long had held off, thinking that H. G. Wells' "Æpyornis Island" had preempted him. When Roof's story appeared (and received the cover illustration for that issue of* Weird Tales), *Lovecraft berated Long: "But what makes me maddest about this issue, damn it, is the dinosaur's egg story given first place and cover design. Rotten—cheap— puerile—yet winning prime distinction because of the subject matter. Now didn't Grandpa tell a bright young man just eight years ago this month to write a story like that?" (*Selected Letters, *III, 186). It could be said that* At the Mountains of Madness *is Lovecraft's "dinosaur egg story," involving as it does the awakening of entities from the dim ages of earth's history. Of course, it is unlikely that any single event could have led to the composition of this richly textured work; no doubt something of the sort had been percolating in Lovecraft's mind for decades.*

Lovecraft was very proud of this work. He refers to it unequivo-
cally as "my best story" in 1932 (Selected Letters, IV, 24), and
elsewhere terms it "my most ambitious story" (Selected Letters,
IV, 84). Clearly he put a great deal of effort into the novel, especially in establishing verisimilitude at the beginning with authentic geological and paleontological information and building gradually to a powerful climax. This is perhaps why he was so embit-
tered when Weird Tales rejected the work; and to add insult to
injury, when the novel was finally published in Astounding Stories, cuts were made (especially at the end) that infuriated
Lovecraft. Referring to F. Orlin Tremaine as a "goddamn'd dung
of a hyaena," Lovecraft fumed: "I'll be hang'd if I can consider the
story as published at all—the last instalment is a joke, with whole
passages missing.... I pass over certain affected changes in sen-
tence-structure, but see red again when I think of theparagraphing.
Venom of Tsathoggua! Have you seen the damn thing? All my
paragraphs cut up into little chunks like the juvenile stuff the
other pulp hacks write. Rhythm, emotional modulations, & minor
climactic effects thereby destroyed.... Tremaine has tried to make
'snappy action' stuff out of old-fashioned leisurely prose" (Lovecraft
to R. H. Barlow, June 4, 1936; ms., John Hay Library). (In all fair-
ness, it was probably not Tremaine himself who made these
changes and cuts, although they were no doubt made with his
approval.)

   This adulteration of the novel has produced some difficulties
in establishing the proper text of the work. Lovecraft corrected
his own copies of the Astounding serialization, but it is evident
that he did not correct many of the errors, in particular the Ameri-
canization of his customary British spellings. What is more, he
made the corrections with reference to his autograph manuscript,
thereby apparently forgetting some changes he himself had made
when preparing his typescript. At some point prior to its submis-
sion to Astounding Lovecraft himself must have further changed
this typescript, since by this time (say, 1935) Lovecraft had discovered some scientific errors in his description of Antarctica; he
was especially keen to remove his erroneous hypothesis that the
Antarctic continent was in fact two land masses separated by a
frozen sea. These corrections must have been made on the copy
sent to Astounding, as they do not appear on the typescript among
Lovecraft's papers (now in the John Hay Library). Given this difficult situation, my text is based on this typescript, except in places
where demonstrable revisions have taken place. The text sent to

Astounding has apparently been destroyed, so that it is now impossible to know exactly what Lovecraft's final revisions on the novel were; but by following his original typescript, one can at least present the text with a minimum of editorial tampering.

Whenever I think of Antartica I think of Ancient Ones in suspended animation lurking in carvernous places hidden under the ice. Ancient aliens of protean and mind-numbing aspect, too awful to discern clearly. Undeniably John W. Campbell got the idea from Lovecraft for "Who Goes There?"—with its Antarctic research station menaced by a shape-shifting alien. And of course "Who Goes There?" eventually became John Carpenter's The Thing, *which restored the shape-shifting business, omitted by the earlier movie made in the days before high-tech special effects. The trouble about Ancient Ones with slithery names is that they're really difficult to see with aghast eyes, rather like an unknown color from out of space. Only cursèd visionaries get a glimpse. No wonder those Emperor Penguins stand around in the blizzards trying to pass themselves off as clowns....*

—Ian Watson

There is a party game at which we are asked, "If David Letterman had a vanity license plate, what would it say?" "If Betty Boop were real where would she eat?" "If H. P. Lovecraft were a comic book which would it be?" The last is the only one I can answer, but I do know that. Lovecraft would be The Sandman. "Comic book" is, of course, a poor description of The Sandman, and "graphic novel" isn't much closer; all of which fits perfectly, because none of the labels pinned on Lovecraft—I mean the labels meant to pigeon-hold his magificent stories—describe him very well. He was certainly not a pulp writer, merely one whose works appeared in a pulp magazine. Nor was he a horror writer, though there are horrors to be found in his stories now and then, especially if one does not look for them. Rather he was a tall and lonely man with many friends, whose soul dwelt in a haunted palace beyond the world, a man who walked by night and always walked alone: a lord of dreams. A song of Lovecraft's time says that dreams come true in Blue Hawaii, but those are daydreams and too often they don't. C. S. Lewis has a bit in which people visit a region where dreams (real dreams like Lovecraft's and ours) actually do come true; and those people return white and shaken. They were lucky, I think—very lucky to return at all through the gates of horn and ivory, the gates that are opened, sometimes, by the silver key.

What do you think, Mr. Carter?

—Gene Wolfe

At the Mountains
of Madness

I.

I[1] am forced into speech because men of science[2] have
refused to follow my advice without knowing why. It is
altogether against my will that I tell my reasons for oppos-
ing this contemplated invasion of the antarctic—with its
vast fossil-hunt and its wholesale boring and melting of the

---

[1] The narrator of *At the Mountains of Madness* is never explicitly named in the text, but in
"The Shadow out of Time" (1934–35) he is identified as Professor William Dyer of the geology department of Miskatonic University.

[2] *men of science*: See note 22 to "The Colour Out of Space."

ancient ice-cap—and I am the more reluctant because my warning may be in vain. Doubt of the real facts, as I must reveal them, is inevitable; yet if I suppressed what will seem extravagant and incredible there would be nothing left. The hitherto withheld photographs, both ordinary & aërial, will count in my favour; for they are damnably vivid and graphic. Still, they will be doubted because of the great lengths to which clever fakery can be carried. The ink drawings, of course, will be jeered at as obvious impostures; notwithstanding a strangeness of technique which art experts ought to remark and puzzle over.

In the end I must rely on the judgment and standing of the few scientific leaders who have, on the one hand, sufficient independence of thought to weigh my data on its own hideously convincing merits or in the light of certain primordial and highly baffling myth-cycles; and on the other hand, sufficient influence to deter the exploring world in general from any rash and overambitious programme in the region of those mountains of madness.[3] It is an unfortunate fact that relatively obscure men like myself and my associates, connected only with a small university,[4] have little chance of making an impression where matters of a wildly bizarre or highly controversial nature are concerned.

It is further against us that we are not, in the strictest sense, specialists in the fields which came primarily to be concerned. As a geologist my object in leading the Miskatonic University Expedition was wholly that of securing deep-level specimens of rock and soil from various

---

[3] *mountains of madness*: This phrase is found in the work of Lord Dunsany: "'And we came at last to those ivory hills that are named the Mountains of Madness'" ("The Hashish Man," in *A Dreamer's Tales* [1910; rpt. Boston: John W. Luce, 1916], 125). Lovecraft may have arrived at the phrase independently.

[4] It is interesting to note Lovecraft's deprecation of Miskatonic University here, since in "The Dunwich Horror" he ranks its library with some of the most prestigious libraries in the world. Perhaps there is no real contradiction, since in that story he is discussing those libraries that hold the *Necronomicon*, and Miskatonic is presumed to have made a specialty of books on occult lore.

parts of the antarctic continent, aided by the remarkable drill devised by Prof. Frank H. Pabodie[5] of our engineering department. I had no wish to be a pioneer in any other field than this; but I did hope that the use of this new mechanical appliance at different points along previously explored paths would bring to light materials of a sort hitherto unreached by the ordinary methods of collection. Pabodie's drilling apparatus, as the public already knows from our reports, was unique and radical in its lightness, portability, and capacity to combine the ordinary artesian drill principle with the principle of the small circular rock drill in such a way as to cope quickly with strata of varying hardness. Steel head, jointed rods, gasoline motor, collapsible wooden derrick, dynamiting paraphernalia, cording, rubbish-removal auger, and sectional piping for bores five inches wide and up to 1000 feet deep all formed, with needed accessories, no greater load than three seven-dog sledges could carry; this being made possible by the clever aluminum alloy[6] of which most of the metal objects were fashioned. Four large Dornier aëroplanes,[7] designed especially for the tremendous altitude flying necessary on the antarctic plateau and with added fuel-warming and quick-starting devices

---

[5] *Pabodie*: Lovecraft later came in touch with Frederic Jay Pabody, who inquired as to the origin of the name. Lovecraft replied: "… let me say that—although I am not personally acquainted with anyone of this patronymic—I chose it as a name typical of good old New England stock, yet not sufficiently common to sound conventional or hackneyed" (*Selected Letters*, V, 228). The more common spelling is Peabody. Lovecraft frequently visited the Peabody Museum in Salem and the Peabody Museum in Cambridge.

[6] *aluminum alloy*: Perhaps an allusion to duralumin, an alloy of aluminum, copper, manganese, and magnesium used in the construction of Dornier airplanes (see note 7 below).

[7] *Dornier aëroplanes*: More exactly, as Jason C. Eckhardt ("Behind the Mountains of Madness: Lovecraft and the Antarctic in 1930," *Lovecraft Studies* No. 14 [Spring 1987]:31–38) points out, Dornier Do-J "Wal" airplanes, a twin-engine, single-wing flying boat used primarily for passenger service. Eckhardt quotes Lincoln Ellsworth's explanation for the use of these planes for flying over the Nheeorth Pole in 1924 as cited in his book, *Beyond Horizons* (Garden City, NY: Doubleday, Doran, 1938), 145–46: "In the first place, he [the pilot] sought a ship with a duralumin hull. Wooden hulls he deemed unsuitable for landing on rough ice or in water filled with broken ice, because of the danger of stripping the bottom. Duralumin, even lighter than steel, will bend or dent under ordinary

worked out by Pabodie, could transport our entire expedition from a base at the edge of the great ice barrier to various suitable inland points, and from these points a sufficient quota of dogs would serve us.

We planned to cover as great an area as one antarctic season—or longer, if absolutely necessary—would permit, operating mostly in the mountain-ranges and on the plateau south of Ross Sea;[8] regions explored to varying degree by Shackleton, Amundsen, Scott, and Byrd.[9] With frequent

---

collisions but will not break much more readily than wood.... What determined the choice of the Dornier-Wal was the design of the hull itself. The lines of other hulls were such that in snow they would push the snow aside, in the manner of a plow. The Dornier-Wal had a lift forward that would enable it to climb over snow, like a toboggan, and was the only hull of that design in Europe."

The Dornier-Wal planes were capable of carrying 7000 pounds of cargo. Eckhardt, basing his calculations on those supplied by Byrd, has conjectured that the total cargo of the Miskatonic Expedition may have come to about 21,000 pounds (12 men = 2400 lbs.; 36 dogs [80 lbs. each] = 2880 lbs.; human food = 2160 lbs.; dog food = 3888 lbs.; gasoline = 9000 lbs.; miscellaneous cargo = 1300 lbs.), well within the capacity of the four planes.

[8] *Ross Sea*: The body of water just outside the Ross Ice Shelf, an enormous frozen sea at the edge of the antarctic continent facing the Pacific Ocean; discovered by the English explorer James Clark Ross (1800–1862) in his expedition of 1839–43. Lovecraft wrote a nonextant juvenile work (c. 1902) entitled *Voyages of Capt. Ross, R.N.*

[9] The English explorers Robert Falcon Scott (1868–1912) and Ernest Henry Shackleton (1874–1922) had explored the Ross Ice Shelf in an expedition of 1901–04; at one point they nearly died on a sled journey over it. On a later expedition (1907–09) Shackleton climbed Mt. Erebus on Ross Island. The Norwegian explorer Roald Amundsen (1872–1928)

changes of camp, made by aëroplane and involving distances great enough to be of geological significance, we expected to unearth a quite unprecedented amount of material; especially in the pre-Cambrian[10] strata of which so narrow a range of antarctic specimens had previously been secured. We wished also to obtain as great as possible a variety of the upper fossiliferous rocks, since the primal life-history of this bleak realm of ice and death is of the highest importance to our knowledge of the earth's past. That the antarctic continent was once temperate and even tropical, with a teeming vegetable and animal life of which the lichens, marine fauna, arachnida,[11] and penguins of the northern edge are the only survivals, is a matter of common information;[12] and we hoped to expand that information in variety, accuracy, and detail. When a simple boring revealed fossiliferous signs, we should enlarge the aperture by blasting in order to get specimens of suitable size and condition.

Our borings, of varying depth according to the promise held out on by the upper soil or rock, were to be confined to

---

undertook an expedition to Antarctica (1910–12) and on December 14, 1911, became the first man to reach the South Pole. Scott had attempted to beat him to the pole, but he failed to do so; on his return trip he died on the Ross Ice Shelf on March 29, 1912, leaving a poignant diary of his journey. Its final entry states: "I do not think we can hope for any better things now. We shall stick it out to the end, but we are getting weaker, of course, and the end cannot be far. It seems a pity, but I do not think I can write more. For God's sake look after our people" (see Walker Chapman, *The Loneliest Continent: The Story of Antarctic Discovery* [Greenwich, CT: New York Graphic Society, 1964], 189). The American Richard Evelyn Byrd (1888–1957) on his first Antarctic Expedition (1928–30) landed on the Ross Ice Shelf, where he established Little America I.

[10] The period (now more commonly termed Proterozoic) following the Archean and preceding the Cambrian; roughly 2500 to 570 million years B.C. The exact extent and dates of eons, eras, periods, and epochs as understood in Lovecraft's day sometimes differs considerably from modern estimates.

[11] *arachnida*: The class of invertebrate animals to which spiders and scorpions belong.

[12] It had become common information only with the Shackleton expedition of 1907–09, when the discovery of deep seams of coal established that the continent had once been warm. Consider also a remark made by Lovecraft in a letter of April 1930: "As for the arctic climate in past ages—despite the recent Berry conclusions I think the question must still be considered an open one. The same problem exists in the Antarctic also, geologists of the Byrd expedition having found many fossils indicating a tropical past" (*Selected Letters*, III, 144).

exposed or nearly exposed land surfaces—these inevitably being sloped and ridges because of the mile or two-mile thickness of solid ice overlying the lower levels.[13] We could not afford to waste drilling depth on any considerable amount of mere glaciation, though Pabodie had worked out a plan for sinking copper electrodes in thick clusters of borings and melting off limited areas of ice with current from a gasoline-driven dynamo. It is this plan—which we could not put into effect except experimentally on an expedition such as ours—that the coming Starkweather-Moore Expedition proposes to follow despite the warnings I have issued since our return from the antarctic.

The public knows of the Miskatonic Expedition through our frequent wireless reports to the *Arkham Advertiser*[14] and Associated Press,[15] and through the later articles of Pabodie and myself. We consisted of four men from the University—Pabodie, Lake of the biology department, Atwood of the physics department (also a meteorologist), and I representing geology and having nominal command—besides sixteen assistants; seven graduate students from Miskatonic and nine skilled mechanics.[16] Of these sixteen, twelve were qualified aëroplane pilots, all but two of whom were competent wireless operators. Eight of them understood navigation with compass and sextant, as did Pabodie, Atwood, and I. In addition, of course, our two ships—wooden ex-whalers, reinforced for ice conditions and having auxil-

---

[13] It is closer to three miles (4776 meters) near the pole.

[14] *Arkham Advertiser*: See note 49 to "The Dunwich Horror."

[15] *Associated Press*: See note 99 to "The Dunwich Horror."

[16] This sequence of names and titles, although common in stories of exploration, seems similar to that found in M. P. Shiel's *The Purple Cloud*, which in its early pages narrates an expedition to the Arctic: "We were seventeen, all told, the five Heads (so to speak) of the undertaking being Clark (our Chief), John Mew (commander), Aubrey Maitland (meteorologist), Wilson (electrician), and myself (doctor, botanist, and assistant meteorologist)" (*The Purple Cloud* [1901; rpt. New York: Vanguard Press, 1930], 21). Lovecraft read the work in early 1929 (see Lovecraft to August Derleth, January 21, [1929]; ms., State Historical Society of Wisconsin).

iary steam—were fully manned. The Nathaniel Derby Pickman Foundation,[17] aided by a few special contributions, financed the expedition; hence our preparations were extremely thorough despite the absence of great publicity. The dogs, sledges, machines, camp materials, and unassembled parts of our five planes were delivered in Boston, and there our ships were loaded. We were marvelously well-equipped for our specific purposes, and in all matters pertaining to supplies, regimen, transportation, and camp construction we profited by the excellent example of our many recent and exceptionally brilliant predecessors. It was the unusual number and fame of these predecessors which made our own expedition—ample though it was—so little noticed by the world at large.

As the newspapers told, we sailed from Boston Harbour on September 2, 1930; taking a leisurely course down the coast and through the Panama Canal, and stopping at Samoa and Hobart, Tasmania, at which latter place we took on final supplies.[18] None of our exploring party had ever been in the polar regions before, hence we all relied greatly on our ship captains—J. B. Douglas, commanding the brig

---

[17] *Nathaniel Derby Pickman Foundation*: A conglomeration of good New England names (see note 5 above). In "The Shadow Out of Time" (1934–35) Lovecraft's protagonist is named Nathaniel Wingate Peaslee; in "The Thing on the Doorstep" (1933) a leading character is Edward Derby; and in "Pickman's Model" (1926) the central figure is Richard Upton Pickman.

[18] As Eckhardt (note 7 above) points out, Byrd's 1928–30 expedition left New York Harbor on August 25, 1928, passed through the Panama Canal, and stopped at Dunedin, New Zealand, for supplies. Tasmania was formerly a common site for refueling or resupplying by expeditions either going to or returning from the Antarctic: John Briscoe (1831), James Clark Ross (1839), Charles Wilkes (1841), Douglas Mawson (1911), and others stopped there.

Arkham,[19] and serving as commander of the sea party, and Georg Thorfinnssen,[20] commanding the barque *Miskatonic*—both veteran whalers in antarctic waters. As we left the inhabited world behind the sun sank lower and lower in the north, and stayed longer and longer above the horizon each day. At about 62° South Latitude we sighted our first icebergs—table-like objects with vertical sides— and just before reaching the Antarctic Circle,[21] which we crossed on October 20 with appropriately quaint ceremonies,[22] we were considerably troubled with field ice. The falling temperature bothered me considerably after our long voyage through the tropics, but I tried to brace up for the worse rigours to come. On many occasions the curious atmospheric effects enchanted me vastly; these including a strikingly vivid mirage—the first I had ever seen—in which distant bergs became the battlements of unimaginable cosmic castles.

Pushing through the ice, which was fortunately neither extensive nor thickly packed, we regained open water at South Latitude 67°, East Longitude 175°. On the morning of October 26, a strong "land blink"[23] appeared on the south, and before noon we all felt a thrill of excitement at beholding a vast, lofty, and snow-clad mountain chain which

---

[19] *Arkham*: Perhaps another tip of the hat to Byrd, one of whose ships in his 1928–30 expedition was named *City of New York* (Richard E. Byrd, *Little America* [New York: G. P. Putnam's Sons, 1930], 11). It is not certain that Lovecraft actually read *Little America*, but it is evident that he closely followed newspaper accounts of Byrd's expedition, as there are frequent mentions of Byrd in Lovecraft's letters from 1929 to 1931.

[20] *Georg Thorfinnsen*: The captain of a whale ship, the *C. A. Larsen*, that assisted Byrd's expedition was also a Scandinavian, Captain Nilsen (Byrd, 1930, 16).

[21] *Antarctic Circle*: 66½° South Latitude.

[22] Such ceremonies for crossing the equator date to at least the early sixteenth century, and usually involve one crewman playing King Neptune and others playing other traditional roles. See William Poundstone, "The Equator-Crossing Ritual," in *Biggest Secrets* (New York: William Morrow, 1993), 245–51.

[23] *"land blink"*: "An atmospheric glow seen from a distance over snow-covered land in the arctic regions" (*Oxford English Dictionary*). Byrd reports seeing a "Barrier blink" caused by the ice of what he called the Ross Ice Barrier (Byrd, 1930, 77).

opened out and covered the whole vista ahead. At last we had encountered an outpost of the great unknown continent and its cryptic world of frozen death. These peaks were obviously the Admiralty Range[24] discovered by Ross, and it would now be our task to round Cape Adare and sail down the east coast of Victoria Land to our contemplated base on the shore of McMurdo Sound at the foot of the volcano Erebus in South Latitude 77° 9'.[25]

The last lap of the voyage was vivid and fancy-stirring, great barren peaks of mystery looming up constantly against the west as the low northern sun of noon or the still lower horizon-grazing southern sun of midnight poured its hazy reddish rays over the white snow, bluish ice and water lanes, and black bits of exposed granite slope. Through the desolate summits swept raging intermittent gusts of the terrible antarctic wind; whose cadences sometimes held vague suggestions of a wild and half-sentient musical piping, with notes extending over a wide range, and which for some subconscious mnemonic[26] reason seemed to me disquieting and even dimly terrible. Something about the scene reminded me of the strange and disturbing Asian paintings of Nicholas Roerich,[27] and of the still stranger and more disturbing

---

[24] *Admiralty Range*: The range of mountains at the eastern end of Victoria Land; the tallest peak is Mt. Sabine (12,201 feet above sea level).

[25] The camp would be placed at the opposite end of the Ross Ice Shelf from where Byrd's contemporaneous expedition had established Little America.

[26] *mnemonic*: Pertaining to memory (from the Greek *mnema*, memory).

[27] Nikolai Roerich (1874–1947), a Russian painter who went to Tibet from 1923 to 1928 and painted many landscape vistas of the Himalayas; he also wrote several books on Buddhism. Many of his paintings are in the Nicholas Roerich Museum, which opened in 1930 at Riverside Drive and 103rd Street and is now at 319 West 107th Street in New York City. Lovecraft saw it soon after it opened, remarking in a letter: "Possibly I have mentioned to you at various times my admiration for the work of Nicholas Roerich—the mystical Russian artist who has devoted his life to the study & portrayal of the unknown uplands of Central Asia, with their vague suggestions of cosmic wonder & terror ... Surely Roerich is one of those rare fantastic souls who have glimpsed the grotesque, terrible secrets outside space & beyond time, & who have retained some ability to hint at the marvels they have seen" (Lovecraft to Lillian D. Clark, May 21–22, 1930; ms., John Hay Library).

descriptions of the evilly fabled plateau of Leng[28] which occur in the dreaded *Necronomicon*[29] of the mad Arab Abdul Alhazred. I was rather sorry, later on, that I had ever looked into that monstrous book at the college library.

On the seventh of November, sight of the westward range having been temporarily lost, we passed Franklin Island; and the next day descried the cones of Mts. Erebus and Terror on Ross Island[30] ahead, with the long line of the Parry Mountains beyond. There now stretched off to the east the low, white line of the great ice barrier; rising perpendicularly to a height of 200 feet like the rocky cliffs of Quebec,[31] and marking the end of southward navigation. In the afternoon we entered McMurdo Sound and stood off the coast in the lee of smoking Mt. Erebus. The scoriac[32] peak towered up some 12,700 feet against the eastern sky, like a Japanese print of the sacred Fujiyama; while beyond it rose the white, ghost-like height of Mt. Terror, 10,900 feet in altitude, and now extinct as a volcano. Puffs of smoke from Erebus came intermittently, and one of the graduate assistants—a brilliant young fellow named Danforth—pointed out what looked like lava on the snowy slope; remarking that this

---

[28] *plateau of Leng*: See note 96 below.

[29] *Necronomicon*: See note 60 to "The Dunwich Horror."

[30] Ross Island is at the very southeastern tip of the Ross Ice Shelf. Mt. Erebus is 12,448 feet above sea level, Mt. Terror 10,702 feet above sea level.

[31] Lovecraft had first visited Quebec in September 1930, and had been captivated by its scenic grandeur and archaic architecture. He subsequently wrote a lengthy travelogue, *A Description of the Town of Quebeck* (1930–31), in which he states: "The antient wall'd city of *Quebeck* ... lyes on a promontory on the north bank of the River *St. Lawrence*; forming a small peninsula with the *St. Lawrence* on the south & east sides, & the confluent River *St. Charles* on the north. Most of this peninsula is a very lofty table-land, rising above a narrow shoar strip in the sheer cliffs of rock. ... The average height of the cliffs is about 300 feet ..." (*To Quebec and the Stars* [West Kingston, RI: Donald M. Grant, 1976], 115).

[32] *scoriac*: Related to *scoriae*, or jagged blocks of loose lava produced by released gases that form bubbles in the lava. The word occurs in line 14 of Poe's "Ulalume" (see note 34 below).

mountain, discovered in 1840,[33] had undoubtedly been the source of Poe's image when he wrote seven years later of

> *"—the lavas that restlessly roll*
> *Their sulphurous currents down Yaanek*
> *In the ultimate climes of the pole—*
> *That groan as they roll down Mount Yaanek*
> *In the realms of the boreal pole."[34]*

Danforth was a great reader of bizarre material, and had talked a good deal of Poe. I was interested myself because of the antarctic scene of Poe's only long story—the disturbing and enigmatical *Arthur Gordon Pym*.[35] On the barren shore, and on the lofty ice barrier in the background, myriads of grotesque penguins squawked and flapped their fins; while many fat seals[36] were visible on the water, swimming or sprawling across large cakes of slowly drifting ice.

---

[33] *discovered in 1840*: By Ross.

[34] From "Ulalume" (ll. 15–19). The poem was written probably in July 1847 and first published in the *American Review* for December 1847. The identification of Yaanek with Mt. Erebus was first made here by Lovecraft and represents one of his several contributions to Poe scholarship. See, in general, Thomas Ollive Mabbott, "Lovecraft as a Student of Poe," *Fresco* 8, No. 3 (Spring 1958):37–39.

[35] The first book publication of *The Narrative of Arthur Gordon Pym, of Nantucket* by Edgar Allan Poe (1809–1849) is dated 1838 but was copyrighted in June 1837. Two installments had appeared in the January and February 1837 issues of the *Southern Literary Messenger*, at that time edited by Poe. Lovecraft is here concerned only with the latter portion of the novel, which takes place on a group of islands in the Antarctic Ocean.

[36] *fat seals*: Much of the Antarctic exploration in the early to middle nineteenth century was inspired by, or resulted in, the extensive hunting of seals in the region. By the 1880s much of the seal population had been wiped out.

Using small boats, we effected a difficult landing on Ross
Island shortly after midnight on the morning of the 9th,
carrying a line of cable from each of the ships and preparing
to unload supplies by means of a breeches-buoy arrangement.[37] Our sensations on first treading antarctic soil were
poignant and complex, even though at this particular point
the Scott and Shackleton expeditions had preceded us. Our
camp on the frozen shore below the volcano's slope was only
a provisional one; headquarters being kept aboard the
Arkham. We landed all our drilling apparatus, dogs,[38] sledges,
tents, provisions, gasoline tanks, experimental ice-melting
outfit, cameras both ordinary and aërial, aëroplane parts,
and other accessories, including three small portable wireless outfits (besides those in the planes) capable of communicating with the *Arkham*'s large outfit from any part of the
antarctic continent that we would be likely to visit. The
ship's outfit, communicating with the outside world, was
to convey press reports to the *Arkham Advertiser*'s powerful wireless station on Kingsport Head, Mass.[39] We hoped to
complete our work during a single antarctic summer;[40] but
if this proved impossible we would winter on the *Arkham,*

---

[37] *breeches-buoy:* "A life-saving apparatus consisting of a life-buoy with suspended canvas
support resembling breeches through which the legs are put" (*Oxford English Dictionary*).

[38] It was Amundsen who pioneered the use of sled dogs, and he was followed by later
explorers. Scott's use of ponies and tractors ended in disaster and contributed to the
ultimate tragedy of his 1911–12 expedition, when he died in the Antarctic.

[39] *Kingsport Head, Mass.:* Mythical. Lovecraft had invented the city of Kingsport in "The
Terrible Old Man" (1920), but did not identify it with the city of Marblehead until "The
Festival" (1923), a year after visiting that quaint Massachusetts seaport for the first time.
The word "Head" refers to a purported headland or cliff overlooking the sea.

[40] *antarctic summer:* In other words, November to March.

[41] The freezing of the ice can have very serious consequences for an expedition, as the
following account of Sir Ernest Shackleton's voyage of 1914–16 attests: "Running before
a raging blizzard, the 'Endeavour' entered the ice-packed waters of the Weddell Sea.
Here on January 18, 1915, she was frozen in. She lay helpless for eight months and was
crushed and sunk late in October. In the 281 days of her imprisonment she had drifted
1,500 miles, and the members of the crew whom she had left to the mercy of the ice were
now about 350 miles south-southeast of Paulette Island" (Francis Trevelyan Miller,
Byrd's Great Adventure [Philadelphia: John C. Winston Co., 1930], 304).

sending the *Miskatonic* north before the freezing of the ice[41] for another summer's supplies.

I need not repeat what the newspapers have already published about our early work: of our ascent of Mt. Erebus; our successful mineral borings at several points on Ross Island and the singular speed with which Pabodie's apparatus accomplished them, even through solid rock layers; our provisional test of the small ice-melting equipment; our perilous ascent of the great barrier with sledges and supplies; and our final assembling of five huge aëroplanes at the camp atop the barrier. The health of our land party—twenty men and 55 Alaskan sledge dogs—was remarkable, though of course we had so far encountered no really destructive temperatures or windstorms. For the most part, the thermometer varied between zero and 20° or 25° above,[42] and our experience with New England winters had accustomed us to rigours of this sort. The barrier camp was semi-permanent, and destined to be a storage cache for gasoline, provisions, dynamite, and other supplies. Only four of our planes were needed to carry the actual exploring material, the fifth being left with a pilot and two men from the ships at the storage cache to form a means of reaching us from the *Arkham* in case all our exploring planes were lost. Later, when not using all the other planes for moving apparatus, we would employ one or two in a shuttle transportation service between this cache and another permanent base on the great plateau from 600 to 700 miles southward, beyond Beardmore Glacier.[43] Despite the almost unanimous accounts of appalling winds and

---

[42] In fact, the average temperature in Antarctica during summer ranges from 32° F on the coast to -30° F in the interior, and during winter from -4° F on the coast to -94° F in the interior. Lovecraft was himself notoriously sensitive to cold, although the causes for his ailment are not well understood. He was uncomfortable when the temperature dropped below 70°, and would lose consciousness in temperatures below 20°.

[43] *Beardmore Glacier.* A large glacier to the southeast of the Ross Ice Shelf. It is near Mt. Kilpatrick, which, at 14,856 feet above sea level, is one of the highest points on the Antarctic continent.

tempests that pour down from the plateau, we determined to dispense with intermediate bases; taking our chances in the interest of economy and probably efficiency.

Wireless reports have spoken of the breath-taking four-hour non-stop flight[44] of our squadron on November 21 over the lofty shelf ice, with vast peaks rising on the west, and the unfathomed silences echoing to the sound of our engines. Wind troubled us only moderately, and our radio compasses helped us through the one opaque fog we encountered. When the vast rise loomed ahead, between Latitudes 83° and 84°, we knew we had reached Beardmore Glacier, the largest valley glacier in the world, and that the frozen sea was now giving place to a frowning and mountainous coastline. At last we were truly entering the white, aeon-dead world of the ultimate south, and even as we realised it we saw the peak of Mt. Nansen in the eastern distance, towering up to its height of almost 15,000 feet.[45]

The successful establishment of the southern base above the glacier in Latitude 86° 7', East Longitude 174° 23', and the phenomenally rapid and effective borings and blastings made at various points reached by our sledge trips and short aëroplane flights, are matters of history; as is the arduous and triumphant ascent of Mt. Nansen by Pabodie and two of the graduate students—Gedney and Carroll—on December 13–15. We were some 8500 feet above sea-level, and when experimental drillings revealed solid ground only twelve feet down through the snow and ice at certain points, we made considerable use of the small melting apparatus and sunk bores and performed dynamiting at many places where no previous explorer had ever thought of securing mineral specimens. The pre-Cambrian granites and beacon sandstones thus obtained confirmed our belief that this plateau was

---

[44] Lovecraft's emphasis here is not on the duration of the flight—Dornier airplanes routinely made transatlantic flights of longer than four hours—but on the wonder of traversing relatively unexplored stretches of the Antarctic continent.

[45] Mt. Fridtjof Nansen is in fact only 13,350 feet above sea level.

homogeneous with the great bulk of the continent to the west, but somewhat different from the parts lying eastward below South America—which we then thought to form a separate and smaller continent divided from the larger one by a frozen junction of Ross and Weddell Seas, though Byrd has since disproved the hypothesis.[46]

In certain of the sandstones, dynamited and chiselled after boring revealed their nature, we found some highly interesting fossil markings and fragments—notably ferns, seaweeds, trilobites, crinoids, and such molluscs as lingulae and gasteropods[47]—all of which seemed of real significance in connexion with the region's primordial history. There was also a queer triangular, striated[48] marking about a foot in greatest diameter which Lake pieced together form three fragments of slate brought up from a deep-blasted aperture. These fragments came from a point to the westward, near the Queen Alexandra Range; and Lake, as a biologist, seemed to find their curious marking unusually

---

[46] As originally written, this passage read: " ... west, but radically different from the parts lying eastward below South America, which in all probability form a separate and smaller continent divided from the larger by a frozen junction of Ross and Weddell Seas." Lovecraft must have revised the passage at some point before sending the tale (through his agent Julius Schwartz) to *Astounding Stories* in late 1935. The notion that the antarctic continent was two separate land masses was a minority opinion throughout the nineteenth century, although Ross had believed that Antarctica may be several different land masses. Lovecraft is wrong in thinking that Byrd disproved the hypothesis: Lincoln Ellsworth and Herbert Hollick-Kenyon disproved it on the first airplane crossing of the continent from the Weddell to the Ross Sea in November 1935.

[47] *trilobites*: "Subphylum of aquatic arthropods known from the Cambrian to the Permian" (R. J. Lincoln and G. A. Boxshall, *The Cambridge Illustrated Dictionary of Natural History* [Cambridge: Cambridge University Press, 1987]).

crinoids: "Sea lilies, feather stars; class of shallow to deep-water echinoderms" (Lincoln and Boxshall, 1987). Cf. note 81 below.

lingulae: A genus of mollusc that "has existed unchanged for 400 million years" (Lincoln and Boxshall, 1987). Lovecraft's ms. reads "linguellae," an apparent error.

gasteropods: "Snails; a large class of aquatic, terrestrial or parasitic molluscs" (Lincoln and Boxshall, 1987); more commonly spelled *gastropod*.

[48] *striated*: "Marked or characterized by striae, furrowed, streaked" (*Oxford English Dictionary*).

puzzling and provocative, though to my geological eye it looked not unlike some of the ripple effects reasonably common in the sedimentary rocks. Since slate is no more than a metamorphic formation into which a sedimentary stratum is pressed,[49] and since the pressure itself produces odd distorting effects on any markings which may exist, I saw no reason for extreme wonder over the striated depression.

On January 6, 1931, Lake, Pabodie, Daniels, all six of the students, four mechanics, and I flew directly over the south pole in two of the great planes,[50] being forced down once by a sudden high wind which fortunately did not develop into a typical storm. This was, as the papers have stated, one of several observation flights; during others of which we tried to discern new topographical features in areas unreached by previous explorers. Our early flights were disappointing in this latter respect; though they afforded us some magnificent examples of the richly fantastic and deceptive mirages of the polar regions, of which our sea voyage had given us some brief foretastes. Distant mountains floated in the sky as enchanted cities, and often the whole white world would dissolve into a gold, silver, and scarlet land of Dunsanian[51] dreams and adventurous expectancy[52] under the magic of the low midnight sun. On cloudy days we had considerable

---

[49] Specifically, slate is the result of the metamorphism (i.e., subjection to high temperatures and pressures) of shale.

[50] The first airplane flight to the South Pole had been effected by Byrd on November 28, 1929 (Byrd, 1930, 326–45).

[51] *Dunsanian*: A reference to Edward John Moreton Drax Plunkett, Lord Dunsany (1878–1957), whose fantastic tales had captivated Lovecraft when he read them in 1919.

[52] *adventurous expectancy*: A central element in Lovecraft's aesthetic of the imagination, and a concept to which he attached peculiar significance. "What has haunted my dreams for nearly forty years is *a strange sense of adventurous expectancy connected with landscape and architecture and sky-effects.* ... I wish I could get the idea on paper—the sense of marvel and liberation hiding in obscure dimensions and problematically reachable at rare instants through vistas of ancient streets, across leagues of strange hill country, or up endless flights of marble steps culminating in tiers of balustraded terraces. Odd stuff—and needing a greater poet than I for effective aesthetic utilisation" (*Selected Letters*, III, 100).

trouble in flying, owing to the tendency of snowy earth and sky to merge into one mystical opalescent[53] void with no visible horizon to mark the junction of the two.

At length we resolved to carry out our original plan of flying 500 miles eastward with all four exploring planes and establishing a fresh sub-base at a point which would probably be on the smaller continental division, as we mistakenly conceived it.[54] Geological specimens obtained there would be desirable for purposes of comparison. Our health so far had remained excellent; lime-juice[55] well offsetting the steady diet of tinned and salted food, and temperatures generally above zero enabling us to do without our thickest furs. It was now midsummer, and with haste and care we might be able to conclude work by March and avoid a tedious wintering through the long antarctic night. Several savage windstorms had burst upon us from the west, but we had escaped damage through the skill of Atwood in devising rudimentary aëroplane shelters and windbreaks of heavy snow blocks, and reinforcing the principal camp buildings with snow. Our good luck and efficiency had indeed been almost uncanny.

The outside world knew, of course, of our programme, and was told also of Lake's strange and dogged insistence on a westward—or rather, northwestward—prospecting trip before our radical shift to the new base. It seems he had pondered a great deal, and with alarmingly radical daring, over that triangular striated marking in the slate; reading

---

[53] *opalescent*: "Exhibiting a play of various colours like that of the opal; having a milky iridescence" (*Oxford English Dictionary*).

[54] *as we mistakenly conceived it*: The phrase was added to the text at a later date (see note 46 above).

[55] *lime-juice*: Lovecraft was surely aware that many previous Antarctic expeditions foundered because scurvy and other diseases had developed from the lack of fresh fruit. As early as 1772, Captain James Cook had shown that citrus fruits—particularly limes and lemons—would help to ward off scurvy, but several later expeditions had failed to stock these essential foodstuffs.

into it certain contradictions in Nature[56] and geological period which whetted his curiosity to the utmost, and made him avid to sink more borings and blastings in the west-stretching formation to which the exhumed fragments evidently belonged. He was strangely convinced that the marking was the print of some bulky, unknown, and radically unclassifiable organism of considerably advanced evolution, notwithstanding that the rock which bore it was of so vastly ancient a date—Cambrian[57] if not actually pre-Cambrian—as to preclude the probable existence not only of all highly evolved life, but of any life at all above the unicellular or at most the trilobite stage. These fragments, with their odd markings, must have been 500 million to a thousand million years old.

II.

Popular imagination, I judge, responded actively to our wireless bulletins of Lake's start northwestward into regions never trodden by human foot or penetrated by human imagination; though we did not mention his wild hopes of revolutionising the entire sciences of biology and geology. His preliminary sledging and boring journey of January 11–18 with Pabodie and five others—marred by the loss of two dogs in an upset when crossing one of the great pressure-ridges in the ice—had brought up more and more of the

---

[56] *contradictions in Nature*: A central conception in Lovecraft's theory of weird fiction. Cf. "Supernatural Horror in Literature": "The true weird tale has something more than secret murder, bloody bones, or a sheeted form clanking chains according to rule. A certain atmosphere of breathless and unexplained dread of outer, unknown forces must be present; and there must be a hint, expressed with a seriousness and portentousness becoming its subject, of that most terrible conception of the human brain—a malign and particular suspension or defeat of those fixed laws of Nature which are our only safeguard against the assaults of chaos and the daemons of unplumbed space" (*Dagon and Other Macabre Tales*, 368).

[57] The Cambrian period extends from roughly 570 to 500 million years ago.

Archaean[58] slate; and even I was interested by the singular profusion of evident fossil markings in that unbelievably ancient stratum. These markings, however, were of very primitive life-forms involving no great paradox except that any life-forms should occur in rock as definitely pre-Cambrian as this seemed to be; hence I still failed to see the good sense of Lake's demand for an interlude in our time-saving programme—an interlude requiring the use of all four planes, many men, and the whole of the expedition's mechanical apparatus. I did not, in the end, veto the plan; though I decided not to accompany the northwestward party despite Lake's plea for my geological advice. While they were gone, I would remain at the base with Pabodie and five men and work out final plans for the eastward shift. In preparation for this transfer one of the planes had begun to move up a good gasoline supply from McMurdo Sound; but this could wait temporarily. I kept with me one sledge and nine dogs, since it is unwise to be at any time without possible transportation in an utterly tenantless world of aeon-long death.

Lake's sub-expedition into the unknown, as everyone will recall, sent out its own reports from the short-wave transmitters[59] on the planes; these being simultaneously picked up by our apparatus at the southern base and by the *Arkham* at McMurdo Sound, whence they were relayed to the outside world on wave-lengths up to fifty metres. The start was made January 22 at 4 a.m.; and the first wireless message we received came only two hours later, when Lake spoke of descending and starting a small-scale ice-melting and bore at a point some 300 miles away from us. Six hours after that a second and very excited message told of

---

[58] The Archean era extends from 4000 to 2500 million years ago. The first microorganisms are thought to have emerged around 3000 million years ago.

[59] The use of short-wave radio had been pioneered by the Australian Douglas Mawson (1882–1958) on his Antarctic voyage of 1911–12. On Byrd's first expedition (1928–30) a reporter for the *New York Times* sent daily reports, while Byrd himself also made regular radio broadcasts to the public.

the frantic, beaver-like work whereby a shallow shaft had been sunk and blasted; culminating in the discovery of slate fragments with several markings approximately like the one which had caused the original puzzlement.

Three hours later a brief bulletin announced the resumption of the flight in the teeth of a raw and piercing gale; and when I despatched a message of protest against further hazards, Lake replied curtly that his new specimens made any hazard worth taking. I saw that his excitement had reached the point of mutiny, and that I could do nothing to check this headlong risk of the whole expedition's success; but it was appalling to think of his plunging deeper and deeper into that treacherous and sinister white immensity of tempests and unfathomed mysteries which stretched off for some 1500 miles to the half-known, half-suspected coastline of Queen Mary and Knox Lands.[60]

Then, in about an hour and a half more, came that doubly excited message from Lake's moving plane which almost reversed my sentiments and made me wish I had accompanied the party.

> *"10:05 p.m. On the wing. After snowstorm, have spied mountain-range ahead higher than any hitherto seen. May equal Himalayas[61] allowing for height of plateau. Probable Latitude 76° 15', Longitude 113° 10' E. Reaches far as can see to right and left. Suspicion of two smoking cones. All peaks black and bare of snow. Gale blowing off them impedes navigation."*

After that Pabodie, the men, and I hung breathlessly over

---

[60] *Queen Mary and Knox Lands*: Now termed Queen Mary Coast and Knox Coast, located at the southeastern end of Wilkes Land, near Masson Island and the Shackleton Ice Shelf.

[61] *Himalayas*: The tallest of the Himalayan mountain chain in Nepal, Mt. Everest, is 29,028 feet above sea level. It was first scaled in 1953 by Sir Edmund Hilary and Tenzing Norgay. In reality, the highest point on the Antarctic continent is the Vinson Massif (16,864 feet above sea level).

the receiver. Thought of this titanic mountain rampart 700 miles away inflamed our deepest sense of adventure; and we rejoiced that our expedition, if not ourselves personally, had been its discoverers. In half an hour Lake called us again.

> "*Moulton's plane forced down on plateau in foothills, but nobody hurt and perhaps can repair. Shall transfer essentials to other three for return or further moves if necessary, but no more heavy plane travel needed just now. Mountains surpass anything in imagination. Am going up scouting in Carroll's plane, with all weight out. You can't imagine anything like this. Highest peaks must go over 35,000 feet. Everest out of the running. Atwood to work out height with theodolite[62] while Carroll and I go up. Probably wrong about cones, for formations look stratified. Possibly pre-Cambrian slate with other strata mixed in. Queer skyline effects—regular sections of cubes clinging to highest peaks. Whole thing marvellous in red-gold light of low sun. Like land of mystery in a dream or gateway to forbidden world of untrodden wonder. Wish you were here to study.*"

Though it was technically sleeping-time, not one of us listeners thought for a moment of retiring. It must have been a good deal the same at McMurdo Sound, where the supply cache and the *Arkham* were also getting the messages; for Capt. Douglas gave out a call congratulating everybody on the important find, and Sherman, the cache operator, seconded his sentiments. We were sorry, of course, about the damaged aëroplane; but hoped it could be easily mended. Then, at 11 p.m., came another call from Lake.

---

[62] *theodolite*: Primarily a surveying instrument, originally designed to measure horizontal angles; but it could also be used to measure altitudes by the method of triangulation.

"*Up with Carroll over highest foothills. Don't dare try really tall peaks in present weather, but shall later. Frightful work climbing, and hard going at this altitude, but worth it. Great range fairly solid, hence can't get any glimpses beyond. Main summits exceed Himalayas, and very queer. Range looks like pre-Cambrian slate, with plain signs of many other upheaved strata. Was wrong about volcanism. Goes farther in either direction than we can see. Swept clear of snow above about 21,000 feet. Odd formations on slopes of highest mountains. Great low square blocks with exactly vertical sides, and rectangular lines of low vertical ramparts, like the old Asian castles clinging to steep mountains in Roerich's paintings. Impressive from distance. Flew close to some, and Carroll thought they were formed of smaller separate pieces, but that is probably weathering. Most edges crumbled and rounded off as if exposed to storms and climate changes for millions of years. Parts, especially upper parts, seem to be of lighter-coloured rock than any visible strata on slopes proper, hence an evidently crystalline origin. Close flying shews many cave-mouths, some unusually regular in outline, square or semicircular. You must come and investigate. Think I saw rampart squarely on top of one peak. Height seems about 30,000 to 35,000 feet. Am up 21,500 myself, in devilish gnawing cold. Wind whistles and pipes through passes and in and out of caves, but no flying danger so far.*"

From then on for another half-hour Lake kept up a running fire of comment, and expressed his intention of climbing some of the peaks on foot. I replied that I would join him as soon as he could send a plane, and that Pabodie and I would work out the best gasoline plan—just where and how to concentrate our supply in view of the expedition's altered character. Obviously, Lake's boring operations, as

well as his aëroplane activities, would need a great deal delivered for the new base which he was to establish at the foot
of the mountains; and it was possible that the eastward flight
might not be made after all this season. In connexion with
this business I called Capt. Douglas and asked him to get as
much as possible out of the ships and up the barrier with
the single dog-team we had left there. A direct route across
the unknown region between Lake and McMurdo Sound was
what we really ought to establish.

Lake called me later to say that he had decided to let the
camp stay where Moulton's plane had been forced down,
and where repairs had already progressed somewhat. The
ice-sheet was very thin, with dark ground here and there
visible, and he would sink some borings and blasts at that
very point before making any sledge trips or climbing expeditions. He spoke of the ineffable majesty of the whole scene,
and the queer state of his sensations at being in the lee of
vast silent pinnacles whose ranks shot up like a wall reaching the sky at the world's rim. Atwood's theodolite observations had placed the height of the five tallest peaks at from
30,000 to 34,000 feet. The windswept nature of the terrain
clearly disturbed Lake, for it argued the occasional existence of prodigious gales violent beyond anything we had so
far encountered.[63] His camp lay a little more than five miles
from where the higher foothills abruptly rose. I could almost
trace a note of subconscious alarm in his words—flashed
across a glacial void of 700 miles—as he urged that we all
hasten with the matter and get the strange new region

---

[63] Antarctic winds are indeed no laughing matter, and can blow as hard as 200 miles per hour.
One of the most serious types of winds is the katabatic wind: "A special wind mediates between the interior and the coast. Between inversion winds and cyclonal winds, there exists a
transitional regime of powerful, gravity-driven winds known as katabatic winds.... Ordinary
katabatic winds erupt for periods of hours, perhaps days, then give way to periods of simple
inversion winds or even calm. Extraordinary katabatic winds, however, can persist for days
or even weeks ... Katabatics are best developed over East Antarctica. Here the polar plateau is
so massive and elevated that storms from the thin Antarctic atmosphere can barely penetrate
anywhere into the interior" (Stephen J. Pyne, *The Ice: A Journey to Antarctica* [New York:
Ballantine Books, 1986], 44–46).

disposed of as soon as possible. He was about to rest now, after a continuous day's work of almost unparalleled speed, strenuousness, and results.

In the morning I had a three-cornered wireless talk with Lake and Capt. Douglas at their widely separated bases; and it was agreed that one of Lake's planes would come to my base for Pabodie, the five men, and myself, as well as for all the fuel it could carry. The rest of the fuel question, depending on our decision about an easterly trip, could wait for a few days; since Lake had enough for immediate camp heat and borings. Eventually the old southern base ought to be restocked; but if we postponed the easterly trip we would not use it till the next summer, and meanwhile Lake must send a plane to explore a direct route between his new mountains and McMurdo Sound.

Pabodie and I prepared to close our base for a short or long period, as the case might be. If we wintered in the antarctic we would probably fly straight from Lake's base to the *Arkham* without returning to this spot. Some of our conical tents had already been reinforced by blocks of hard snow, and now we decided to complete the job of making a permanent Esquimau[64] village. Owing to a very liberal tent supply, Lake had with him all that his base would need even after our arrival. I wirelessed that Pabodie and I would be ready for the northwestward move after one day's work and one night's rest.

Our labours, however, were not very steady after 4 p.m.; for about that time Lake began sending in the most extraordinary and excited messages. His working day had started unpropitiously; since an aëroplane survey of the nearly exposed rock surfaces shewed an entire absence of those Archaean and primordial strata for which he was looking, and which formed so great a part of the colossal peaks that loomed up at a tantalising distance from the camp. Most of

---

[64] *Esquimau*: Lovecraft always preferred this now archaic spelling for "Eskimo."

the rocks glimpsed were apparently Jurassic and Comanchian sandstones and Permian and Triassic schists,[65] with now and then a glossy black outcropping suggesting a hard and slaty coal. This rather discouraged Lake, whose plans all hinged on unearthing specimens more than 500 million years older. It was clear to him that in order to recover the Archaean slate vein in which he had found the odd markings, he would have to make a long sledge trip from these foothills to the steep slopes of the gigantic mountains themselves.

He had resolved, nevertheless, to do some local boring as part of the expedition's general programme; hence set up the drill and put five men to work with it while the rest finished settling the camp and repairing the damaged aëroplane. The softest visible rock—a sandstone about a quarter of a mile from the camp—had been chosen for the first sampling; and the drill made excellent progress without much supplementary blasting. It was about three hours afterward, following the first really heavy blast of the operation, that the shouting of the drill crew was heard; and that young Gedney—the acting foreman—rushed into the camp with the startling news.

They had struck a cave. Early in the boring the sandstone had given place to a vein of Comanchian limestone full of minute fossil cephalopods, corals, echini, and spirifera, and with occasional suggestions of siliceous sponges and marine

---

[65] *Jurassic*: The Jurassic period extends from 190 to 136 million years ago.

Comanchian: The term Comanchian (or Comanchean) formerly designated a geological period between the Jurassic and Cretaceous (136 to 65 million years ago); it was already archaic by 1930.

Permian: A period extending from 280 to 225 million years ago.

Triassic: A period extending from 225 to 190 million years ago.

schists: "Probably the most widely occurring of the metamorphic rocks.... Schists may be made from a wide variety of rocks by recrystallization under high temperature and pressure" (E. Laurence Palmer, *Fieldbook of Natural History*, 2nd ed. [New York: McGraw-Hill, 1975]).

vertebrate bones—the latter probably of teliosts, sharks, and ganoids.[66] This in itself was important enough, as affording the first vertebrate fossils the expedition had yet secured; but when shortly afterward the drill-head dropped through the stratum into apparent vacancy, a wholly new and doubly intense wave of excitement spread among the excavators. A good-sized blast had laid open the subterrene secret; and now, through a jagged aperture perhaps five feet across and three feet thick, there yawned before the avid searchers a section of shallow limestone hollowing worn more than fifty million years ago by the trickling ground waters of a bygone tropic world.

The hollowed layer was not more than seven or eight feet deep, but extended off indefinitely in all directions and had a fresh, slightly moving air which suggested its membership in an extensive subterranean system. Its roof and floor were abundantly equipped with large stalactites and stalagmites, some of which met in columnar form; but important above all else was the vast deposit of shells and bones which in places nearly choked the passage. Washed down from unknown jungles of Mesozoic[67] tree-ferns and fungi, and

---

[66] *cephalopods:* "Octopus, squid, cuttlefish; a class of marine carnivorous molluscs characterized by the specialization of the head-foot into a ring of arms (tentacles) generally equipped with suckers or hooks" (Lincoln and Boxshall, 1987).

echini: Sea urchins.

spirifera: "Extinct order of articulate brachiopods with spiral brachidia; known from the Ordovician to the Jurassic" (Lincoln and Boxshall, 1987).

siliceous: "Containing or consisting of silica [the dioxide of silicon, which in the form of quartz enters into the composition of many rocks, and is contained in sponges and certain plants]" (*Oxford English Dictionary*).

teliosts: "Loose assemblage of bony fishes (Osteichthyes)" (Lincoln and Boxshall, 1987) (more commonly spelled *teleost*).

ganoids: An order of largely extinct fish whose bodies are covered with bony plates or scales. The term is no longer in common use.

[67] *Mesozoic:* An era (encompassing the Triassic, Jurassic, and Cretaceous periods) extending from 225 to 65 million years ago.

forests of Tertiary cycads,[68] fan-palms, and primitive angiosperms,[69] this osseous[70] medley contained representatives of more Cretaceous, Eocene,[71] and other animal species than the greatest palaeontologist could have counted or classified in a year. Molluscs, crustacean armour, fishes, amphibians, reptiles, birds, and early mammals—great and small, known and unknown. No wonder Gedney ran back to the camp shouting, and no wonder everyone else dropped work and rushed headlong through the biting cold to where the tall derrick marked a new-found gateway to secrets of inner earth and vanished aeons.

When Lake had satisfied the first keen edge of his curiosity he scribbled a message in his notebook and had young Moulton run back to the camp to despatch it by wireless. This was my first word of the discovery, and it told of the identification of early shells, bones of ganoids and placoderms, remnants of labyrinthodonts and thecodonts, great mososaur skull fragments, dinosaur vertebrae and armour-plates, pterodactyl teeth and wing-bones, archaeopteryx debris, Miocene sharks' teeth, primitive bird-skulls, and skulls, vertebrae, and other bones of archaic mammals such as palaeotheres, xiphodons, dinoceroses, eohippi, oreodons, and titanotheres.[72] There was nothing as recent

---

[68] *Tertiary*: A period extending from 65 to 2.5 million years ago. *cycads*: "Subdivision of Gymnosperms [see note 147 below] (Pinophyta); evergreen, perennial shrubs or trees with stems that are usually unbranched but thickened by some secondary growth" (Lincoln and Boxshall, 1987).

[69] *angiosperms*: "Flowering plants; the major division of seed plants (Spermatophyta)" (Lincoln and Boxshall, 1987).

[70] *osseous*: Pertaining to bones (from the Latin *ossa*).

[71] *Cretaceous*: See note 65 above.

Eocene: An epoch within the Tertiary period extending from 54 to 38 million years ago.

[72] *placoderms*: "Class of primitive, heavily armoured, jawed fishes (Gnathostomata) known primarily from the Devonian [i.e., 395 to 345 million years ago]" (Lincoln and Boxshall, 1987).

labyrinthodonts: "Extinct subclass of primitive amphibians known from the Palaeozoic and Triassic" (Lincoln and Boxshall, 1987).

as a mastodon, elephant, true camel, deer, or bovine animal; hence Lake concluded that the last deposits had occurred during the Oligocene age,[73] and that the hollowed stratum had lain in its present dried, dead, and inaccessible state for at least thirty million years.

On the other hand, the prevalence of very early life-forms was singular in the highest degree. Though the limestone formation was, on the evidence of such typical imbedded fossils as ventriculites,[74] positively and unmistakably Comanchian and not a particle earlier; the free fragments in the hollow space included a surprising proportion from

---

thecodonts: "Primitive order of archosaurian reptiles with teeth set in sockets; probably ancestral to dinosaurs, pterosaurs, and crocodiles; known from the Upper Permian to the Upper Triassic" (Lincoln and Boxshall, 1987).

mososaur: An extinct Leipdosaurian marine reptile known from the Cretaceous; ancestor of various species of lizard. More commonly spelled *mosasaur.*

tterodactyl: A well-known extinct winged reptile of the suborder Pterodactyloidea, known from the Upper Jurassic to the Cretaceous.

archaeopteryx: "The oldest known fossil bird, having a long vertebrate tail" (*Oxford English Dictionary*). Fossil remains dating from the Late Jurassic have been found.

Miocene: An epoch within the Tertiary period extending from 26 to 7 million years ago.

palaeotheres: "Extinct family of horse-like mammals (Perissodactyla) known from the Eocene and Oligocene" (Lincoln and Boxshall, 1987).

xiphodons: "Extinct family of primitive artiodactyls [diverse order of mostly large herbivorous or omnivorous terrestrial mammals] known from the Eocene and Oligocene of Europe" (Lincoln and Boxshall, 1987).

dinocerases: "Extinct suborder of mainly North American ungulates [any large hoof-bearing, grazing animal] known from the late Palaeocene to Eocene" (Lincoln and Boxshall, 1987).

eohippi: The oldest known genus of the horse family. The term is now largely archaic and, when used, refers only to the North American specimens of the extinct genus Hyracotherium.

oreodons: An extinct mammal of the artiodactyl order known from the Oligocene to Miocene periods in North America.

titanotheres: An extinct rhinoceroslike ungulate mammal known from the Lower Eocene to the Middle Oligocene.

[73] *Oligocene age:* More properly, the Oligocene epoch, a part of the Tertiary period extending from 38 to 26 million years ago.

[74] *ventriculites:* A type of sponge known from the Upper Cretaceous.

organisms hitherto considered as peculiar to far older periods—even rudimentary fishes, molluscs, and corals as remote as the Silurian or Ordovician.[75] The inevitable inference was that in this part of the world there had been a remarkable and unique degree of continuity between the life of over 300 million years ago and that of only thirty million years ago. How far this continuity had extended beyond the Oligocene age when the cavern was closed, was of course past all speculation. In any event, the coming of the frightful ice in the Pleistocene[76] some 500,000 years ago—a mere yesterday as compared with the age of this cavity—must have put an end to any of the primal forms which had locally managed to outlive their common terms.

Lake was not content to let his first message stand, but had another bulletin written and despatched across the snow to the camp before Moulton could get back. After that Moulton stayed at the wireless in one of the planes, transmitting to me—and to the *Arkham* for relaying to the outside world—the frequent postscripts which Lake sent him by a succession of messengers. Those who followed the newspapers will remember the excitement created among men of science by that afternoon's reports—reports which have finally led, after all these years, to the organisation of that very Starkweather-Moore Expedition which I am so anxious to dissuade from its purposes. I had better give the messages literally as Lake sent them, and as our base operator McTighe translated them from his pencil shorthand.

"Fowler makes discovery of highest importance in sandstone and limestone fragments from blasts. Several distinct triangular striated prints like those in

---

[75] *Silurian*: A period extending from 430 to 395 million years ago.

Ordovician: A period extending from 500 to 430 million years ago.

[76] *Pleistocene*: An epoch within the Quaternary period extending from 2.5 million to 10,000 years ago.

Archaean slate, proving that source survived from
over 600 million years ago to Comanchian times
without more than moderate morphological changes
and decrease in average size. Comanchian prints
apparently more primitive or decadent, if anything,
than older ones. Emphasise importance of discovery
in press. Will mean to biology what Einstein[77] has
meant to mathematics and physics. Joins up with
my previous work and amplifies conclusions.
Appears to indicate, as I suspected, that earth has
seen whole cycle or cycles of organic life before
known one that begins with Archaeozoic[78] cells. Was
evolved and specialised not later than thousand million years ago, when planet was young and recently
uninhabitable for any life-forms or normal protoplasmic structure. Question arises when, where, and how
development took place."

————————

"Later. Examining certain skeletal fragments of large
land and marine saurians and primitive mammals,
find singular local wounds or injuries to bony

————————————————————

[77] *Einstein*: Lovecraft's initial reaction to the theory of relativity propounded by Albert Einstein (1879–1955) was one of shock and philosophical confusion. In May 1923 he stated: "My cynicism and scepticism are increasing, and from an entirely new cause—the Einstein theory.… All is chance, accident, and ephemeral illusion—a fly may be greater than Arcturus, and Durfee Hill may surpass Mount Everest—assuming them to be removed from the present plane and differently environed in the continuum of space-time" (*Selected Letters*, I, 231). Later Lovecraft came to terms with relativity, remarking in 1929: "Distances among the planets and nearer stars are, allowing for all possible variations, constant enough to make our picture of them as roughly true as our picture of the distances among the various cities of America.… The given area *isn't big enough* to let relativity get in its major effects—*hence we can rely on the never-failing laws of earth to give absolutely reliable results in the nearer heavens*" (*Selected Letters*, II, 264–65). Einstein is referred to fleetingly in several of Lovecraft's stories. In "The Whisperer in Darkness" (1930) one character states provocatively: "'Do you know that Einstein is wrong, and that certain objects and forces *can* move with a velocity greater than that of light?'" (*The Dunwich Horror and Others*, 259).

[78] *Archaeozoic*: "Pertaining to the era of the earliest living beings on our planet" (*Oxford English Dictionary*). Now archaic.

structure not attributable to any known predatory or carnivorous animal of any period. Of two sorts— straight, penetrant bores, and apparently hacking incisions. One or two cases of cleanly severed bone. Not many specimens affected. Am sending to camp for electric torches. Will extend search area underground by hacking away stalactites."

"Still later. Have found peculiar soapstone fragment about six inches across and an inch and a half thick, wholly unlike any visible local formation. Greenish, but no evidences to place its period. Has curious smoothness and regularity. Shaped like five-pointed star with tips broken off, and signs of other cleavage at inward angles and in centre of surface. Small, smooth depression in centre of unbroken surface. Arouses much curiosity as to source and weathering. Probably some freak of water action. Carroll, with magnifier, thinks he can make out additional markings of geologic significance. Groups of tiny dots in regular patterns. Dogs growing uneasy as we work, and seem to hate this soapstone. Must see if it has any peculiar odour. Will report again when Mills gets back with light and we start on underground area."

"10:15 p.m. Important discovery. Orrendorf and Watkins, working underground at 9:45 with light, found monstrous barrel-shaped fossil of wholly unknown nature; probably vegetable unless overgrown specimen of unknown marine radiata.[79] Tissue

---

[79] *radiata*: Latinized plural noun form of the adjective "radiate," referring to creatures (e.g., starfish) whose bodies are characterized by radial symmetry.

evidently preserved by mineral salts. Tough as leather, but astonishing flexibility retained in places. Marks of broken-off parts at ends and around sides. Six feet end to end, 3.5 feet central diameter, tapering to 1 foot at each end. Like a barrel with five bulging ridges in place of staves. Lateral breakages, as of thinnish stalks, are at equator in middle of these ridges. In furrows between ridges are curious growths. Combs or wings that fold up and spread out like fans. All greatly damaged but one, which gives almost seven-foot wing spread. Arrangement reminds one of certain monsters of primal myth, especially fabled Elder Things[80] in Necronomicon. These wings seem to be membraneous, stretched on framework of glandular tubing. Apparent minute orifices in frame tubing at wing tips. Ends of body shrivelled, giving no clue to interior or to what has been broken off there. Must dissect when we get back to camp. Can't decide whether vegetable or animal. Many features obviously of almost incredible primitiveness. Have set all hands cutting stalactites and looking for further specimens. Additional scarred bones found, but these must wait. Having trouble with dogs. They can't endure the new specimen, and would probably tear it to pieces if we didn't keep it at a distance from them."

"11:30 p.m. Attention, Dyer, Pabodie, Douglas. Matter of highest—I might say transcendent—importance. Arkham must relay to Kingsport Head Station at once. Strange barrel growth is the Archaean thing that left prints in rocks. Mills, Boudreau, and

---

[80] There is a fleeting mention of "Elder Things" in "The Dunwich Horror" (p. 158), but it is not at all clear that they are the same or similar entities to those described here.

Fowler discover cluster of thirteen more at under-
ground point forty feet from aperture. Mixed with
curiously rounded and configured soapstone frag-
ments smaller than one previously found—star-
shaped but no marks of breakage except at some of
the points. Of organic specimens, eight apparently
perfect, with all appendages. Have brought all to sur-
face, leading off dogs to distance. They cannot stand
the things. Give close attention to description and
repeat back for accuracy. Papers must get this right.

"*Objects are eight feet long all over. Six-foot five-*
ridged barrel torso 3.5 feet central diameter, 1 foot
end diameters. Dark grey, flexible, and infinitely
tough. Seven-foot membraneous wings of same
colour, found folded, spread out of furrows between
ridges. Wing framework tubular or glandular, of
lighter grey, with orifices at wing tips. Spread wings
have serrated edge. Around equator, one at central
apex of each of the five vertical, stave-like ridges, are
five systems of light grey flexible arms or tentacles
found tightly folded to torso but expansible to maxi-
mum length of over 3 feet. Like arms of primitive
crinoid. Single stalks 3 inches diameter branch after
6 inches into five sub-stalks, each of which branches
after 8 inches into five small, tapering tentacles or
tendrils, giving each stalk a total of 25 tentacles.

"*At top of torso blunt bulbous neck of lighter grey*
with gill-like suggestions holds yellowish five-
pointed starfish-shaped apparent head covered with
three-inch wiry cilia of various prismatic colours.
Head thick and puffy, about 2 feet point to point,
with three-inch flexible yellowish tubes projecting
from each point. Slit in exact centre of top probably
breathing aperture. At end of each tube is spherical
expansion where yellowish membrane rolls back on
handling to reveal glassy, red-irised globe, evidently
an eye. Five slightly longer reddish tubes start from

inner angles of starfish-shaped head and end in sac-like swellings of same colour which upon pressure open to bell-shaped orifices 2 inches maximum diameter and lined with sharp white tooth-like projections. Probable mouths. All these tubes, cilia, and points of starfish-head found folded tightly down; tubes and points clinging to bulbous neck and torso. Flexibility surprising despite vast toughness.

"At bottom of torso rough but dissimilarly functioning counterparts of head arrangements exist. Bulbous light-grey pseudo-neck, without gill suggestions, holds greenish five-pointed starfish-arrangement. Tough, muscular arms 4 feet long and tapering from 7 inches diameter at base to about 2.5 at point. To each point is attached small end of a greenish five-veined membraneous triangle 8 inches long and 6 wide at farther end. This is the paddle, fin, or pseudo-foot which has made prints in rocks from a thousand million to fifty or sixty million years old. From inner angles of starfish-arrangement project two-foot reddish tubes tapering from 3 inches diameter at base to 1 at tip. Orifices at tips. All these parts infinitely tough and leathery, but extremely flexible. Four-foot arms with paddles undoubtedly used for locomotion of some sort, marine or otherwise. When moved, display suggestions of exaggerated muscularity. As found, all these projections tightly folded over pseudo-neck and end of torso, corresponding to projections at other end.

"Cannot yet assign positively to animal or vegetable kingdom, but odds now favour animal. Probably represents incredibly advanced evolution of radiata without loss of certain primitive features. Echinoderm[81] resemblances unmistakable despite local

---

[81] *echinoderm*: A phylum of marine animals including sea lilies, starfish, sea urchins, and sea cucumbers, all of which bear five-fold rotational symmetry.

contradictory evidences. Wing structure puzzles in view of probable marine habitat, but may have use in water navigation. Symmetry is curiously vegetable-like, suggesting vegetable's essentially up-and-down structure rather than animal's fore-and-aft structure. Fabulously early date of evolution, preceding even simplest Archaean protozoa hitherto known, baffles all conjecture as to origin.

"Complete specimens have such uncanny resemblance to certain creatures of primal myth that suggestion of ancient existence outside antarctic becomes inevitable. Dyer and Pabodie have read Necronomicon *and seen Clark Ashton Smith's[82] nightmare paintings based on text, and will understand when I speak of Elder Things supposed to have created all earth-life as jest or mistake. Students have always thought conception formed from morbid imaginative treatment of very ancient tropical radiata. Also like prehistoric folklore things Wilmarth[83] has spoken of—Cthulhu cult appendages,[84] etc.*

---

[82] Clark Ashton Smith (1893–1961) remained Lovecraft's close colleague and correspondent for fifteen years; they had first got in touch in 1922. Smith was a poet, fiction writer, painter, and sculptor whose work in all these media Lovecraft much admired. In sending some of Smith's paintings to Frank Belknap Long, Lovecraft remarked: "GAWD! THOSE COLOURS!! Opium madness unleashed … Oh, boy! 'Twilight'—'Sunset in Lemuria'—'The Witch's Wood'—and the Dunsany design! Sancta Pegana, but I don't know that it's right to loose such diabolic provocation upon a young person already addicted to rhapsodick extravagances of diction!" (*Selected Letters*, II, 45).

[83] *Wilmarth*: Albert N. Wilmarth, instructor of literature at Miskatonic University, is the narrator of "The Whisperer in Darkness."

[84] *Cthulhu cult appendages*: It is not entirely clear what is meant by this phrase. Cthulhu, the extraterrestrial entity trapped in his sunken city of R'lyeh in the Pacific, was created in "The Call of Cthulhu" (1926); he has a band of human worshipers scattered across the earth who seek to bring about his resurrection. Here the term seems to refer to the entities (mentioned in the story as the Great Old Ones) who accompanied Cthulhu on his cosmic voyage from the depths of space to the earth, and who are presumably similar in shape to the octopoid Cthulhu. They are not, however, explicitly described in the tale, and at one point it is said: "The carven idol was great Cthulhu, but none might say whether or not the others were precisely like him"; later it is mentioned that they are not "composed altogether of flesh and blood" (*The Dunwich Horror and Others*, 139–40).

"Vast field of study opened. Deposits probably of late Cretaceous or early Eocene period, judging from associated specimens. Massive stalagmites deposited above them. Hard work hewing out, but toughness prevented damage. State of preservation miraculous, evidently owing to limestone action. No more found so far, but will resume search later. Job now to get fourteen huge specimens to camp without dogs, which bark furiously and can't be trusted near them. With nine men—three left to guard the dogs—we ought to manage the three sledges fairly well, though wind is bad. Must establish plane communication with McMurdo Sound and begin shipping material. But I've got to dissect one of these things before we take any rest. Wish I had a real laboratory here. Dyer better kick himself for having tried to stop my westward trip. First the world's greatest mountains, and then this. If this last isn't the high spot of the expedition, I don't know what is. We're made scientifically. Congrats, Pabodie, on the drill that opened up the cave. Now will Arkham please repeat description?"

The sensations of Pabodie and myself at receipt of this report were almost beyond description, nor were our companions much behind us in enthusiasm. McTighe, who had hastily translated a few high spots as they came from the droning receiving set, wrote out the entire message from his shorthand version as soon as Lake's operator signed off. All appreciated the epoch-making significance of the discovery, and I sent Lake congratulations as soon as the *Arkham*'s operator had repeated back the descriptive parts as requested; and my example was followed by Sherman from his station at the McMurdo Sound supply cache, as well as by Capt. Douglas of the *Arkham*. Later, as head of the expedition, I added some remarks to be relayed through the *Arkham* to the outside world. Of course, rest was an absurd thought amidst this excitement; and my only wish was to get to Lake's camp as quickly as I could. It disappointed me when he sent word that a rising mountain gale made early aërial travel impossible.

But within an hour and a half interest again rose to banish disappointment. Lake was sending more messages, and told of the completely successful transportation of the fourteen great specimens to the camp. It had been a hard pull, for the things were surprisingly heavy; but nine men had accomplished it very neatly. Now some of the party were hurriedly building a snow corral at a safe distance from the camp, to which the dogs could be brought for convenience in feeding. The specimens were laid out on the hard snow near the camp, save for one on which Lake was making crude attempts at dissection.

This dissection seemed to be a greater task than had been expected; for despite the heat of a gasoline stove in the newly raised laboratory tent, the deceptively flexible tissues of the chosen specimen—a powerful and intact one—lost nothing of their more than leathery toughness. Lake was puzzled as to how he might make the requisite incisions without violence destructive enough to upset all the structural niceties he was looking for. He had, it is true, seven more perfect specimens; but these were too few to use up recklessly unless the cave might later yield an unlimited supply. Accordingly he removed the specimen and dragged in one which, though having remnants of the starfish-arrangements at both ends, was badly crushed and partly disrupted along one of the great torso furrows.

Results, quickly reported over the wireless, were baffling and provocative indeed. Nothing like delicacy or accuracy was possible with instruments hardly able to cut the anomalous tissue, but the little that was achieved left us all awed and bewildered. Existing biology would have to be wholly revised, for this thing was no product of any cell-growth science knows about. There had been scarcely any mineral replacement, and despite an age of perhaps forty million years the internal organs were wholly intact. The leathery, undeteriorative, and almost indestructible quality was an inherent attribute of the thing's form of organisation; and pertained to some palaeogean cycle of invertebrate evolution utterly beyond our powers of speculation. At first all that Lake found was dry, but as the heated tent produced its thawing effect, organic moisture of pungent and offensive odour was encountered toward the thing's uninjured side. It was not blood, but a thick, dark-green fluid apparently answering the same purpose. By the time Lake reached this stage all 37 dogs had been brought to the still uncompleted corral near the camp; and even at that distance set up a savage barking and show of restlessness at the acrid, diffusive smell.

Far from helping to place the strange entity, this provisional dissection merely deepened its mystery. All guesses about its external members had been correct, and on the evidence of these one could hardly hesitate to call the thing animal; but internal inspection brought up so many vegetable evidences that Lake was left hopelessly at sea. It had digestion and circulation, and eliminated waste matter through the reddish tubes of its starfish-shaped base. Cursorily, one would say that its respiratory apparatus handled oxygen rather than carbon dioxide; and there were odd evidences of air-storage chambers and methods of shifting respiration from the external orifice to at least two other fully developed breathing-systems—gills and pores. Clearly, it was amphibian and probably adapted to long airless hibernation-periods as well. Vocal organs seemed present in connexion with the main respiratory system, but they presented anomalies beyond immediate solution. Articulate speech, in the sense of syllable-utterance, seemed barely conceivable; but musical piping notes covering a wide range were highly probable. The muscular system was almost preternaturally developed.

The nervous system was so complex and highly developed as to leave Lake aghast. Though excessively primitive and archaic in some respects, the thing had a set of ganglial centres and connectives arguing the very extremes of specialised development. Its five-lobed brain was surprisingly advanced; and there were signs of a sensory equipment, served in part through the wiry cilia of the head, involving factors alien to any other terrestrial organism. Probably it had more than five senses, so that its habits could not be predicted from any existing analogy. It must, Lake thought, have been a creature of keen sensitiveness and delicately differentiated functions in its primal world; much like the ants and bees of today. It reproduced like the vegetable cryptogams,[85] especially the pteridophytes;[86] having spore-cases at the tips of the wings and evidently developing from a thallus or prothallus.[87]

But to give it a name at this stage was mere folly. It looked like a radiate, but was clearly something more. It was partly vegetable, but had three-fourths of the essentials of animal structure. That it was marine in origin, its symmetrical contour and certain other attributes clearly indicated; yet one could not be exact as to the limit of its later adaptations. The wings, after all, held a persistent suggestion of the aërial. How it could have undergone its tremendously complex evolution on a new-born earth in time to leave prints in Archaean rocks was so far beyond conception as

---

[85] *cryptogams*: "A lower plant, lacking conspicuous reproductive structures such as flowers or cones" (Lincoln and Boxshall, 1987).

[86] *pteridophytes*: "Ferns; classified under the term Filicophyta [division of vascular plants which reproduce by spores produced in sporangia borne on the leaves, usually in clusters]" (Lincoln and Boxshall, 1987).

[87] *thallus or prothallus*: A thallus is a primitive plant body consisting of relatively undifferentiated cells. Prothallus is a variant of *prothallium*. The *Oxford English Dictionary* quotes Miles Joseph Berkeley's *Introduction to Cryptogamic Botany* (1857): "The spores germinate and produce a more or less foliaceous [i.e., leaflike] mass, which after impregnation bears fruit containing bodies like the original spores, or a plant capable of bearing such spores, in which case it is called a prothallus."

to make Lake whimsically recall the primal myths about Great Old Ones[88] who filtered down from the stars and concocted earth-life as a joke or mistake; and the wild tales of cosmic hill things from Outside told by a folklorist colleague in Miskatonic's English department.[89]

Naturally, he considered the possibility of the pre-Cambrian prints' having been made by a less evolved ancestor of the present specimens; but quickly rejected this too facile theory upon considering the advanced structural qualities of the older fossils. If anything, the later contours shewed decadence rather than higher evolution. The size of the pseudo-feet had decreased, and the whole morphology seemed coarsened and simplified. Moreover, the nerves and organs just examined held singular suggestions of retrogression from forms still more complex. Atrophied and vestigial parts were surprisingly prevalent. Altogether, little could be said to have been solved; and Lake fell back on mythology for a provisional name—jocosely dubbing his finds "The Elder Ones".[90]

At about 2:30 a.m., having decided to postpone further work and get a little rest, he covered the dissected organism with a tarpaulin, emerged from the laboratory tent, and studied the intact specimens with renewed interest. The ceaseless antarctic sun had begun to limber up their

---

[88] *Great Old Ones*: The phrase is repeatedly used by Lovecraft in "The Call of Cthulhu" to denote the creatures that accompanied Cthulhu in his flight through interstellar space to the Earth; although in that tale there is no suggestion that they "concocted earth-life as a joke or mistake." The term "Great Ones" is used to denote the "mild gods of earth" in *The Dream-Quest of Unknown Kadath* (1926–27), while "Old Ones" is used in several stories but apparently in reference to quite different entities.

[89] Albert N. Wilmarth (see note 83 above). "The Whisperer in Darkness" deals with creatures labelled the fungi from Yuggoth who have come from the planet Yuggoth (= Pluto) to the Earth and besiege a lonely farmer in the Vermont wilderness.

[90] *"The Elder Ones"*: This term had also been used in several previous stories by Lovecraft, but again it appears to denote quite different entities. The term first occurs in "The Strange High House in the Mist" (1926) and then in *The Dream-Quest of Unknown Kadath*, evidently referring to the gods of the dream-world, or the "Great Ones" (see note 88 above).

tissues a trifle,[91] so that the head-points and tubes of two or three shewed signs of unfolding; but Lake did not believe there was any danger of immediate decomposition in the almost sub-zero air. He did, however, move all the undissected specimens closer together and throw a spare tent over them in order to keep off the direct solar rays. That would also help to keep their possible scent away from the dogs, whose hostile unrest was really becoming a problem even at their substantial distance and behind the higher and higher snow walls which an increased quota of the men were hastening to raise around their quarters. He had to weight down the corners of the tent-cloth with heavy blocks of snow to hold it in place amidst the rising gale, for the titan mountains seemed about to deliver some gravely severe blasts. Early apprehensions about sudden antarctic winds were revived, and under Atwood's super-vision precautions were taken to bank the tents, new dog-corral, and crude aëroplane shelters with snow on the mountainward side. These latter shelters, begun with hard snow blocks during odd moments, were by no means as high as they should have been; and Lake finally detached all hands from other tasks to work on them.

It was after four when Lake at last prepared to sign off and advised us all to share the rest period his outfit would take when the shelter walls were a little higher. He held some friendly chat with Pabodie over the ether,[92] and re-peated his praise of the really marvellous drills that had helped him make his discovery. Atwood also sent greetings and praises. I gave Lake a warm word of congratulation, owning up that he was right about the western trip; and

---

[91] This seems implausible given the generally low temperatures prevailing on the Antarctic continent, but solar radiation can indeed warm objects no matter how cold the air is.

[92] *ether.* The ether was believed to be a superfine material substance that made possible the transmission of particles of light. Here the term is perhaps being used more idiomatically for the transmission of radio signals through the atmosphere. The ether is used in a more tech-nical sense later in the novel; see note 162 below.

we all agreed to get in touch by wireless at ten in the morning. If the gale was then over, Lake would send a plane for the party at my base. Just before retiring I despatched a final message to the *Arkham* with instructions about toning down the day's news for the outside world, since the full details seemed radical enough to rouse a wave of incredulity until further substantiated.

III.

None of us, I imagine, slept very heavily or continuously that morning; for both the excitement of Lake's discovery and the mounting fury of the wind were against such a thing. So savage was the blast, even where we were, that we could not help wondering how much worse it was at Lake's camp, directly under the vast unknown peaks that bred and delivered it. McTighe was awake at ten o'clock and tried to get Lake on the wireless, as agreed, but some electrical condition in the disturbed air to the westward seemed to prevent communication. We did, however, get the *Arkham*, and Douglas told me that he had likewise been vainly trying to reach Lake. He had not known about the wind, for very little was blowing at McMurdo Sound despite its persistent rage where we were.

Throughout the day we all listened anxiously and tried to get Lake at intervals, but invariably without results. About noon a positive frenzy of wind stampeded out of the west, causing us to fear for the safety of our camp; but it eventually died down, with only a moderate relapse at 2 p.m. After three o'clock it was very quiet, and we redoubled our efforts to get Lake. Reflecting that he had four planes, each provided with an excellent short-wave outfit, we could not imagine any ordinary accident capable of crippling all his wireless equipment at once. Nevertheless the stony silence continued; and when we thought of the delirious force the wind must cave had in his locality we could not help making the most direful conjectures.

By six o'clock our fears had become intense and definite, and after a wireless consultation with Douglas and Thorfinnssen I resolved to take steps toward investigation. The fifth aëroplane, which we had left at the McMurdo Sound supply cache with Sherman and two sailors, was in good shape and ready for instant use; and it seemed that the very emergency for which it had been saved was now upon us. I got Sherman by wireless and ordered him to join me with the plane and the two sailors at the southern base as quickly as possible; the air conditions being apparently highly favourable. We then talked over the personnel of the coming investigation party; and decided that we would include all hands, together with the sledge and dogs which I had kept with me. Even so great a load would not be too much for one of the huge planes built to our especial orders for heavy machinery transportation. At intervals I still tried to reach Lake with the wireless, but all to no purpose.

Sherman, with the sailors Gunnarsson and Larsen,[93] took off at 7:30; and reported a quiet flight from several points on the wing. They arrived at our base at midnight, and all hands at once discussed the next move. It was risky business sailing over the antarctic in a single aëroplane without any line of bases, but no one drew back from what seemed like the plainest necessity. We turned in at two o'clock for a brief rest after some preliminary loading of the plane, but were up again in four hours to finish the loading and packing.

At 7:15 a.m., January 25th, we started flying northwestward under McTighe's pilotage with ten men, seven dogs, a sledge, a fuel and food supply, and other items including the plane's wireless outfit. The atmosphere was clear, fairly

---

[93] Recall the name of the whaling ship accompanying Byrd's expedition, the *C. A. Larsen* (note 20 above).

quiet, and relatively mild in temperature; and we anticipated very little trouble in reaching the latitude and longitude designated by Lake as the site of his camp. Our apprehensions were over what we might find, or fail to find, at
the end of our journey; for silence continued to answer all
calls despatched to the camp.

Every incident of that four-and-a-half-hour flight is
burned into my recollection because of its crucial position
in my life. It marked my loss, at the age of fifty-four, of all
that peace and balance which the normal mind possesses
through its accustomed conception of external Nature and
Nature's laws. Thenceforward the ten of us—but the student Danforth and myself above all others—were to face a
hideously amplified[94] world of lurking horrors which nothing can erase from our emotions, and which we would
refrain from sharing with mankind in general if we could.
The newspapers have printed the bulletins we sent from
the moving plane; telling of our non-stop course, our two
battles with treacherous upper-air gales, our glimpse of the
broken surface where Lake had sunk his mid-journey shaft
three days before, and our sight of a group of those strange
fluffy snow-cylinders noted by Amundsen and Byrd as loll-
ing in the wind across the endless leagues of frozen plateau. There came a point, though, when our sensations
could not be conveyed in any words the press would understand; and a later point when we had to adopt an actual
rule of strict censorship.[95]

---

[94] The significance of the word "amplified" here may not be immediately obvious, but it
appears to relate to Lovecraft's evolving theory of weird fiction as expressed in a contemporaneous letter (quoted in part in the Introduction): "The time has come when the normal revolt against time, space, & matter must assume a form not overtly incompatible with what is
known of reality—when it must be gratified by images forming *supplements* rather than *contradictions* of the visible & mensurable universe. And what, if not a form of *non-supernatural
cosmic art*, is to pacify this sense of revolt—as well as gratify the cognate sense of curiosity?"
(*Selected Letters*, III, 295–96). The "amplified world" encountered by the protagonists is an
instance of a "supplement rather than a contradiction" of the known universe.

The sailor Larsen was first to spy the jagged line of witch-like cones and pinnacles ahead, and his shouts sent every-one to the windows of the great cabined plane. Despite our speed, they were very slow in gaining prominence; hence we knew that they must be infinitely far off, and visible only because of their abnormal height. Little by little, how-ever, they rose grimly into the western sky; allowing us to distinguish various bare, bleak, blackish summits, and to catch the curious sense of phantasy which they inspired as seen in the reddish antarctic light against the provocative background of iridescent ice-dust clouds. In the whole spec-tacle there was a persistent, pervasive hint of stupendous secrecy and potential revelation; as if these stark, nightmare spires marked the pylons of a frightful gateway into forbid-den spheres of dream, and complex gulfs of remote time, space, and ultra-dimensionality. I could not help feeling that they were evil things—mountains of madness whose far-ther slopes looked out over some accursed ultimate abyss. That seething, half-luminous cloud-background held inef-fable suggestions of a vague, ethereal *beyondness* far more than terrestrially spatial; and gave appalling reminders of the utter remoteness, separateness, desolation, and aeon-long death of this untrodden and unfathomed astral world.

It was young Danforth who drew our notice to the curi-ous regularities of the higher mountain skyline—regulari-ties like clinging fragments of perfect cubes, which Lake had mentioned in his messages, and which indeed justi-fied his comparison with the dream-like suggestions of pri-mordial temple-ruins on cloudy Asian mountain-tops so

---

[95] A similar type of censorship (externally enforced) is found in "The Shadow over Innsmouth" (1931). The narrator reports that "Complaints from many liberal organisations" concerning the events at Innsmouth "were met with long confidential discussions, and rep-resentatives were taken on trips to certain camps and prisons. As a result, these societies became surprisingly passive and reticent. Newspaper men were harder to manage, but seemed largely to coöperate with the government in the end" (*The Dunwich Horror and Others*, 304).

subtly and strangely painted by Roerich. There was indeed something hauntingly Roerich-like about this whole unearthly continent of mountainous mystery. I had felt it in October when we first caught sight of Victoria Land, and I felt it afresh now. I felt, too, another wave of uneasy consciousness of Archaean mythical resemblances; of how disturbingly this lethal realm corresponded to the evilly famed plateau of Leng in the primal writings. Mythologists have placed Leng[96] in Central Asia; but the racial memory of man—or of his predecessors—is long, and it may well be that certain tales have come down from lands and mountains and temples of horror earlier than Asia and earlier than any human world we know. A few daring mystics have hinted at a pre-Pleistocene origin for the fragmentary Pnakotic Manuscripts,[97] and have suggested that the devotees of Tsathoggua were as alien to mankind as Tsathoggua[98] itself. Leng, wherever in space or time it might brood, was not a region I would care to be in or near; nor

---

[96] *Leng*: First cited in Lovecraft's "Celephaïs" (1920) but apparently in a dream-world there; in "The Hound" (1922) it is situated in "Central Asia" (*Dagon and Other Macabre Tales*, 174). In *The Dream-Quest of Unknown Kadath* (1926–27) Leng is a sinister region next to Kadath in the Cold Waste: " ... finally they came to a windswept table-land which seemed the very roof of a blasted and tenantless world" (*At the Mountains of Madness and Other Novels*, 370). In that novel, of course, Leng is in a dream-world. In his transference of Leng from the realm of dream or legend to that of reality, Lovecraft seems to be performing the same sort of "demythologizing" that he will eventually do for the Old Ones themselves (see Introduction, p. 18).

[97] *Pnakotic Manuscripts*: Chronologically, the first of Lovecraft's mythical books, preceding even the *Necronomicon*. They are first cited in "Polaris" (1918), a tale about the ancient arctic world of Lomar (see note 133 below). Extensive use is made of them in *The Dream-Quest of Unknown Kadath* (1926–27), where it is remarked that "parts of the Pnakotic Manuscripts [are] too ancient to be read" (*At the Mountains of Madness and Other Novels*, 312). The comment about their "pre-Pleistocene origin" refers to the possibility that they were composed before the earliest primitive human beings had evolved from hominids, about two million years ago.

[98] *Tsathoggua*: An invention of Lovecraft's friend Clark Ashton Smith (see note 82 above); it was first cited in the story "The Tale of Satampra Zeiros" (written in 1929, but not published until it appeared in *Weird Tales*, November 1931). Lovecraft made his first reference to the entity in "The Mound," a tale ghostwritten for Zealia Bishop in 1929–30 but not published until 1940: "It [a temple] had been built in imitation of certain temples depicted in the vaults of Zin, to house a very terrible black toad-idol found in the red-litten world [of Yoth] and

did I relish the proximity of a world that had ever bred such ambiguous and Archaean monstrosities as those Lake had just mentioned. At the moment I felt sorry that I had ever read the abhorred *Necronomicon,* or talked so much with that unpleasantly erudite folklorist Wilmarth at the university.[99]

This mood undoubtedly served to aggravate my reaction to the bizarre mirage which burst upon us from the increasingly opalescent zenith as we drew near the mountains and began to make out the cumulative undulations of the foothills. I had seen dozens of polar mirages during the preceding weeks, some of them quite as uncanny and fantastically vivid as the present sample; but this one had a wholly novel and obscure quality of menacing symbolism, and I shuddered as the seething labyrinth of fabulous walls and towers and minarets loomed out of the troubled ice-vapours above our heads.

The effect was that of a Cyclopean[100] city of no architecture known to man or to human imagination, with vast aggregations of night-black masonry embodying monstrous perversions of geometrical laws and attaining the most grotesque extremes of sinister bizarrerie. There were truncated cones, sometimes terraced or fluted, surmounted by tall cylindrical shafts here and there bulbously enlarged and often capped with tiers of thinnish scalloped discs; and strange, beetling, table-like constructions suggesting piles of multitudinous rectangular slabs or circular plates or five-pointed stars with each one overlapping the one beneath.

called Tsathoggua in the Yothic manuscripts" (Lovecraft, *The Horror in the Museum and Other Revisions* [Sauk City, WI: Arkham House, 1989], 140). Tsathoggua is cited again in "The Whisperer in Darkness" (1930), where Lovecraft clearly tips his hat to Smith: "'It's from N'kai that frightful Tsathoggua came—you know, the amorphous, toad-like god-creature mentioned in the Pnakotic Manuscripts and the *Necronomicon* and the Commoriom myth-cycle preserved by the Atlantean high-priest Klarkash-Ton'" (*The Dunwich Horror and Others,* 254).

[99] For the *Necronomicon,* see note 60 to "The Dunwich Horror"; for Wilmarth, see note 83 above.

[100] *Cyclopean:* See note 97 to "The Dunwich Horror."

There were composite cones and pyramids either alone or surmounting cylinders or cubes or flatter truncated cones and pyramids, and occasional needle-like spires in curious clusters of five. All of these febrile structures seemed knit together by tubular bridges crossing from one to the other at various dizzy heights, and the implied scale of the whole was terrifying and oppressive in its sheer giganticism. The general type of mirage was not unlike some of the wilder forms observed and drawn by the Arctic whaler Scoresby in 1820;[101] but at this time and place, with those dark, unknown mountain peaks soaring stupendously ahead, that anomalous elder-world discovery in our minds, and the pall of probable disaster enveloping the greater part of our expedition, we all seemed to find in it a taint of latent malignity and infinitely evil portent.

I was glad when the mirage began to break up, though in the process the various nightmare turrets and cones assumed distorted temporary forms of even vaster hideousness. As the whole illusion dissolved to churning opalescence we began to look earthward again, and saw that our journey's end was not far off. The unknown mountains ahead rose dizzyingly up like a fearsome rampart of giants, their curious regularities shewing with startling clearness even without a field-glass. We were over the lowest foothills now, and could see amidst the snow, ice, and bare patches of their main plateau a couple of darkish spots which we took to be Lake's camp and boring. The higher foothills shot up between five and six miles away, forming a range almost distinct from the terrifying line of more than Himalayan peaks beyond them. At length Ropes—the student who had relieved McTighe at the controls—began to head downward toward the left-hand dark spot whose size marked it

---

[101] William Scoresby (1789–1857) undertook yearly voyages to Greenland between 1803 and 1822 and wrote many books of his travels, illustrated with his own drawings. Among them are *On the Greenland Polar Ice* (1815?), *An Account of the Arctic Regions* (1820), and *Journal of a Voyage to the Northern Whale-Fishery* (1823).

as the camp. As he did so, McTighe sent out the last uncensored wireless message the world was to receive from our expedition.

Everyone, of course, has read the brief and unsatisfying bulletins of the rest of our antarctic sojourn. Some hours after our landing we sent a guarded report of the tragedy we found, and reluctantly announced the wiping out of the whole Lake party by the frightful wind of the preceding day, or of the night before that. Eleven known dead, young Gedney missing. People pardoned our hazy lack of details through realisation of the shock the sad event must have caused us, and believed us when we explained that the mangling action of the wind had rendered all eleven bodies unsuitable for transportation outside. Indeed, I flatter myself that even in the midst of our distress, utter bewilderment, and soul-clutching horror, we scarcely went beyond the truth in any specific instance. The tremendous significance lies in what we dared not tell—what I would not tell now but for the need of warning others off from nameless terrors.

It is a fact that the wind had wrought dreadful havoc. Whether all could have lived through it, even without the other thing, is gravely open to doubt. The storm, with its fury of madly driven ice-particles, must have been beyond anything our expedition had encountered before. One aëroplane shelter—all, it seems, had been left in a far too flimsy and inadequate state—was nearly pulverised; and the derrick at the distant boring was entirely shaken to pieces. The exposed metal of the grounded planes and drilling machinery was bruised into a high polish, and two of the small tents were flattened despite their snow banking. Wooden surfaces left out in the blast were pitted and denuded of paint, and all signs of tracks in the snow were completely obliterated. It is also true that we found none of the Archaean biological objects in a condition to take outside as a whole. We did gather some minerals from a vast tumbled pile, including several of the greenish soapstone fragments whose odd five-pointed rounding and faint patterns of grouped dots caused so many doubtful comparisons; and some fossil bones, among which were the most typical of the curiously injured specimens.

None of the dogs survived, their hurriedly built snow enclosure near the camp being almost wholly destroyed. The wind may have done that, though the greater break-age on the side next the camp, which was not the wind-ward one, suggests an outward leap or break of the frantic beasts themselves. All three sledges were gone, and we have tried to explain that the wind may have blown them off into the unknown. The drill and ice-melting machinery at the boring were too badly damaged to warrant salvage, so we used them to choke up that subtly disturbing gateway to the past which Lake had blasted. We likewise left at the camp the two most shaken-up of the planes; since our surviving party had only four real pilots—Sherman, Danforth, McTighe, and Ropes—in all, with Danforth in a poor nervous shape to navigate. We brought back all the books, scientific equipment, and other incidentals we could find, though much was rather unaccountably blown away. Spare tents and furs were either missing or badly out of condition.

It was approximately 4 p.m., after wide plane cruising had forced us to give Gedney up for lost, that we sent our guarded message to the *Arkham* for relaying; and I think we did well to keep it as calm and non-committal as we suc-ceeded in doing. The most we said about agitation concerned our dogs, whose frantic uneasiness near the biological speci-mens was to be expected from poor Lake's accounts. We did not mention, I think, their display of the same uneasiness when sniffing around the queer greenish soapstones and certain other objects in the disordered region; objects including scientific instruments, aëroplanes, and machin-ery both at the camp and at the boring, whose parts had been loosened, moved, or otherwise tampered with by winds that must have harboured singular curiosity and investi-gativeness.

About the fourteen biological specimens we were pardonably indefinite. We said that the only ones we discovered were damaged, but that enough was left of them to prove Lake's description wholly and impressively accurate. It was hard work keeping our personal emotions out of this matter—and we did not mention numbers or say exactly how we had found those which we did find. We had by that time agreed not to transmit anything suggesting madness on the part of Lake's men, and it surely looked like madness to find six imperfect monstrosities carefully buried upright in nine-foot snow graves under five-pointed mounds punched over with groups of dots in patterns exactly like those on the queer greenish soapstones dug up from Mesozoic or Tertiary times. The eight perfect specimens mentioned by Lake seemed to have been completely blown away.

We were careful, too, about the public's general peace of mind; hence Danforth and I said little about that frightful trip over the mountains the next day. It was the fact that only a radically lightened plane could possibly cross a range of such height which mercifully limited that scouting tour to the two of us. On our return at 1 a.m. Danforth was close to hysterics, but kept an admirably stiff upper lip. It took no persuasion to make him promise not to shew our sketches and the other things we brought away in our pockets, not to say anything more to the others than what we had agreed to relay outside, and to hide our camera films for private development later on; so that part of my present story will be as new to Pabodie, McTighe, Ropes, Sherman, and the rest as it will be to the world in general. Indeed—Danforth is closer mouthed than I; for he saw—or thinks he saw—one thing he will not tell even me.

As all know, our report included a tale of a hard ascent; a confirmation of Lake's opinion that the great peaks are of Archaean slate and other very primal crumpled strata unchanged since at least middle Comanchian times; a conventional comment on the regularity of the clinging cube and rampart formations; a decision that the cave-mouths indicate dissolved calcareous[102] veins; a conjecture that certain slopes and passes would permit of the scaling and crossing of the entire range by seasoned mountaineers; and a remark that the mysterious other side holds a lofty and immense super-plateau as ancient and unchanging as the mountains themselves—20,000 feet in elevation, with grotesque rock formations protruding through a thin glacial layer and with low gradual foothills between the general plateau surface and the sheer precipices of the highest peaks.

This body of data is in every respect true so far as it goes, and it completely satisfied the men at the camp. We laid our absence of sixteen hours—a longer time than our announced flying, landing, reconnoitring, and rock-collecting programme called for—to a long mythical spell of adverse wind conditions; and told truly of our landing on the farther foothills. Fortunately our tale sounded realistic and prosaic enough not to tempt any of the others into emulating our flight. Had any tried to do that, I would have used every ounce of my persuasion to stop them—and I do not know what Danforth would have done. While we were gone, Pabodie, Sherman, Ropes, McTighe, and Williamson had worked like beavers over Lake's two best planes; fitting them again for use despite the altogether unaccountable juggling of their operative mechanism.

We decided to load all the planes the next morning and start back for our old base as soon as possible. Even though indirect, that was the safest way to work toward McMurdo Sound; for a straight-line flight across the most utterly unknown stretches of the aeon-dead continent would involve many additional hazards. Further exploration was hardly feasible in view of our tragic decimation and the ruin of our drilling machinery; and the doubts and horrors around us—which we did not reveal—made us wish only

---

[102] *calcareous:* "Containing or composed of lime or limestone" (*Oxford English Dictionary*).

to escape from this austral world of desolation and brooding madness as swiftly as we could.

As the public knows, our return to the world was accomplished without further disasters. All planes reached the old base on the evening of the next day—January 27th—after a swift non-stop flight; and on the 28th we made McMurdo Sound in two laps, the one pause being very brief, and occasioned by a faulty rudder in the furious wind over the ice-shelf after we had cleared the great plateau. In five days more the *Arkham* and *Miskatonic*, with all hands and equipment on board, were shaking clear of the thickening field ice and working up Ross Sea with the mocking mountains of Victoria Land looming westward against a troubled antarctic sky and twisting the wind's wails into a wide-ranged musical piping which chilled my soul to the quick. Less than a fortnight later we left the last hint of polar land behind us, and thanked heaven that we were clear of a haunted, accursed realm where life and death, space and time, have made black and blasphemous alliances in the unknown epochs since matter first writhed and swam on the planet's scarce-cooled crust.

Since our return we have all constantly worked to discourage antarctic exploration, and have kept certain doubts and guesses to ourselves with splendid unity and faithfulness. Even young Danforth, with his nervous breakdown, has not flinched or babbled to his doctors—indeed, as I have said, there is one thing he thinks he alone saw which he will not tell even me, though I think it would help his psychological state if he would consent to do so. It might explain and relieve much, though perhaps the thing was no more than the delusive aftermath of an earlier shock. That is the impression I gather after those rare irresponsible moments when he whispers disjointed things to me—things which he repudiates vehemently as soon as he gets a grip on himself again.

It will be hard work deterring others from the great white south, and some of our efforts may directly harm our cause by drawing inquiring notice. We might have known from the first that human curiosity[103] is undying, and that the results we announced would be enough to spur others ahead on the same age-long pursuit of the unknown. Lake's reports of those biological monstrosities had aroused naturalists and palaeontologists to the highest pitch; though we were sensible enough not to shew the detached parts we had taken from the actual buried specimens, or our photographs of those specimens as they were found. We also refrained from shewing the more puzzling of the scarred bones and greenish soapstones; while Danforth and I have closely guarded the pictures we took or drew on the super-plateau across the range, and the crumpled things we smoothed, studied in terror, and brought away in our pockets. But now that Starkweather-Moore party is organising, and with a thoroughness far beyond anything our outfit attempted. If not dissuaded, they will get to the innermost nucleus of the antarctic and melt and bore till they bring up that which may end the world we know. So I must break through all reticences at last—even about that ultimate nameless thing beyond the mountains of madness.

IV. [104]

It is only with vast hesitancy and repugnance that I let my mind go back to Lake's camp and what we really found

---

[103] The notion of curiosity is one of the most persistent and complex ideas in Lovecraft's fiction, and occurs in his very earliest works: in "The Tomb" (1917) the narrator declares, "But in that instant of curiosity was born ... madly unreasoning desire" (*Dagon and Other Macabre Tales*, 5). The possible psychological dangers of excessive curiosity are frequently stressed in Lovecraft's tales, and is perhaps encapsulated in an early letter: "All rationalism tends to minimise the value and importance of life, and to decrease the sum total of human happiness. In many cases the truth may cause suicidal or nearly suicidal depression" (*Selected Letters*, I, 65). And elsewhere: "To the scientist there is the joy in pursuing truth which nearly counteracts the depressing revelations of truth" (*Selected Letters*, I, 27).

[104] The second installment of the *Astounding Stories* serialization (March 1936) begins here.

there—and to that other thing beyond the frightful mountain wall. I am constantly tempted to shirk the details, and to let hints stand for actual facts and ineluctable deductions. I hope I have said enough already to let me glide briefly over the rest; the rest, that is, of the horror at the camp. I have told of the wind-ravaged terrain, the damaged shelters, the disarranged machinery, the varied uneasinesses of our dogs, the missing sledges and other items, the deaths of men and dogs, the absence of Gedney, and the six insanely buried biological specimens, strangely sound in texture for all their structural injuries, from a world forty million years dead. I do not recall whether I mentioned that upon checking up the canine bodies we found one dog missing. We did not think much about that till later—indeed, only Danforth and I have thought of it at all.

The principal things I have been keeping back relate to the bodies, and to certain subtle points which may or may not lend a hideous and incredible kind of rationale to the apparent chaos. At the time I tried to keep the men's minds off those points; for it was so much simpler—so much more normal—to lay everything to an outbreak of madness on the part of some of Lake's party. From the look of things, that daemon mountain wind must have been enough to drive any man mad in the midst of this centre of all earthly mystery and desolation.

The crowning abnormality, of course, was the condition of the bodies—men and dogs alike. They had all been in some terrible kind of conflict, and were torn and mangled in fiendish and altogether inexplicable ways. Death, so far as we could judge, had in each case come from strangulation or laceration. The dogs had evidently started the trouble, for the state of their ill-built corral bore witness to its forcible breakage from within. It had been set some distance from the camp because of the hatred of the animals for those hellish Archaean organisms, but the precaution seemed to have been taken in vain. When left alone in that monstrous wind behind flimsy walls of

insufficient height they must have stampeded—whether
from the wind itself, or from some subtle, increasing odour
emitted by the nightmare specimens, one could not say.
Those specimens, of course, had been covered with a tent-
cloth; yet the low antarctic sun had beat steadily upon
that cloth, and Lake had mentioned that solar heat tended
to make the strangely sound and tough tissues of the
things relax and expand. Perhaps the wind had whipped
the cloth from over them, and jostled them about in such
a way that their more pungent olfactory qualities became
manifest despite their unbelievable antiquity.[105]

But whatever had happened, it was hideous and revolt-
ing enough. Perhaps I had better put squeamishness aside
and tell the worst at last—though with a categorical statement of opinion, based on the first-hand observations and
most rigid deductions of both Danforth and myself, that the
then missing Gedney was in no way responsible for the
loathsome horrors we found. I have said that the bodies
were frightfully mangled. Now I must add that some were
incised and subtracted from in the most curious, cold-
blooded, and inhuman fashion. It was the same with dogs
and men. All the healthier, fatter bodies, quadrupedal or
bipedal, had had their most solid masses of tissue cut out
and removed, as by a careful butcher; and around them was
a strange sprinkling of salt—taken from the ravaged pro-
vision-chests on the planes—which conjured up the most
horrible associations. The thing had occurred in one of the
crude aëroplane shelters from which the plane had been
dragged out, and subsequent winds had effaced all tracks
which could have supplied any plausible theory. Scattered

---

[105] The last two sentences ("Those specimens ... antiquity") are found in Lovecraft's
typescript; they were cut in the *Astounding* serialisation and were *not* restored by Lovecraft
in his copies of the magazine. I believe this is an oversight by Lovecraft (this section is,
as just noted, near the beginning of the second installment, and Lovecraft does not seem
to have noticed the heavy editing of his story until the third installment) and that this
passage belongs in the text. See note 107 below.

bits of clothing, roughly slashed from the human incision-subjects, hinted no clues. It is useless to bring up the half-impression of certain faint snow-prints in one shielded corner of the ruined enclosure—because that impression did not concern human prints at all, but was clearly mixed up with all the talk of fossil prints which poor Lake had been giving throughout the preceding weeks. One had to be careful of one's imagination in the lee of those overshadowing mountains of madness.

As I have indicated, Gedney and one dog turned out to be missing in the end. When we came on that terrible shelter we had missed two dogs and two men; but the fairly unharmed dissecting tent, which we entered after investigating the monstrous graves, had something to reveal. It was not as Lake had left it, for the covered parts of the primal monstrosity had been removed from the improvised table. Indeed, we had already realised that one of the six imperfect and insanely buried things we had found—the one with the trace of a peculiarly hateful odour—must represent the collected sections of the entity which Lake had tried to analyse. On and around that laboratory table were strown[106] other things, and it did not take long for us to guess that those things were the carefully though oddly and inexpertly dissected parts of one man and one dog. I shall spare the feelings of survivors by omitting mention of the man's identity. Lake's anatomical instruments were missing, but there were evidences of their careful cleansing. The gasoline stove was also gone, though around it we found a curious litter of matches. We buried the human parts beside the other ten men, and the canine parts with the other 35 dogs. Concerning the bizarre smudges on the laboratory table, and on the jumble of roughly handled illustrated books scattered near it, we were much too bewildered to speculate.

This formed the worst of the camp horror, but other

---

[106] *strown*: Archaic spelling of *strewn*.

things were equally perplexing. The disappearance of Gedney, the one dog, the eight uninjured biological specimens, the three sledges, and certain instruments, illustrated technical and scientific books, writing materials, electric torches and batteries, food and fuel, heating apparatus, spare tents, fur suits, and the like, was utterly beyond sane conjecture; as were likewise the spatter-fringed inkblots on certain pieces of paper, and the evidences of curious alien fumbling and experimentation around the planes and all other mechanical devices both at the camp and at the boring. The dogs seemed to abhor this oddly disordered machinery. Then, too, there was the upsetting of the larder, the disappearance of certain staples, and the jarringly comical heap of tin cans pried open in the most unlikely ways and at the most unlikely places. The profusion of scattered matches, intact, broken, or spent, formed another minor enigma; as did the two or three tent-cloths and fur suits which we found lying about with peculiar and unorthodox slashings conceivably due to clumsy efforts at unimaginable adaptations. The maltreatment of the human and canine bodies, and the crazy burial of the damaged Archaean specimens, were all of a piece with this apparent disintegrative madness. In view of just such an eventuality as the present one, we carefully photographed all the main evidences of insane disorder at the camp; and shall use the prints to buttress our pleas against the departure of the proposed Starkweather-Moore Expedition.

Our first act after finding the bodies in the shelter was to photograph and open the row of insane graves with the five-pointed snow mounds. We could not help noticing the resemblance of these monstrous mounds, with their clusters of grouped dots, to poor Lake's descriptions of the strange greenish soapstones; and when we came on some of the soapstones themselves in the great mineral pile we found the likeness very close indeed. The whole general formation, it must be made clear, seemed abominably suggestive of the starfish-head of the Archaean entities; and we agreed that the suggestion must have worked potently upon the sensitised minds of Lake's overwrought party. Our own first sight of the actual buried entities formed a horrible moment, and sent the imaginations of Pabodie and myself back to some of the shocking primal myths we had read and heard. We all agreed that the mere sight and continued presence of the things must have coöperated with the oppressive polar solitude and daemon mountain wind in driving Lake's party mad.[107]

For madness—centring in Gedney as the only possible surviving agent—was the explanation spontaneously adopted by everybody so far as spoken utterance was concerned; though I will not be so naive as to deny that each of us may have harboured wild guesses which sanity forbade him to formulate completely. Sherman, Pabodie, and McTighe made an exhaustive aëroplane cruise over all the surrounding territory in the afternoon, sweeping the horizon with field-glasses in quest of Gedney and of the various missing things; but nothing came to light. The party reported that the titan barrier range extended endlessly to right and left alike, without any diminution in height or essential structure. On some of the peaks, though, the regular cube and rampart formations were bolder and plainer; having doubly fantastic similitudes to Roerich-painted Asian hill ruins. The distribution of cryptical cave-mouths on the black snow-denuded summits seemed roughly even as far as the range could be traced.

In spite of all the prevailing horrors we were left with enough sheer scientific zeal and adventurousness to wonder about the unknown realm beyond those mysterious

---

[107] The preceding two sentences ("Our own first sight ... Lake's party mad"), found in Lovecraft's typescript, were also omitted in the *Astounding* serialization and not restored in Lovecraft's copies. Here the omission is clearly an error, since the first sentence of the next paragraph, with its reference to madness, would not have the proper antecedent if these sentences were omitted.

[108] Cf. "Dagon" (1917): "Dazed and frightened, yet not without a certain thrill of the scientist's or archaeologist's delight, I examined my surroundings more closely" (*Dagon and Other Macabre Tales*, 17).

mountains.[108] As our guarded messages stated, we rested
at midnight after our day of terror and bafflement; but not
without a tentative plan for one or more range-crossing altitude flights in a lightened plane with aërial camera and
geologist's outfit, beginning the following morning. It was
decided that Danforth and I try it first, and we awaked at 7
a.m. intending an early trip; though heavy winds—mentioned in our brief bulletin to the outside world—delayed
our start till nearly nine o'clock.

I have already repeated the non-committal story we told
the men at camp—and relayed outside—after our return sixteen hours later. It is now my terrible duty to amplify this
account by filling in the merciful blanks with hints of what
we really saw in the hidden trans-montane world—hints of
the revelations which have finally driven Danforth to a nervous collapse. I wish he would add a really frank word about
the thing which he thinks he alone saw—even though it
was probably a nervous delusion—and which was perhaps
the last straw that put him where he is; but he is firm against
that. All I can do is to repeat his later disjointed whispers
about what set him shrieking as the plane soared back
through the wind-tortured mountain pass after that real and
tangible shock which I shared. This will form my last word.
If the plain signs of surviving elder horrors in what I disclose be not enough to keep others from meddling with the
inner antarctic—or at least from prying too deeply beneath
the surface of that ultimate waste of forbidden secrets and
unhuman,[109] aeon-cursed desolation—the responsibility for
unnamable and perhaps immensurable[110] evils will not be
mine.

---

[109] Note the subtle change from "inhuman" (a term with significant moral overtones and emotive properties) to the somewhat more neutral "unhuman." This might be thought to begin the moral rehabilitation of the Old Ones from objects to fear to objects of admiration with a significant psychological and cultural linkage to human-ity; the culmination of this transformation is reached toward the end of the novel (see p. 316).

[110] *immensurable*: A legitimate variant of *immeasurable*.

Danforth and I, studying the notes made by Pabodie in his afternoon flight and checking up with a sextant,[111] had calculated that the lowest available pass in the range lay somewhat to the right of us, within sight of camp, and about 23,000 or 24,000 feet above sea-level. For this point, then, we first headed in the lightened plane as we embarked on our flight of discovery. The camp itself, on foothills which sprang from a high continental plateau, was some 12,000 feet in altitude; hence the actual height increase necessary was not so vast as it might seem. Nevertheless we were acutely conscious of the rarefied air and intense cold as we rose; for on account of visibility conditions we had to leave the cabin windows open.[112] We were dressed, of course, in our heaviest furs.

As we drew near the forbidding peaks, dark and sinister above the line of crevasse-riven snow and interstitial glaciers, we noticed more and more the curiously regular formations clinging to the slopes; and thought again of the strange Asian paintings of Nicholas Roerich. The ancient and wind-weathered rock strata fully verified all of Lake's bulletins, and proved that these hoary pinnacles had been towering up in exactly the same way since a surprisingly early time in earth's history—perhaps over fifty million years. How much higher they had once been, it was futile to guess; but everything about this strange region pointed to obscure atmospheric influences unfavourable to change, and calculated to retard the usual climatic processes of rock disintegration.

But it was the mountainside tangle of regular cubes, ramparts, and cave-mouths which fascinated and disturbed us

---

[111] *sextant*: "An astronomical instrument ... used for measuring angular distances between objects, esp. for observing altitudes of celestial objects in ascertaining latitude at sea" (*Oxford English Dictionary*).

[112] Dyer and Danforth are at the very limit of breathability without external aid: human beings ordinarily require an oxygen supply above 25,000 feet.

most. I studied them with a field-glass and took aërial photographs whilst Danforth drove; and at times relieved him
at the controls—though my aviation knowledge was purely
an amateur's—in order to let him use the binoculars. We
could easily see that much of the material of the things was
a lightish Archaean quartzite, unlike any formation visible
over broad areas of the general surface; and that their regularity was extreme and uncanny to an extent which poor
Lake had scarcely hinted.

As he had said, their edges were crumbled and rounded
from untold aeons of savage weathering; but their preternatural solidity and tough material had saved them from
obliteration. Many parts, especially those closest to the
slopes, seemed identical in substance with the surrounding
rock surface. The whole arrangement looked like the ruins
of Machu Picchu in the Andes,[113] or the primal foundation-
walls of Kish as dug up by the Oxford—Field Museum Expedition in 1929;[114] and both Danforth and I obtained that
occasional impression of *separate Cyclopean blocks* which
Lake had attributed to his flight-companion Carroll. How
to account for such things in this place was frankly beyond
me, and I felt queerly humbled as a geologist. Igneous

---

[113] *Machu Picchu*: A city of the Incas fifty miles northwest of Cuzco, situated on a narrow
ridge 2000 feet above the Vilcanota River. It was probably built sometime early in the first
millennium A.D. (c. 1000–1400). It was rediscovered in 1911 by Hiram Bingham, an
American explorer.

[114] *Kish*: An ancient Sumerian city near Babylon that flourished in the third millennium B.C.
Oxford University and the Field Museum (Chicago) undertook a joint expedition to the site
in 1923–29; several monographs detailing their excavations were subsequently published.

[115] *Giants' Causeway*: A geological formation on the northern coast of County Antrim,
Northern Ireland. It consists of a lava flow that is at least twelve million years old, 700 feet
long, and 40 feet wide. As the flat surface of the lava cooled, cracks formed a very regular
pattern of hexagons; the downward extension of these cracks produced a forest of closely
packed hexagonal columns 20 feet tall. Mythological tales attribute the formation of the
"causeway" to the giant Finn MacCool, who supposedly built it as a bridge between
Ireland and Britain. Cf. *The Dream-Quest of Unknown Kadath* (1926–27): "Dylath-Leen
with its thin angular towers looks in the distance like a bit of the Giants' Causeway" (*At
the Mountains of Madness and Other Novels*, 315).

formations often have strange regularities—like the famous Giants' Causeway in Ireland[115]—but this stupendous range, despite Lake's original suspicion of smoking cones, was above all else non-volcanic in evident structure.

The curious cave-mouths, near which the odd formations seemed most abundant, presented another albeit a lesser puzzle because of their regularity of outline. They were, as Lake's bulletin had said, often approximately square or semicircular; as if the natural orifices had been shaped to greater symmetry by some magic hand. Their numerousness and wide distribution were remarkable, and suggested that the whole region was honeycombed with tunnels dissolved out of limestone strata. Such glimpses as we secured did not extend far within the caverns, but we saw that they were apparently clear of stalactites and stalagmites. Outside, those parts of the mountain slopes adjoining the apertures seemed invariably smooth and regular; and Danforth thought that the slight cracks and pittings of the weathering tended toward unusual patterns. Filled as he was with the horrors and strangenesses discovered at the camp, he hinted that the pittings vaguely resembled those baffling groups of dots sprinkled over the primeval greenish soapstones, so hideously duplicated on the madly conceived snow mounds above those six buried monstrosities.

We had risen gradually in flying over the higher foothills and along toward the relatively low pass we had selected. As we advanced we occasionally looked down at the snow and ice of the land route, wondering whether we could have attempted the trip with the simpler equipment of earlier days. Somewhat to our surprise we saw that the terrain was far from difficult as such things go; and that despite the crevasses and other bad spots it would not have been likely to deter the sledges of a Scott, a Shackleton, or an Amundsen. Some of the glaciers appeared to lead up to wind-bared passes with unusual continuity, and upon reaching our chosen pass we found that its case formed no exception.

Our sensations of tense expectancy as we prepared to round the crest and peer out over an untrodden world can hardly be described on paper; even though we had no cause to think the regions beyond the range essentially different from those already seen and traversed. The touch of evil mystery in these barrier mountains, and in the beckoning sea of opalescent sky glimpsed betwixt their summits, was a highly subtle and attenuated matter not to be explained in literal words. Rather was it an affair of vague psychological symbolism and aesthetic association—a thing mixed up with exotic poetry and paintings, and with archaic myths lurking in shunned and forbidden volumes. Even the wind's burden held a peculiar strain of conscious malignity; and for a second it seemed that the composite sound included a bizarre musical whistling or piping over a wide range as the blast swept in and out of the omnipresent and resonant cave-mouths. There was a cloudy note of reminiscent repulsion in this sound, as complex and unplaceable as any of the other dark impressions.

We were now, after a slow ascent, at a height of 23,570 feet according to the aneroid;[116] and had left the region of clinging snow definitely below us. Up here were only dark, bare rock slopes and the start of rough-ribbed glaciers—but with those provocative cubes, ramparts, and echoing cave-mouths to add a portent of the unnatural, the fantastic, and the dream-like. Looking along the line of high peaks, I thought I could see the one mentioned by poor Lake, with a rampart exactly on top. It seemed to be half-lost in a queer antarctic haze; such a haze, perhaps, as had been responsible for Lake's early notion of volcanism. The pass loomed directly before us, smooth and windswept between its jagged and malignly frowning pylons. Beyond it was a sky fretted with swirling vapours and lighted by the low polar

---

[116] *aneroid*: Short for aneroid barometer, "in which the pressure of the air is measured, not by the height of a column of mercury or other fluid which it sustains, but by its action on the elastic lid of a box exhausted of air" (*Oxford English Dictionary*).

sun—the sky of that mysterious farther realm upon which we felt no human eye had ever gazed.

A few more feet of altitude and we would behold that realm. Danforth and I, unable to speak except in shouts amidst the howling, piping wind that raced through the pass and added to the noise off the unmuffled engines, exchanged eloquent glances. And then, having gained those last few feet, we did indeed stare across the momentous divide and over the unsampled secrets of an elder and utterly alien earth.

V.

I think that both of us simultaneously cried out in mixed awe, wonder, terror, and disbelief in our own senses as we finally cleared the pass and saw what lay beyond. Of course we must have had some natural theory in the back of our heads to steady our faculties for the moment. Probably we thought of such things as the grotesquely weathered stones of the Garden of the Gods in Colorado,[117] or the fantastically symmetrical wind-carved rocks of the Arizona desert.[118] Perhaps we even half thought the sight a mirage like that we had seen the morning before on first approaching those mountains of madness. We must have had some such normal notions to fall back upon as our eyes swept that limitless, tempest-scarred plateau and grasped the almost endless labyrinth of colossal, regular, and geometrically eurhythmic[119] stone masses which reared their crumbled and

---

[117] *Garden of the Gods:* A park northwest of Colorado Springs, consisting of red and white sandstone formations, some of which stand upright and are over 300 feet tall. The site is of late Palaeozoic origin and was produced by erosion from wind and water.

[118] Presumably a reference to the Grand Canyon. Lovecraft, of course, having never gone west of New Orleans, did not know these sites in Colorado and Arizona at first-hand.

[119] *eurhythmic:* "Of or pertaining to well-arranged proportion, esp. in architecture" (*Oxford English Dictionary*).

pitted crests above a glacial sheet not more than forty or fifty feet deep at its thickest, and in places obviously thinner.

The effect of the monstrous sight was indescribable, for some fiendish violation of known natural law[120] seemed certain at the outset. Here, on a hellishly ancient table-land fully 20,000 feet high, and in a climate deadly to habitation since a pre-human age not less than 500,000 years ago, there stretched nearly to the vision's limit a tangle of orderly stone which only the desperation of mental self-defence[121] could possibly attribute to any but a conscious and artificial cause. We had previously dismissed, so far as serious thought was concerned, any theory that the cubes and ramparts of the mountainsides were other than natural in origin. How could they be otherwise, when man himself could scarcely have been differentiated from the great apes at the time when this region succumbed to the present unbroken reign of glacial death?

Yet now the sway of reason seemed irrefutably shaken, for this Cyclopean maze of squared, curved, and angled blocks had features which cut off all comfortable refuge. It was, very clearly, the blasphemous city of the mirage in stark, objective, and ineluctable reality. That damnable portent had had a material basis after all—there had been some horizontal stratum of ice-dust in the upper air, and this shocking stone survival had projected its image across the mountains according to the simple laws of reflection. Of course the phantom had been twisted and exaggerated, and had contained things which the real source did not contain; yet now, as we saw that real source, we thought it even more hideous and menacing than its distant image.

---

[120] See note 56 above.

[121] This phrase seems a fairly exact encapsulation of Freud's conception of the "defense mechanism." Lovecraft had first read Freud in 1921, at which time he remarked: "Dr. Sigmund Freud of Vienna, whose system of psycho-analysis I have begun to investigate, will probably prove the end of idealistic thought. In details, I think he has his limitations; and I am inclined to accept the modifications of Adler, who in placing the ego above the eros makes a scientific return to the position which Nietzsche assumed for wholly philosophical reasons" (*Selected Letters*, I, 134).

Only the incredible, unhuman massiveness of these vast stone towers and ramparts had saved the frightful thing from utter annihilation in the hundreds of thousands—perhaps millions—of years it had brooded there amidst the blasts of a bleak upland. "Corona Mundi ... Roof of the World ..."[122] All sorts of fantastic phrases sprang to our lips as we looked dizzily down at the unbelievable spectacle. I thought again of the eldritch primal myths that had so persistently haunted me since my first sight of this dead antarctic world—of the daemoniac plateau of Leng, of the Mi-Go, or Abominable Snow-Men of the Himalayas,[123] of the Pnakotic Manuscripts with their pre-human implications, of the Cthulhu cult,[124] of the *Necronomicon,* and of the Hyperborean legends of formless Tsathoggua[125] and the worse than formless star-spawn associated with that semi-entity.

For boundless miles in every direction the thing stretched off with very little thinning; indeed, as our eyes followed it to the right and left along the base of the low, gradual foothills which separated it from the actual mountain rim, we decided that we could see no thinning at all except for an interruption at the left of the pass through which we had come. We had merely struck, at random, a limited part

---

[122] *"Corona Mundi ...":* "A name given to the Pamirs, the great region of mountains covering 30,000 square miles, devoid of trees and shrubs, and most of it in the [former] Soviet Socialist Republic of Tadzhikistan" (*Brewer's Dictionary of Phrase and Fable*).

[123] The Mi-Go, Yeti, or Abominable Snowmen are a real folk myth in Nepal and Tibet. They are supposed to be huge human beings who dwell at the snowline in the Himalayas; their snowprints have purportedly been seen, but these are probably the prints of bears. The term *Mi-Go* is a Tibetan compound: *mi,* "man," and *go* (or *gyo*), "swift," hence "fast-moving manlike creature." This mention, however, is a clear nod to "The Whisperer in Darkness" (1930), where the stories of the fungi from Yuggoth in the Vermont hills are said to be analogous to the "belief of the Nepalese hill tribes in the dreaded *Mi-Go* or 'Abominable Snow-Men' who lurk hideously amidst the ice and rock pinnacles of the Himalayan summits"; later the fungi are explicitly identified with the Mi-Go (*The Dunwich Horror and Others,* 214, 224).

[124] See note 84 above.

[125] For Tsathoggua, see note 98 above. "Hyperborean" refers to the story cycle involving the mythical ancient northern continent of Hyperborea (at the North Pole) written by Clark Ashton Smith, of which "The Tale of Satampra Zeiros" is a part.

of something of incalculable extent. The foothills were more sparsely sprinkled with grotesque stone structures, linking the terrible city to the already familiar cubes and ramparts which evidently formed its mountain outposts. These latter, as well as the queer cave-mouths, were as thick on the inner as on the outer sides of the mountains.

The nameless stone labyrinth consisted, for the most part, of walls from 10 to 150 feet in ice-clear height, and of a thickness varying from five to ten feet. It was composed mostly of prodigious blocks of dark primordial slate, schist, and sandstone—blocks in many cases as large as $4 \times 6 \times 8$ feet—though in several places it seemed to be carved out of a solid, uneven bed-rock of pre-Cambrian slate. The buildings were far from equal in size; there being innumerable honeycomb-arrangements of enormous extent as well as smaller separate structures. The general shape of these things tended to be conical, pyramidal, or terraced; though there were many perfect cylinders, perfect cubes, clusters of cubes, and other rectangular forms, and a peculiar sprinkling of angled edifices whose five-pointed ground plan roughly suggested modern fortifications. The builders had made constant and expert use of the principle of the arch,[126] and domes had probably existed in the city's heyday.[127]

The whole tangle was monstrously weathered, and the glacial surface from which the towers projected was strown with fallen blocks and immemorial debris. Where the glaciation was transparent we could see the lower parts

---

[126] Cf. the description of the city of the Great Race in Australia in "The Shadow out of Time": " ... the principle of the arch was known as fully and used as extensively as by the Romans" (*The Dunwich Horror and Others*, 379).

[127] The Old Ones' city corresponds very roughly to the city described in A. Merritt's "The People of the Pit" (1917): "'Straight beneath me was the—city. I looked down upon mile after mile of closely packed cylinders. They lay upon their sides in pyramids of three, of five—of dozens—piled upon each other.... [T]hey were topped by towers, by minarets, by flares, by fans, and twisted monstrosities." The city is postulated as existing underground somewhere in the Yukon. See A. Merritt, *The Fox Woman and Other Stories* (1949; rpt. New York: Avon, 1977), 67–68.

of the gigantic piles, and noticed the ice-preserved stone bridges which connected the different towers at varying distances above the ground. On the exposed walls we could detect the scarred places where other and higher bridges of the same sort had existed. Closer inspection revealed countless largish windows; some of which were closed with shutters of a petrified material originally wood, though most gaped open in a sinister and menacing fashion. Many of the ruins, of course, were roofless, and with uneven though wind-rounded upper edges; whilst others, of a more sharply conical or pyramidal model or else protected by higher surrounding structures, preserved intact outlines despite the omnipresent crumbling and pitting. With the field-glass we could barely make out what seemed to be sculptural decorations in horizontal bands—decorations including those curious groups of dots whose presence on the ancient soap-stones now assumed a vastly larger significance.

In many places the buildings were totally ruined and the ice-sheet deeply riven from various geologic causes. In other places the stonework was worn down to the very level of the glaciation. One broad swath, extending from the plateau's interior to a cleft in the foothills about a mile to the left of the pass we had traversed, was wholly free from buildings; and probably represented, we concluded, the course of some great river which in Tertiary times—millions of years ago—had poured through the city and into some prodigious subterranean abyss of the great barrier range. Certainly, this was above all a region of caves, gulfs, and underground secrets beyond human penetration.

Looking back to our sensations, and recalling our dazedness at viewing this monstrous survival from aeons we had thought pre-human, I can only wonder that we preserved the semblance of equilibrium which we did. Of course we knew that something—chronology, scientific theory, or our own consciousness—was woefully awry; yet we kept enough poise to guide the plane, observe many things quite minutely, and take a careful series of photographs which may yet serve both us and the world in good stead. In my case, ingrained scientific habit may have helped; for above all my bewilderment and sense of menace there burned a dominant curiosity to fathom more of this age-old secret—to know what sort of beings had built and lived in this incalculably gigantic place, and what relation to the general world of its time or of other times so unique a concentration of life could have had.

For this place could be no ordinary city. It must have formed the primary nucleus and centre of some archaic and unbelievable chapter of earth's history whose outward ramifications, recalled only dimly in the most obscure and distorted myths, had vanished utterly amidst the chaos of terrene convulsions long before any human race we know had shambled out of apedom. Here sprawled a palaeogean[128] megalopolis compared with which the fabled Atlantis[129] and Lemuria,[130] Commoriom[131] and Uzuldaroum,[132] and Olathoë in the land of Lomar[133] are recent things of today—not even of yesterday; a megalopolis ranking with such whispered

---

[128] *palaeogean*: Not a technical geological term, but one referring generally to prior ages of the earth's surface.

[129] *Atlantis*: Lovecraft did not believe in the existence of a sunken Atlantic continent, but this did not prevent him from using the idea in fiction. The narrator of "The Temple" (1920) claims that he is "confronted at last with the Atlantis I had formerly deemed largely a myth" (*Dagon and Other Macabre Tales*, 67). Lovecraft discusses the myth of Atlantis in a late letter (*Selected Letters*, V, 267–69).

[130] *Lemuria*: A continent once thought to have existed in the Indian Ocean; hypothesized by Ernst Haeckel (see note 48 to "The Rates in the Walls") to account for the presence of lemurs and other animals and plants in southern Africa and the Malay Peninsula. Lovecraft, although philosophically influenced by Haeckel, learned of Lemuria primarily from W. Scott-Elliot's *The Story of Atlantis and the Lost Lemuria* (1925), which is mentioned in "The Call of Cthulhu" (1926). Although he passed it off as a myth "developed by modern occultists & the sophistical charlatans," he nevertheless found the idea "ineffably pregnant with fantastic suggestion" (*Selected Letters*, II, 58).

[131] *Commoriom*: A city in the land of Hyperborea invented by Clark Ashton Smith in "The Tale of Satampra Zeiros" (see note 98 above).

[132] *Uzuldaroum*: Another city in Hyperborea invented by Clark Ashton Smith; first cited in "The Tale of Satampra Zeiros" (see note 98 above).

[133] A reference to Lovecraft's own tale, "Polaris" (see note 97 above).

[134] *Valusia*: a kingdom in prehistoric Europe invented by Lovecraft's friend Robert E.

pre-human blasphemies as Valusia,[134] R'lyeh,[135] Ib[136] in the land of Mnar, and the Nameless City of Arabia Deserta.[137] As we flew above that tangle of stark titan towers my imagination sometimes escaped all bounds and roved aimlessly in realms of fantastic associations—even weaving links betwixt this lost world and some of my own wildest dreams concerning the mad horror at the camp.

The plane's fuel-tank, in the interest of greater lightness, had been only partly filled; hence we now had to exert caution in our explorations. Even so, however, we covered an enormous extent of ground—or rather, air—after swooping down to a level where the wind became virtually negligible. There seemed to be no limit to the mountain-range, or to the length of the frightful stone city which bordered

---

Howard (1906–1936). Cf. "The Hyborian Age": "Valusia was the western-most kingdom of the Thurian Continent [i.e., Europe] ..." (Robert E. Howard, *Skull-Face and Others* [Sauk City, WI: Arkham House, 1946], 190). In Howard's fiction Valusia is ruled by King Kull, and an entire series of tales—including "The Shadow Kingdom" (*Weird Tales*, August 1929) and "The Mirrors of Tuzun Thune" (*Weird Tales*, September 1929)—are set in this realm.

[135] *R'lyeh*: The sunken city housing Cthulhu in "The Call of Cthulhu" (1926).

[136] *Ib*: The primeval city that was destroyed by Sarnath in Lovecraft's "The Doom That Came to Sarnath" (1920). It is said there that the city existed "in the immemorial years when the world was young" (*Dagon and Other Macabre Tales*, 43).

[137] *the Nameless City of Arabia Deserta*: A reference to Lovecraft's own "The Nameless City" (1921). "It must have been thus before the first stones of Memphis were laid, and while the bricks of Babylon were yet unbaked. There is no legend so old as to give it a name, or to recall that it was ever alive ..." (*Dagon and Other Macabre Tales*, 98).

[138] Cf. Lovecraft's "The Festival" (1923): " ... I saw that it was a burying-ground where black gravestones stuck ghoulishly through the snow like the decayed fingernails of a gigantic corpse" (*Dagon and Other Macabre Tales*, 209). This is a lightly fictionalized description of the Hill Burying Ground in Marblehead, Massachusetts.

its inner foothills. Fifty miles of flight in each direction shewed no major change in the labyrinth of rock and masonry that clawed up corpse-like through the eternal ice.[138] There were, though, some highly absorbing diversifications; such as the carvings on the canyon where that broad river had once pierced the foothills and approached its sinking-place in the great range. The headlands at the stream's entrance had been boldly carved into Cyclopean pylons; and something about the ridgy, barrel-shaped designs stirred up oddly vague, hateful, and confusing semi-remembrances in both Danforth and me.

We also came upon several star-shaped open spaces, evidently public squares; and noted various undulations in the terrain. Where a sharp hill rose, it was generally hollowed out into some sort of rambling stone edifice; but there were at least two exceptions. Of these latter, one was too badly weathered to disclose what had been on the jutting eminence, while the other still bore a fantastic conical monument carved out of the solid rock and roughly resembling such things as the well-known Snake Tomb in the ancient valley of Petra.[139]

Flying inland from the mountains, we discovered that the city was not of infinite width, even though its length along the foothills seemed endless. After about thirty miles the grotesque stone buildings began to thin out, and in ten more miles we came to an unbroken waste virtually without signs of sentient artifice. The course of the river beyond the city seemed marked by a broad depressed line; while the land assumed a somewhat greater ruggedness, seeming to slope slightly upward as it receded in the mist-hazed west.

So far we had made no landing, yet to leave the plateau without an attempt at entering some of the monstrous

---

[139] *Petra*: The Greek name (meaning simply "rock") for an ancient city in the southern desert of modern-day Jordan, founded by the Edomites late in the second millennium B.C. It is probably to be identified with the biblical city of Sela. It was conquered by the Nabataeans around 312 B.C. and then by the Romans in A.D. 106. The Snake Tomb is a tomb, built by the Nabataeans, carved out of a mountain and surmounted by the figure of a coiled snake.

structures would have been inconceivable. Accordingly we decided to find a smooth place on the foothills near our navigable pass, there grounding the plane and preparing to do some exploration on foot. Though these gradual slopes were partly covered with a scattering of ruins, low flying soon disclosed an ample number of possible landing-places. Selecting that nearest to the pass, since our next flight would be across the great range and back to camp, we succeeded about 12:30 p.m. in coming down on a smooth, hard snowfield wholly devoid of obstacles and well adapted to a swift and favourable takeoff later on.

It did not seem necessary to protect the plane with a snow banking for so brief a time and in so comfortable an absence of high winds at this level; hence we merely saw that the landing skis were safely lodged, and that the vital parts of the mechanism were guarded against the cold. For our foot journey we discarded the heaviest of our flying furs, and took with us a small outfit consisting of pocket compass, hand camera, light provisions, voluminous notebooks and paper, geologist's hammer and chisel, specimen-bags, coil of climbing rope, and powerful electric torches with extra batteries; this equipment having been carried in the plane on the chance that we might be able to effect a landing, take ground pictures, make drawings and topographical sketches, and obtain rock specimens from some bare slope, outcropping, or mountain cave. Fortunately we had a supply of extra paper to tear up, place in a spare specimen-bag, and use on the ancient principle of hare-and-hounds for marking our course in any interior mazes we might be able to penetrate. This had been brought in case we found some cave system with air quiet enough to allow such a rapid and easy method in place of the usual rock-chipping method of trail-blazing.

Walking cautiously downhill over the crusted snow toward the stupendous stone labyrinth that loomed against the opalescent west, we felt almost as keen a sense of imminent marvels as we had felt on approaching the unfathomed mountain pass four hours previously. True, we had become visually familiar with the incredible secret concealed by the barrier peaks; yet the prospect of actually entering primordial walls reared by conscious beings perhaps millions of years ago—before any known race of men could have existed—was none the less awesome and potentially terrible in its implications of cosmic abnormality. Though the thinness of the air at this prodigious altitude made exertion somewhat more difficult than usual; both Danforth and I found ourselves bearing up very well, and felt equal to almost any task which might fall to our lot. It took only a few steps to bring us to a shapeless ruin worn level with the snow, while ten or fifteen rods[140] farther on there was a huge roofless rampart still complete in its gigantic five-pointed outline and rising to an irregular height of ten or eleven feet. For this latter we headed; and when at last we were able actually to touch its weathered Cyclopean blocks, we felt that we had established an unprecedented and almost blasphemous link with forgotten aeons normally closed to our species.

This rampart, shaped like a star and perhaps 300 feet from point to point, was built of Jurassic sandstone blocks of irregular size, averaging 6 × 8 feet in surface. There was a row of arched loopholes or windows about four feet wide and five feet high; spaced quite symmetrically along the points of the star and at its inner angles, and with the bottoms about four feet from the glaciated surface. Looking through these, we could see that the masonry was fully five feet thick, that there were no partitions remaining within, and that there were traces of banded carvings or bas-reliefs on the interior walls; facts we had indeed guessed before, when flying low over this rampart and others like it. Though lower parts must have originally existed, all traces

---

[140] *rods*: Unit of measurement equalling 5½ yards or 16½ feet.

[141] *outré*: "Beyond the bounds of what is usual or considered correct and proper; unusual, eccentric, out-of-the-way; exaggerated" (*Oxford English Dictionary*). From the French (past participle of *outrer*, to go beyond), but usually not italicized by Lovecraft.

of such things were now wholly obscured by the deep layer of ice and snow at this point.

We crawled through one of the windows and vainly tried to decipher the nearly effaced mural designs, but did not attempt to disturb the glaciated floor. Our orientation flights had indicated that many buildings in the city proper were less ice-choked, and that we might perhaps find wholly clear interiors leading down to the true ground level if we entered those structures still roofed at the top. Before we left the rampart we photographed it carefully, and studied its mortarless Cyclopean masonry with complete bewilderment. We wished that Pabodie were present, for his engineering knowledge might have helped us guess how such titanic blocks could have been handled in that unbelievably remote age when the city and its outskirts were built up.

The half-mile walk downhill to the actual city, with the upper wind shrieking vainly and savagely through the skyward peaks in the background, was something whose smallest details will always remain engraved on my mind. Only in fantastic nightmares could any human beings but Danforth and me conceive such optical effects. Between us and the churning vapours of the west lay that monstrous tangle of dark stone towers; its outré[141] and incredible forms impressing us afresh at every new angle of vision. It was a mirage in solid stone, and were it not for the photographs I would still doubt that such a thing could be. The general type of masonry was identical with that of the rampart we had examined; but the extravagant shapes which this masonry took in its urban manifestations were past all description.

Even the pictures illustrate only one or two phases of its infinite bizarrerie, endless variety, preternatural massiveness, and utterly alien exoticism. There were geometrical forms for which an Euclid[142] could scarcely find a name—

---

[142] *Euclid*: A mathematician who flourished around 300 B.C. in Greece and wrote the *Stoicheia* (*Elements*), a landmark work on the principles of geometry. In high school Lovecraft, although having difficulty with algebra, did quite well in geometry: he received

cones of all degrees of irregularity and truncation; terraces
of every sort of provocative disproportion; shafts with odd
bulbous enlargements; broken columns in curious groups;
and five-pointed or five-ridged arrangements of mad grotesqueness. As we drew nearer we could see beneath certain
transparent parts of the ice-sheet, and detect some of the
tubular stone bridges that connected the crazily sprinkled
structures at various heights. Of orderly streets there seemed
to be none, the only broad open swath being a mile to the left,
where the ancient river had doubtless flowed through the
town into the mountains.

Our field-glasses shewed the external horizontal bands of
nearly effaced sculptures and dot-groups to be very prevalent, and we could half-imagine what the city must once
have looked like—even though most of the roofs and tower-
tops had necessarily perished. As a whole, it had been a
complex tangle of twisted lanes and alleys; all of them deep
canyons, and some little better than tunnels because of
the overhanging masonry or overarching bridges.[143] Now,
outspread below us, it loomed like a dream-phantasy
against a westward mist through whose northern end the
low, reddish antarctic sun of early afternoon was struggling to shine; and when for a moment that sun encountered a denser obstruction and plunged the scene into temporary shadow, the effect was subtly menacing in a way I
can never hope to depict. Even the faint howling and piping of the unfelt wind in the great mountain passes behind

---

a 92 in Plane Geometry during his sophomore year (1906–07) at Hope Street High
School. His tales contain frequent references to "non-Euclidean" geometry, especially in
architecture.

[143] Cf. Lovecraft's "The Music of Erich Zann" (1921): "The houses were tall, peaked-
roofed, incredibly old, and crazily leaning backward, forward, and sidewise. Occasionally an opposite pair, both leaning forward, almost met across the street like an arch ...
There were a few overhead bridges from house to house across the street" (*The Dunwich
Horror and Others*, 84). The story takes place in France, and the city described (although
never named) is presumably Paris; but Lovecraft may have been thinking of several New
England cities that feature this type of architecture. Cf. "The Festival": "The upper part
[of the house] overhung the narrow grass-grown street and nearly met the overhanging

us took on a wilder note of purposeful malignity. The last
stage of our descent to the town was unusually steep and
abrupt, and a rock outcropping at the edge where the grade
changed led us to think that an artificial terrace had once
existed there. Under the glaciation, we believed, there
must be a flight of steps or its equivalent.

When at last we plunged into the labyrinthine town
itself, clambering over fallen masonry and shrinking from
the oppressive nearness and dwarfing height of omnipresent crumbling and pitted walls, our sensations again became such that I marvel at the amount of self-control we
retained. Danforth was frankly jumpy, and began making
some offensively irrelevant speculations about the horror
at the camp—which I resented all the more because I could
not help sharing certain conclusions forced upon us by many
features of this morbid survival from nightmare antiquity.
The speculations worked on his imagination, too; for in one
place—where a debris-littered alley turned a sharp corner—
he insisted that he saw faint traces of ground markings which
he did not like; whilst elsewhere he stopped to listen to a
subtle imaginary sound from some undefined point—a
muffled musical piping, he said, not unlike that of the wind
in the mountain caves yet somehow disturbingly different. The ceaseless *five-pointedness*[144] of the surrounding
architecture and of the few distinguishable mural

---

part of the house opposite, so that I was almost in a tunnel, with the low stone doorstep
wholly free from snow" (*Dagon and Other Macabre Tales*, 210). This story is a fictional-
ization of Lovecraft's first visit to Marblehead, Massachusetts, in December 1922; there
is an actual house in Marblehead upon which this somewhat exaggerated description is
based.

[144] *five-pointedness*: One wonders whether Lovecraft meant to suggest the pentagram, commonly used by occultists in incantations. See Lewis Spence, *An Encyclopaedia of Occultism*
(New York: Dodd, Mead, 1920), 261: "The Pentagram, the sign of the Microcosm, was held
to be the most powerful means of conjuration in any rite. It may represent evil as well as
good, for while with one point in the ascendant it was the sign of Christ, with two points in the
ascendant it was the sign of Satan. By the use of the pentagram in these positions the powers
of light or darkness were evoked. The pentagram was said to be the star which led the Magi
to the manger where the infant Christ was laid."

arabesques[145] had a dimly sinister suggestiveness we could not escape; and gave us a touch of terrible subconscious certainty concerning the primal entities which had reared and dwelt in this unhallowed place.

Nevertheless our scientific and adventurous souls were not wholly dead; and we mechanically carried out our programme of chipping specimens from all the different rock types represented in the masonry. We wished a rather full set in order to draw better conclusions regarding the age of the place. Nothing in the great outer walls seemed to date from later than the Jurassic and Comanchian periods, nor was any piece of stone in the entire place of a greater recency than the Pliocene age.[146] In stark certainty, we were wandering amidst a death which had reigned at least 500,000 years, and in all probability even longer.

As we proceeded through this maze of stone-shadowed twilight we stopped at all available apertures to study interiors and investigate entrance possibilities. Some were above our reach, whilst others led only into ice-choked ruins as unroofed and barren as the rampart on the hill. One, though spacious and inviting, opened on a seemingly bottomless abyss without visible means of descent. Now and then we had a chance to study the petrified wood of a surviving shutter, and were impressed by the fabulous antiquity implied in the still discernible grain. These

---

[145] *arabesques*: When lower-cased, "A species of mural or surface decoration in colour or low relief, composed in flowing lines of branches, leaves, and scroll-work fancifully intertwined" (*Oxford English Dictionary*). When capitalized and as an adjective (the original usage), the word means simply "Arabian," and is occasionally so used by Lovecraft. Cf. Poe's *Tales of the Grotesque and Arabesque* (1840).

[146] *Pliocene age*: More properly, the Pliocene epoch, extending from 7 to 2.5 million years ago.

[147] *gymnosperms*: Now termed Pinophyta: "Ancient division of seed-bearing vascular plants extending from the Devonian to Recent" (Lincoln and Boxshall, 1987).

conifers: Literally, "cone-bearers"; now classified under the term Pinatae: "The largest group of extant Gymnosperms; usually evergreen shrubs and trees" (Lincoln and Boxshall, 1987).

things had come from Mesozoic gymnosperms and conifers[147]—especially Cretaceous cycads—and from fan-palms
and early angiosperms of plainly Tertiary date. Nothing definitely later than the Pliocene could be discovered. In the
placing of these shutters—whose edges shewed the former
presence of queer and long-vanished hinges—usage seemed
to be varied; some being on the outer and some on the inner
side of the deep embrasures. They seemed to have become
wedged in place, thus surviving the rusting of their former
and probably metallic fixtures and fastenings.

After a time we came across a row of windows—in the
bulges of a colossal five-ridged cone of undamaged apex—
which led into a vast, well-preserved room with stone floor-
ing; but these were too high in the room to permit of descent without a rope. We had a rope with us, but did not
wish to bother with this twenty-foot drop unless obliged
to—especially in this thin plateau air where great demands
were made upon the heart action. This enormous room was
probably a hall or concourse of some sort, and our electric
torches shewed bold, distinct, and potentially startling sculptures arranged round the walls in broad, horizontal bands
separated by equally broad strips of conventional arabesques.
We took careful note of this spot, planning to enter here
unless a more easily gained interior were encountered.

Finally, though, we did encounter exactly the opening we
wished; an archway about six feet wide and ten feet high,
marking the former end of an aërial bridge which had spanned
an alley about five feet above the present level of glaciation.
These archways, of course, were flush with upper-story floors;
and in this case one of the floors still existed. The building
thus accessible was a series of rectangular terraces on our
left facing westward. That across the alley, where the other
archway yawned, was a decrepit cylinder with no windows
and with a curious bulge about ten feet above the aperture. It
was totally dark inside, and the archway seemed to open on
a well of illimitable emptiness.

Heaped debris made the entrance to the vast left-hand

building doubly easy, yet for a moment we hesitated before taking advantage of the long-wished chance. For though we had penetrated into this tangle of archaic mystery, it required fresh resolution to carry us actually inside a complete and surviving building of a fabulous elder world whose nature was becoming more and more hideously plain to us. In the end, however, we made the plunge; and scrambled up over the rubble into the gaping embrasure. The floor beyond was of great slate slabs, and seemed to form the outlet of a long, high corridor with sculptured walls.

Observing the many inner archways which led off from it, and realising the probable complexity of the nest of apartments within, we decided that we must begin our system of hare-and-hound trail-blazing. Hitherto our compasses, together with frequent glimpses of the vast mountain-range between the towers in our rear, had been enough to prevent our losing our way; but from now on, the artificial substitute would be necessary. Accordingly we reduced our extra paper to shreds of suitable size, placed these in a bag to be carried by Danforth, and prepared to use them as economically as safety would allow. This method would probably gain us immunity from straying, since there did not appear to be any strong air-currents inside the primordial masonry. If such should develop, or if our paper supply should give out, we could of course fall back on the more secure though more tedious and retarding method of rock-chipping.

Just how extensive a territory we had opened up, it was impossible to guess without a trial. The close and frequent connexion of the different buildings made it likely that we might cross from one to another on bridges underneath the ice except where impeded by local collapses and geologic rifts, for very little glaciation seemed to have entered the massive constructions. Almost all the areas of transparent ice had revealed the submerged windows as tightly shuttered, as if the town had been left in that uniform state until the glacial sheet came to crystallise the lower part for all succeeding time. Indeed, one gained a curious impression that this place had been deliberately closed and deserted in some dim, bygone aeon, rather than overwhelmed by any sudden calamity or even gradual decay. Had the coming of the ice been foreseen, and had a nameless population left en masse to seek a less doomed abode? The precise physiographic conditions attending the formation of the ice-sheet at this point would have to wait for later solution. It had not, very plainly, been a grinding drive. Perhaps the pressure of accumulated snows had been responsible; and perhaps some flood from the river, or from the bursting of some ancient glacial dam in the great range, had helped to create the special state now observable. Imagination could conceive almost anything in connexion with this place.

VI.

It would be cumbrous to give a detailed, consecutive account of our wanderings inside that cavernous, aeon-dead honeycomb of primal masonry; that monstrous lair of elder secrets which now echoed for the first time, after uncounted epochs, to the tread of human feet. This is especially true because so much of the horrible drama and revelation came from a mere study of the omnipresent mural carvings. Our flashlight photographs of those carvings will do much toward proving the truth of what we are now disclosing, and it is lamentable that we had not a larger film supply with us. As it was, we made crude notebook sketches of certain salient features after all our films were used up.

The building which we had entered was one of great size and elaborateness, and gave us an impressive notion of the architecture of that nameless geologic past. The inner partitions were less massive than the outer walls, but on the lower levels were excellently preserved. Labyrinthine complexity, involving curiously irregular differences in floor levels, characterised the entire arrangement; and we should certainly have been lost at the very outset but for the trail of torn paper left behind us. We decided to explore the more decrepit upper parts first of all, hence climbed aloft in the maze for a distance of some 100 feet, to where the topmost tier of chambers yawned snowily and ruinously open to the polar sky. Ascent was effected over the steep, transversely ribbed stone ramps or inclined planes which everywhere served in lieu of stairs. The rooms we encountered were of all imaginable shapes and proportions, ranging from five-pointed stars to triangles and perfect cubes. It might be safe to say that their general average was about 30 × 30 feet in floor area, and 20 feet in height; though many larger apartments existed. After thoroughly examining the upper regions and the glacial level we descended story by story into the submerged part, where indeed we soon saw we were in a continuous maze of connected chambers and passages probably leading over unlimited areas outside this particular building. The Cyclopean massiveness and giganticism of everything about us became curiously oppressive; and there was something vaguely but deeply unhuman in all the contours, dimensions, proportions, decorations, and constructional nuances of the blasphemously archaic stonework. We soon realised from what the carvings revealed that this monstrous city was many million years old.

We cannot yet explain the engineering principles used in the anomalous balancing and adjustment of the vast rock masses, though the function of the arch was clearly much relied on. The rooms we visited were wholly bare of all portable contents, a circumstance which sustained our belief in the city's deliberate desertion. The prime decorative feature was the almost universal system of mural sculpture; which tended to run in continuous horizontal bands three feet wide and arranged from floor to ceiling in alternation with bands of equal width given over to geometrical arabesques. There

---

[148] *cartouches*: A tablet for an inscription or for ornament" (*Oxford English Dictionary*).

were exceptions to this rule of arrangement, but its preponderance was overwhelming. Often, however, a series of smooth cartouches[148] containing oddly patterned groups of dots would be sunk along one of the arabesque bands.

The technique, we soon saw, was mature, accomplished, and aesthetically evolved to the highest degree of civilised mastery; though utterly alien in every detail to any known art tradition of the human race.[149] In delicacy of execution no sculpture I have ever seen could approach it. The minutest details of elaborate vegetation, or of animal life, were rendered with astonishing vividness despite the bold scale of the carvings; whilst the conventional designs were marvels of skilful intricacy. The arabesques displayed a profound use of mathematical principles, and were made up of obscurely symmetrical curves and angles based on the quantity of five. The pictorial bands followed a highly formalised tradition, and involved a peculiar treatment of perspective; but had an artistic force that moved us profoundly notwithstanding the intervening gulf of vast geologic periods. Their method of design hinged on a singular juxtaposition of the cross-section with the two-dimensional silhouette, and embodied an analytical psychology beyond that of any known race of antiquity. It is useless to try to compare this art with any represented in our museums. Those who see our photographs will probably find its closest analogue in certain grotesque conceptions of the most daring futurists.[150]

The arabesque tracery consisted altogether of depressed

---

[149] Cf. the description of the jewelry fashioned by the Deep Ones in "The Shadow over Innsmouth" (1931): "It clearly belonged to some settled technique of infinite maturity and perfection, yet that technique was utterly remote from any—Eastern or Western, ancient or modern—which I had ever heard of or seen exemplified. It was as if the workmanship were that of another planet" (*The Dunwich Horror and Others*, 311).

[150] *futurists*: A short-lived artistic movement founded by the Italian poet Filippo Marinetti in 1909. It purported to address directly the phenomena of the modern world (especially machinery, speed, and violence) by attempting to depict movement rather than static still-life. Although it had died out by around 1916, its principles were incorporated in part by the Dadaists and Vorticists. Lovecraft satirized the movement in a poem, "Futurist Art" (1917).

lines whose depth on unweathered walls varied from one to two inches. When cartouches with dot-groups appeared—evidently as inscriptions in some unknown and primordial language and alphabet—the depression of the smooth surface was perhaps an inch and a half, and of the dots perhaps a half-inch more. The pictorial bands were in counter-sunk low relief, their background being depressed about two inches from the original wall surface. In some specimens marks of a former colouration could be detected, though for the most part the untold aeons had disintegrated and banished any pigments which may have been applied.[151] The more one studied the marvellous technique the more one admired the things. Beneath their strict conventionalisation one could grasp the minute and accurate observation and graphic skill of the artists; and indeed, the very conventions themselves served to symbolise and accentuate the real essence or vital differentiation of every object delineated. We felt, too, that besides these recognisable excellences there were others lurking beyond the reach of our perceptions. Certain touches here and there gave vague hints of latent symbols and stimuli which another mental and emotional background, and a fuller or different sensory equipment, might have made of profound and poignant significance to us.

The subject-matter of the sculptures obviously came from the life of the vanished epoch of their creation, and contained a large proportion of evident history. It is this abnormal historic-mindedness of the primal race—a chance circumstance operating, through coincidence, miraculously in our favour—which made the carvings so awesomely informative to us, and which caused us to place

---

[151] Perhaps Lovecraft was thinking of ancient Greek statuary, which was once vividly colored but whose tints have been worn off through the passage of time.

[152] This use of art to deduce the history of an alien species was first used by Lovecraft in "The Nameless City" (1921): "Rich, vivid, and daringly fantastic designs and pictures formed a continuous scheme of mural painting whose lines and colours were beyond description.... I thought I could trace roughly a wonderful epic of the nameless city; the tale of a mighty sea-coast metropolis that ruled the world before Africa rose out of the

their photography and transcription above all other considerations.[152] In certain rooms the dominant arrangement was varied by the presence of maps, astronomical charts, and other scientific designs on an enlarged scale—these things giving a naive and terrible corroboration to what we gathered from the pictorial friezes and dadoes.[153] In hinting at what the whole revealed, I can only hope that my account will not arouse a curiosity greater than sane caution on the part of those who believe me at all. It would be tragic if any were to be allured to that realm of death and horror by the very warning meant to discourage them.

Interrupting these sculptured walls were high windows and massive twelve-foot doorways; both now and then retaining the petrified wooden planks—elaborately carved and polished—of the actual shutters and doors. All metal fixtures had long ago vanished, but some of the doors remained in place and had to be forced aside as we progressed from room to room. Window-frames with odd transparent panes—mostly elliptical—survived here and there, though in no considerable quantity. There were also frequent niches of great magnitude, generally empty, but once in a while containing some bizarre object carved from green soapstone which was either broken or perhaps held too inferior to warrant removal. Other apertures were undoubtedly connected with bygone mechanical facilities—heating, lighting, and the like—of a sort suggested in many of the carvings. Ceilings tended to be plain, but had sometimes been inlaid with green soapstone or other tiles, mostly fallen now. Floors were also paved with such tiles, though plain stonework predominated.

As I have said, all furniture and other moveables were

---

waves, and of its struggles as the sea shrank away, and the desert crept into the fertile valley that held it" (*Dagon and Other Macabre Tales*, 104–5).

[153] *dadoes*: "Any lining, painting, or papering of the lower part of an interior wall, of a different material or colour from that of the upper part" (*Oxford English Dictionary*).

absent; but the sculptures gave a clear idea of the strange devices which had once filled these tomb-like, echoing rooms. Above the glacial sheet the floors were generally thick with detritus,[154] litter, and debris; but farther down this condition decreased. In some of the lower chambers and corridors there was little more than gritty dust or ancient incrustations, while occasional areas had an uncanny air of newly swept immaculateness. Of course, where rifts or collapses had occurred, the lower levels were as littered as the upper ones. A central court—as in other structures we had seen from the air—saved the inner regions from total darkness; so that we seldom had to use our electric torches[155] in the upper rooms except when studying sculptured details. Below the ice-cap, however, the twilight deepened; and in many parts of the tangled ground level there was an approach to absolute blackness.

To form even a rudimentary idea of our thoughts and feelings as we penetrated this aeon-silent maze of unhuman masonry one must correlate a hopelessly bewildering chaos of fugitive moods, memories, and impressions. The sheer appalling antiquity and lethal desolation of the place were enough to overwhelm almost any sensitive person, but added to these elements were the recent unexplained horror at the camp, and the revelations all too soon effected by the terrible mural sculptures around us. The moment we came upon a perfect section of carving, where no ambiguity of interpretation could exist, it took only a brief study to give us the hideous truth[156]—a truth which it would be naive to claim

---

[154] *detritus*: "Matter produced by the detrition or wearing away of exposed surfaces, especially the gravel, sand, clay, or other material eroded and washed away by aqueous agency; a mass or formation of this nature" (*Oxford English Dictionary*).

[155] *torches*: Lovecraft uses the American "flashlight" and the British "torch" interchangeably here as elsewhere in his work.

[156] Cf. the central section of Lovecraft's poem, "The Poe-et's Nightmare" (1916), entitled "Aletheia Phrikodes" (Greek for "the frightful truth").

Danforth and I had not independently suspected before, though we had carefully refrained from even hinting it to each other. There could now be no further merciful doubt about the nature of the beings which had built and inhabited this monstrous dead city millions of years ago, when man's ancestors were primitive archaic mammals, and vast dinosaurs roamed the tropical steppes of Europe and Asia.[157]

We had previously clung to a desperate alternative and insisted—each to himself—that the omnipresence of the five-pointed motif meant only some cultural or religious exaltation of the Archaean natural object which had so patently embodied the quality of five-pointedness; as the decorative motifs of Minoan Crete exalted the sacred bull,[158] those of Egypt the scarabaeus,[159] those of Rome the wolf and the eagle,[160] and those of various savage tribes some

---

[157] The period of the dinosaurs is thought to extend from roughly 200 to 65 million years ago (the Jurassic and Cretaceous periods). The first archaic mammals appeared roughly 190 million years ago.

[158] *Minoan Crete*: The pre-Greek civilisation that had been established upon the island of Crete from c. 3000 to 1000 B.C. The name Minoan was coined by Sir Arthur Evans from Minos, the mythical king of Crete.

sacred bull: The Minotaur ("the bull of Minos") was a monster said to dwell in a labyrinth at the palace of Minos at Knossos. Bull-leaping and bull-baiting were common sports in Minoan culture.

[159] *scarabaeus*: Lovecraft had long been fascinated by ancient Egyptian culture, and had ghostwritten a tale for Harry Houdini on the subject, "Under the Pyramids" (1924). Cf. also the original conception of Lovecraft's god Nyarlathotep (see note 51 to "The Rats in the Walls"). The scarabaeus (scarab) was an ornament carved in the shape of the sacred scarab beetle. It had a variety of religious and ritualistic functions; it was, for example, placed on the breast of a mummy to prevent the heart from testifying against the deceased, and it also served to ward off sickness and the evil eye.

[160] This passage is clearly a reworking of a similar one in "The Nameless City" (1921), where an investigator similarly encounters depictions of anomalous nonhuman entities on the walls of an underground temple: "These creatures, I said to myself, were to the men of the nameless city what the she-wolf was to Rome, or some totem-beast is to a tribe of Indians" (*Dagon and Other Macabre Tales*, 105). Late in life Lovecraft declared: "To me the Roman Empire will always seem the central incident of human history" (*Selected Letters*, V, 266). The wolf had been an important symbol in Roman culture from the earliest times, as the Romans fostered the myth of their founders Remus and Romulus being nurtured by a she-wolf. The eagle was considered sacred to Jupiter; the figure of an eagle surmounted the standards of the Roman legions.

chosen totem-animal. But this lone refuge was now stripped from us, and we were forced to face definitely the reason-shaking realisation which the reader of these pages has doubtless long ago anticipated. I can scarcely bear to write it down in black and white even now, but perhaps that will not be necessary.

The things once rearing and dwelling in this frightful masonry in the age of dinosaurs were not indeed dinosaurs, but far worse. Mere dinosaurs were new and almost brainless objects—but the builders of the city were wise and old, and had left certain traces in rocks even then laid down well-nigh a thousand million years ... rocks laid down before the true life of earth had advanced beyond plastic groups of cells ... rocks laid down before the true life of earth had existed at all. They were the makers and enslavers of that life, and above all doubt the originals of the fiendish elder myths which things like the Pnakotic Manuscripts and the *Necronomicon* frightedly hint about. They were the Great Old Ones that had filtered down from the stars when the earth was young—the beings whose substance an alien evolution had shaped, and whose powers were such as this planet had never bred. And to think that only the day before Danforth and I had actually looked upon fragments of their millennially fossilised substance ... and that poor Lake and his party had seen their complete outlines....

It is of course impossible for me to relate in proper order the stages by which we picked up what we know of that monstrous chapter of pre-human life. After the first shock of the certain revelation we had to pause a while to recuperate, and it was fully three o'clock before we got started on our actual tour of systematic research. The sculptures in the building we entered were of relatively late date—perhaps two million years ago—as checked up by geological, biological, and astronomical features; and embodied an art which would be called decadent in comparison with that of specimens we found in older buildings after crossing bridges under the glacial sheet. One edifice hewn from the solid rock seemed to go back forty or possibly fifty million years—to the lower Eocene or upper Cretaceous—and contained bas-reliefs of an artistry surpassing anything else, with one tremendous exception, that we encountered. That was, we have since agreed, the oldest domestic structure we traversed.

Were it not for the support of those snapshots[161] soon to be made public, I would refrain from telling what I found and inferred, lest I be confined as a madman. Of course, the infinitely early parts of the patchwork tale—representing the pre-terrestrial life of the star-headed beings on other planets, and in other galaxies, and in other universes—can readily be interpreted as the fantastic mythology of those beings themselves; yet such parts sometimes involved designs and diagrams so uncannily close to the latest findings of mathematics and astrophysics that I scarcely know what to think. Let others judge when they see the photographs I shall publish.

Naturally, no one set of carvings which we encountered told more than a fraction of any connected story; nor did we even begin to come upon the various stages of that story in their proper order. Some of the vast rooms were independent units so far as their designs were concerned, whilst in other cases a continuous chronicle would be carried through a series of rooms and corridors. The best of the maps and diagrams were on the walls of a frightful abyss below even the ancient ground level—a cavern perhaps 200 feet square and sixty feet high, which had almost undoubtedly been an educational centre of some sort. There were many provoking repetitions of the same material in different rooms and buildings; since certain chapters of experience, and certain summaries or phases of racial history, had evidently been favourites with different decorators or dwellers. Sometimes, though, variant versions of the

---

[161] *snapshots*: In both his autograph manuscript and his typescript, Lovecraft has written "flashlights" here; but this seems to be a slip of the pen.

same theme proved useful in settling debatable points and filling in gaps.

I still wonder that we deduced so much in the short time at our disposal. Of course, we even now have only the barest outline; and much of that was obtained later on from a study of the photographs and sketches we made. It may be the effect of this later study—the revived memories and vague impressions acting in conjunction with his general sensitiveness and with that final supposed horror-glimpse whose essence he will not reveal even to me—which has been the immediate source of Danforth's present breakdown. But it had to be; for we could not issue our warning intelligently without the fullest possible information, and the issuance of that warning is a prime necessity. Certain lingering influences in that unknown antarctic world of disordered time and alien natural law make it imperative that further exploration be discouraged.

VII.

The full story, so far as deciphered, will shortly appear in an official bulletin of Miskatonic University. Here I shall sketch only the salient high lights in a formless, rambling way. Myth or otherwise, the sculptures told of the coming of those star-headed things to the nascent, lifeless earth out of cosmic space—their coming, and the coming of many other alien entities such as at certain times embark upon spatial pioneering. They seemed able to traverse the interstellar ether on their vast membraneous wings[162]—thus oddly confirming some

---

[162] This idea seems to us preposterous, especially since the ether is no longer believed to exist. The luminiferous ("light-bearing") ether was a conception of nineteenth-century science, derived ultimately from Aristotle. Working on the belief that light could not travel through a vacuum, it was thought that an ether—what Ernst Haeckel termed "an extremely attenuated medium, filling the whole of space outside of ponderable matter"—was required to allow the particles (as they were then conceived) of light to travel

curious hill folklore long ago told me by an antiquarian colleague. They had lived under the sea a good deal, building fantastic cities and fighting terrific battles with nameless adversaries by means of intricate devices employing unknown principles of energy. Evidently their scientific and mechanical knowledge far surpassed man's today,[163] though they made use of its more widespread and elaborate forms only when obliged to. Some of the sculptures suggested that they had passed through a stage of mechanised life on other planets, but had receded upon finding its effects emotionally unsatisfying.[164] Their

---

through space. Haeckel continues: "The existence of ether (or cosmic ether) as a real element is a *positive fact*, and has been known as such for the last twelve years. ... Although, however, the existence of ether is now regarded as a positive fact by nearly all physicists, and although many effects of this remarkable substance are familiar to us through an extensive experience ... yet we are still far from being clear and confident as to its real character." Haeckel attempts to prove that ether fills the whole of space that is not occupied by matter, and that it has no chemical quality and is not composed of atoms. See Ernst Haeckel, *The Riddle of the Universe*, tr. Joseph McCabe (New York: Harper & Brothers, 1900), 225–28. Einstein's theory of relativity was the death blow to the ether, and it soon dropped out of physics. But in 1936 Lovecraft heard a lecture by Professor Dayton C. Miller who continued to deny Einstein and assert the existence of the ether. Lovecraft concluded: "If Miller is right, the whole fabrick of relativity collapses, and we have once more the absolute dimensions and real time which we had before 1905" (*Selected Letters*, V, 255).

The idea of the Old Ones flying through the ether on wings also strikes us as ridiculous, but Lovecraft used the same idea for the fungi from Yuggoth in "The Whisperer in Darkness" (1930); this is what Lovecraft here refers to as "curious hill folklore ... told me by an antiquarian colleague" (i.e., Albert N. Wilmarth).

[163] Cf. "The Whisperer in Darkness" (1930) on the fungi from Yuggoth: "Their brain-capacity exceeds that of any other surviving life-form" (*The Dunwich Horror and Others*, 240). See also "The Shadow Out of Time" (1934–35) on the Great Race: "their intelligence was enormously greater than man's" (*The Dunwich Horror and Others*, 393).

[164] This single sentence points to a central concern in Lovecraft's later political philosophy: the psychological and cultural effects of mechanized industrialism upon human beings. In 1929 he wrote: "Mechanical invention has, for better or for worse, permanently altered mankind's relationship to his setting & to the forces of nature generally; & has just as inevitably begun to produce a new type of organisation among his own numbers as a result of changed modes of housing, transportation, manufacture, agriculture, commerce, & economic adjustment" (*Selected Letters*, II, 280–81). In speaking of the Old Ones' abandonment of mechanization, Lovecraft echoes what he says in "The Mound" (1929–30), suggesting that human civilisation can somehow overcome the machine: "Many of the old mechanical devices were still in use, though others had been abandoned when it was seen that they failed to give pleasure ... Industry, being found

preternatural toughness of organisation and simplicity of natural wants made them peculiarly able to live on a high plane without the more specialised fruits of artificial manufacture, and even without garments except for occasional protection against the elements.

It was under the sea, at first for food and later for other purposes, that they first created earth-life—using available substances according to long-known methods. The more elaborate experiments came after the annihilation of various cosmic enemies. They had done the same thing on other planets; having manufactured not only necessary foods, but certain multicellular protoplasmic masses capable of moulding their tissues into all sorts of temporary organs under hypnotic influence and thereby forming ideal slaves to perform the heavy work of the community. These viscous masses were without doubt what Abdul Alhazred whispered about as the "shoggoths"[165] in his frightful *Necronomicon,* though even that mad Arab had not hinted that any existed on earth except in the dreams of those who had chewed a certain alkaloidal herb. When the star-headed Old Ones on this planet had synthesised their simple food forms and bred a good supply of shoggoths they allowed other cell-groups to develop into other forms of animal and vegetable life for sundry purposes; extirpating any whose presence became troublesome.

With the aid of the shoggoths, whose expansions could

---

fundamentally futile except for the supplying of basic needs and the gratification of inescapable yearnings, had become very simple. Physical comfort was ensured by an urban mechanisation of standardised and easily maintained pattern ..." (*The Horror in the Museum and Other Revisions,* 134).

[165] *shoggoths:* These creatures were first cited in "Night-Gaunts," sonnet XX of *Fungi from Yuggoth* (1929-30): "And down the nether pits to that foul lake / Where the puffed shoggoths splash in doubtful sleep." Almost simultaneously they appear (without being named) in "The Mound" (1929–30): " ... when the men of K'n-yan went down into N'kai's black abyss with their great atom-power searchlights they found living things— living things that oozed along stone channels and worshipped onyx and basalt images of Tsathoggua. But they were not toads like Tsathoggua himself. Far worse—they were amorphous lumps of viscous black slime that took temporary shapes for various purposes" (*The Horror in the Museum and Other Revisions,* 141). See Will Murray, "The Trouble with Shoggoths," *Crypt of Cthulhu* No. 32 (St. John's Eve 1985):35–38.

be made to lift prodigious weights, the small, low cities under the sea grew to vast and imposing labyrinths of stone not unlike those which later rose on land. Indeed, the highly adaptable Old Ones had lived much on land in other parts of the universe, and probably retained many traditions of land construction. As we studied the architecture of all these sculptured palaeogean cities, including that whose aeon-dead corridors we were even then traversing, we were impressed by a curious coincidence which we have not yet tried to explain, even to ourselves. The tops of the buildings, which in the actual city around us had of course been weathered into shapeless ruins ages ago, were clearly displayed in the bas-reliefs; and shewed vast clusters of needle-like spires, delicate finials on certain cone and pyramid apexes, and tiers of thin, horizontal scalloped discs capping cylindrical shafts. This was exactly what we had seen in that monstrous and portentous mirage, cast by a dead city whence such skyline features had been absent for thousands and tens of thousands of years, which loomed on our ignorant eyes across the unfathomed mountains of madness as we first approached poor Lake's ill-fated camp.

Of the life of the Old Ones, both under the sea and after part of them migrated to land, volumes could be written. Those in shallow water had continued the fullest use of the eyes at the ends of their five main head tentacles, and had practiced the arts of sculpture and of writing in quite the usual way—the writing accomplished with a stylus on waterproof waxen surfaces. Those lower down in the ocean depths, though they used a curious phosphorescent organism to furnish light, pieced out their vision with obscure special senses operating through the prismatic cilia on their heads—senses which rendered all the Old Ones partly independent of light in emergencies. Their forms of sculpture and writing had changed curiously during the descent, embodying certain apparently chemical coating processes—probably to secure phosphorescence—which the bas-reliefs could not make clear to us. The beings moved in the sea partly by swimming—using the lateral crinoid arms—and partly by wriggling with the lower tier of tentacles containing the pseudo-feet. Occasionally they accomplished long swoops with the auxiliary use of two or more sets of their fan-like folding wings. On land they locally used the pseudo-feet, but now and then flew to great heights or over long distances with their wings. The many slender tentacles into which the crinoid arms branched were infinitely delicate, flexible, strong, and accurate in muscular-nervous coordination; ensuring the utmost skill and dexterity in all artistic and other manual operations.

The toughness of the things was almost incredible. Even the terrific pressures of the deepest sea-bottoms appeared powerless to harm them. Very few seemed to die at all except by violence, and their burial-places were very limited. The fact that they covered their vertically inhumed dead with five-pointed inscribed mounds set up thoughts in Danforth and me which made a fresh pause and recuperation necessary after the sculptures revealed it. The beings multiplied by means of spores[166]—like vegetable pteridophytes as Lake had suspected—but owing to their prodigious toughness and longevity, and consequent lack of replacement needs, they did not encourage the large-scale development of new prothalli except when they had new regions to colonise. The young matured swiftly, and received an education evidently beyond any standard we can imagine. The prevailing intellectual and aesthetic life was highly evolved, and produced a tenaciously enduring set of customs and institutions which I shall describe more fully in my coming monograph. These varied slightly according to sea or land residence, but had the same foundations and essentials.

---

[166] Cf. the Great Race in "The Shadow Out of Time" (1934-35): "They had no sex, but reproduced through seeds or spores which clustered on their bases and could be developed only under water" (*The Dunwich Horror and Others*, 399).

Though able, like vegetables, to derive nourishment from inorganic substances; they vastly preferred organic and especially animal food. They ate uncooked marine life under the sea, but cooked their viands on land. They hunted game and raised meat herds—slaughtering with sharp weapons whose odd marks on certain fossil bones our expedition had noted. They resisted all ordinary temperatures marvellously; and in their natural state could live in water down to freezing. When the great chill of the Pleistocene drew on, however—nearly a million years ago—the land dwellers had to resort to special measures including artificial heating; until at last the deadly cold appears to have driven them back into the sea. For their prehistoric flights through cosmic space, legend said, they had absorbed certain chemicals and became almost independent of eating, breathing, or heat conditions; but by the time of the great cold they had lost track of the method. In any case they could not have prolonged the artificial state indefinitely without harm.

Being non-pairing and semi-vegetable in structure, the Old Ones had no biological basis for the family phase of mammal life; but seemed to organise large households on the principles of comfortable space-utility and—as we deduced from the pictured occupations and diversions of co-dwellers—congenial mental association.[167] In furnishing their homes they kept everything in the centre of the huge rooms, leaving all the wall spaces free for decorative treatment. Lighting, in the case of the land inhabitants, was accomplished by a device probably electro-chemical in nature. Both on land and under water they used curious tables, chairs, and couches like cylindrical frames—for they rested and slept upright with folded-down tentacles—and racks for the hinged sets of dotted surfaces forming their books.

---

[167] Cf. the Great Race in "The Shadow Out of Time" (1934–35): "Family organisation was not overstressed, though ties among persons of common descent were recognised, and the young were generally reared by their parents" (*The Dunwich Horror and Others*, 399).

Government was evidently complex and probably socialistic,[168] though no certainties in this regard could be deduced from the sculptures we saw. There was extensive commerce, both local and between different cities; certain small, flat counters, five-pointed and inscribed, serving as money. Probably the smaller of the various greenish soapstones found by our expedition were pieces of such currency. Though the culture was mainly urban, some agriculture and much stock-raising existed. Mining and a limited amount of manufacturing were also practiced. Travel was very frequent, but permanent migration seemed relatively rare except for the vast colonising movements by which the race expanded. For personal locomotion no external aid was used; since in land, air, and water movement alike the Old Ones seemed to possess excessively vast capacities for speed. Loads, however, were drawn by beasts of burden—shoggoths under the sea, and a curious variety of primitive vertebrates in the later years of land existence.

These vertebrates, as well as an infinity of other life-forms— animal and vegetable, marine, and aërial—were the products of unguided evolution acting on life-cells made by the Old Ones but escaping beyond their radius of attention. They had been suffered to develop unchecked because they had not come in conflict with the dominant beings. Bothersome forms, of course, were mechanically exterminated. It interested us to see in some of the very last and most decadent sculptures a shambling[169] primitive mammal, used

---

[168] An indication that Lovecraft himself had converted to a moderate, non-Marxist socialism by this time. In July 1931, speaking of the effects of "technological unemployment" (whereby machines have permanently replaced human beings in many occupations), Lovecraft stated that the artificial shortening of working hours for all individuals is the only solution against a revolt of the unemployed. "If the existing social order is to last, more money must be distributed in some way or other, regardless of normal principles of profit. Socialistic measures like those already in force in England—old age pensions & unemployment insurance—the so-called 'dole'—will be as necessary as fire-engines at a fire" (*Selected Letters*, III, 386–87).

[169] Cf. a phrase earlier in this work: " ... long before any human race we know had shambled out of apedom" (p. 250).

sometimes for food and sometimes as an amusing buffoon by the land dwellers, whose vaguely simian and human foreshadowings were unmistakable. In the building of land cities the huge stone blocks of the high towers were generally lifted by vast-winged pterodactyls of a species heretofore unknown to palaeontology.

The persistence with which the Old Ones survived various geologic changes and convulsions of the earth's crust was little short of miraculous. Though few or none of their first cities seem to have remained beyond the Archaean age, there was no interruption in their civilisation or in the transmission of their records. Their original place of advent to the planet was the Antarctic Ocean, and it is likely that they came not long after the matter forming the moon was wrenched from the neighbouring South Pacific.[170] According to one of the sculptured maps, the whole globe was then under water, with stone cities scattered farther and farther from the antarctic as aeons passed. Another map shews a vast bulk of dry land around the south pole, where it is evident that some of the beings made experimental settlements though their main centres were transferred to the nearest sea-bottom. Later maps, which display this land mass as cracking and drifting, and sending certain detached parts northward, uphold in a striking way the theories of continental drift lately advanced by Taylor, Wegener, and Joly.[171]

---

[170] This theory of the moon's origin was commonly held in Lovecraft's day, although ironically it was the continental drift theory, which Lovecraft here also embraces (see n. 171 below), that cast doubt on it, since continental drift renders the Pacific Ocean a merely ephemeral feature in geological time. One scholar, Peter H. Cadogan, now regards this "fission hypothesis" as "clearly the least-popular theory for lunar origin" (*The Moon—Our Sister Planet* [Cambridge: Cambridge University Press, 1981], 356).

[171] Lovecraft was in a distinct minority in supporting the continental drift theory at this time, as it was doubted by many geologists; it must also be stated that the proponents of continental drift had failed to provide a proper rationale for the theory, and such a rationale was not forthcoming until the 1960s.

In 1910 Frank Bursley Taylor (1860–1938) published a paper, "Bearing of the Tertiary Mountain Belt on the Origin of the Earth's Plan," in *Bulletin of the Geological Society of*

With the upheaval of new land in the South Pacific tremendous events began. Some of the marine cities were
hopelessly shattered, yet that was not the worst misfortune.
Another race—a land race of beings shaped like octopi and
probably corresponding to the fabulous pre-human spawn
of Cthulhu—soon began filtering down from cosmic infinity and precipitated a monstrous war which for a time drove
the Old Ones wholly back to the sea—a colossal blow in
view of the increasing land settlements.[172] Later peace was
made, and the new lands were given to the Cthulhu spawn
whilst the Old Ones held the sea and the older lands. New
land cities were founded—the greatest of them in the antarctic, for this region of first arrival was sacred. From then
on, as before, the antarctic remained the centre of the Old
Ones' civilisation, and all the discoverable cities built there
by the Cthulhu spawn were blotted out. Then suddenly the
lands of the Pacific sank again, taking with them the frightful stone city of R'lyeh and all the cosmic octopi, so that
the Old Ones were again supreme on the planet except for
one shadowy fear about which they did not like to speak.
At a rather later age their cities dotted all the land and water areas of the globe—hence the recommendation in my
coming monograph that some archaeologist make system-

America, outlining the theory. But it was the German geologist Alfred Lothar Wegener
(1880–1930) who became the theory's chief exponent: he delivered a paper in 1912
(almost certainly conceived independently of Taylor) on the subject and then published
a book, Die Enstehung der Kontinente und Ozeane (1915), translated in 1924 as The Origins
of Continents and Oceans. John Joly (1857–1933) took up Wegener's work in The Surface
History of the Earth (1925). Conferences on continental drift were held in 1922, 1923, and
1926; at the last conference a majority decided against the theory. The chief difficulty was
in devising a plausible mechanism for drift. Wegener's belief that the continents merely
floated like rafts to their current positions proved to be untenable. It was only in 1961
that R. S. Dietz published a paper placing the source of drift much lower under the
earth's crust than Wegener, thereby answering many geologists' objections to the theory.
See Gabriel Gohau, A History of Geology (New Brunswick, NJ: Rutgers University Press,
1990), 187–200.

[172] The "pre-human spawn of Cthulhu" are clearly the "Great Old Ones" referred to in
"The Call of Cthulhu" (see note 88 above). In that story it is not made clear when the
spawn of Cthulhu arrived on the earth; it is merely said that "the Great Old Ones ... lived
ages before there were any men" (The Dunwich Horror and Others, 139).

atic borings with Pabodie's type of apparatus in certain widely separated regions.

The steady trend down the ages was from water to land; a movement encouraged by the rise of new land masses, though the ocean was never wholly deserted. Another cause of the landward movement was the new difficulty in breeding and managing the shoggoths upon which successful sea-life depended. With the march of time, as the sculptures sadly confessed, the art of creating new life from inorganic matter had been lost; so that the Old Ones had to depend on the moulding of forms already in existence. On land the great reptiles proved highly tractable; but the shoggoths of the sea, reproducing by fission and acquiring a dangerous degree of accidental intelligence, presented for a time a formidable problem.

They had always been controlled through the hypnotic suggestion of the Old Ones, and had modelled their tough plasticity into various useful temporary limbs and organs; but now their self-modelling powers were sometimes exercised independently, and in various imitative forms implanted by past suggestion. They had, it seems, developed a semi-stable brain whose separate and occasionally stubborn volition echoed the will of the Old Ones without always obeying it. Sculptured images of these shoggoths filled Danforth and me with horror and loathing. They were normally shapeless entities composed of a viscous jelly which looked like an agglutination of bubbles; and each averaged about fifteen feet in diameter when a sphere. They had, however, a constantly shifting shape and volume; throwing out temporary developments or forming apparent organs of sight, hearing, and speech in imitation of their masters, either spontaneously or according to suggestion.

They seem to have become peculiarly intractable toward the middle of the Permian age, perhaps 150 million years ago,[173] when a veritable war of re-subjugation was waged

---

[173] The Permian period is now thought to extend from 280 to 225 million years ago. A date 150 million years ago would now be regarded as part of the Upper Jurassic.

upon them by the marine Old Ones. Pictures of this war, and of the headless, slime-coated fashion in which the shoggoths typically left their slain victims, held a marvellously fearsome quality despite the intervening abyss of untold ages. The Old Ones had used curious weapons of molecular disturbance against the rebel entities, and in the end had achieved a complete victory. Thereafter the sculptures shewed a period in which shoggoths were tamed and broken by armed Old Ones as the wild horses of the American west were tamed by cowboys. Though during the rebellion the shoggoths had shewn an ability to live out of water, this transition was not encouraged; since their usefulness on land would hardly have been commensurate with the trouble of their management.

During the Jurassic age the Old Ones met fresh adversity in the form of a new invasion from outer space—this time by half-fungous, half-crustacean creatures from a planet identifiable as the remote and recently discovered Pluto;[174] creatures undoubtedly the same as those figuring in certain whispered hill legends of the north, and remembered in the Himalayas as the Mi-Go, or Abominable Snow-Men.[175] To fight these beings the Old Ones attempted, for the first time since their terrene advent, to sally forth again into the planetary ether; but despite all traditional preparations found it no longer possible to leave the earth's atmosphere. Whatever the old secret of interstellar travel

---

[174] The phrase "from a planet … Pluto," appearing in Lovecraft's typescript, was omitted in the *Astounding* appearance and not restored by Lovecraft. It is possible that this was a deliberate omission on Lovecraft's part, since by 1936 he may no longer have regarded Pluto as "recently" discovered (Pluto had been discovered in early 1930).

[175] A clear reference to the fungi from Yuggoth from "The Whisperer in Darkness" (see note 123 above). Again, it is not made clear in that story when the fungi first came to earth from Yuggoth; it is only mentioned that "'they were here long before the fabulous epoch of Cthulhu was over, and remember all about sunken R'lyeh when it was above the waters'" (*The Dunwich Horror and Others*, 254). This statement itself suggests a possible conflict with an earlier portion of this story, since the sinking of R'lyeh appears to have occurred at an earlier epoch (see p. 278). But Lovecraft rarely felt obliged to adhere to data cited in earlier stories, and this is probably a willful change on his part.

had been, it was now definitely lost to the race. In the end the Mi-Go drove the Old Ones out of all the northern lands, though they were powerless to disturb those in the sea. Little by little the slow retreat of the elder race to their original antarctic habitat was beginning.

It was curious to note from the pictured battles that both the Cthulhu spawn and the Mi-Go seem to have been composed of matter more widely different from that which we know than was the substance of the Old Ones. They were able to undergo transformations and reintegrations impossible for their adversaries, and seem therefore to have originally come from even remoter gulfs of cosmic space. The Old Ones, but for their abnormal toughness and peculiar vital properties, were strictly material, and must have had their absolute origin within the known space-time continuum; whereas the first sources of the other beings can only be guessed at with bated breath. All this, of course, assuming that the non-terrestrial linkages and the anomalies ascribed to the invading foes are not pure mythology. Conceivably, the Old Ones might have invented a cosmic framework to account for their occasional defeats; since historical interest and pride obviously formed their chief psychological element. It is significant that their annals failed to mention many advanced and potent races of beings whose mighty cultures and towering cities figure persistently in certain obscure legends.[176]

The changing state of the world through long geologic ages appeared with startling vividness in many of the sculptured maps and scenes. In certain cases existing science will require revision, while in other cases its bold deductions are magnificently confirmed. As I have said,

---

[176] This sentence does not appear in Lovecraft's autograph ms. or typescript, but appears in the *Astounding* text; it must have been added by hand in the typescript sent to *Astounding*. This supposition is supported by the fact that *Astounding* rendered the word "cities" as "ethics" (it was corrected by hand in Lovecraft's copy of the appearance), perhaps because *Astounding*'s typesetters could not read Lovecraft's handwriting here.

the hypothesis of Taylor, Wegener, and Joly that all the continents are fragments of an original antarctic land mass which cracked from centrifugal force and drifted apart over a technically viscous lower surface—an hypothesis suggested by such things as the complementary outlines of Africa and South America, and the way the great mountain chains are rolled and shoved up—receives striking support from this uncanny source.

Maps evidently shewing the Carboniferous[177] world of an hundred million or more years ago displayed significant rifts and chasms destined later to separate Africa from the once continuous realms of Europe (then the Valusia of hellish primal legend), Asia, the Americas, and the antarctic continent. Other charts—and most significantly one in connexion with the founding fifty million years ago of the vast dead city around us—shewed all the present continents well differentiated. And in the latest discoverable specimen—dating perhaps from the Pliocene age—the approximate world of today appeared quite clearly despite the linkage of Alaska with Siberia, of North America with Europe through Greenland, and of South America with the antarctic continent[178] through Graham Land. In the Carboniferous map the whole globe—ocean floor and rifted land mass alike—bore symbols of the Old Ones' vast stone cities, but in the later charts the gradual recession toward the antarctic became very plain. The final Pliocene specimen shewed no land cities except on the antarctic continent and the tip of South America, nor any ocean cities north of the fiftieth parallel of South Latitude. Knowledge and interest in the northern world, save for a study of coast-lines probably

---

[177] *Carboniferous*: A period extending from 345 to 280 million years ago. The term is now generally archaic, it being replaced by two geological periods, the Mississippian (345 to 325 million years ago) and the Pennsylvanian (325 to 280 million years ago).

[178] Lovecraft's autograph ms. and typescript read "with a still undivided antarctic continent" (see note 46 above).

made during long exploration flights on those fan-like
membraneous wings, had evidently declined to zero
among the Old Ones.

Destruction of cities through the upthrust of mountains,
the centrifugal rending of continents, the seismic convulsions of land or sea-bottom, and other natural causes was
a matter of common record; and it was curious to observe
how fewer and fewer replacements were made as the ages
wore on. The vast dead megalopolis that yawned around
us seemed to be the last general centre of the race; built
early in the Cretaceous age after a titanic earth-buckling[179]
had obliterated a still vaster predecessor not far distant. It
appeared that this general region was the most sacred spot
of all, where reputedly the first Old Ones had settled on a
primal sea-bottom. In the new city—many of whose features we could recognise in the sculptures, but which
stretched fully an hundred miles along the mountain-range
in each direction beyond the farthest limits of our aërial
survey—there were reputed to be preserved certain sacred
stones forming part of the first sea-bottom city, which were
thrust up to light after long epochs in the course of the
general crumpling of strata.

VIII.

Naturally, Danforth and I studied with especial interest
and a peculiarly personal sense of awe everything pertaining to the immediate district in which we were. Of this
local material there was naturally a vast abundance; and
on the tangled ground level of the city we were lucky
enough to find a house of very late date whose walls, though

---

[179] Lovecraft's autograph ms. and typescript read: "earth-buckling—the one which had
sundered the antarctic continent and joined Ross and Weddell Seas—" (see note 46
above).

somewhat damaged by a neighbouring rift, contained sculptures of decadent workmanship carrying the story of the region much beyond the period of the Pliocene map whence we derived our last general glimpse of the pre-human world. This was the last place we examined in detail, since what we found there gave us a fresh immediate objective.

Certainly, we were in one of the strangest, weirdest, and most terrible of all the corners of earth's globe. Of all existing lands it was infinitely the most ancient; and the conviction grew upon us that this hideous upland must indeed be the fabled nightmare plateau of Leng which even the mad author of the *Necronomicon* was reluctant to discuss. The great mountain chain was tremendously long—starting as a low range at Luitpold Land[180] on the coast of Weddell Sea and virtually crossing the entire continent. The really high part stretched in a mighty arc from about Latitude 82°, E. Longitude 60° to Latitude 70°, E. Longitude 115°, with its concave side toward our camp and its seaward end in the region of that long, ice-locked coast whose hills were glimpsed by Wilkes[181] and Mawson at the Antarctic Circle.

Yet even more monstrous exaggerations of Nature seemed disturbingly close at hand. I have said that these peaks are higher than the Himalayas, but the sculptures forbid me to say that they are earth's highest. That grim honour is beyond doubt reserved for something which half the sculptures hesitated to record at all, whilst others approached it with obvious repugnance and trepidation. It seems that there was one part of the ancient land—the first part that ever rose from the waters after the earth had flung off the moon and the Old Ones had seeped down from the stars—which had come to be shunned as vaguely

---

[180] Now termed Luitpold Coast, located in Coats Land facing the Weddell Sea.

[181] Charles Wilkes (1798–1877), American explorer who went to Antarctica in 1838–40 to test John Cleves Symmes's theory of the hollow earth. One of Lovecraft's nonextant juvenile treatises was *Wilkes's Explorations* (c. 1902).

and namelessly evil. Cities built there had crumbled before their time, and had been found suddenly deserted. Then when the first great earth-buckling had convulsed the region in the Comanchian age, a frightful line of peaks had shot suddenly up amidst the most appalling din and chaos—and earth had received her loftiest and most terrible mountains.

If the scale of the carvings was correct, these abhorred things must have been much over 40,000 feet high—radically vaster than even the shocking mountains of madness we had crossed. They extended, it appeared, from about Latitude 77°, E. Longitude 70° to Latitude 70°, E. Longitude 100°—less than 300 miles away from the dead city, so that we would have spied their dreaded summits in the dim western distance had it not been for that vague opalescent haze. Their northern end must likewise be visible from the long Antarctic Circle coast-line at Queen Mary Land.

Some of the Old Ones, in the decadent days, had made strange prayers to those mountains; but none ever went near them or dared to guess what lay beyond. No human eye had ever seen them, and as I studied the emotions conveyed in the carvings I prayed that none ever might. There are protecting hills along the coast beyond them—Queen Mary and Kaiser Wilhelm Lands[182]—and I thank heaven no one has been able to land and climb those hills. I am not as sceptical about old tales and fears as I used to be, and I do not laugh now at the pre-human sculptor's notion that lightning paused meaningfully now and then at each of the brooding crests, and that an unexplained glow shone from one of those terrible pinnacles all through the long polar night. There may be a very real and very monstrous meaning in the old Pnakotic whispers about Kadath in the Cold Waste.[183]

---

[182] For Queen Mary Land, see note 60 above. Kaiser Wilhelm II Land is now termed Leopold and Castrid Coast; it is to the east of Queen Mary Coast, facing the West Ice Shelf.

[183] For Kadath, see note 66 to "The Dunwich Horror."

But the terrain close at hand was hardly less strange, even if less namelessly accursed. Soon after the founding of the city the great mountain-range became the seat of the principal temples, and many carvings shewed what grotesque and fantastic towers had pierced the sky where now we saw only the curiously clinging cubes and ramparts. In the course of ages the caves had appeared, and had been shaped into adjuncts of the temples. With the advance of still later epochs all the limestone veins of the region were hollowed out by ground waters, so that the mountains, the foothills, and the plains below them were a veritable network of connected caverns and galleries. Many graphic sculptures told of explorations deep underground, and of the final discovery of the Stygian[184] sunless sea that lurked at earth's bowels.

This vast nighted gulf had undoubtedly been worn by the great river which flowed down from the nameless and horrible westward mountains, and which had formerly turned at the base of the Old Ones' range and flowed beside that chain into the Indian Ocean between Budd and Totten Lands[185] on Wilkes's coast-line. Little by little it had eaten away the limestone hill base at its turning, till at last its sapping currents reached the caverns of the ground waters and joined with them in digging a deeper abyss. Finally its whole bulk emptied into the hollow hills and left the old bed toward the ocean dry. Much of the later city as we now found it had been built over that former bed. The Old Ones, understanding what had happened, and exercising their always keen artistic sense, had carved into ornate pylons those headlands of the foothills where the great stream began its descent into eternal darkness.

This river, once crossed by scores of noble stone bridges, was plainly the one whose extinct course we had seen in

---

[184] *Stygian*: Adjectival form of Styx, one of the five rivers in the Greek underworld.

[185] Budd Land is now termed Budd Coast, located in Wilkes Land to the west of Knox Coast. Totten Land is a region west of Budd Coast and is now termed the Sabrina Coast.

our aëroplane survey. Its position in different carvings of
the city helped us to orient ourselves to the scene as it
had been at various stages of the region's age-long, aeon-
dead history; so that we were able to sketch a hasty but
careful map of the salient features—squares, important
buildings, and the like—for guidance in further explorations. We could soon reconstruct in fancy the whole stupendous thing as it was a million or ten million or fifty
million years ago,[186] for the sculptures told us exactly what
the buildings and mountains and squares and suburbs and
landscape setting and luxuriant Tertiary vegetation had
looked like. It must have had a marvellous and mystic
beauty, and as I thought of it I almost forgot the clammy
sense of sinister oppression with which the city's inhuman age and massiveness and deadness and remoteness
and glacial twilight had choked and weighed on my spirit.
Yet according to certain carvings the denizens of that city
had themselves known the clutch of oppressive terror; for
there was a sombre and recurrent type of scene in which
the Old Ones were shewn in the act of recoiling
affrightedly from some object—never allowed to appear in
the design—found in the great river and indicated as having been washed down through waving, vine-draped cycad-
forests from those horrible westward mountains.

It was only in the one late-built house with the decadent
carvings that we obtained any foreshadowing of the final
calamity leading to the city's desertion. Undoubtedly there
must have been many sculptures of the same age elsewhere,
even allowing for the slackened energies and aspirations of
a stressful and uncertain period; indeed, very certain evidence of the existence of others came to us shortly afterward. But this was the first and only set we directly
encountered. We meant to look farther later on; but as I
have said, immediate conditions dictated another present

---

[186] Cf. a similar usage in "The Rats in the Walls": " ... the events which must have taken place there three hundred, or a thousand, or two thousand, or ten thousand years ago" (p. 50).

objective. There would, though, have been a limit—for after all hope of a long future occupancy of the place had perished among the Old Ones, there could not but have been a complete cessation of mural decoration. The ultimate blow, of course, was the coming of the great cold which once held most of the earth in thrall, and which has never departed from the ill-fated poles—the great cold that, at the world's other extremity, put an end to the fabled lands of Lomar and Hyperborea.[187]

Just when this tendency began in the antarctic it would be hard to say in terms of exact years. Nowadays we set the beginning of the general glacial periods at a distance of about 500,000 years from the present, but at the poles the terrible scourge must have commenced much earlier. All quantitative estimates are partly guesswork; but it is quite likely that the decadent sculptures were made considerably less than a million years ago, and that the actual desertion of the city was complete long before the conventional opening of the Pleistocene—500,000 years ago—as reckoned in terms of the earth's whole surface.

In the decadent sculptures there were signs of thinner vegetation everywhere, and of a decreased country life on the part of the Old Ones. Heating devices were shewn in the houses, and winter travellers were represented as muffled in protective fabrics. Then we saw a series of cartouches (the continuous band arrangement being frequently interrupted in these late carvings) depicting a constantly growing migration to the nearest refuges of greater warmth—some fleeing to cities under the sea off the far-away coast, and some clambering down through networks of limestone caverns in the hollow hills to the neighbouring black abyss of subterrene waters.

In the end it seems to have been the neighbouring abyss which received the greatest colonisation. This was partly

---

[187]   For Lomar, see note 133 above; for Hyperborea, note 125 above.

due, no doubt, to the traditional sacredness of this especial region; but may have been more conclusively determined by the opportunities it gave for continuing the use
of the great temples on the honeycombed mountains, and
for retaining the vast land city as a place of summer residence and base of communication with various mines. The
linkage of old and new abodes was made more effective by
means of several gradings and improvements along the
connecting routes, including the chiselling of numerous
direct tunnels from the ancient metropolis to the black
abyss—sharply down-pointing tunnels whose mouths we
carefully drew, according to our most thoughtful estimates,
on the guide map we were compiling. It was obvious that
at least two of these tunnels lay within a reasonable exploring distance of where we were; both being on the
mountainward edge of the city, one less than a quarter-mile
toward the ancient river-course, and the other perhaps
twice that distance in the opposite direction.

The abyss, it seems, had shelving shores of dry land at
certain places; but the Old Ones built their new city under
water—no doubt because of its greater certainty of uniform warmth. The depth of the hidden sea appears to have
been very great, so that the earth's internal heat could
ensure its habitability for an indefinite period. The beings
seem to have had no trouble in adapting themselves to
part-time—and eventually, of course, whole-time—residence under water; since they had never allowed their gill
systems to atrophy. There were many sculptures which
shewed how they had always frequently visited their submarine kinsfolk elsewhere, and how they had habitually
bathed on the deep bottom of their great river. The darkness of inner earth could likewise have been no deterrent
to a race accustomed to a long antarctic nights.

Decadent though their style undoubtedly was, these latest carvings had a truly epic quality where they told of the
building of the new city in the cavern sea. The Old Ones
had gone about it scientifically; quarrying insoluble rocks

from the heart of the honeycombed mountains, and employing expert workers from the nearest submarine city to perform the construction according to the best methods. These
workers brought with them all that was necessary to establish the new venture—shoggoth-tissue from which to breed
stone-lifters and subsequent beasts of burden for the cavern
city, and other protoplasmic matter to mould into phosphorescent organisms for lighting purposes.

At last a mighty metropolis rose on the bottom of that
Stygian sea; its architecture much like that of the city above,
and its workmanship displaying relatively little decadence
because of the precise mathematical element inherent in
building operations. The newly bred shoggoths grew to enormous size and singular intelligence, and were represented as
taking and executing orders with marvellous quickness. They
seemed to converse with the Old Ones by mimicking their
voices—a sort of musical piping over a wide range, if poor
Lake's dissection had indicated aright—and to work more
from spoken commands than from hypnotic suggestions as
in earlier times. They were, however, kept in admirable con-
trol. The phosphorescent organisms supplied light with vast
effectiveness, and doubtless atoned for the loss of the familiar polar auroras of the outer-world night.

Art and decoration were pursued, though of course with
a certain decadence. The Old Ones seemed to realise this
falling off themselves; and in many cases anticipated the
policy of Constantine the Great by transplanting especially
fine blocks of ancient carving from their land city, just as
the emperor, in a similar age of decline, stripped Greece
and Asia of their finest art to give his new Byzantine capital greater splendours than its own people could create.[188]
That the transfer of sculptured blocks had not been more

---

[188] Constantine I (Flavius Valerius Constantinus), Emperor of Rome from 306 to 337,
founded Constantinople ("the city of Constantine"; now Istanbul) in A.D. 324 on the site of
the former Greek city of Byzantium, making it the eastern capital of the Roman Empire.
Although founded as a Christian city, it was adorned with many works of art taken from pagan
temples. Constantinople later became the capital of the Byzantine Empire.

extensive, was doubtless owing to the fact that the land city was not at first wholly abandoned. By the time total abandonment did occur—and it surely must have occurred before the polar Pleistocene was far advanced—the Old Ones had perhaps become satisfied with their decadent art—or had ceased to recognise the superior merit of the older carvings. At any rate, the aeon-silent ruins around us had certainly undergone no wholesale sculptural denudation; though all the best separate statues, like other moveables, had been taken away.

The decadent cartouches and dadoes telling this story were, as I have said, the latest we could find in our limited search. They left us with a picture of the Old Ones shuttling back and forth betwixt the land city in summer and the sea-cavern city in winter, and sometimes trading with the sea-bottom cities off the antarctic coast. By this time the ultimate doom of the land city must have been recognised, for the sculptures shewed many signs of the cold's malign encroachments. Vegetation was declining, and the terrible snows of the winter no longer melted completely even in midsummer. The saurian livestock were nearly all dead, and the mammals were standing it none too well. To keep on with the work of the upper world it had become necessary to adapt some of the amorphous and curiously cold-resistant shoggoths to land life; a thing the Old Ones had formerly been reluctant to do. The great river was now lifeless, and the upper sea had lost most of its denizens except the seals and whales. All the birds had flown away, save only the great, grotesque penguins.

What had happened afterward we could only guess. How long had the new sea-cavern city survived? Was it still down there, a stony corpse in eternal blackness? Had the subterranean waters frozen at last? To what fate had the ocean-bottom cities of the outer world been delivered? Had any of the Old Ones shifted north ahead of the creeping ice-cap? Existing geology shews no trace of their presence. Had the frightful Mi-Go been still a menace in the outer land world of the north? Could one be sure of what might or might not linger even to this day in the lightless and unplumbed abysses of earth's deepest waters? Those things had seemingly been able to withstand any amount of pressure—and men of the sea have fished up curious objects at times. And has the killer-whale theory really explained the savage and mysterious scars on antarctic seals noticed a generation ago by Borchgrevingk?[189]

The specimens found by poor Lake did not enter into these guesses, for their geologic setting proved them to have lived at what must have been a very early date in the land city's history. They were, according to their location, certainly not less than thirty million years old; and we reflected that in their day the sea-cavern city, and indeed the cavern itself, had no existence. They would have remembered an older scene, with lush Tertiary vegetation everywhere, a younger land city of flourishing arts around them, and a great river sweeping northward along the base of the mighty mountains toward a far-away tropic ocean.

And yet we could not help thinking about these specimens— especially about the eight perfect ones that were missing from Lake's hideously ravaged camp. There was something abnormal about that whole business—the strange things we had tried so hard to lay to somebody's madness—those frightful graves—the amount *and nature* of the missing material—Gedney—the unearthly

---

[189] Carsten Egeberg Borchgrevink (or Borchgrevingk) (1864–1934), a Norwegian explorer, undertook an expedition to the Antarctic in 1898–1900. In February 1899 he established the first camp on Antarctic soil, and a year later (February 19, 1900) he became the first man to walk on the Ross Ice Shelf. See his book, *First on the Antarctic Continent* (London: George Newnes, 1901). Lovecraft reports that when he was ten years old "The Borchgrevink expedition, which had just made a new record in South Polar achievement, greatly stimulated" his interest in the Antarctic (*Selected Letters*, I, 37). The mention of "scars on antarctic seals" derives from Karl Fricker's *The Antarctic Regions* (London: Swan Sonnenschein & Co., 1900), a book Lovecraft owned: "Though Borchgrevingk lately noticed scars of wounds upon some seals, which led him to believe in the existence of some mysterious, powerful beast of prey, it has been most conclusively proved that these wounds were inflicted by the teeth of a ferocious cetacean—the orca gladiator" (p. 269).

toughness of those archaic monstrosities, and the queer vital freaks the sculptures now shewed the race to have. . . . Danforth and I had seen a good deal in the last few hours, and were prepared to believe and keep silent about many appalling and incredible secrets of primal Nature.

IX. [190]

I have said that our study of the decadent sculptures brought about a change in our immediate objective. This of course had to do with the chiselled avenues to the black inner world, of whose existence we had not known before, but which we were now eager to find and traverse. From the evident scale of the carvings we deduced that a steeply descending walk of about a mile through either of the neighbouring tunnels would bring us to the brink of the dizzy sunless cliffs above the great abyss; down whose side adequate paths, improved by the Old Ones, led to the rocky shore of the hidden and nighted ocean. To behold this fabulous gulf in stark reality was a lure which seemed impossible of resistance once we knew of the thing—yet we realised we must begin the quest at once if we expected to include it on our present flight.

It was now 8 p.m., and we had not enough battery replacements to let our torches burn on forever. We had done so much of our studying and copying below the glacial level that our battery supply had had at least five hours of nearly continuous use; and despite the special dry cell formula would obviously be good for only about four more—though by keeping one torch unused, except for especially interesting or difficult places, we might manage to eke out a

---

[190] The third installment of the *Astounding Stories* serialization (April 1936) begins here.

safe margin beyond that. It would not do to be without a light in these Cyclopean catacombs, hence in order to make the abyss trip we must give up all further mural deciphering. Of course we intended to revisit the place for days and perhaps weeks of intensive study and photography—curiosity having long ago got the better of horror—but just now we must hasten. Our supply of trail-blazing paper was far from unlimited, and we were reluctant to sacrifice spare notebooks or sketching paper to augment it; but we did let one large notebook go. If worst came to worst, we could resort to rock-chipping—and of course it would be possible, even in case of really lost direction, to work up to full daylight by one channel or another if granted sufficient time for plentiful trial and error. So at last we set off eagerly in the indicated direction of the nearest tunnel.

According to the carvings from which we had made our map, the desired tunnel-mouth could not be much more than a quarter-mile from where we stood; the intervening space shewing solid-looking buildings quite likely to be penetrable still at a sub-glacial level. The opening itself would be in the basement—on the angle nearest the foothills—of a vast five-pointed structure of evidently public and perhaps ceremonial nature, which we tried to identify from our aërial survey of the ruins. No such structure came to our minds as we recalled our flight, hence we concluded that its upper parts had been greatly damaged, or that it had been totally shattered in an ice-rift we had noticed. In the latter case the tunnel would probably turn out to be choked, so that we would have to try the next nearest one—the one less than a mile to the north. The intervening river-course prevented our trying any of the more southerly tunnels on this trip; and indeed, if both of the neighbouring ones were choked it was doubtful whether our batteries would warrant an attempt on the next northerly one—about a mile beyond our second choice.

As we threaded our dim way through the labyrinth with the aid of map and compass—traversing rooms and corridors in every stage of ruin or preservation, clambering up ramps, crossing upper floors and bridges and clambering down again, encountering chocked doorways and piles of debris, hastening now and then along finely preserved and uncannily immaculate stretches, taking false leads and retracing our way (in such cases removing the blind paper trail we had left), and once in a while striking the bottom of an open shaft through which daylight poured or trickled down—we were repeatedly tantalised by the sculptured walls along our route. Many must have told tales of immense historical importance, and only the prospect of later visits reconciled us to the need of passing them by. As it was, we slowed down once in a while and turned on our second torch. If we had more films we would certainly have paused briefly to photograph certain bas-reliefs, but time-consuming hand copying was clearly out of the question.

I come now once more to a place where the temptation to hesitate, or to hint rather than state, is very strong. It is necessary, however, to reveal the rest in order to justify my course in discouraging further exploration.[191] We had wormed our way very close to the computed site of the tunnel's mouth—having crossed a second-story bridge to what seemed plainly the tip of a pointed wall, and descended to a ruinous corridor especially rich in decadently elaborate and apparently ritualistic sculptures of late workmanship—when, about 8:30 p.m., Danforth's keen young nostrils gave us the first hint of something unusual. If we had a dog with us, I suppose we would have been warned before. At first we could not precisely say what was wrong with the formerly crystal-pure air, but after a few seconds our memories reacted only too definitely. Let me try to state the thing without flinching. There was an odour—and that odour was vaguely, subtly, and unmistakably akin to what had nauseated us upon opening the insane grave of the horror poor Lake had dissected.

---

[191] The passage "Many must have told ... further exploration" was omitted in *Astounding* (restored in Lovecraft's copy).

Of course the revelation was not as clearly cut at the time as it sounds now. There were several conceivable explanations, and we did a good deal of indecisive whispering. Most important of all, we did not retreat without further investigation; for having come this far, we were loath to be balked by anything short of certain disaster. Anyway, what we must have suspected was altogether too wild to believe. Such things did not happen in any normal world. It was probably sheer irrational instinct which made us dim our single torch—tempted no longer by the decadent and sinister sculptures that leered menacingly from the oppressive walls—and which softened our progress to a cautious tiptoeing and crawling over the increasingly littered floor and heaps of debris.

Danforth's eyes as well as nose proved better than mine, for it was likewise he who first noticed the queer aspect of the debris after we had passed many half-choked arches leading to chambers and corridors on the ground level. It did not look quite as it ought after countless thousands of years of desertion, and when we cautiously turned on more light we saw that a kind of swath seemed to have been lately tracked through it. The irregular nature of the litter precluded any definite marks, but in the smoother places there were suggestions of the dragging of heavy objects. Once we thought there was a hint of parallel tracks, as if of runners. This was what made us pause again.

It was during that pause that we caught—simultaneously this time—the other odour ahead. Paradoxically, it was both a less frightful and a more frightful odour—less frightful intrinsically, but infinitely appalling in this place under the known circumstances ... unless, of course, Gedney.... For the odour was the plain and familiar one of common petrol—every-day gasoline.

Our motivation after that is something I will leave to psychologists. We knew now that some terrible extension of the camp horrors must have crawled into this nighted burial-place of the aeons, hence could not doubt any longer the existence of nameless conditions—present or at least recent—just ahead. Yet in the end we did let sheer burning curiosity—or anxiety—or auto-hypnotism—or vague thoughts of responsibility toward Gedney—or what not—drive us on. Danforth whispered again of the print he thought he had seen at the alley-turning in the ruins above; and of the faint musical piping—potentially of tremendous significance in the light of Lake's dissection report despite its close resemblance to the cave-mouth echoes of the windy peaks—which he thought he had shortly afterward half heard from unknown depths below. I, in my turn, whispered of how the camp was left—of what had disappeared, and of how the madness of a lone survivor might have conceived the inconceivable—a wild trip across the monstrous mountains and a descent into the unknown primal masonry—

But we could not convince each other, or even ourselves, of anything definite. We had turned off all light as we stood still, and vaguely noticed that a trace of deeply filtered upper day kept the blackness from being absolute. Having automatically begun to move ahead, we guided ourselves by occasional flashes from our torch. The disturbed debris formed an impression we could not shake off, and the smell of gasoline grew stronger. More and more ruin met our eyes and hampered our feet, until very soon we saw that the forward way was about to cease. We had been all too correct in our pessimistic guess about that rift glimpsed from the air. Our tunnel quest was a blind one, and we were not even going to be able to reach the basement out of which the abyssward aperture opened.

The torch, flashing over the grotesquely carven walls of the blocked corridor in which we stood, shewed several doorways in various states of obstruction; and from one of them the gasoline odour—quite submerging that other hint of odour—came with especial distinctness. As we looked more steadily, we saw that beyond a doubt there had been a slight and recent clearing away of debris from that particular opening. Whatever the lurking horror might be, we believed the direct avenue toward it was now plainly manifest. I do not think anyone will wonder that we waited an appreciable time before making any further motion.

And yet, when we did venture inside that black arch, our first impression was one of anticlimax. For amidst the littered expanse of that sculptured crypt—a perfect cube with sides of about twenty feet—there remained no recent object of instantly discernible size; so that we looked instinctively, though in vain, for a farther doorway. In another moment, however, Danforth's sharp vision had descried a place where the floor debris had been disturbed; and we turned on both torches full strength. Though what we saw in that light was actually simple and trifling, I am none the less reluctant to tell of it because of what it implied. It was a rough levelling of the debris, upon which several small objects lay carelessly scattered, and at one corner of which a considerable amount of gasoline must have been spilled lately enough to leave a strong odour even at this extreme super-plateau altitude. In other words, it could not be other than a sort of camp—a camp made by questing beings who like us had been turned back by the unexpectedly choked way to the abyss.

Let me be plain. The scattered objects were, so far as substance was concerned, all from Lake's camp; and consisted of tin cans as queerly opened as those we had seen at that ravaged place, many spent matches, three illustrated books more or less curiously smudged, an empty ink bottle with its pictorial and instructional carton, a broken fountain pen, some oddly snipped fragments of fur and tent-cloth, a used electric battery with circular of directions, a folder that came with our type of tent heater, and a sprinkling of crumpled papers. It was all bad enough, but when we smoothed out the papers and looked at what was on them we felt we had come to the worst. We had found certain inexplicably blotted papers at the camp which might have prepared us, yet the effect of the sight down there in the pre-human vaults of a nightmare city was almost too much to bear.

A mad Gedney might have made the groups of dots in

imitation of those found on the greenish soapstones, just as the dots on those insane five-pointed grave-mounds might have been made; and he might conceivably have prepared rough, hasty sketches—varying in their accuracy or lack of it—which outlined the neighbouring parts of the city and traced the way from a circularly represented place outside our previous route—a place we identified as a great cylindrical tower in the carvings and as a vast circular gulf glimpsed in our aërial survey—to the present five-pointed structure and the tunnel-mouth therein. He might, I repeat, have prepared such sketches; for those before us were quite obviously compiled as our own had been from late sculptures somewhere in the glacial labyrinth, though not from the ones which we had seen and used. But what this art-blind bungler could never have done was to execute those sketches in a strange and assured technique perhaps superior, despite haste and carelessness, to any of the decadent carvings from which they were taken—the characteristic and unmistakable technique of the Old Ones themselves in the dead city's heyday.

There are those who will say Danforth and I were utterly mad not to flee for our lives after that; since our conclusions were now—notwithstanding their wildness—completely fixed, and of a nature I need not even mention to those who have read my account as far as this. Perhaps we were mad—for have I not said those horrible peaks were mountains of madness? But I think I can detect something of the same spirit—albeit in a less extreme form—in the men who stalk deadly beasts through African jungles to photograph them or study their habits. Half-paralysed with terror though we were, there was nevertheless fanned within us a blazing flame of awe and curiosity which triumphed in the end.

Of course we did not mean to face that—or those—which we knew had been there, but we felt that they must be gone by now. They would by this time have found the other neighbouring entrance to the abyss, and have passed within to whatever night-black fragments of the past might await them in the ultimate gulf—the ultimate gulf they had never seen. Or if that entrance, too, was blocked, they would have gone on to the north seeking another. They were, we remembered, partly independent of light.

Looking back to that moment, I can scarcely recall just what precise form our new emotions took—just what change of immediate objective it was that so sharpened our sense of expectancy. We certainly did not mean to face what we feared—yet I will not deny that we may have had a lurking, unconscious wish to spy certain things from some hidden vantage-point.[192] Probably we had not given up our zeal to glimpse the abyss itself, though there was interposed a new goal in the form of that great circular place shewn on the crumpled sketches we had found. We had at once recognised it as a monstrous cylindrical tower figuring in the very earliest carvings, but appearing only as a prodigious round aperture from above. Something about the impressiveness of its rendering, even in these hasty diagrams, made us think that its sub-glacial levels must still form a feature of peculiar importance. Perhaps it embodied architectural marvels as yet unencountered by us. It was certainly of incredible age according to the sculptures in which it figured—being indeed among the first things built in the city. Its carvings, if preserved, could not but be highly significant. Moreover, it might form a good present link with the upper world—a shorter route than the one we were so carefully blazing, and probably that by which those others had descended.

---

[192] This is reminiscent of the conclusion of "Under the Pyramids" (1924), the tale Lovecraft ghostwrote for Harry Houdini. The narrator (supposed to be Houdini himself) climbs to the top of an immense staircase in order to peer down at some enormous underground temple under the Sphinx: "At length I succeeded in reaching the steps and began to climb ... Though the staircase was huge and steep ... the ascent seemed virtually interminable.... I had intended, on reaching the landing, to climb immediately onward along whatever upper staircase might mount from there; stopping for no last look at the carrion abominations that pawed and genuflected some seventy or eighty feet below ..." (*Dagon and Other Macabre Tales*, 242).

At any rate, the thing we did was to study the terrible sketches—which quite perfectly confirmed our own—and start back over the indicated course to the circular place; the course which our nameless predecessors must have traversed twice before us. The other neighbouring gate to the abyss would lie beyond that. I need not speak of our journey—during which we continued to leave an economical trail of paper—for it was precisely the same in kind as that by which we had reached the cul de sac;[193] except that it tended to adhere more closely to the ground level and even descend to basement corridors. Every now and then we could trace certain disturbing marks in the debris or litter under foot; and after we had passed outside the radius of the gasoline scent we were again faintly conscious—spasmodically— of that more hideous and more persistent scent. After the way had branched from our former course we sometimes gave the rays of our single torch a furtive sweep along the walls; noting in almost every case the well-nigh omnipresent sculptures, which indeed seem to have formed a main aesthetic outlet for the Old Ones.

About 9:30 p.m., while traversing a vaulted corridor whose increasingly glaciated floor seemed somewhat below the ground level and whose roof grew lower as we advanced, we began to see strong daylight ahead and were able to turn off our torch. It appeared that we were coming to the vast circular place, and that our distance from the upper air could not be very great. The corridor ended in an arch surprisingly low for these megalithic ruins,[194] but we could see much through it even before we emerged. Beyond there stretched a prodigious round space—fully 200 feet in diameter—strown with debris and

---

[193] *cul de sac*: Dead end; French for "bottom of [a] bag."

[194] *megalithic*: "Consisting or constructed of great stones" (*Oxford English Dictionary*), usually referring to a period of European history when such structures (e.g., Stonehenge) were built (c. 1900–1400 B.C.); here used literally.

containing many choked archways corresponding to the one we were about to cross. The walls were—in available spaces—boldly sculptured into a spiral band of heroic proportions; and displayed, despite the destructive weathering caused by the openness of the spot, an artistic splendour far beyond anything we had encountered before. The littered floor was quite heavily glaciated, and we fancied that the true bottom lay at a considerably lower depth.

But the salient object of the place was the titanic stone ramp which, eluding the archways by a sharp turn outward into the open floor, wound spirally up the stupendous cylindrical wall like an inside counterpart of those once climbing outside the monstrous towers or ziggurats of antique Babylon.[195] Only the rapidity of our flight, and the perspective which confounded the descent with the tower's inner wall, had prevented our noticing this feature from the air, and thus caused us to seek another avenue to the sub-glacial level. Pabodie might have been able to tell what sort of engineering held it in place, but Danforth and I could merely admire and marvel. We could see mighty stone corbels[196] and pillars here and there, but what we saw seemed inadequate to the function performed. The thing was excellently preserved up to the present top of the tower—a highly remarkable circumstance in view of its exposure—and its shelter had done much to protect the bizarre and disturbing cosmic sculptures on the walls.

As we stepped out into the awesome half-daylight of this monstrous cylinder-bottom—fifty million years old, and without doubt the most primally ancient structure ever to

---

[195] The ziggurats or temple towers were constructed in Babylon and other cities in Sumeria beginning in the middle of the third millennium B.C. One of these towers may be the origin of the "Tower of Babel," as it is scornfully referred to in the Old Testament (Genesis 11:9).

[196] *corbels*: "A projection of stone, brick, timber, iron, or other constructional material, jutting out from (not merely attached to) the face of a wall, to support a superincumbent weight" (*Oxford English Dictionary*).

meet our eyes—we saw that the ramp-traversed sides stretched dizzily up to a height of fully sixty feet. This, we recalled from our aërial survey, meant an outside glaciation of some forty feet; since the yawning gulf we had seen from the plane had been at the top of an approximately twenty-foot mound of crumbled masonry, somewhat sheltered for three-fourths of its circumference by the massive curving walls of a line of higher ruins. According to the sculptures the original tower had stood in the centre of an immense circular plaza; and had been perhaps 500 or 600 feet high, with tiers of horizontal discs near the top, and a row of needle-like spires along the upper rim. Most of the masonry had obviously toppled outward rather than inward—a fortunate happening, since otherwise the ramp might have been shattered and the whole interior choked. As it was, the ramp shewed sad battering; whilst the choking was such that all the archways at the bottom seemed to have been recently half-cleared.

It took us only a moment to conclude that this was indeed the route by which those others had descended, and that this would be the logical route for our own ascent despite the long trail of paper we had left elsewhere. The tower's mouth was no farther from the foothills and our waiting plane than was the great terraced building we had entered, and any further sub-glacial exploration we might make on this trip would lie in this general region. Oddly, we were still thinking about possible later trips—even after all we had seen and guessed. Then as we picked our way cautiously over the debris of the great floor, there came a sight which for the time excluded all other matters.

It was the neatly huddled array of three sledges in that farther angle of the ramp's lower and outward-projecting course which had hitherto been screened from our view. There they were—the three sledges missing from Lake's camp—shaken by a hard usage which must have included forcible dragging along great reaches of snowless masonry and debris, as well as much hand portage over utterly unnavigable places. They were carefully and intelligently packed and strapped, and contained things memorably familiar enough—the gasoline stove, fuel cans, instrument cases, provision tins, tarpaulins obviously bulging with books, and some bulging with less obvious contents—everything derived from Lake's equipment. After what we had found in that other room, we were in a measure prepared for this encounter. The really great shock came when we stepped over and undid one tarpaulin whose outlines had peculiarly disquieted us. It seems that others as well as Lake had been interested in collecting typical specimens; for there were two here, both stiffly frozen, perfectly preserved, patched with adhesive plaster where some wounds around the neck had occurred, and wrapped with patent[197] care to prevent further damage. They were the bodies of young Gedney and the missing dog.

X.

Many people will probably judge us callous as well as mad for thinking about the northward tunnel and the abyss so soon after our sombre discovery, and I am not prepared to say that we would have immediately revived such thoughts but for a specific circumstance which broke in upon us and set up a whole new train of speculations. We had replaced the tarpaulin over poor Gedney and were standing in a kind of mute bewilderment when the sounds finally reached our consciousness—the first sounds we had heard since descending out of the open where the mountain wind whined faintly from its unearthly heights. Well known and mundane though they were, their presence in this remote world of death was more unexpected and unnerving than any grotesque or fabulous tones could possibly have been—

---

[197] *patent*: Clear or obvious. The use of this word in relation to the Old Ones goes far in absolving them of moral guilt in the killing of Lake's party.

since they gave a fresh upsetting to all our notions of cosmic harmony.

Had it been some trace of that bizarre musical piping over a wide range which Lake's dissection report had led us to expect in those others—and which, indeed, our overwrought fancies had been reading into every wind-howl we had heard since coming on the camp horror—it would have had a kind of hellish congruity with the aeon-dead region around us. A voice from other epochs belongs in a graveyard of other epochs. As it was, however, the noise shattered all our profoundly seated adjustments—all our tacit acceptance of the inner antarctic as a waste as utterly and irrevocably void of every vestige of normal life as the sterile disc of the moon.[198] What we heard was not the fabulous note of any buried blasphemy of elder earth from whose supernal toughness an age-denied polar sun had evoked a monstrous response. Instead, it was a thing so mockingly normal and so unerringly familiarised by our sea days off Victoria Land and our camp days at McMurdo Sound that we shuddered to think of it here, where such things ought not to be. To be brief—it was simply the raucous squawking of a penguin.

The muffled sound floated from sub-glacial recesses nearly opposite to the corridor whence we had come—regions manifestly in the direction of that other tunnel to the vast abyss. The presence of a living water-bird in such a direction—in a world whose surface was one of age-long and uniform lifelessness—could lead to only one conclusion; hence our first thought was to verify the objective reality of the sound. It was, indeed, repeated; and seemed at times to come from more than one throat. Seeking its source, we entered an archway from which much debris had been cleared; resuming our trail-blazing—with an added paper-supply taken with curious

---

[198]   The sentence is printed as per Lovecraft's typescript. In the *Astounding* appearance, the sentence reads: " ... waste utterly and irrevocably devoid of every vestige of normal life." Lovecraft has failed to correct this reading, but this may be an oversight.

repugnance from one of the tarpaulin bundles on the sledges—when we left daylight behind.

As the glaciated floor gave place to a litter of detritus, we plainly discerned some curious dragging tracks; and once Danforth found a distinct print of a sort whose description would be only too superfluous. The course indicated by the penguin cries was precisely what our map and compass prescribed as an approach to the more northerly tunnel-mouth, and we were glad to find that a bridgeless thoroughfare on the ground and basement levels seemed open. The tunnel, according to the chart, ought to start from the basement of a large pyramidal structure which we seemed vaguely to recall from our aërial survey as remarkably well preserved. Along our path the single torch shewed a customary profusion of carvings, but we did not pause to examine any of these.

Suddenly a bulky white shape loomed up ahead of us, and we flashed on the second torch. It is odd how wholly this new quest had turned our minds from earlier fears of what might lurk near. Those other ones, having left their supplies in the great circular place, must have planned to return after their scouting trip toward or into the abyss; yet we had now discarded all caution concerning them as completely as if they had never existed. This white, waddling thing was fully six feet high, yet we seemed to realise at once that it was not one of those others. They were larger and dark, and according to the sculptures their motion over land surfaces was a swift, assured matter despite the queerness of their sea-born tentacle equipment. But to say that the white thing did not profoundly frighten us would be vain. We were indeed clutched for an instant by a primitive dread almost sharper than the worst of our reasoned fears regarding those others. Then came a flash of anticlimax as the white shape sidled into a lateral archway to our left to join two others of its kind which had summoned it in raucous tones. For it was only a penguin—albeit of a huge, unknown species larger than the greatest of the known king penguins,[199] and monstrous in its combined albinism and virtual eyelessness.

When we had followed the thing into the archway and turned both our torches on the indifferent and unheeding group of three we saw that they were all eyeless albinos of the same unknown and gigantic species. Their size reminded us of some of the archaic penguins depicted in the Old Ones' sculptures, and it did not take us long to conclude that they were descended from the same stock— undoubtedly surviving through a retreat to some warmer inner region whose perpetual blackness had destroyed their pigmentation and atrophied their eyes to mere useless slits. That their present habitat was the vast abyss we sought, was not for a moment to be doubted; and this evidence of the gulf's continued warmth and habitability filled us with the most curious and subtly perturbing fancies.

We wondered, too, what had caused these three birds to venture out of their usual domain. The state and silence of the great dead city made it clear that it had at no time been an habitual seasonal rookery, whilst the manifest indifference of the trio to our presence made it seem odd that any passing party of those others should have startled them. Was it possible that those others had taken some aggressive action or tried to increase their meat supply? We doubted whether that pungent odour which the dogs had hated could cause an equal antipathy in these penguins; since their ancestors had obviously lived on excellent terms with the Old Ones—an amicable relationship which must have survived in the abyss below as long as any of the Old Ones remained. Regretting—in a flareup of the old spirit of pure science— that we could not photograph these anomalous creatures, we shortly left them to their squawking and pushed on toward the abyss whose openness was now so positively

---

[199] *king penguins*: *Aptenodytes forsteri*, usually 37 inches tall and weighing 33 pounds. It is curious that Lovecraft does not mention the emperor penguin (*Aptenodytes patagonica*), which is found only in Antarctica; it is usually 44 inches tall and weighs 66 pounds.

proved to us, and whose exact direction occasional penguin tracks made clear.

Not long afterward a steep descent in a long, low, doorless, and peculiarly sculptureless corridor led us to believe that we were approaching the tunnel-mouth at last. We had passed two more penguins, and heard others immediately ahead.[200] Then the corridor ended in a prodigious open space which made us gasp involuntarily—a perfect inverted hemisphere, obviously deep underground; fully an hundred feet in diameter and fifty feet high, with low archways opening around all parts of the circumference but one, and that one yawning cavernously with a black arched aperture which broke the symmetry of the vault to a height of nearly fifteen feet. It was the entrance to the great abyss.

In this vast hemisphere, whose concave roof was impressively though decadently carved to a likeness of the primordial celestial dome, a few albino penguins waddled—aliens there, but indifferent and unseeing. The black tunnel yawned indefinitely off at a steep descending grade, its aperture adorned with grotesquely chiselled jambs and lintel. From that cryptical mouth we fancied a current of slightly warmer air and perhaps even a suspicion of vapour proceeded; and we wondered what living entities other than penguins the limitless void below, and the contiguous honeycombings of the land and the titan mountains, might conceal. We wondered, too, whether the trace of mountain-top smoke at first suspected by poor Lake, as well as the odd haze we had ourselves perceived around the rampart-crowned peak, might not be caused by the tortuous-channelled rising of some such vapour from the unfathomed regions of earth's core.

Entering the tunnel, we saw that its outline was—at least at the start—about fifteen feet each way; sides, floor, and arched roof composed of the usual megalithic masonry.

---

[200] This sentence is rendered in *Astounding* as: "We had heard two more penguins."

The sides were sparsely decorated with cartouches of conventional designs in a late, decadent style; and all the construction and carving were marvellously well preserved. The floor was quite clear, except for a slight detritus bearing outgoing penguin tracks and the inward tracks of those others. The farther one advanced, the warmer it became; so that we were soon unbuttoning our heavy garments. We wondered whether there were any actually igneous manifestations below, and whether the waters of that sunless sea were hot. After a short distance the masonry gave place to solid rock, though the tunnel kept the same proportions and presented the same aspect of carved regularity. Occasionally its varying grade became so steep that grooves were cut in the floor. Several times we noted the mouths of small lateral galleries not recorded in our diagrams; none of them such as to complicate the problem of our return, and all of them welcome as possible refuges in case we met unwelcome entities on their way back from the abyss. The nameless scent of such things was very distinct. Doubtless it was suicidally foolish to venture into that tunnel under the known conditions, but the lure of the unplumbed is stronger in certain persons than most suspect—indeed, it was just such a lure which had brought us to this unearthly polar waste in the first place. We saw several penguins as we passed along, and speculated on the distance we would have to traverse. The carvings had led us to expect a steep downhill walk of about a mile to the abyss, but our previous wanderings had shewn us that matters of scale were not wholly to be depended on.

After about a quarter of a mile that nameless scent became greatly accentuated, and we kept very careful track of the various lateral openings we passed. There was no visible vapour as at the mouth, but this was doubtless due to the lack of contrasting cooler air. The temperature was rapidly ascending, and we were not surprised to come upon a careless heap of material shudderingly familiar to us. It was composed of furs and tent-cloth taken from Lake's camp, and we did not pause to study the bizarre forms into which the fabrics had been slashed. Slightly beyond this point we noticed a decided increase in the size and number of the side-galleries, and concluded that the densely honeycombed region beneath the higher foothills must now have been reached. The nameless scent was now curiously mixed with another and scarcely less offensive odour—of what nature we could not guess, though we thought of decaying organisms and perhaps unknown subterrene fungi. Then came a startling expansion of the tunnel for which the carvings had not prepared us—a broadening and rising into a lofty, natural-looking elliptical cavern with a level floor; some 75 feet long and 50 broad, and with many immense side-passages leading away into cryptical darkness.

Though this cavern was natural in appearance, an inspection with both torches suggested that it had been formed by the artificial destruction of several walls between adjacent honeycombings. The walls were rough, and the high vaulted roof was thick with stalactites; but the solid rock floor had been smoothed off, and was free from all debris, detritus, or even dust to a positively abnormal extent. Except for the avenue through which we had come, this was true of the floors of all the great galleries opening off from it; and the singularity of the condition was such as to set us vainly puzzling. The curious new foetor[201] which had supplemented the nameless scent was excessively pungent here; so much so that it destroyed all trace of the other. Something about this whole place, with its polished and almost glistening floor, struck us as more vaguely baffling and horrible than any of the monstrous things we had previously encountered.

The regularity of the passage immediately ahead, as well as the larger proportion of penguin-droppings there, prevented all confusion as to the right course amidst this

---

[201] *foetor:* Archaic or British spelling of *fetor,* an offensive smell or stench.

plethora[202] of equally great cave-mouths. Nevertheless we resolved to resume our paper trail-blazing if any further complexity should develop; for dust tracks, of course, could no longer be expected. Upon resuming our direct progress we cast a beam of torchlight over the tunnel walls—and stopped short in amazement at the supremely radical change which had come over the carvings in this part of the passage. We realised, of course, the great decadence of the Old Ones' sculpture at the time of the tunnelling; and had indeed noticed the inferior workmanship of the arabesques in the stretches behind us. But now, in this deeper section beyond the cavern, there was a sudden difference wholly transcending explanation—a difference in basic nature as well as in mere quality, and involving so profound and calamitous a degradation of skill that nothing in the hitherto observed rate of decline could have led one to expect it.

This new and degenerate work was coarse, bold, and wholly lacking in delicacy of detail. It was counter-sunk with exaggerated depth in bands following the same general line as the sparse cartouches of the earlier sections, but the height of the reliefs did not reach the level of the general surface. Danforth had the idea that it was a second carving—a sort of palimpsest[203] formed after the obliteration of a previous design. In nature it was wholly decorative and conventional; and consisted of crude spirals and angles roughly following the quintile mathematical tradition of the Old Ones, yet seeming more like a parody than a perpetuation of that tradition. We could not get it out of our minds that some subtly but profoundly alien element had been added to the

---

[202] *plethora*: "Over-fullness in any respect, superabundance; any unhealthy repletion or excess" (*Oxford English Dictionary*).

[203] *palimpsest*: From the Greek *palimpsestos* ("scraped again"), originally meaning a paper or parchment that has been erased or otherwise obliterated and written over; later used to denote such erasure and rewriting or recarving on brass, stone, or other substances. The practice was common in classical antiquity and the Middle Ages because of the relative shortage of papyrus or parchment.

aesthetic feeling behind the technique—an alien element, Danforth guessed, that was responsible for the manifestly laborious substitution. It was like, yet disturbingly unlike, what we had come to recognise as the Old Ones' art; and I was persistently reminded of such hybrid things as the ungainly Palmyrene sculptures fashioned in the Roman manner.[204] That others had recently noticed this belt of carving was hinted by the presence of a used torch battery on the floor in front of one of the most characteristic designs.[205]

Since we could not afford to spend any considerable time in study, we resumed our advance after a cursory look; though frequently casting beams over the walls to see if any further decorative changes developed. Nothing of the sort was perceived, though the carvings were in places rather sparse because of the numerous mouths of smooth-floored lateral tunnels.[206] We saw and heard fewer penguins, but thought we caught a vague suspicion of an infinitely distant chorus of them somewhere deep within the earth. The new and inexplicable odour was abominably strong, and we could detect scarcely a sign of that other nameless scent. Puffs of visible vapour ahead bespoke increasing contrasts in temperature, and the relative nearness of the sunless sea-cliffs of the great abyss. Then, quite unexpectedly, we saw certain obstructions on the polished floor ahead—obstructions which were quite definitely not penguins—and turned on our second torch after making sure that the objects were quite stationary.

---

[204] Palmyra was a city in northern Arabia that for a brief period in the later third century A.D. attained celebrity when a succession of Roman emperors favored it with their patronage. It was destroyed by the Emperor Aurelian in 273. The statuary and architecture of Palmyra are a fusion of Graeco-Roman and Middle Eastern styles.

[205] The passage "We could not ... designs" was omitted in *Astounding* (restored in Lovecraft's copy).

[206] The passage "though frequently ... lateral tunnels" was omitted in *Astounding* (restored in Lovecraft's copy).

XI.

Still another time have I come to a place where it is very difficult to proceed. I ought to be hardened by this stage; but there are some experiences and intimations which scar too deeply to permit of healing, and leave only such an added sensitiveness that memory reinspires all the original horror. We saw, as I have said, certain obstructions on the polished floor ahead; and I may add that our nostrils were assailed almost simultaneously by a very curious intensification of the strange prevailing foetor, now quite plainly mixed with the nameless stench of those others which had gone before us. The light of the second torch left no doubt of what the obstructions were, and we dared approach them only because we could see, even from a distance, that they were quite as past all harming power as had been the six similar specimens unearthed from the monstrous star-mounded graves at poor Lake's camp.

They were, indeed, as lacking in completeness as most of those we had unearthed—though it grew plain from the thick, dark-green pool gathering around them that their incompleteness was of infinitely greater recency. There seemed to be only four of them, whereas Lake's bulletins would have suggested no less than eight as forming the group which had preceded us. To find them in this state was wholly unexpected, and we wondered what sort of monstrous struggle had occurred down here in the dark.

Penguins, attacked in a body, retaliate savagely with their beaks; and our ears now made certain the existence of a rookery far beyond. Had those others disturbed such a place and aroused murderous pursuit? The obstructions did not suggest it, for penguin beaks against the tough tissues Lake had dissected could hardly account for the terrible damage our approaching glance was beginning to make out.

Besides, the huge blind birds we had seen appeared to be singularly peaceful.

Had there, then, been a struggle among those others, and were the absent four responsible? If so, where were they? Were they close at hand and likely to form an immediate menace to us? We glanced anxiously at some of the smooth-floored lateral passages as we continued our slow and frankly reluctant approach. Whatever the conflict was, it had clearly been that which had frightened the penguins into their unaccustomed wandering. It must, then, have arisen near that faintly heard rookery in the incalculable gulf beyond, since there were no signs that any birds had normally dwelt here. Perhaps, we reflected, there had been a hideous running fight, with the weaker party seeking to get back to the cached sledges when their pursuers finished them. One could picture the daemoniac fray between namelessly monstrous entities as it surged out of the black abyss with great clouds of frantic penguins squawking and scurrying ahead.

I say that we approached those sprawling and incomplete obstructions slowly and reluctantly. Would to heaven we had never approached them at all, but had run back at top speed out of that blasphemous tunnel with the greasily smooth floors and the degenerate murals aping and mocking the things they had superseded—run back, before we had seen what we did see, and before our minds were burned with something which will never let us breathe easily again![207]

Both of our torches were turned on the prostrate objects, so that we soon realised the dominant factor in their incompleteness. Mauled, compressed, twisted, and ruptured as they were, their chief common injury was total decapita-

---

[207] A frequently expressed sentiment in Lovecraft's fiction. Cf. "The Call of Cthulhu": "I have looked upon all that the universe has to hold of horror, and even the skies of spring and the flowers of summer must ever afterward be poison to me" (*The Dunwich Horror and Others*, 154).

tion. From each one the tentacled starfish-head had been removed; and as we drew near we saw that the manner of removal looked more like some hellish tearing or suction than like any ordinary form of cleavage. Their noisome dark-green ichor[208] formed a large, spreading pool; but its stench was half overshadowed by that newer and stranger stench, here more pungent than at any other point along our route. Only when we had come very close to the sprawling obstructions could we trace that second, unexplainable foetor to any immediate source—and the instant we did so Danforth, remembering certain very vivid sculptures of the Old Ones' history in the Permian age 150 million years ago, gave vent to a nerve-tortured cry which echoed hysterically through that vaulted and archaic passage with the evil palimpsest carvings.

I came only just short of echoing his cry myself; for I had seen those primal sculptures, too, and had shudderingly admired the way the nameless artist had suggested that hideous slime-coating found on certain incomplete and prostrate Old Ones—those whom the frightful shoggoths had characteristically slain and sucked to a ghastly headlessness in the great war of re-subjugation. They were infamous, nightmare sculptures even when telling of age-old, bygone things; for shoggoths and their work ought not to be seen by human beings or portrayed by any beings. The mad author of the *Necronomicon* had nervously tried to swear that none had been bred on this planet, and that only drugged dreamers had ever conceived them. Formless protoplasm able to mock and reflect all forms and organs and processes—viscous agglutinations of bubbling cells—rubbery fifteen-foot spheroids infinitely plastic and ductile—slaves of suggestion, builders of cities—more and more sullen, more and more intelligent, more and more

---

[208] *ichor:* "A watery acid discharge issuing from certain wounds or sores" (*Oxford English Dictionary*); here referring merely to a sort of watery substance that serves the function of blood. See also note 75 to "The Dunwich Horror."

amphibious, more and more imitative—Great God! What madness made even those blasphemous Old Ones willing to use and to carve such things?

And now, when Danforth and I saw the freshly glistening and reflectively iridescent black slime which clung thickly to those headless bodies and stank obscenely with that new unknown odour whose cause only a diseased fancy could envisage—clung to those bodies and sparkled less voluminously on a smooth part of the accursedly re-sculptured wall *in a series of grouped dots*—we understood the quality of cosmic fear to its uttermost depths. It was not fear of those four missing others—for all too well did we suspect they would do no harm again. Poor devils! After all, they were not evil things of their kind. They were the men of another age and another order of being. Nature had played a hellish jest on them—as it will on any others that human madness, callousness, or cruelty may hereafter drag up in that hideously dead or sleeping polar waste—and this was their tragic homecoming.

They had not been even savages—for what indeed had they done? That awful awakening in the cold of an unknown epoch—perhaps an attack by the furry, frantically barking quadrupeds, and a dazed defence against them and the equally frantic white simians with the queer wrappings and paraphernalia ... poor Lake, poor Gedney ... and poor Old Ones![209] Scientists to the last—what had they done that we would not have done in their place? God, what intelligence and persistence! What a facing of the incredible, just as those carven kinsmen and forbears had faced things only a little less incredible! Radiates, vegetables, monstrosities, star-spawn—whatever they had been, they were men!

They had crossed the icy peaks on whose templed slopes they had once worshipped and roamed among the tree-ferns. They had found their dead city brooding under its curse, and had read its carven latter days as we had done. They had tried

---

[209] This passage is rendered in *Astounding* as " ... paraphernalia. Poor Lake. Poor Gedney. And poor Old Ones!" (restored in Lovecraft's copy).

to reach their living fellows in fabled depths of blackness they had never seen—and what had they found? All this flashed in unison through the thoughts of Danforth and me as we looked from those headless, slime-coated shapes to the loathsome palimpsest sculptures and the diabolical dot-groups of fresh slime on the wall beside them—looked and understood what must have triumphed and survived down there in the Cyclopean water-city of that nighted, penguin-fringed abyss, whence even now a sinister curling mist had begun to belch pallidly as if in answer to Danforth's hysterical scream.

The shock of recognising that monstrous slime and head-lessness had frozen us into mute, motionless statues, and it is only through later conversations that we have learned of the complete identity of our thoughts at that moment. It seemed aeons that we stood there, but actually it could not have been more than ten or fifteen seconds. That hateful, pallid mist curled forward as if veritably driven by some remoter advancing bulk—and then came a sound which upset much of what we had just decided, and in so doing broke the spell and enabled us to run like mad past squawk-ing, confused penguins over our former trail back to the city, along ice-sunken megalithic corridors to the great open circle, and up that archaic spiral ramp in a frenzied auto-matic plunge for the sane outer air and light of day.

The new sound, as I have intimated, upset much that we had decided; because it was what poor Lake's dissec-tion had led us to attribute to those we had just judged dead. It was, Danforth later told me, precisely what he had caught in infinitely muffled form when at that spot be-yond the alley-corner above the glacial level; and it cer-tainly had a shocking resemblance to the wind-pipings we had both heard around the lofty mountain caves. At the risk of seeming puerile[210] I will add another thing, too; if only because of the surprising way Danforth's impression

---

[210] *puerile*: From the Latin *puer* ("boy"); "merely boyish or childish, juvenile; immature, trivial" (*Oxford English Dictionary*).

chimed with mine. Of course common reading is what prepared us both to make the interpretation, though Danforth has hinted at queer notions about unsuspected and forbidden sources to which Poe may have had access when writing his *Arthur Gordon Pym*[211] a century ago. It will be remembered that in that fantastic tale there is a word of unknown but terrible and prodigious significance connected with the antarctic and screamed eternally by the gigantic, spectrally snowy birds of that malign region's core. *"Tekeli-li! Tekeli-li!"*[212] That, I may admit, is exactly what we thought we heard conveyed by that sudden sound behind the advancing white mist—that insidious musical piping over a singularly wide range.

We were in full flight before three notes or syllables had been uttered, though we knew that the swiftness of the Old Ones would enable any scream-roused and pursuing survivor of the slaughter to overtake us in a moment if it really wished to do so. We had a vague hope, however, that nonaggressive conduct and a display of kindred reason might cause such a being to spare us in case of capture; if only from scientific curiosity. After all, if such an one had nothing to fear for itself it would have no motive in harming us. Concealment being futile at this juncture, we used our torch for a running glance behind, and perceived that the mist was thinning. Would we see, at last, a complete and living specimen of those others? Again came that insidious musical piping—*"Tekeli-li! Tekeli-li!"*

Then, noting that we were actually gaining on our pursuer, it occurred to us that the entity might be wounded.

---

[211] See note 35 above.

[212] This cry is as unexplained in Poe as it is in Lovecraft. It is first uttered by savages dwelling on some islands off the coast of Antarctica, and later by birds: "The darkness had materially increased, relieved only by the glare of the water thrown back from the white curtain before us. Many gigantic and pallidly white birds flew continuouusly now from beyond the veil, and their scream was the eternal *Tekeli-li!* as they retreated from our vision" (Edgar Allan Poe, *The Narrative of Arthur Gordon Pym of Nantucket* [Harmondsworth, UK: Penguin Books, 1975], 238–39).

We could take no chances, however, since it was very obviously approaching in answer to Danforth's scream rather than in flight from any other entity. The timing was too close to admit of doubt. Of the whereabouts of that less conceivable and less mentionable nightmare—that foetid, unglimpsed mountain of slime-spewing protoplasm whose race had conquered the abyss and sent land pioneers to re-carve and squirm through the burrows of the hills—we could form no guess; and it cost us a genuine pang to leave this probably crippled Old One—perhaps a lone survivor—to the peril of recapture and a nameless fate.

Thank heaven we did not slacken our run. The curling mist had thickened again, and was driving ahead with increased speed; whilst the straying penguins in our rear were squawking and screaming and displaying signs of a panic really surprising in view of their relatively minor confusion when we had passed them. Once more came that sinister, wide-ranged piping—*"Tekeli-li! Tekeli-li!"* We had been wrong. The thing was not wounded, but had merely paused on encountering the bodies of its fallen kindred and the hellish slime inscription above them. We could never know what that daemon message was—but those burials at Lake's camp had shewn how much importance the beings attached to their dead. Our recklessly used torch now revealed ahead of us the large open cavern where various ways converged, and we were glad to be leaving those morbid palimpsest sculptures—almost felt even when scarcely seen—behind.

Another thought which the advent of the cave inspired was the possibility of losing our pursuer at this bewildering focus of large galleries. There were several of the blind albino penguins in the open space, and it seemed clear that their fear of the oncoming entity was extreme to the point of unaccountability. If at that point we dimmed our torch to the very lowest limit of travelling need, keeping it strictly in front of us, the frightened squawking motions of the huge birds in the mist might muffle our footfalls, screen our true course, and somehow set up a false lead. Amidst the churning, spiralling fog the littered and unglistening floor of the main tunnel beyond this point, as differing from the other morbidly polished burrows, could hardly form a highly distinguishing feature; even, so far as we could conjecture, for those indicated special senses which made the Old Ones partly though imperfectly independent of light in emergencies. In fact, we were somewhat apprehensive lest we go astray ourselves in our haste. For we had, of course, decided to keep straight on toward the dead city; since the consequences of loss in those unknown foothill honeycombings would be unthinkable.

The fact that we survived and emerged is sufficient proof that the thing did take a wrong gallery whilst we providentially hit on the right one. The penguins alone could not have saved us, but in conjunction with the mist they seem to have done so. Only a benign fate kept the curling vapours thick enough at the right moment, for they were constantly shifting and threatening to vanish. Indeed, they did lift for a second just before we emerged from the nauseously resculptured tunnel into the cave; so that we actually caught one first and only half-glimpse of the oncoming entity as we cast a final, desperately fearful glance backward before dimming the torch and mixing with the penguins in the hope of dodging pursuit. If the fate which screened us was benign, that which gave us the half-glimpse was infinitely the opposite; for to that flash of semi-vision can be traced a full half of the horror which has ever since haunted us.

Our exact motive in looking back again was perhaps no more than the immemorial instinct of the pursued to gauge the nature and course of its pursuer; or perhaps it was an automatic attempt to answer a subconscious question raised by one of our senses. In the midst of our flight, with all our faculties centred on the problem of escape, we were in no condition to observe and analyse details; yet even so our latent brain-cells must have wondered at the message brought them by our nostrils. Afterward we realised what it was—that our retreat from the foetid slime-coating on those headless obstructions, and the coincident approach of the pursuing entity, had not brought us the exchange of stenches which logic called for. In the neighbourhood of the prostrate things that new and lately unexplainable foetor had been wholly dominant; but by this time it ought to have largely given place to the nameless stench associated with those others. This it had not done—for instead, the newer and less bearable smell was now virtually undiluted, and growing more and more poisonously insistent each second.

So we glanced back—simultaneously, it would appear; though no doubt the incipient motion of one prompted the imitation of the other. As we did so we flashed both torches full strength at the momentarily thinned mist; either from sheer primitive anxiety to see all we could, or in a less primitive but equally unconscious effort to dazzle the entity before we dimmed our light and dodged among the penguins of the labyrinth-centre ahead. Unhappy act! Not Orpheus himself,[213] or Lot's wife,[214] paid much more dearly for a backward glance. And again came that shocking, wide-ranged piping—*"Tekeli-li! Tekeli-li!"*

I might as well be frank—even if I cannot bear to be quite direct—in stating what we saw; though at the time we felt that it was not to be admitted even to each other. The words reaching the reader can never even suggest the awfulness of the sight itself. It crippled our consciousness

---

[213] *Orpheus:* Orpheus' wife, fleeing from Aristaeus, stepped on a serpent and died. Orpheus descended to Tartarus and made a plea to Hades, ruler of the underworld, to restore Eurydice to life. Hades granted the request on the condition that he not look back at her until she had left the underworld. Orpheus observed the condition until the last moment, when he looked back to see if she was still behind him; he then lost her forever. The story is told in Ovid's *Metamorphoses* 10, 1–77.

[214] *Lot's wife:* When angels came to Lot to announce the imminent destruction of Sodom, Lot and his family fled, with the angelic injunction not to look back at the city; but his wife looked back at their abandoned property and as punishment was turned into a pillar of rock salt. See Genesis 19:1–26; also note 69 to "The Colour Out of Space."

so completely that I wonder we had the residual sense to dim our torches as planned, and to strike the right tunnel toward the dead city. Instinct alone must have carried us through—perhaps better than reason could have done; though if that was what saved us, we paid a high price. Of reason we certainly had little enough left.[215] Danforth was totally unstrung, and the first thing I remember of the rest of the journey was hearing him light-headedly chant an hysterical formula in which I alone of mankind could have found anything but insane irrelevance. It reverberated in falsetto echoes among the squawks of the penguins; reverberated through the vaultings ahead, and—thank God—through the now empty vaultings behind. He could not have begun it at once—else we would not have been alive and blindly racing. I shudder to think of what a shade of difference in his nervous reactions might have brought.

"South Station Under—Washington Under—Park Street Under—Kendall—Central—Harvard...." The poor fellow was chanting the familiar stations of the Boston-Cambridge tunnel that burrowed through our peaceful native soil thousands of miles away in New England, yet to me the ritual had neither irrelevance nor home-feeling.[216] It had only horror, because I knew unerringly the monstrous, nefandous[217] analogy that had suggested it. We had expected, upon looking back, to see a terrible and in-

---

[215] The passage "I might as well ... enough left" was omitted in *Astounding* (restored in Lovecraft's copy).

[216] This exact subway line is still in operation today as part of the Red Line to Harvard. It is one of the oldest subway lines in the nation, and the entire run from South Station to Harvard was completed on December 3, 1916. Lovecraft had visited Boston in 1920; he is likely to have ridden the subway at that time, and on many subsequent occasions. The "Washington Under" stop (i.e., under Washington Street) is now called Downtown Crossing; and there is now an additional stop, Charles/MGH (i.e., at the foot of Longfellow Bridge near the Charles River and the Massachusetts General Hospital) prior to the three stops in Cambridge (Kendall, Central, and Harvard). In the late 1980s, several further stops opened: Porter Square, Davis, and Alewife.

[217] *nefandous*: From the Latin *nefandus* (derived from *ne-fari*, "not to be mentioned, unmentionable" [Lewis and Short, *A Latin Dictionary*]), hence unspeakable or abominable.

credibly moving entity if the mists were thin enough; but of that entity we had formed a clear idea. What we did see—for the mists were indeed all too malignly thinned—was something altogether different, and immeasurably more hideous and detestable. It was the utter, objective embodiment of the fantastic novelist's 'thing that should not be'; and its nearest comprehensible analogue is a vast, onrushing subway train as one sees it from a station platform—the great black front looming colossally out of infinite subterraneous distance, constellated with strangely coloured lights and filling the prodigious burrow as a piston fills a cylinder.

But we were not on a station platform. We were on the track ahead as the nightmare plastic column of foetid black iridescence oozed tightly onward through its fifteen-foot sinus; gathering unholy speed and driving before it a spiral, re-thickening cloud of the pallid abyss-vapour. It was a terrible, indescribable thing vaster than any subway train—a shapeless congeries[218] of protoplasmic bubbles, faintly self-luminous, and with myriads of temporary eyes forming and unforming as pustules[219] of greenish light all over the tunnel-filling front that bore down upon us, crushing the penguins and slithering over the glistening floor that it and its kind had swept so evilly free of all litter. Still came that eldritch, mocking cry— *"Tekeli-li! Tekeli-li!"* And at last we remembered that the daemoniac shoggoths—given life, thought, and plastic organ patterns solely by the Old Ones, and having no language save that which the dot-groups expressed—*had likewise no voice save the imitated accents of their bygone masters.*

---

[218] *congeries*: A word taken directly into English from Latin: "A collection of things merely massed or heaped together; a mass, heap" (*Oxford English Dictionary*). Pronounced "kon-JEER-i-eez." Cf. "The Book," sonnet I of *Fungi from Yuggoth* (1929-30): " ... the books, in piles like twisted trees, / Rotting from floor to roof—congeries / Of crumbling elder lore at little cost."

[219] *pustules*: Warts or pimples.

XII.

Danforth and I have recollections of emerging into the great sculptured hemisphere and of threading our back trail through the Cyclopean rooms and corridors of the dead city; yet these are purely dream-fragments involving no memory of volition, details, or physical exertion. It was as if we floated in a nebulous world or dimension without time, causation, or orientation. The grey half-daylight of the vast circular space sobered us somewhat; but we did not go near those cached sledges or look again at poor Gedney and the dog. They have a strange and titanic mausoleum, and I hope the end of this planet will find them still undisturbed.

It was while struggling up the colossal spiral incline that we first felt the terrible fatigue and short breath which our race through the thin plateau air had produced; but not even the fear of collapse could make us pause before reaching the normal outer realm of sun and sky.[220] There was something vaguely appropriate about our departure from those buried epochs; for as we wound our panting way up the sixty-foot cylinder of primal masonry we glimpsed beside us a continuous procession of heroic sculptures in the dead race's early and undecayed technique—a farewell from the Old Ones, written fifty million years ago.

Finally scrambling out at the top, we found ourselves on a great mound of tumbled blocks; with the curved walls of higher stone-work rising westward, and the brooding peaks of the great mountains shewing beyond the more crumbled structures toward the east. The low antarctic sun of

---

[220] The passage "It was as if ... sun and sky" was omitted in *Astounding* (restored in Lovecraft's copy).

midnight peered redly from the southern horizon through rifts in the jagged ruins, and the terrible age and deadness of the nightmare city seemed all the starker by contrast with such relatively known and accustomed things as the features of the polar landscape.[221] The sky above was a churning and opalescent mass of tenuous ice-vapours, and the cold clutched at our vitals. Wearily resting the outfit-bags to which we had instinctively clung throughout our desperate flight, we rebuttoned our heavy garments for the stumbling climb down the mound and the walk through the aeon-old stone maze to the foothills where our aëroplane waited. Of what had set us fleeing from the darkness of earth's secret and archaic gulfs we said nothing at all.[222]

In less than a quarter of an hour we had found the steep grade to the foothills—the probable ancient terrace—by which we had descended, and could see the dark bulk of our great plane amidst the sparse ruins on the rising slope ahead. Half way uphill toward our goal we paused for a momentary breathing-spell, and turned to look again at the fantastic palaeogean tangle of incredible stone shapes below us—once more outlined mystically against an unknown west. As we did so we saw that the sky beyond had lost its morning haziness; the restless ice-vapours having moved up to the zenith, where their mocking outlines seemed on the point of settling into some bizarre pattern which they feared to make quite definite or conclusive.

There now lay revealed on the ultimate white horizon behind the grotesque city a dim, elfin line of pinnacled violet whose needle-pointed heights loomed dream-like against the beckoning rose-colour of the western sky. Up toward this shimmering rim sloped the ancient table-land, the depressed course of the bygone river traversing it as an irregular ribbon of shadow. For a second we gasped in

---

[221] This sentence was omitted by *Astounding* (restored in Lovecraft's copy).

[222] The passage "Wearily resting ... nothing at all" was omitted in *Astounding* (restored in Lovecraft's copy).

admiration of the scene's unearthly cosmic beauty, and then vague horror began to creep into our souls. For this far violet line could be nothing else than the terrible mountains of the forbidden land—highest of earth's peaks and focus of earth's evil; harbourers of nameless horrors and Archaean secrets; shunned and prayed to by those who feared to carve their meaning; untrodden by any living thing of earth, but visited by the sinister lightnings and sending strange beams across the plains in the polar night—beyond doubt the unknown archetype of that dreaded Kadath in the Cold Waste beyond abhorrent Leng, whereof unholy primal legends hint evasively. We were the first human beings ever to see them—and I hope to God we may be the last.[223]

If the sculptured maps and pictures in that pre-human city had told truly, these cryptic violet mountains could not be much less than 300 miles away; yet none the less sharply did their dim elfin essence jut above that remote and snowy rim, like the serrated edge of a monstrous alien planet about to rise into unaccustomed heavens. Their height, then, must have been tremendous beyond all known comparison—carrying them up into tenuous atmospheric strata peopled by such gaseous wraiths as rash flyers have barely lived to whisper of after unexplainable falls.[224] Looking at them, I thought nervously of certain sculptured hints of what the great bygone river had washed down into the city from their accursed slopes—and wondered how much sense and how much folly had lain in the fears of those Old Ones who carved them so reticently. I recalled how

---

[223] This sentence first appears in Lovecraft's typescript; it is absent from his autograph ms. It was omitted in the *Astounding* appearance, and Lovecraft—correcting that text with his autograph ms., not the typescript—did not notice its omission and failed to restore it.

[224] This sentence (omitted in *Astounding* but restored in Lovecraft's copy) appears to be an encapsulation of the basic plot of Sir Arthur Conan Doyle's story "The Horror of the Heights" (in *Danger! and Other Stories* [1918]; rpt. in *Tales of Terror and Mystery* [1922]). Lovecraft reports reading Conan Doyle's horror stories in the collection of W. Paul Cook in the summer of 1928 (see Lovecraft to Lillian D. Clark, June 25, 1928; ms., John Hay Library).

their northerly end must come near the coast at Queen Mary Land, where even at that moment Sir Douglas Mawson's expedition was doubtless working less than a thousand miles away;[225] and hoped that no evil fate would give Sir Douglas and his men a glimpse of what might lie beyond the protecting coastal range. Such thoughts formed a measure of my overwrought condition at the time—and Danforth seemed to be even worse.

Yet long before we had passed the great star-shaped ruin and reached our plane our fears had become transferred to the lesser but vast enough range whose re-crossing lay ahead of us. From these foothills the black, ruin-crusted slopes reared up starkly and hideously against the east, again reminding us of those strange Asian paintings of Nicholas Roerich; and when we thought of the damnable honeycombs inside them, and of the frightful amorphous entities that might have pushed their foetidly squirming way even to the topmost hollow pinnacles, we could not face without panic the prospect of again sailing by those suggestive skyward cave-mouths where the wind made sounds like an evil musical piping over a wide range. To make matters worse, we saw distinct traces of local mist around several of the summits—as poor Lake must have done when he made that early mistake about volcanism— and thought shiveringly of that kindred mist from which we had just escaped; of that, and of the blasphemous, horror-fostering abyss whence all such vapours came.

All was well with the plane, and we clumsily hauled on our heavy flying furs. Danforth got the engine started without trouble, and we made a very smooth takeoff over the nightmare city. Below us the primal Cyclopean masonry spread out as it had done when first we saw it—so short, yet infinitely long, a time ago—and we began rising and

---

[225] Sir Douglas Mawson (see note 59 above) commanded an expedition to the Antarctic in 1929–31 that explored Kemp Land and Enderby Land.

turning to test the wind for our crossing through the pass.[226]
At a very high level there must have been great disturbance, since the ice-dust clouds of the zenith were doing
all sorts of fantastic things; but at 24,000 feet, the height
we needed for the pass, we found navigation quite practicable. As we drew close to the jutting peaks the wind's
strange piping again became manifest, and I could see
Danforth's hands trembling at the controls. Rank amateur
though I was, I thought at that moment that I might be a
better navigator than he in effecting the dangerous crossing between pinnacles; and when I made motions to change
seats and take over his duties he did not protest. I tried to
keep all my skill and self-possession about me, and stared
at the sector of reddish farther sky betwixt the walls of
the pass—resolutely refusing to pay attention to the puffs
of mountain-top vapour, and wishing that I had wax-
stopped ears like Ulysses' men off the Sirens' coast[227] to
keep that disturbing wind-piping from my consciousness.[228]

But Danforth, released from his piloting and keyed up to
a dangerous nervous pitch, could not keep quiet. I felt him
turning and wriggling about as he looked back at the terrible receding city, ahead at the cave-riddled, cube-barnacled
peaks, sidewise at the bleak sea of snowy, rampart-strown
foothills, and upward at the seething, grotesquely clouded
sky. It was then, just as I was trying to steer safely through
the pass, that his mad shrieking brought us so close to
disaster by shattering my tight hold on myself and causing me to fumble helplessly with the controls for a moment. A second afterward my resolution triumphed and

---

[226] This sentence was omitted in *Astounding*; it was restored by Lovecraft in his copy
except for the phrase "—so short, yet infinitely long, a time ago—", as this phrase is
found only in Lovecraft's typescript, and he had evidently forgotten its inclusion there.

[227] The celebrated tale is first told in Homer's *Odyssey* 12, 142–200. Edward Lucas White
has elaborated upon the myth in "The Song of the Sirens," in *The Song of the Sirens and
Other Stories* (New York: E. P. Dutton, 1919), which Lovecraft read in 1921.

[228] The passage "—resolutely refusing ... consciousness" was omitted in *Astounding*
(restored in Lovecraft's copy).

we made the crossing safely—yet I am afraid that Danforth will never be the same again.

I have said that Danforth refused to tell me what final horror made him scream out so insanely—a horror which, I feel sadly sure, is mainly responsible for his present breakdown. We had snatches of shouted conversation above the wind's piping and the engine's buzzing as we reached the safe side of the range and swooped slowly down toward the camp, but that had mostly to do with the pledges of secrecy we had made as we prepared to leave the nightmare city. Certain things, we had agreed, were not for people to know and discuss lightly— and I would not speak of them now but for the need of heading off that Starkweather-Moore Expedition, and others, at any cost. It is absolutely necessary, for the peace and safety of mankind, that some of earth's dark, dead corners and unplumbed depths be let alone; lest sleeping abnormalities wake to resurgent life, and blasphemously surviving nightmares squirm and splash out of their black lairs to newer and wider conquests.[229]

All that Danforth has ever hinted is that the final horror was a mirage. It was not, he declares, anything connected with the cubes and caves of echoing, vaporous, wormily honeycombed mountains of madness which we crossed; but a single fantastic, daemoniac glimpse, among the churning zenith-clouds, of what lay back of those other violet westward mountains which the Old Ones had shunned and feared. It is very probable that the thing was a sheer delusion born of the previous stresses we had passed through, and of the actual though unrecognised mirage of the dead transmontane city experienced near Lake's camp the day before; but it was so real to Danforth that he suffers from it still.[230]

---

[229] The passage "Certain things ... wider conquests" was omitted in *Astounding* (restored in Lovecraft's copy).

[230] The following fragmentary utterances by Danforth were intended by Lovecraft to be vague and inconclusive, so as to end the novel on a note of portentous mystery. In his notes to the novel Lovecraft has written: "Danf. screams at what he sees in sky—over mts—PIPING? VAPOURS? ... End." Cf. Lovecraft to August Derleth, May 16, 1931: "Now as to the end of the thing—of course I'm not satisfied myself, but I am very oddly unable to decide whether more or *less* definiteness is needed. Remember Arthur Gordon Pym.

He has on rare occasions whispered disjointed and irresponsible things about "the black pit", "the carven rim", "the proto-shoggoths", "the windowless solids with five dimensions", "the nameless cylinder", "the elder pharos",[231] "Yog-Sothoth",[232] "the primal white jelly", "the colour out of space",[233] "the wings", "the eyes in darkness", "the moon-ladder", "the original, the eternal, the undying", and other bizarre conceptions; but when he is fully himself he repudiates all this and attributes it to his curious and macabre reading of earlier years. Danforth, indeed, is known to be among the few who have ever dared go completely through that worm-riddled copy of the *Necronomicon* kept under lock and key in the college library.

The higher sky, as we crossed the range, was surely vaporous and disturbed enough; and although I did not see the zenith I can well imagine that its swirls of ice-dust may have taken strange forms. Imagination, knowing how vividly distant scenes can sometimes be reflected, refracted, and magnified by such layers of restless cloud, might easily

---

In my tale the shoggoth provides a concrete & tangible climax—& what I wished to add was merely a vague hint of further spiritual horrors—as Poe hinted with his white bird screaming '*Tekeli-li! Tekeli-li!*' I wanted to leave the *actuality* of the glimpse very unsettled, so that it might easily pass off as an hallucination. Possibly I ought to have left it *vaguer still*—& then again I had an idea that the thing ought to be developed at full length—perhaps as a sequel to the present thing, or perhaps as an expansion of that thing to full book length ... What the thing was supposed to be, of course, was a region containing vestiges of some utterly primal cosmic force or process ruling or occupying the earth (among other planets) even before its solidification, & upheaved from the sea-bottom when the great Antarctic land mass arose. Lack of *interest* in the world beyond the inner mountains would account for its non-reconquest of the sphere. But then again, there may have been no such thing! Those Others may well have had their superstitions—& of course Danforth was strangely read, nervously organised, & fresh from a terrific shock.... Anyhow, what I did set down was a sort of weak compromise betwixt the two ways I vaguely & ineffectively thought it ought to be" (ms., State Historical Society of Wisconsin).

[231] *the elder pharos*: The title of sonnet XXVII of *Fungi from Yuggoth*, which incidentally mentions Leng (see note 96 above). Pharos means lighthouse (from Pharos, the name of the island in the Bay of Alexandria upon which was a famous lighthouse).

[232] *Yog-Sothoth*: See note 42 to "The Dunwich Horror."

[233] *the colour out of space*: The title of one of Lovecraft's most celebrated stories (1927).

have supplied the rest—and of course Danforth did not hint any of those specific horrors till after his memory had had a chance to draw on his bygone reading. He could never have seen so much in one instantaneous glance.

At the time his shrieks were confined to the repetition of a single mad word of all too obvious source:

"Tekeli-li! Tekeli-li!"

The Adjectives of Erich Zann
A Tale of Horror

In my lifetime, I have read only one story by H. P. Lovecraft. Yet that story I remember well, if only because I came upon it shortly after my twin brother committed suicide.

Somehow, talk of Lovecraft implies hushed talk of the past— awful attics or seedy cellars in which dreadful things lurk, waiting to emerge from long ago or far away, or both. From what I have heard, it is useless for anyone in the Lovecraftian universe to struggle. Lift a finger, and evil forces will come bursting in. It was with a compulsion greater than myself that I decided I must—whether I liked it or not—read once more that special story of his which has remained with me throughout so many years.

So, bearing a flambeau, I climb the stairs to a dusty attic where my precious few books are kept. On the way, I ponder the kindly if damp spirit of Lovecraft. This was the man who once declared, in words to be echoed by HAL in the movie 2001 almost half a century later, "Existence seems of little value and I wish it might be terminated."

Remembrance told me how L. Sprague de Camp, in his 1975 biography of Lovecraft, had quoted the master as announcing that mankind were "wolves, hyenas, swine, fools, and madmen." What sort of wisdom might we not expect from a man who had torn thus aside the tissue of lies behind which we hide our frailties? Even as I reached the chill attic, pulling my shawl more securely round my shoulders, I was aware of fear welling up inside me in a cascade of adjectives.

There on an upper shelf ... I reach out ... ah!, got it! That aged black book, from which I blow the dust. I open its pages with trembling fingers.

No, no it's not the Necronomicon, Cthulhu be praised! It's a volume entitled Modern Tales of Horror, selected by Dashiell Hammett. The volume was published in London in 1932, by Victor Gollancz.

A precocious lad, I was seven when I bought it. For many years, it was my favorite book—favorite because it scared the life out of me. Also precious to me because at that age I was trying to become on good terms with my mother, and had discovered that she was not averse to a good horror story. So I read aloud to her in our scullery while she did the ironing.

Two stories in the Hammett collection I read her over and over. They were Paul Suter's "Beyond the Door" and Michael Joyce's "Perchance to Dream." (Thirty years later, I included that marvelous latter story in my Best Fantasy Stories, published by Faber & Faber.) We both trembled, my mother and I, in those long cosy peacetime afternoons. As long as she kept ironing and I kept reading, she never said another word about sending me off to an orphanage.

One story in the Hammett collection made us scream. It was "The Music of Erich Zann," written by H. P. Lovecraft. We screamed with laughter. After all these years, it's hard to see why we found it so funny; of course, it was a nervous time for us: the police were still investigating. The very name of Erich Zann broke us up. Then again, Zann, the crazy old musician, played a viol. Come on, guys, viola is serious. Violin is serious. Viol is FUNNY! Sounds like VILE, right?

This is my dictionary's definition of a viol: "held between the knees when played." You imagine someone playing a kind of violin, gripping it with his knees ... I was also reading funnies to my mother, to keep her amiable, like Saki and Stephen Leacock. You remember Leacock's "My Financial Career"? That broke us up. I thought she would hav one of her fits. Lovecraft's story is a kind of "My Musical Career." I know that what I am saying will offend the devout, and that it just goes to show I was a hopeless neurotic aged seven, but that's how it was. That's what Zann did up in that peaked garret.

How was Zann's playing on this instrument of his? Fantastic, delirious, hysterical, is the answer. Okay, but later?

Oh, later, the frantic playing became a blind mechanical unrecognisable orgy, is the answer. And what was Zann doing while he played? He was dripping with an uncanny perspiration and twisted like a monkey, is the answer. You see, he was playing a wild Hungarian dance. Hence the uncanny perspiration. Are all Hungarian dances like that? Hope not, is the answer.

Something broke the glass and came in through the window while Zann was in this state. We never figured out what actually came in, apart from the blackness—though it's true the blackness screamed with shocking music. The Hungarians at it again, we supposed. Mother loved that bit. Perhaps she was thinking that my so-called father might be going to break in and attack us again. The idea certainly entered my mind. There was a hysterical edge to our laughter. Even as I read, I was dripping with uncanny perspiration.

It's all long ago. We were living in New England then. How foolish we were, how innocent, how—unread!

Even now, grey-haired and no longer quite so neurotic, I still see how whole sentences in that wonderful story must have struck those two thirties idiots as funny. "My liking for him did not grow." "I had a curious desire to look out of that window, over the wall and down the unseen slope at the glittering roofs and spires which must lie outspread there." Well, all I can say is that when we looked out of our kitchen window we gazed down unseen slopes onto a banana yard.

To top it all, poor old Erich Zann was dumb and deaf. We had no idea of political correctness in our house. We were Presbyterians. We found deafness funny, particularly in a musician. (Beethoven was not on our curriculum.) Funny too, we thought in our perverted way, was the fate that overcame the old deaf wistful shabby grotesque strange satyrlike distorted nearly bald—with what youthful zeal I shouted out the adjectives!— viol-player. There's the divinely hilarious moment when the unnamed hero feels "strange currents of wind" and clutches Zann's ice-cold stiffened unbreathing face, whose bulging eyes bulged uselessly into the void. I could hardly get the words out. Mother burnt a pair of pink bloomers with the iron.

Jesus, how we laughed. How silly I was at seven. Didn't know a bit of good hokum when I saw it ...

—Brian W. Aldiss

Lovecraft is notable for being both a skilled practitioner and theorist of weird fiction. Aside from such formal essays as "Supernatural Horror in Literature" and "Notes on Writing Weird Fiction," some of his most perspicacious comments on the theory and purpose of weird fiction is found in his letters. The following extracts present some of his more provocative views on the subject, emphasizing the need for a "non-supernatural cosmic art" that effects a union between traditional horror and science fiction.

Lovecraft
on Weird Fiction

Popular authors do not and apparently cannot appreciate the fact that true art is obtainable only by rejecting normality and conventionality in toto, and approaching a theme purged utterly of any usual or preconceived point of view. Wild and "different" as they may consider their quasi-weird products, it remains a fact that the bizarrerie is on the surface alone; and that basically they reiterate the same old conventional values and motives and perspectives. Good and evil, teleological illusion,[1] sugary sentiment, anthropocentric[2] psychology—the usual superficial stock

---

[1] Teleology is "The doctrine or study of ends or final causes, esp. as related to the evidences of design or purpose in nature" (*Oxford English Dictionary*). By "teleological illusion," therefore, Lovecraft refers to what he believes is the mistaken assumption that everything in nature is designed for the ultimate benefit of human beings.

[2] *anthropocentric:* "Centring in man; regarding man as the central fact of the universe, to which all surrounding facts have reference" (*Oxford English Dictionary*).

in trade, and all shot through with the eternal and ines-capable commonplace. Take a werewolf story, for instance—who ever wrote a story from the point of view of the wolf, and sympathising strongly with the devil to whom he has sold himself?[3] Who ever wrote a story from the point of view that man is a blemish on the cosmos, who ought to be eradicated? As an example—a young man I know[4] lately told me that he means to write a story about a scientist who wishes to dominate the earth, and who to accomplish his ends trains and overdevelops germs (à la Anthony Rud's "Ooze"[5]), and leads on armies of them in the manner of the Egyptian plagues. I told him that although this theme has promise, it is made utterly com-monplace by assigning the scientist a normal motive. There is nothing outré about wanting to conquer the earth; Alexander, Napoleon, and Wilhelm II wanted to do that. Instead, I told my friend, he should conceive a man with a morbid, frantic, shuddering hatred of the life-principle itself, who wishes to extirpate from the planet every trace of biological organism, animal and vegetable alike, includ-ing himself. That would be tolerably original. But after all, originality lies within the author. One can't write a weird story of real power without perfect psychological detach-ment from the human scene, and a magic prism of imagination which suffuses theme and style alike with that grotesquerie and disquieting distortion characteris-tic of morbid vision. Only a cynic can create horror— for being every masterpiece of the sort must reside a driving daemonic force that despises the human race and

---

[3] H. Warner Munn, reading this passage, was inspired by it to write "The Werewolf of Ponkert" (*Weird Tales*, July 1925), but he seems to have misunderstood Lovecraft's idea, since he has the werewolf react with self-loathing at his condition.

[4] Perhaps Frank Belknap Long or C. M. Eddy, Jr.

[5] See note 39 to "The Dunwich Horror."

its illusions, and longs to pull them to pieces and mock them.

—*Letter to Edwin Baird (c. October 1923),*
Weird Tales *3, No. 3 (March 1924): 86, 88*

In accordance with your suggestion I am re-submitting "The Call of Cthulhu",[6] though possibly you will still think it a trifle too bizarre for a clientele who demand their weirdness in name only, and who like to keep both feet pretty solidly on the ground of the known and the familiar....

Now all my tales are based on the fundamental premise that common human laws and interests and emotions have no validity or significance in the vast cosmos-at-large. To me there is nothing but puerility in a tale in which the human form—and the local human passions and conditions and standards—are depicted as native to other worlds or other universes. To achieve the essence of real externality, whether of time or space or dimension, one must forget that such things as organic life, good and evil, love and hate, and all such local attributes of a negligible and temporary race called mankind, have any existence at all. Only the human scenes and characters must have human qualities. *These* must be handled with unsparing *realism,* (not catch-penny *romanticism*) but when we cross the line to the boundless and hideous unknown—the shadow-haunted *Outside*—we must remember to leave our humanity and terrestrialism at the threshold.

So much for theory. In practice, I presume that few commonplace readers would have any use for a story written on these psychological principles. They want their conventional best-seller values and motives kept paramount throughout

---

[6] The story had been rejected by Farnsworth Wright of *Weird Tales* when first submitted around October 1926.

the abysses of apocalyptic vision and extra-Einsteinian[7] chaos, and would not deem an "interplanetary" tale in the least interesting if it did not have its Martian (or Jovian or Venerian[8] or Saturnian) heroine fall in love with the young voyager from Earth, and thereby incur the jealousy of the inevitable Prince Kongros (or Zeelar or Hoshgosh or Norkog) who at once proceeds to usurp the throne etc.; or if it did not have its Martian (or etc.) nomenclature follow a closely terrestrial pattern, with an Indo-Germanic "-a" name for the Princess, and something disagreeable and Semitic for the villain.[9] Now I couldn't grind out that sort of junk if my life depended on it. If I were writing an "interplanetary" tale it would deal with beings organised very differently from mundane mammalia, and obeying motives wholly alien to anything we know upon Earth—the exact degree of alienage depending, of course, on the scene of the tale; whether laid in the solar system, the visible galactic universe outside the solar system, or the *utterly unplumbed* gulfs still farther out—the nameless vortices of never-dreamed-of strangeness, where form and symmetry, light and heat, even matter and energy themselves, may be unthinkably metamorphosed or totally wanting. I have merely got at the edge of this in "Cthulhu", where I have been careful to avoid terrestrialism in the few linguistic and nomenclatural specimens from Outside which I present. All very well—but will the readers

---

[7] For Lovecraft's reaction to Albert Einstein, see note 77 to *At the Mountains of Madness.*

[8] "Jovian" is the adjectival form of "Jupiter"; "Venerian" is the adjectival form of "Venus."

[9] This sarcastic description corresponds very well to the space-operas of Edgar Rice Burroughs. What Lovecraft does not indicate here is how much he enjoyed Burroughs's work when he first read it in the *All-Story* and other magazines of the Munsey chain. A letter by Lovecraft to the editor of the *All-Story*, published in the March 7, 1914, issue, reads: "At or near the head of your list of writers Edgar Rice Burroughs undoubtedly stands. I have read very few recent novels by others wherein is displayed an equal ingenuity in plot, and verisimilitude in treatment" (*H. P. Lovecraft in the Argosy* [West Warwick, RI: Necronomicon Press, 1994], 34). Fifteen years later Lovecraft's response was very different: "I shall sooner or later get around to the interplanetary field myself—& you may depend upon it that I shall not choose Edmond Hamilton, Ray Cummings, or Edgar Rice Burroughs as my model!" (*Selected Letters*, III, 88).

stand for it? That's all they're likely to get from me in the future—except when I deal with definitely terrestrial scenes—and I am the last one to urge the acceptance of material of doubtful value to the magazine's particular purpose. Even when I deal with the mundanely weird, moreover, I shan't be likely to stress the popular artificial values and emotions of cheap fiction.

—*Letter to Farnsworth Wright (editor of*Weird Tales*), July 5, 1927;* Selected Letters 1925-1929, *ed. August Derleth and Donald Wandrei (Sauk City, WI: Arkham House, 1968), pp. 149–51*

Fantastic literature cannot be treated as a single unit, because it is a composite resting on widely divergent bases. I really agree that "Yog-Sothoth" is a basically immature conception, & unfitted for really serious literature. The fact is, I have never approached serious literature as yet. But I consider the use of actual folk-myths as even more childish than the use of new artificial myths, since in employing the former one is forced to retain many blatant puerilities & contradictions of experience which could be subtilised or smoothed over if the supernaturalism were modelled to order for the given case. The only permanently artistic use of Yog-Sothothery, I think, is in symbolic or associative phantasy of the frankly poetic type; in which fixed dream-patterns of the natural organism are given an embodiment & crystallisation. The reasonable permanence of this phase of poetic phantasy as a *possible* art form (whether or not favoured by current fashion) seems to me a highly strong probability. It will, however, demand ineffable adroitness— the vision of a Blackwood joined to the touch of a de la Mare[10]—& is probably beyond my utmost powers of

---

[10] Algernon Blackwood (1869–1951), prolific British author whom Lovecraft eventually ranked as the greatest weird writer of his day. His best-known works are "The Willows" (in *The Listener and Other Stories* [London: Eveleigh Nash, 1907]), "The Wendigo" (in *The Lost Valley and Other Strories* [London: Eveleigh Nash, 1910]), and *John Silence—Physician Extraordi-*

achievement. I hope to see material of this sort in time, though I hardly expect to produce anything even remotely approaching it myself. I am too saturated in the empty gestures & pseudo-moods of an archaic & vanished world to have any successful traffick with symbols of an expanded dream-reality. But there is another phase of cosmic phantasy (which may or may not include frank Yog-Sothothery) whose foundations appear to me as better grounded than those of ordinary oneiroscopy; personal limitation regarding the *sense of outsideness*. I refer to the aesthetic crystallisation of that burning & inextinguishable feeling of mixed wonder & oppression which the sensitive imagination experiences upon scaling itself & its restrictions against the vast & provocative abyss of the unknown. This has always been the chief emotion in my psychology; & whilst it obviously figures less in the psychology of the majority, it is clearly a well-defined & permanent factor from which very few sensitive persons are wholly free. Here we have a natural biological phenomenon so untouched & untouchable by intellectual disillusion that it is difficult to envisage its total death as a factor in the most serious art. Reason as we may, we cannot destroy a normal perception of the highly limited & fragmentary nature of our visible world of perception & experience as scaled against the outside abyss of unthinkable galaxies & unplumbed dimensions—an abyss wherein our solar system is the merest dot (by the same *local* principle that makes a sand-grain a dot as compared with the whole planet earth) *no matter what relativisitic system we may use in conceiving the cosmos as a whole*—& this perception cannot fail to act potently upon the natural physical instinct of *pure curiosity*; an instinct just as basic & primitive, & as impossible of

---

nary (London: Eveleigh Nash, 1908). Walter de la Mare (1893–1956), British author who wrote the weird novel *The Return* (1910) and the collections *The Riddle and Other Stories* (1923) and *The Connoisseur and Other Stories* (1926) among a large array of fiction, poetry, and miscellany.

destruction by any philosophy whatsoever, as the parallel instincts of hunger, sex, ego-expansion, & fear. ... A great part of religion is merely a childish & diluted pseudo-gratification of this perpetual gnawing toward the ultimate illimitable void. Superadded to this simple curiosity is the galling sense of *intolerable restraint* which all sensitive people (except self-blinded earth-gazers like little Augie Derleth[11]) feel as they survey their natural limitations in time & space as scaled against the freedoms & expansions & comprehensions & adventurous expectancies which the mind can formulate as abstract conceptions. ... The time has come when the normal revolt against time, space, & matter must assume a form not overtly incompatible with what is known of reality—when it must be gratified by images forming *supplements* rather than *contradictions* of the visible & mensurable universe. And what, if not a form of *non-supernatural cosmic art*, is to pacify this sense of revolt—as well as gratify the cognate sense of curiosity?

> —*Letter to Frank Belknap Long, 22 February 1931;* Selected Letters 1929-1931, *ed. August Derleth and Donald Wandrei (Sauk City, WI: Arkham House, 1971), pp. 293-96*

To my mind, the *sense of the unknown* is an authentic & virtually permanent—even though seldom dominant—part of human personality; an element too basic to be destroyed by the modern world's knowledge that the supernatural does not exist. It is true that we no longer credit the existence of discarnate[12] intelligence & super-physical forces around us,

---

[11] Although August Derleth (1909–1971) was instrumental in rescuing Lovecraft's work from the pulp magazines and publishing it in hardcover, Lovecraft found Derleth's own weird writing to be relatively conventional and limited in scope. He had great admiration, however, for Derleth's mainstream work, such as *Place of Hawks* (1935) and *Evening in Spring* (1941), drafts of both of which he read before publication.

[12] *discarnate*: Lacking a physical body. The reference is to the belief in an immaterial soul.

& that consequently the traditional "gothick tale" of spectres & vampires has lost a large part of its power to move our emotions. But in spite of this disillusion there remain two factors largely unaffected—& in one case actually *increased*—by the change: first, a sense of impatient rebellion against the rigid & ineluctable tyranny of time, space, & natural law—a sense which drives our imaginations to devise all sorts of plausible hypothetic defeats of that tyranny—& second, a burning curiosity concerning the vast reaches of unplumbed & unplumbable cosmic space which press down tantalisingly on all sides of our pitifully tiny sphere of the known. Between these two surviving factors I believe that the field of the weird must necessarily continue to have a reason for existence, & that the nature of man must necessarily still seek occasional expression (even though in limited degree) in symbols & phantasies involving the hypothetical frustration of physical law, & the imaginative extrusion of knowledge & adventure beyond the bounds imposed by reality. That this must be done more subtly than in the past, goes without saying; but I insist that it still must be done now & then. The emotional need for escape from terrestrial certainties is still, with a definite & permanent minority, a genuine & sometimes acute one.

In my own efforts to crystallise this spaceward outreaching, I try to utilise as many as possible of the elements which have, under earlier mental & emotional conditions, given man a symbolic feeling of the unreal, the ethereal, & the mystical—choosing those least attacked by the realistic mental & emotional conditions of the present. Darkness—sunset—dreams—mists—fever—madness—the tomb—the hills—the sea—the sky—the wind—all these, & many other things have seemed to me to retain a certain imaginative potency despite our actual scientific analyses of them. Accordingly I have tried to weave them into a kind of shadowy phantasmagoria which may have the same sort of vague coherence as a cycle of traditional myth or legend—with nebulous backgrounds of Elder Forces & trans-galactic entities which lurk about this infinitesimal planet, (& of course about others as well) establishing outposts thereon, & occasionally brushing aside other accidental forms of life (like human beings) in order to take up full habitation. This is essentially the sort of notion prevalent in most racial mythologies—but an artificial mythology can become subtler & more plausible than a natural one, because it can recognise & adapt itself to the information & moods of the present. The best artificial mythology, of course, is Lord Dunsany's elaborate & consistently developed pantheon of Pegana's gods.[13] Having formed a cosmic pantheon, it remains for the fantaisiste to link this "outside" element to the earth in a suitably dramatic & convincing fashion. This, I have thought, is best done through glancing allusions to immemorially ancient cults & idols & documents attesting the recognition of the "outside" forces by men—or by those terrestrial entities which preceded man. The actual climaxes of tales based on such elements naturally have to do with sudden latter-day intrusions of forgotten elder forces on the placid surface of the known—either active intrusions, or revelations caused by the feverish & presumptuous probing of men into the unknown. Often the merest *hint* that such a forgotten elder force *may* exist is the most effective sort of a climax—indeed, I am not sure but that this may be the *only* climax possible in a truly mature fantasy. I have had many severe criticisms because of the *concrete & tangible* nature of some of my "cosmic horrors". Variants of the general theme include defeats of the visible laws of time—strange juxtapositions of widely separated aeons—& transcensions of the boundary-lines of Euclidean space; these, & the always-fruitful device of a human voyage into forbidden celestial deeps. In every one of these seemingly

---

[13] Lord Dunsany (1878–1957), Irish writer who had devised an internally coherent pseudomythology in his first two volumes of tales, *The Gods of Pegana* (1905) and *Time and the Gods* (1906).

extravagant conceptions there is a certain amount of imaginative satisfaction for a very genuine emotional need of mankind—if only the subject be handled with adequate subtlety & convincingness.

—Letter to Harold S. Farnese, September 22, 1932; Selected Letters 1932-1934, ed. *August Derleth and James Turner (Sauk City, WI: Arkham House, 1976), pp. 69–71*

H. P. Lovecraft re-invented the horror story for the 20th century. Rejecting the religiously-based horrors of the past, he turned an unflinching eye on the chaotic universe revealed by science, in which mankind has but a small and perhaps transient role to play. Lovecraft's universe is beyond good and evil; the horrors are material because there is no spirituality—that being one more anthrocentric concept of no general relevance. Lovecraft's antecedents are in Nietzsche as much as they are in Poe. His importance is not so much in his style—which can be admirable—but in his thematic approach. He is a thinking man's horror writer, whose work expresses a coherent philosophical outlook, a writer in many ways more akin to H. G. Welles or Olaf Stapledon than to the graveyard-variety spookmonger

—Darrell Schweitzer

Appendix:
Lovecraft in the Media

Lovecraft's opinion of film was not high. Although he enjoyed *The Phantom of the Opera*, he had nothing but scorn for the average run of horror films in his day:

As a thorough soporific I recommend the average popularly "horrible" play or cinema or radio dialogue. They are all the same—flat, hackneyed, synthetic, essentially atmosphereless jumbles of conventional shrieks and mutterings and superficial, mechanical situations. The Bat made me drowse back in the early 1920's—and last year an alleged Frankenstein on the screen would have made me drowse had not a posthumous sympathy for poor Mrs. Shelley made me

see red instead. Ugh! And the screen Dracula *in
1931—I saw the beginning of that in Miami, Fla.—
but couldn't bear to watch it drag to its full term of
dreariness, hence walked out into the fragrant tropic
moonlight!* (Selected Letters, *IV, 154–55)*

What Lovecraft objected to, evidently, in the latter two
films was both the technical crudity of their acting and
production and their lack of faithfulness to the literary
works on which they were based. He himself did not wish
his own works similarly mangled, and refused to release
radio dramatization rights to "The Dreams in the Witch
House" to Farnsworth Wright of *Weird Tales.*

It would be nice to think that, with the advances that
radio, film, and television have made in the last half-century,
the several adaptations of Lovecraft's own work in various
media might have met Lovecraft's approval; but, sadly
enough, only a few would probably have done so.

Lovecraft appears to have been adapted on radio in the
late 1940s, although information on these items is not easily
forthcoming. A dramatization of "The Dunwich Horror"
for "Suspense" (CBS, 1949) is just the sort of melodramatic,
atmosphereless adaptation that Lovecraft would have
scorned; but perhaps it helped in its small way to bring
Lovecraft's work to a wider audience.

The first actual film adaptation was *The Haunted Palace*
(American International, 1963), produced and directed by
Roger Corman and with a screenplay written by Charles
Beaumont. This film was part of Corman's series of Edgar
Allan Poe adaptations, but it is very clearly derived from
Lovecraft's *The Case of Charles Dexter Ward.* It now seems
very dated, and the special effects are hardly worth the name;
but Vincent Price performs well as both the modern-day
Charles Dexter Ward and his eighteenth-century ancestor,
the alchemist Joseph Curwen, who ultimately gains psychic possession of his descendant and renews his reign of
terror. Lon Chaney, Jr., also has a small role.

Lovecraft's "The Colour Out of Space" was adapted as *Die, Monster, Die* (American International, 1965; entitled *Monster of Terror* in Great Britain), directed by Daniel Haller and with a screenplay by Jerry Sohl. This is a rather sad specimen, the departures from Lovecraft's story being in every instance for the worse, with the result that the film is nothing more than routine Hollywood schlock. First, the setting is transferred from New England to England (the attempt to depict the "blasted heath" is pathetically inadequate); second, a silly romance element has been added; and third, the story ends with a cheerful happy ending. Boris Karloff gamely does his best as the decrepit patriarch Nahum Witley (a name seemingly combined from the original story and from "The Dunwich Horror"!), but his performance is marred by the fatuous Nick Adams and Suzan Farmer.

The Shuttered Room (SevenArts-Troy-Schenck, 1968) is a curious specimen. The film is based upon a story of that title first published in *The Shuttered Room and Other Pieces* (1959) as "by H. P. Lovecraft and August Derleth," but the tale is almost entirely the work of Derleth. The film version is in many ways an improvement upon the original, purging it of its luridness and focusing instead upon a family tragedy: the "shuttered room" conceals the idiot daughter (Carol Lynley) of a decaying New England family. In many ways this scenario captures the sense of physical and moral regression that Lovecraft depicted in such stories as "The Picture in the House" and "The Colour Out of Space." Gig Young and Oliver Reed contribute admirable performances in this film, directed by David Greene with a screenplay by D. B. Ledrov and Nathaniel Tanchuck.

One would like to be charitable to *The Dunwich Horror* (American International, 1970), directed by Daniel Haller (screenplay by Curtis Lee Hanson, Henry Rosenbaum, and Ronald Silkosky); but it is difficult to do so when so many ridiculous liberties are taken with the original text. Instead of a hideous and hulking Wilbur Whateley, we have a suave, handsome, moustached Dean Stockwell playing the role;

and Hollywood's compulsion to have a seductive female is here fulfilled by Sandra Dee. Ed Begley and Sam Jaffe, however, distinguish themselves as Henry Armitage and Old Whateley, respectively. The Old Ones appear in a series of psychedelic interludes, but they seem to be nothing more than hippies dancing in a drug-delirium. At the conclusion, Whateley ties the Sandra Dee character to an altar and attempts to summon his twin brother, but he is foiled at the last minute. But in a final twist (seen only in the uncut version, not in the version usually shown on television) it is shown that Dee has in fact been impregnated by Whateley: perhaps in the course of time this descendant will complete the ceremony that was so abruptly terminated! This ending is authentically Lovecraftian, but it cannot make up for the film's manifest deficiencies.

A very peculiar film is *The Crimson Cult* (Tigon/American International, 1968; entitled *Curse of the Crimson Altar* in Great Britain), an uncredited and very loose adaptation of Lovecraft's "The Dreams in the Witch House." Only the basic core of the story is preserved—the attempt by a witch (here played, implausibly, by the voluptuous Barbara Steele) to gain possession of the spirit of a college student (Mark Eden)—everything else is metamorphosed out of recognition. Christopher Lee and Boris Karloff have amusing bit parts.

Hollywood decided to give Lovecraft a merciful fifteen-year hiatus in the mangling of his work, but in 1985 director Stuart Gordon and producer Brian Yuzna collaborated on the very entertaining *Re-Animator* (Empire), which has spawned a cult-following of its own. This completely over-the-top adaptation of "Herbert West—Reanimator" (the screenplay is by Dennis Paoli, William J. Norris, and Stuart Gordon) is weirdly faithful to the story in spite (or perhaps because) of its exquisite combination of humor and horror and its wild special effects. Although the film is set in the contemporary world, we have the same basic scenario as in the story: the attempt by Dr. Herbert West to reanimate the dead. Jeffrey Combs is admirable in the leading role, and is complemented well by other characters: his friend Dan Cain (Bruce Abbott), his girlfriend Megan Halsey (Barbara Crampton), and his opponent, Dr. Carl Hill (David Gale). No doubt Lovecraft would not have approved of the abuse, both physical and sexual, that poor Megan undergoes, but on the whole the film perfectly captures the self-parodic humor of the original.

From Beyond (Empire, 1986), Gordon and Yuzna's next production, is not nearly as successful. Based upon one of Lovecraft's slightest tales, with a screenplay by Dennis Paoli, Yuzna, and Gordon, the film both lacks the good humor of *Re-Animator* and a coherent plot. Many of the same actors— Combs and Crampton in particular—from the earlier film are here, and the lead role is entrusted to Ted Sorel; but the film simply doesn't come off, lapsing into lurid special-effects and nasty sadomasochism.

But Yuzna (without Gordon) made a splendid return to form in *The Bride of Re-Animator* (Wild Street Pictures/ Reanimator 2 Productions, 1991), which was premiered at the H. P. Lovecraft Centennial Conference in Providence, Rhode Island, in August 1990. Although an explicit sequel to *Re-Animator*, the film (whose screenplay was written by Keith Woody, Rick Fry, and Yuzna) draws again upon "Herbert West—Reanimator" for some of its plot elements and imagery. Combs again excels as Herbert West, along with Bruce Abbott as his sidekick Dan Cain, and David Gale as the resurrected Dr. Carl Hill. This is one of the most outrageously funny horror films in recent years and, even if the genuinely Lovecraftian element is rather small, should not be missed.

The Curse (TransWorld, 1987) is a surprisingly fine adaptation of "The Colour Out of Space," directed by David Keith and with a screenplay by David Chaskin. Although the setting has been transferred to the South, many of the other plot elements are preserved, and the fine acting by the film's lead characters (Claude Akins, Will Wheaton,

Malcolm Danare) and the relative restraint in the use of special effects make this a notable triumph. The film has already generated three sequels, but these have nothing to do either with Lovecraft or with the original film.

The Unnamable (Yankee Classic/K.P., 1988), written and directed by Jean-Paul Ouellette, should perhaps have been called *The Unspeakable*, as it must be close to the nadir of Lovecraft media adaptations. Again based on a very slight story, this film does nothing except display a series of buxom bimbos and their jock boyfriends being terrified by a monster in a haunted house. Mercifully, this abomination went direct to video; unmercifully, there has been at least one sequel to it.

More a success than a failure is *The Resurrected* (Eurobrothers, N.V., 1992), a tolerably faithful adaptation of *The Case of Charles Dexter Ward*. Purportedly based in Providence (but not actually filmed there), this film, directed by Dan O'Bannon, retains the core of Lovecaft's plot and features an admirable acting performance by Chris Sarandon as both Charles Dexter Ward and Joseph Curwen. John Terry plays a private investigator who investigates the case, and his exploration of Ward/Curwen's underground laboratory is both highly effective and very clearly drawn from the analogous scene in Lovecraft's novel.

I have not seen the two most recent adaptations, *The Lurking Fear* (Full Moon, 1994) and *Necronomicon*. *The Lurking Fear* is directed by C. Courtney Joyner and once again features Jeffrey Combs, along with Ashley Laurence and Mike Todd. *Necronomicon* is an anthology film containing very loose adaptations of "The Rats in the Walls," "Cool Air," and "The Whisperer in Darkness," each segment directed by a different director (Brian Yuzna, Christophe Gans, and Shu Kaneko). Jeffrey Combs plays Lovecraft himself and acts as narrator. The film, produced by Yuzna and Samuel Hadida, has not been released as of this writing.

Perhaps the most faithful adaptation of a Lovecraft story,

as well as perhaps the most intrinsically fine film in its own right, is an amateur effort, *The Music of Erich Zann*, written, produced, and directed by a young filmmaker, John Strysik. This short film magnificently captures the Lovecraftian *atmosphere* of insidious horror in its depiction of an aged, mute musician in Paris who strives with his bizarre music either to ward off or perhaps to summon the nameless forces that lurk outside the window of his lofty garret apartment. It was perhaps unwise of Strysik actually to show the scene outside Zann's window: his small special-effects budget makes the scene nothing more than a kaleidoscopic shot of a woman performing a wild Bacchanalian dance. Otherwise, this film is nearly flawless.

Some of the most effective "Lovecraftian" films are those that are only inspired by Lovecraft rather than based on a specific work. John Carpenter has frequently acknowledged his admiration for Lovecraft, and this is very evident in such of his films as *The Fog* (Rank/Avco Embassy, 1979) and *The Thing* (Universal, 1982). The latter draws heavily upon *At the Mountains of Madness* (as the story on which the film was based, John W. Campbell's "Who Goes There?", does as well). The Italian directors Dario Argento and Lucio Fulci also make frequent nods to Lovecraft in their films.

Lovecraft has perhaps fared slightly—but only slightly—better on television. In the 1970s two Lovecraft stories were adapted for Rod Serling's "Night Gallery" (NBC). The results are surprisingly creditable, although with occasional crudities and absurdities. "Pickman's Model" (broadcast on December 1, 1971; teleplay by Alvin Sapinsley) is unfortunately set in the past instead of the contemporary world, and the period atmosphere is not handled well; and we see rather too much of the monsters that Pickman painted—something Lovecraft wisely kept concealed until the very end. Bradford Dillman portrays Pickman ably. "Cool Air" (broadcast on December 8, 1971; teleplay by Rod Serling) is a quite faithful adaptation, although the story is set in Spain instead of New York. The gradual physical dissolution of the body of Dr. Muñoz (played well by Henry Darrow), who is actually dead but is continuing a sort of half-life by artificial preservation, is nicely handled. Both stories are also marred by a supernumerary romance element. Serling's producer Jack Laird created a delightful little 30-second skit, "Professor Peabody's Last Lecture" (broadcast November 10, 1971), in which a professor argues in front of a classroom that the Old Ones have no real existence, only to learn very emphatically the truth of the matter. Some of the students have the names of Lovecraft's friends and colleagues. (Another brief skit by Laird, "Miss Lovecraft Sent Me," broadcast on September 15, 1971, has nothing to do with Lovecraft except the name.)

A very different television production was an HBO special, *Cast a Deadly Spell* (1991), which was initially going to be called *Lovecraft*. In this highly effective two-hour film, Fred Ward plays a tough private eye, H. Phil Lovecraft, who in an alternate-world Los Angeles is on the hunt for the Old Ones. Although not explicitly based on any single Lovecraft story, this program—in spite of its occasional lapses into self-parody—comes surprisingly close to capturing the essence of Lovecraft.

The history of media adaptations of Lovecraft's work is a decidedly mixed bag. In the 1960s and '70s the films suffered both in their faithfulness to their originals and in their general effectiveness from inferior special effects and from Hollywood's insistence on romance and happy endings. The 1980s saw the refinement of special effects, but the Lovecraftian films of this decade—especially those by Stuart Gordon and Brian Yuzna—tended to lapse into self-parody. A *serious* adaptation of one of Lovecraft's great stories has yet to be attempted.

Select Bibliography

Publications by and about Lovecraft have now become so voluminous that it is difficult to keep track of them. Listed below are the most significant texts by Lovecraft and a selection of the best criticism devoted to his life and work.

Works by Lovecraft

Fiction

At the Mountains of Madness and Other Novels. Selected by August Derleth, with texts edited by S. T. Joshi. Sauk City, WI: Arkham House, 1985.

Dagon and Other Macabre Tales. Selected by August Derleth, with texts edited by S. T. Joshi. Sauk City, WI: Arkham House, 1986.

The Dunwich Horror and Others. Selected by August Derleth, with texts edited by S. T. Joshi. Sauk City, WI: Arkham House, 1984.

The Horror in the Museum and Other Revisions. Selected by August Derleth, with texts edited by S. T. Joshi. Sauk City, WI: Arkham House, 1989.

The standard corrected edition of Lovecraft's major fiction. Previous Arkham House editions, as well as all British and American paperback editions, contain many errors.

Poetry

Collected Poems. Selected by August Derleth. Sauk City, WI: Arkham House, 1963.

The Fantastic Poetry. Edited by S. T. Joshi. West Warwick, RI: Necronomicon Press, 1990 (rev. ed. 1993).

Medusa and Other Poems. Edited by S. T. Joshi. Mount Olive, NC: Cryptic Publications, 1986.

Saturnalia and Other Poems. Edited by S. T. Joshi. Bloomfield, NJ: Cryptic Publications, 1984.

A Winter Wish and Other Poems. Edited by Tom Collins. Chapel Hill, NC: Whispers Press, 1977.
These five volumes, taken together, contain nearly the whole of Lovecraft's extensive poetic output. Collected Poems *and* A Winter Wish *contain many textual errors. A complete edition of Lovecraft's poetry is in preparation.*

Essays

Miscellaneous Writings. Edited by S. T. Joshi. Sauk City, WI: Arkham House, 1995.
The most comprehensive collection of Lovecraft's essays; also contains minor fiction not included in the four previous Arkham House editions.

Supernatural Horror in Literature. New York: Ben Abramson, 1945 (rpt. New York: Dover, 1972).
Convenient, if textually unsound, edition of Lovecraft's celebrated essay on weird fiction, first published in 1927. A corrected text is available in Dagon and Other Macabre Tales *(see above).*

To Quebec and the Stars. Edited by L. Sprague de Camp. West Kingston, RI: Donald M. Grant, 1976.
First publication of Lovecraft's lengthy travelogue of Quebec, with other important essays.

Uncollected Prose and Poetry. 3 vols. Edited by S. T. Joshi and Marc A. Michaud. West Warwick, RI: Necronomicon Press, 1978-82.
Reprinting of many obscure essays from amateur journals.

Letters

Letters to Richard F. Searight. Edited by David E. Schultz and S. T. Joshi. West Warwick, RI: Necronomicon Press, 1992.

Letters to Robert Bloch. Edited by David E. Schultz and S. T. Joshi. West Warwick, RI: Necronomicon Press, 1993 (Supplement, 1993).
These two volumes are unabridged and annotated editions of Lovecraft's letters to two later colleagues.

Letters to Samuel Loveman and Vincent Starrett. Edited by S. T. Joshi and David E. Schultz. West Warwick, RI: Necronomicon Press, 1994.

Selected Letters. 5 vols. Edited by August Derleth, Donald Wandrei, and James Turner. Sauk City, WI: Arkham House, 1965-76.
Most extensive selection of Lovecraft's letters, although the editing is at times erratic. A landmark in Lovecraft studies.

Uncollected Letters. Edited by S. T. Joshi. West Warwick, RI: Necronomicon Press, 1986.
Collection of Lovecraft's letters published in magazines during and just after his lifetime; includes his letters to Weird Tales.

Works about Lovecraft

Biographical

Cook, W. Paul. *In Memoriam: Howard Phillips Lovecraft: Recollections, Appreciations, Estimates.* North Montpelier, VT: Driftwind Press, 1941 (rpt. West Warwick, RI: Necronomicon Press, 1977 [rev. ed. 1991]).
Still the best memoir of Lovecraft, by one of his closest friends.

Davis, Sonia H. *The Private Life of H. P. Lovecraft.* Edited by S. T. Joshi. West Warwick, RI: Necronomicon Press, 1985 (rev. ed. 1992).
Fascinating and provocative memoir by Lovecraft's ex-wife.

Joshi, S. T. *H. P. Lovecraft: A Life.* West Warwick, RI: Necronomicon Press, 1996.
Exhaustive biography discussing Lovecraft's life, his literary work, his philosophical thought, and his place in intellectual history.

Long, Frank Belknap. *Howard Phillips Lovecraft: Dreamer*

on the Nightside. Sauk City, WI: Arkham House, 1975. *Lengthy but insubstantial and occasionally unreliable memoir by a longtime friend.*

Bibliographical

Joshi, S. T. *H. P. Lovecraft and Lovecraft Criticism: An Annotated Bibliography.* Kent, OH: Kent State University Press, 1981.

Joshi, S. T., and L. D. Blackmore. *H. P. Lovecraft and Lovecraft Criticism: An Annotated Bibliography: Supplement 1980–1984.* West Warwick, RI: Necronomicon Press, 1985.
The standard bibliography.

Critical

Burleson, Donald R. *H. P. Lovecraft: A Critical Study.* Westport, CT: Greenwood Press, 1983.
Sound general study of Lovecraft's entire work.

Burleson, Donald R. *Lovecraft: Disturbing the Universe.* Lexington: University Press of Kentucky, 1990.
Provocative deconstructionist interpretation of Lovecraft.

Cannon, Peter. *H. P. Lovecraft.* Boston: Twayne, 1989.
Up-to-date general survey with useful references to secondary literature.

Joshi, S. T. *H. P. Lovecraft: The Decline of the West.* Mercer Island, WA: Starmont House, 1990.
Analysis of Lovecraft's philosophy and its incorporation into his fiction.

Joshi, S. T., ed. *H. P. Lovecraft: Four Decades of Criticism.* Athens: Ohio University Press, 1980. *Collection of critical essays on Lovecraft from 1944 to 1978.*

Lévy, Maurice. *Lovecraft ou du fantastique.* Paris: Christian Bourgois (Union Générale d'Editions), 1972. Translated by S. T. Joshi as *Lovecraft: A Study in the Fantastic.* Detroit: Wayne State University Press, 1988. *Still perhaps the best thematic study of Lovecraft.*

St. Armand, Barton L. *The Roots of Horror in the Fiction of H. P. Lovecraft.* Elizabethtown, NY: Dragon Press, 1977. *Comprehensive study of the thematic and psychological aspects of "The Rats in the Walls."*

Schultz, David E. and S. T. Joshi, eds. *An Epicure in the Terrible: A Centennial Anthology in Honor of H. P. Lovecraft.* Rutherford, NJ: Fairleigh Dickinson University Press, 1991. *Large collection of original essays by many leading scholars.*

Schweitzer, Darrell, ed. *Discovering H. P. Lovecraft.* Mercer Island, WA: Starmont House, 1987. *Useful collection of previously published essays on Lovecraft.*

Shreffler, Philip A. *The H. P. Lovecraft Companion.* Westport, CT: Greenwood Press, 1977. *Interesting index of places and characters in Lovecraft's fiction.*

Other Works Cited

Baring-Gould, S. *Curious Myths of the Middle Ages.* 1866-68. Rev. ed. London: Rivington's, 1869.

Byrd, Richard E. *Little America.* New York: G. P. Putnam's Sons, 1930.

The Compact Edition of the Oxford English Dictionary. Oxford: Oxford University Press, 1971 (reprint of the 1933 edition).

Frazer, Sir James George. *The Golden Bough: A Study in Magic and Religion.* New York: Macmillan, 1922.

Lewis, Charlton T. and Charles Short. *A Latin Dictionary.* 1879. Rpt. Oxford: Oxford University Press, 1975.

Liddell, Henry George and Robert Scott. *A Greek-English Lexicon.* Revised and augmented throughout by Sir Henry Stuart Jones with the assistance of Roderick McKenzie. Oxford: Clarendon Press, 1940.

Lincoln, R. J. and G. A. Boxshall. *The Cambridge Illustrated Dictionary of Natural History.* Cambridge: Cambridge University Press, 1987.

Palmer, E. Laurence. *Fieldbook of Natural History.* 2nd ed. (rev. H. Seymour Fowler). New York: McGraw-Hill, 1975.

Skinner, Charles M. *Myths and Legends of Our Own Land.* Philadelphia: J. B. Lippincott Co., 1896. 2 vols.